KU-431-234

Jackie Gingell, and her identical twin, are the eldest of six children. A Kentish maid by birth, spending her formative years in the Medway Towns, Jackie has lived in Somerset for the last thirty years with husband Geoffrey. She has two grown up children Andrew and Samantha and two recycled sheepdogs – Archie and Tizz. Jackie has an OU Degree in English Literature and is a long term and active member of the Yeovil Cre8ive writing group. She works as a School Secretary – taking on the job initially for six months. Twenty-two years and six Headteachers later she is still there.

www.jackiegingell.co.uk

EE EYE ADDYEO
(THE FARMER WANTS A WIFE)

To Stacey

Jackie Gingell

EE EYE ADDYEO
(THE FARMER WANTS A WIFE)

- one of the kindest, hardest
working people I know.
We couldn't have got through
the wedding without your
support

Jackie Gingell

x

Vanguard Press

VANGUARD PAPERBACK

© Copyright 2010
Jackie Gingell

The right of Jackie Gingell to be identified as author of
this work has been asserted by her in accordance with the
Copyright, Designs and Patents Act 1988.

All Rights Reserved

No reproduction, copy or transmission of this publication
may be made without written permission.
No paragraph of this publication may be reproduced,
copied or transmitted save with the written permission of the publisher,
or in accordance with the provisions
of the Copyright Act 1956 (as amended).

Any person who commits any unauthorised act in relation to
this publication may be liable to criminal
prosecution and civil claims for damages.

A CIP catalogue record for this title is
available from the British Library.

ISBN 978 1 843865 964

*Vanguard Press is an imprint of
Pegasus Elliot MacKenzie Publishers Ltd.*
www.pegasuspublishers.com

First Published in 2010

**Vanguard Press
Sheraton House Castle Park
Cambridge England**

Printed & Bound in Great Britain

For Geoffrey, Andrew and Samantha who give me so much love
and support in everything I do.

ACKNOWLEDGEMENTS

The Yeovil Cre8tive Writers group for their encouragement.
The Yeovil International Literary Prize for making me believe I
had something worth working on.
Margaret Graham for always being so positive about my writing.
Janet Black, for taking such care over my photograph.
Samantha Gingell for being such a brilliant proof reader and
whose positive comments have given me so much confidence.
Becky Osborne who has become a much loved member of the
Gingell family.
Yvonne Hughes, my identical twin sister whose literary success
and unconditional love and support was such an incentive.

CHAPTER 1

She heard but didn't see it coming until it was almost too late. There was no pavement so she had to make do with the muddy grass verge. The tractor thundered by, close and very loud, swerving away from her at the very last minute.

"Bloody maniac!" she shouted.

The driver was wearing ear defenders. She doubted he had heard her but it made her feel better. Margot looked down, she had stepped in something and already a brown stain was marking her beige leather shoes.

"Damn, that's all I need."

The shoes had cost her a small fortune even in the January sales. She hopped on to one foot, took off her shoe and sniffed it hoping it was only mud that she had stood in. God, how she hated the countryside. It was a foreign land where the climate was awful and the natives hostile. Her move was not proving to be the rural idyll she hoped for. London had wearied her. She had tired of social gatherings in soulless wine bars and boring dinner parties with inedible food and indigestible conversation. It was spending her forty-second birthday alone, save a large glass of red and the Internet for company that had decided her. The country cottage had looked so inviting and the promise of community that the advertisement offered was almost too good to be true. So she had bought the cottage and made the move within a matter of weeks. However, by day two in her new home she realised that she had made a terrible mistake. Margot had now been living in Middle Chippings for just over a month and if you included the postman she had spoken to a total of thirteen people in all that time. She looked back up the lane but the tractor was gone. It must have turned into the farmyard at the top.

"Silly cow!" Giles yelled as he swerved to avoid the woman. She must have seen him coming or at the very least heard him. He glanced in the rear-view mirror. He guessed that she was the woman from London who had just bought Saddleback Cottage. 'She's got to be rich or stupid or both,' he thought. It was common knowledge that she had paid well over the odds for it. Still, she wouldn't stay long, her sort never did.

Giles switched off the tractor engine, still irritated by the stupid woman who had stepped out in front of him. He parked next to the farm sign. It read 'G. Farmer and Son'. By tradition all the Farmer men were given names beginning with 'G'. There was no rhyme or reason for this but it served a purpose, the sign never had to be replaced. The Farmers were nothing if not thrifty. However, there was a minor problem but one that could not be ignored. It was the word 'Son'. To begat a son one needed a wife, or at least a willing woman. Giles had always been painfully shy amongst women, especially beautiful ones; well to be honest even the ugly ones terrified him. When he was younger his social life revolved around the Young Farmers' clubs but he was way beyond that now. It was a time when he did occasionally get to meet girls. Giles didn't do small talk; in fact he didn't talk much at all. Not a lot of call for it in his profession, particularly as much of his working day was spent alone. Giles's dream date was blonde, with big tits and slim hips. If she could also drive a tractor, muck out animals and discuss the finer points of artificial insemination, well that would be a bonus. Needless to say he was still looking.

Giles stared out of the window and watched his father climb awkwardly from the farm fork lift. The hunched shoulders had less to do with the biting wind and more with the disappointment of having an unmarried son. Giles knew his father was desperate to hand over the farm to him. Godfrey had his sights set on Saddleback Cottage; or rather he did have until it was sold to that woman from London. All the while Giles remained single his father would stay put in the business. A wife and a family would provide the incentive for Giles to maintain Home Farm as a going concern. As a single man on his own he might be tempted to sell off the land for building. Giles frequently reassured his father that he would not succumb to Danny Bragg's offers. What was Bragg calling himself these days? Oh yes a 'property developer'. A jumped-up brickie with a PhD in ducking and diving was closer to the mark. Danny Bragg had approached them last year. He wanted to buy the farm so that he could convert the barns and put up 'affordable housing'. Affordable for whom, that's what Godfrey wanted to know. Home Farm had been in the Farmer family for generations and would continue to be so.

There was nothing else for it; Giles had to get himself a wife. He had been thinking about it for years but how to go about it, that was the difficulty. He looked across the kitchen to Meg the farm collie. She had glued herself to the Aga in the corner. She sensed Giles's attention and thumped the last three inches of her tail in greeting.

"Oh Meg, if only women weren't such complicated creatures. I know which dogs to put with which bitches to produce the best working strain, so why can't I do the same for myself?"

Godfrey pushed open the back door and walked into the kitchen still wearing his muddy wellingtons.

When Giles's mother was alive his father wouldn't have dared step over the threshold in his boots let alone wear them to the table. Giles poured out some tea into two old mugs. His father was looking tired and old.

"Sit down, Dad, take a rest. I'll finish off the bottom paddock. You look all in."

"All in, course I'm bloody all in. Man my age shouldn't be working this hard. I should be sitting here playing with me grandchildren, eating home-made cake baked by my daughter-in-law!"

Giles would not rise to the bait. It was just a continuation of the conversation they had had earlier this morning. In fact it was a conversation they seemed to be having quite regularly. Godfrey took a swig of his tea, then a deep breath to continue the argument. Giles couldn't take any more.

"If you must know, Dad, I've got a date tonight."

Godfrey's jaw dropped.

"What? Since when? You mean a real date, a proper date, with a woman?"

"Yes, and that's all I'm going to tell you about it."

Giles grabbed his old coat and slammed the door as he left the kitchen. He had actually managed to stop the old man in his tracks. The look on his father's face was priceless. Only one slight problem – where the hell was he going to find a woman to take on a date?

Giles drove back down the lane, no sign of the woman this time. He turned into the narrow road leading to the lower paddock when he sensed a car behind him. He looked into the rear-view mirror. He recognised the car as much by the impatience of the driver as by its make – bloody Danny Bragg.

"Thinks he owns the place," thought Giles. "Well he damn well doesn't."

Common courtesy said that he ought to have pulled the tractor over to let the other vehicle pass but Giles ignored the lay-by halfway down the lane. Bragg was only likely to understand the first part of the phrase 'common courtesy'. At the 'T' junction Giles indicated to turn right by sticking his hand through the cab window with a two-fingered gesture. Danny Bragg replied with an indignant blast on the car horn. Giles knew it was a petty triumph. Ever since Bragg's return to Middle Chippings he had been flashing his money around in an attempt to impress. Folk in Middle Chippings had long memories and were not so easily fooled. Giles had no time to waste thinking about Bragg. He had more pressing things on his mind. What was he going to do about this date tonight? He had to think of something and think of it fast.

Giles wasn't totally unfamiliar with the world of women and dating, he just wasn't any good at it. Blind dates he'd gone on invariably ended up in disaster. Double dates were a dead loss – he always ended up with the ugly fat one. Ugly they might have been but desperate they were not so he very rarely made a second date.

Giles's longest relationship, if you could call it that, had been with Samantha Savage although she was Samantha Foster in those days. The reason it had lasted was that for most of the time they only saw each other at weekends. Giles was away at college and Sam, well she was off travelling, only returning to recharge her batteries and her bank balance. Giles had often wondered whether his collection of fourteen post cards actually did constitute a relationship. In the absence of anything else he considered that on balance it did. It always surprised him that

Sam had ended up living back in the village. When she left Middle Chippings Sam swore blind that it was forever. Divorced with a daughter in tow, she had returned to her roots several years ago, ploughing her money into The Quarry Man pub. Giles had tentatively tried to rekindle what they had but without much luck. In all honesty the relationship never really went beyond friendship on her part and a massive crush on his.

The Quarry Man. Yes, that was where he would take his date tonight. Great, he had a venue, all he needed was the girl. Giles reached the top of the paddock and dropped the load of straw attached to the front of the tractor. He would be glad when the spring growth came through properly.

Giles stopped the tractor but kept the engine going, the heater full blast. He took out his mobile phone and flipped it open; he trawled through his contacts: his father, the vet, doctor, dentist, not one female except his sister Jean.

Jean too was single. She never had much luck where men were concerned. Married and divorced twice, not to mention some unsavoury liaisons in between. She had never been a particularly good judge of men. Within the space of five years she had divorced husband number one, remarried and divorced husband number two. Finally she had opted to be a single parent.

Gavin spent all of his school holidays at Home Farm. Giles was really fond of his nephew. It wasn't Gavin's fault that he had such a feckless mother. He was a good lad. It just seemed natural that Gavin should come and work in the family business. Initially it had been just for the summer. The idea was that he could then take a bit of time deciding what he wanted to do with his life. He had already wasted a couple of 'gap' years in dead-end jobs. Gavin had his mother's penchant for short-lived relationships, dumping girls and breaking their hearts. Yes, that was it. Giles could get himself 'dumped'. Well perhaps 'dumped' wasn't quite the right word, but he could get himself stood up.

Giles opened the mobile phone and pretended to speak.

"Yes, OK, no don't worry, these things happen. Another time perhaps?" He tried again, but this time with a bit more regret in his tone.

That sounded OK. All he had to do was raise his voice slightly in the pub and people would start listening. It was one of the best ways to start a rumour in Middle Chippings. He would book a table for two at the pub, go home for a bath and put on his best jacket, maybe even polish his boots. Everything had to be as realistic as possible. Giles smiled; well at least he now had a plan. A rubbish plan but at least it was a plan.

CHAPTER 2

Margot Denning wrapped the pashmina tighter around her shoulders – even the bloody weather was conspiring against her. Middle Chippings was losing its lustre by the minute. Not only were the natives hostile but when they did speak, she barely understood a word they said. Margot tried to arrange to have her newspapers delivered and had been asked, "Where be that to?" She also did not like the fact that everyone seemed to know everyone else's business. Now she had to wait for three days before someone could come out and look at her boiler. Surely no heat in February constituted an emergency, well it did as far as she was concerned.

Margot sighed and turned back to the wooden box continuing to unpack her precious books. The whole of one side of the sitting room consisted of floor to ceiling bookshelves. It had been the first thing that had caught her eye when she came to view the cottage. So enamoured was she that she had failed to notice the damp patches in the bathroom, the appalling wallpaper in the bedroom and the inadequate pokey little kitchen. In her defence the viewing had lasted all of twenty minutes, the agent had been reluctant to let her linger. To be honest she had been more concerned with the book tour and catching her flight to the States. Cash rich and time poor, Margot had employed a company to organise the packing up of her flat in London. The same company also arranged to lease it out. They had found a tenant almost immediately. It was rented to an American – initially for two years. For better or worse Margot was stuck with Saddleback Cottage – for the immediate future at least.

Margot finished emptying the packing case and opened another. It contained hardback and paperback copies of every book she had written so far. Margot lined them on the shelves in chronological order. The names on the spines were different as she had several noms de plume. All were romantic novels. Her earliest books were her particular favourites. They had been printed by a small independent publisher. She had wanted to stay with them out of loyalty and gratitude but the bigger companies came knocking and their blandishments were hard to resist. Margot had a very astute market sense – she could spot trends even before they'd had time to establish. Different names and publishers for different genres helped keep control of her writing empire. They wanted historical romance, she gave them Victorian and Edwardian; they wanted racy, she gave them erotica (but never porn). By dint of sheer hard graft Margot aimed to produce two books a year. Constantly juggling the competing demands of her publishers was exhausting. Margot was very aware that you were only as good as your last book so she worked extremely hard to maintain her output and her high standards – to the detriment of her social life.

The phone rang and startled her, not many people knew the number. It was one of her editors, or rather the twelve-year-old anorexic girl that he employed as his P.A. Margot looked at her watch. She had forgotten the appointment with the local newspaper but would not admit it to this chit of a girl.

"No, of course I haven't, Sasha; just remind me again where am I meeting this journalist?"

Margot grabbed a piece of paper and scribbled, "The Quarry Man, eight o'clock, yes I've got it."

She had just over an hour to get herself ready and presentable. Margot didn't particularly enjoy the promotional side of her job but knew that it was necessary. Journalists were always after a different angle, usually one that involved sex or money or both. Margot was more than happy talking about her novels but questions of a personal nature were definitely off-limits, a point she always made at the start of every interview she gave. It wasn't so much that she had an outrageous personal life but rather the opposite. If the truth be told her life was actually a very boring one. In Margot's experience journalists were often wannabe novel writers themselves. They seemed to think that she had the magic key to making a lot of money. However, there was nothing magical about putting in the hours that she did, just sheer hard work.

Margot had lived her childhood through books. By the time she was twelve she had read most of the popular children's writers. She then progressed to Barbara Cartland's Regency romances and from there to Jane Austen, whom she absolutely adored. Everything that Margot knew about sheep farming in Australia or being a doctor on a remote Scottish island came from romantic fiction. Margot's voracious appetite for the genre continued well into her teenage and adult years. She had learned her craft and learned it very well.

Unfortunately, the genre had also influenced Margot's attitude to relationships. She wasn't stupid and knew that life was not all about tall, dark, handsome men falling in love with shy quiet girls but in her heart she hoped it might happen. Margot had spent virtually all of her adult life searching for Mr Right and had never come anywhere close. She would have settled for Mr Almost, but even he had eluded her.

One of the strengths of Margot's writing was her ability to write credible, raunchy and at the same time romantic sex scenes. She had won prizes for it. There was a general assumption, which Margot made no effort to correct, that much of what she wrote was based on personal experience. However, Margot had a secret that she would have died rather than admit to. At forty-two she was still a virgin. Nice girls never went 'all the way' and Margot's mother had impressed on her the importance of 'saving herself' for marriage. Margot's sexual experience was restricted to heavy petting – the acceptable alternative for a teenager in the late Seventies. The spectre of AIDS in the Eighties put a damper on any promiscuity she might have considered. The longer her celibacy continued the harder it was to forgo. At her fortieth birthday party Margot finally accepted that she had been 'saving herself' for something that was unlikely to happen.

The sexual content of her novels titillated and interested journalists who frequently used it as the focus for interviews. For Margot the sex was but a small part of the whole story. However, she was enough of a business woman to know that sex sold books. Two years previously Margot had received the national accolade of being awarded the 'Mr Darcy' prize for romantic fiction. This had propelled her into the media spotlight.

Margot had been invited to take part in television chat shows, radio programmes and countless newspaper interviews. She had even been asked to take part in a debate on Channel 4 about how sex and romance had been affected by the credit crunch. This she had declined.

The attention over what Margot considered to be just one facet of her writing had become overwhelming, she couldn't wait to get away. The American book tour had come up at just the right moment. Time out of London would give her the break she needed to recharge her batteries and escape the paparazzi. It had been her publisher's suggestion that she relocate to a quiet country retreat. Everything had happened so quickly, which was why she had ended up with such a cursory viewing of Saddleback Cottage. Margot was under no illusion that her publishers were concerned for her welfare. They just wanted to get the latest Margot Denning romance on the shelf. Everyone it seemed wanted a piece of her – including this bloody journalist!

There were no street lights, except in the village's main road and Margot was not prepared to ruin another pair of shoes in the pitch darkness. Who knows what she might be stepping into. Margot rummaged around in her handbag for the card that the Post Office woman had given her. 'Leaker B. Quick's Superior Taxi Service'. She booked the taxi for eight o'clock; she'd just have to be a bit late.

Margot dressed to impress, the journalist might only be a local hack but she liked to give value. The 'V' of her top was just low enough to showcase her ample cleavage without making her look cheap. She wore tailored trousers that flattered her slim but short legs and finished the outfit off with a smart fitted jacket. Margot made up her face carefully in the tiny bathroom mirror, it was amazing what a bit of blusher and a couple of flicks of mascara could do. At ten minutes to eight she heard the doorbell. Margot headed towards the hall but was distracted by the telephone ringing. She hesitated, distracted by a further buzz on the doorbell. It sounded as if someone was leaning on the bell push with all their weight. As she hovered indecisively between the door and the ringing phone, the answerphone kicked in so she headed for the front door. Margot couldn't hear what the phone message was about or who it was from. The person at her door had given up on the bell and started on the knocker.

Margot angrily wrenched open the door.

"Do you have to…?"

She didn't finish, taken aback by the tiny man in front of her. He took off his flat cap.

"Begging your pardon, missus, but did you order a taxi?"

"Yes, I did for," Margot looked pointedly at her watch, "for eight o'clock and you are at least ten minutes early."

"Yes, well, you'm lucky to have me. I normally knock off round about seven so this is a special favour, you understand."

"How can it be a special favour when I'm paying you?"

"Money b'aint everything me dear."

"Hang on, I'll just lock up and set the alarm."

The old man snorted, "Wos wanna do that for? I can't remember the last burglary we had in Middle Chippings. This aint the big city you know."

Margot ignored him, set her alarm and locked the door pointedly. He proffered his arm which she declined. Her shoes slipped and slithered on the uneven path as she followed him. She wished she had accepted his offer. The taxi was old but the leather seats were clean. Margot sat back. She could feel one of her 'heads' coming on and hoped that the driver wouldn't talk too much. She reckoned that the pithy put-downs she gave the London cabbies would not have the same effect on this little man.

Leaker drove her out of, and away from, the village. When they passed the church for the third time Margot realised that she was being taken for a ride, literally as well as figuratively. After about a quarter of an hour they arrived outside The Quarry Man. Mr Quick turned.

"That'll be four pounds and fifty pence please."

Margot had no idea how he had worked out the price but she gave him a fiver and climbed out of the ancient car. She looked up and stared through the window. The pub was busy.

She walked through the pub door. All conversation stopped, all eyes turned towards her. It was only for seconds but Margot had the distinct feeling that she had been sized up and found lacking. She spotted the man at the back of the restaurant area. The buzz of conversation resumed as she hurried towards the table.

Chapter 3

Giles's mother had been right, tell one lie and you have to tell another to cover yourself. He stared at himself in the bathroom mirror, not particularly liking what he saw. This was ridiculous; he was shaving to meet a non-existent girlfriend. Giles quickly finished washing and returned to his bedroom. From his wardrobe he took out a clean shirt and his smartest jacket, well – his only jacket really. Giles knew that he ought to admit to his father that he had been joking, that there was no woman. But he had gone too far to back out now. He had to go through the pretence of a dinner date.

Godfrey sat reading the newspaper and looked up when Giles walked in. Godfrey continued the conversation from where they had left it earlier.

"How old is she then?"

"Old enough, Dad."

"Do I know her?"

"I doubt it. Right, that's me ready. How do I look?"

Godfrey appraised Giles. "You look OK," he paused, "with a good light and the wind behind you."

"Thanks a lot," Giles replied sarcastically then added, "Don't wait up."

Giles picked up his car keys from the dresser and left the farmhouse. He climbed into the Land Rover; it smelled of wet dog. He drove to The Quarry Man and parked at the back of the car park. If he had too much to drink he could always leave the Land Rover here and collect it in the morning. The pub was busy, it usually was on a Saturday night, not a lot else to do in Middle Chippings. Samantha Savage was working tonight; she smiled as Giles walked towards the bar.

"Hi Giles, what can I get you?"

Giles ordered a pint.

"Er did you book me a table?"

"Yeah, just like you asked. Who's the lucky lady then?"

"What makes you think it's a lady?"

"Just something a little bird told me."

"It wouldn't be a little bird with a flat cap and size eight boots by any chance?"

"It might be," she smiled at him.

Godfrey had arrived back at the farm late so Giles guessed that he had called in at The Quarry Man on his way home.

Samantha Savage placed the pint on the bar. Giles handed over the money.

"So?"

"So what?"

"So, who is she?"

"Just a friend."

"Don't tease the bloke, Sam, can't you see he's nervous enough already."

Giles looked along the bar. That was all he needed, bloody Danny Bragg. Giles sipped his pint and tried to ignore him. Bragg pulled out his wallet and extracted a five pound note.

"A fiver says that she won't show," he slapped the note on the bar, throwing a challenging look in Giles's direction.

'How the hell does he know?' thought Giles.

"Don't be mean, Danny." Samantha Savage smiled at Giles. "Just ignore him. I've reserved you the table right at the back. We're fairly full tonight. Here," she passed over a newspaper, "read the local rag whilst you are waiting."

Giles walked to the table at the far end of the eating area. He ran his eyes down the menu which he knew off by heart anyway. He opened the local paper and began to read. Giles glanced up at the bar. Danny Bragg and Samantha Savage were deep in conversation pausing only to look across at his table. Giles guessed that they were talking about him. What had seemed like a joke earlier was rapidly losing its charm. He looked at his watch; it was seven fifty-five, time he was stood up. He jiggled around and made a show of pulling his mobile phone out of his pocket.

"Yes, oh hi," he was about to go into his rehearsed speech when he saw Bragg pick up the fiver, and wave it at the landlady, holding out his other hand.

Giles held Bragg's gaze whilst pretending to listen to a conversation. He finished the fake call and looked across at the expectant pair at the bar. He mouthed the words, "Late, she's gonna be late," and he tapped his wristwatch for added emphasis. There was no mistaking the disappointment on Danny Bragg's face. Giles ordered another pint then continued reading the newspaper. He got to the sports pages at the back, a section he never read normally. Another five minutes and he really would have to get himself stood up.

Giles was not sure whether it was the draught of cold air or the sudden silence that made him look up, but look up he did. She was gorgeous. He stared as she squeezed her way through the packed room. It wasn't until she came closer that Giles realised she was heading straight for his table. The woman looked pointedly at the newspaper he was reading.

"So sorry I'm late," she smiled and waved her hand towards the empty chair opposite him. "Shall I?"

"Yes, of course, er be my guest," Giles remembered his manners and jumped to his feet. Margot unbuttoned her jacket and Giles swiftly moved around the table to help her off with it. She smelled as lovely as she looked. He stood looking around wondering what to do next.

"Shall I take that for you?" Giles hadn't noticed Samantha creep up behind them. She had Danny Bragg's fiver in her hand. "Can I bring you a drink before you order your food?"

"Oh thank you, a dry white wine, please."

Samantha Savage smiled and picked up Giles's empty glass, and he nodded. Margot sat down opposite Giles. She glanced down at the newspaper and waited for him to speak. He seemed tongue tied and ill at ease. She broke the silence.

"Right, shall we begin, you know who I am. I'm sorry I have totally forgotten your name, do forgive me," she smiled and waited.

"Er, Farmer. Giles Farmer," should he shake her hand? He didn't want to broadcast that she was a stranger to him.

"Right, Mr Farmer, fire away."

"Oh please, call me Giles."

"Alright then, in which case you must call me Margot."

'Margot' – well it was a start. At least he now knew her name. He panicked, what should he say now? He was rubbish at chatting up women. He grabbed the menu.

"Perhaps you would like to choose," he looked up. "Here comes your wine." Giles pulled out his wallet. Samantha Savage smiled.

"This one's on the house," she turned and looked pointedly at Danny Bragg.

Mesmerised by the gorgeous woman sitting opposite him Giles's mind went totally blank. She appeared to be waiting for him to say something. 'Do you come here often?' was not only a cheesy line but she obviously didn't or he would have met her before.

"Er, what do you do, I mean why are you here in Middle Chippings?"

"The usual," she smiled, "sex and romance."

Giles gulped; this was going much better than he thought. The waitress arrived for their order. Giles asked for another glass of wine for Margot though she had barely touched the first one. He must slow his drinking down. He was already on his third pint. Giles felt ever so slightly pickled, it was never a good idea to drink on an empty stomach. He smiled at the woman opposite. She was waiting again.

"Er, what sort of er romance. Do you have anyone susspific er I mean specific in mind?" He must concentrate, get his words right.

"Not really, it's early days yet. I shall probably try out several lovers before I decide which one to settle with. Then I'll lock myself away with him in my little cottage. I won't leave until it's all over."

Giles didn't know what to say. He decided to try a different tack.

"Tell me a bit about yourself."

Margot was obviously well rehearsed on the subject of Margot. Giles found himself lulled by her voice and the three pints. He listened carefully, nodding and smiling in what he thought were appropriate places. Giles was more than happy to bask in the glow of her company, relieved that he had to make so little effort. At one point she broke off to say:

"Do you not want to make notes?"

"Why, will I be tested later?"

She looked puzzled but continued. Margot talked about publishers and writers so he guessed that she worked for them or something. Giles was not a great reader himself.

When the food arrived she stopped talking about herself. Instead they discussed the different foods that they liked. Giles was on safer ground here. He even found the confidence to take a more active part in the conversation. They finished their meal.

"Well, that's enough about me, what about you?"

"Me? Oh you don't want to hear about me, my life's boring compared with yours. I've lived in Middle Chippings all my life. I er…"

Giles looked up; Samantha Savage was coming towards them carrying Margot's jacket.

"Excuse me, Miss Denning, your taxi's here."

"Good," thought Giles, "I've now got a surname and she doesn't appear to be married."

"Oh, must you go?" Giles failed to keep the disappointment out of his voice. He took the jacket from Sam and held it up for Margot to put on. She leaned slightly back into him. Her hair smelled so clean. Margot turned and faced him, leaned forward and gently brushed her lips against his cheek.

"Thank you for a lovely evening. I hope that you got what you wanted."

"Oh yes. Yes I did, I most certainly did."

He stood and watched as she made her way back through the packed bar; she turned and gave a wave as she left. Damn, he should have walked her to the taxi, he might then have found out where she lived. He sat down. Giles hadn't got a clue who this Margot Denning was or why she had singled him out, but he was damn pleased she did. He had had a brilliant evening in the company of a beautiful woman. Getting one over Danny Bragg was a bonus.

Samantha Savage brought the bill over herself and placed it on the table in front of him. Giles barely glanced at it, the evening had been priceless.

CHAPTER 4

Margot leaned back in the taxi seat. What on earth had possessed her to give him a kiss? She couldn't believe she had done it, her face burned with the embarrassment. She had had a lovely evening. Giles Farmer had been excellent company and he had bought her dinner even though he would probably claim it on expenses. He certainly wasn't like any other journalist she had come across. He was slightly older than she had imagined, about her own age or perhaps a bit younger. Margot had never been good at guessing ages.

It didn't seem as long getting back; she noticed that they only drove past the village church twice this time. Leaker B. Quick stopped the car right outside her gate.

"Do you want me to walk you to the door, miss?"

"No, that's fine, I can manage."

She parted with another fiver and walked up the front path. The taxi waited until she had opened the door and gone inside.

Margot kicked off her shoes and flexed her toes. If men ever wore stilettos they would never expect women to but when you were as short as she was every inch helped. Margot wished that she hadn't booked the taxi so early. The evening was just beginning to get interesting. She rummaged around in some of the kitchen boxes and found what she was looking for. She poured herself a small brandy and took it into the sitting room.

God what a mess the house was. She needed to get herself straight so that she could get on with her next novel. She had all these ideas whizzing around in her head with never enough hours in the day to get them written down. Margot finished her drink and rinsed the glass in the sink. As she walked past the telephone she noticed that the message light was flashing. She pressed the button.

"Oh hello, Miss Denning. Look I am really, really sorry, but I won't be able to make this evening's meeting at The Quarry Man. Could we reschedule it for another night, please?

You can get me by phoning the exchange at the Gazette. I do hope that you get this message and that you don't have a wasted journey. I am so looking forward to meeting you; I'm such a fan of yours."

Margot stared at the answer machine and listened to the message a second and a third time. If the man on the phone was from the Gazette then who the hell had she just spent the evening with? If Giles Farmer wasn't a journalist then that would explain quite a lot. She had been puzzled as to why he knew absolutely nothing about her – although he did seem rather keen and appeared to hang on to her every word. She wondered why Giles Farmer had let her talk so much about herself. OK, so she had launched almost immediately into her well rehearsed speech about her body of work and plans for the future but surely at some point he could have just stopped her and clarified who exactly he was. She wouldn't have minded. She might have felt a bit stupid but not half as foolish as she felt now. Margot looked at her watch; it was too late to phone anyone, and anyway she was so tired that she couldn't think straight. She would deal with it in the morning.

Margot overslept and woke with one of her 'heads'. Knowing that she would be unable to concentrate on writing she pottered around trying to get some sort of order out of the chaos that was her lounge. The telephone rang incessantly – her agent phoned her twice, she had a call about a television interview and a local radio station asked if they could interview her on their breakfast programme. In addition that morning alone she had three visitors. The vicar called, so did someone from the WI and a scruffy-looking man asked if she needed any gardening work done. As a consequence of all of these interruptions Margot failed to do any of the jobs that she had planned. In an attempt to get rid of her callers, and ingratiate herself in the village she had made a donation to the church tower fund, volunteered to give a talk to the WI and was now a bona fide employer with a gardener to pay.

She telephoned the man from the Gazette and rearranged her meeting for later in the week. He wanted to hold the interview in The Quarry Man but Margot declined. How would it look if she turned up there again two days later with someone different? It would not do and anyway, it had cost her a fortune in taxi fares, so she arranged for them to meet during the day at the local tea shop.

With the interview rescheduled all that she had to do was to try to work out who this Giles Farmer was, and why he had treated her to dinner the night before. Normally Margot loved a mystery, but mainly because she had written it and knew all the answers – this she hadn't a clue about. All she did know was that Giles Farmer was rather sweet, quite nice looking and she wouldn't mind meeting him again.

Later in the morning Margot felt better and decided to get on with her writing. Margot's original plan had been to install her computer and a work station in the dining room, which she would use as a study. Almost as soon as she had set it up she realised that it would not work. The phone rang again; she ignored it. She would have to do something; she couldn't work with these constant interruptions. Margot opened the back door and walked into the garden to get a bit of peace and quiet. She needed to think. The cottage was far too noisy. It had been quieter in her flat in London.

To one side of the cottage was a low building, some of the roof tiles were missing but the walls, which consisted of large slabs, looked sound. The door was heavy and had two large iron hinges. It was stiff but opened after a hefty shove. Inside, it was divided into pens. Margot vaguely remembered the estate agent mumbling something about an old piggery in the garden. This was the first chance she had to look at it properly. Saddleback Cottage had once belonged to the big farm up the road. Margot remembered some research she had done for one of her historical sagas. Farm workers often kept their own livestock either to sell or to feed their large families. She stood for a few moments; there was a calmness about the building.

That was it, just what she needed. Not a piggery but a proper office, a quiet space far away from visitors, phones and the hundred and one other distractions that prevented her from writing. Margot knew next to nothing about the building trade but reckoned that the piggery could be made into a viable working space. The walls were sound, and although there was a slight smell of damp she felt sure that it could be sorted. She

31

would then have the luxury of her own dedicated writing space. It was something that she had always wanted. In London it had just not been possible. All she needed now was a reliable builder who could do the conversion for her.

Margot had a late lunch and saw from the state of her cupboards that she needed to do some shopping. Margot had never learned to drive, living in London there had been no need but she was used to walking. She put on her flattest pair of shoes and a warm coat. Saddleback Cottage was near the bottom of the unmade lane. She and the people in the farm at the top were the only ones who needed to use it. Good job really as it was in a bad state of repair. Margot couldn't remember the name of the farm. It was probably written in her deeds somewhere.

By the time she got to the road and the narrow pavement running alongside it her shoes were filthy. She turned left towards the village high street, passing a couple of people who nodded a return to her smile. Margot had only been walking for about five minutes when she saw the sign on the opposite side of the road; it read: 'The Quarry Man next turning 100 yards'. A hundred yards, a hundred bloody yards. That taxi driver had taken a good quarter of an hour to drive her to the pub and looking at the distance involved it would have been quicker to have walked it. Just because she was from London, it didn't mean she could be taken advantage of. Margot continued her walk and passed the village school, judging by the noise it was playtime. She walked on for a few more minutes then came across the shop. She walked past; she might as well explore the rest of the village before she did her shopping.

A quarter of an hour later and she was back outside the village stores. She had found the tea shop where she was to meet the proper journalist and had worked out where the church and the village hall were. The Post Office was at the back of the shop and there was only one other customer – Margot's WI visitor from earlier in the day.

"Emma, this was the lady I was telling you about. She is a famous writer; she's going to come to WI to give us a talk."

"Really?" Emma came out of her little post office cage, locked up and turned towards Margot to have a better look. The woman walked behind the counter and faced Margot. Behind the woman there were rows of wine bottles and cans of beer and cider. Margot had intended on buying a bottle of brandy but had a feeling that her purchase would be noted and discussed later; so she thought better of it.

"Yes, I'm looking forward to it. Now, I just need a few bits and pieces to tide me over. Could I have a loaf of bread, some eggs and some milk, please?"

Emma bustled around collecting things from the shelves and placing everything in a carrier bag recycled from one of the big supermarket chains.

"I need to have some work done on my cottage and wondered if you knew of any good builders around here?"

The two ladies looked at each other.

"Well there is Danny Bragg, course he doesn't actually do the building himself. These days, he's got quite a few men who work for him. Got his finger in lots of pies has Danny."

Emma rummaged under the counter and pulled out a magazine.

"This is last month's parish magazine. All the local people advertise in here. They don't really need to but it helps the vicar out with his tower appeal. I think Danny is in there, you could always give him a ring."

Margot thanked the two ladies and left the shop. She didn't have many groceries but they felt heavy after she had been carrying them for a while. She turned off the main road and down into her lane. She had seconds to react as the tractor pulled out. The driver swerved missing her by inches. What he didn't miss was the deep water-filled rut. As his tyre tractor hit it square on he sprayed mud and water all over Margot.

"What the hell," she twisted around but the tractor had already gone, disappearing down the main road. Margot looked at her mud spattered coat and rubbed ineffectively at the marks with a crumpled tissue. She would never get the marks off. The bloody man hadn't even stopped to apologise.

CHAPTER 5

That was the second time the stupid woman had jumped out in front of him and he had almost killed her this time. It was lucky that he had such good reflexes. Giles guessed it was the new owner of Saddleback Cottage. Dad had said that someone with more money than sense had bought it. At least it hadn't been sold to Danny Bragg, despite his attempts to bribe the estate agent. Whoever the new owner was, if they continued to step out into the road without looking they wouldn't last long.

Giles caught sight of himself in the mirror. The remnants of his hangover were still visible in the dark bags under his eyes. He had woken late and not had time for a shave; he looked and felt lousy. Godfrey had waited up for him last night and despite an interrogation worthy of the Spanish inquisition Giles had given nothing away.

"Well are you seeing her again?" Godfrey had finally asked.

"May be, may be not, who knows," Giles had replied and then to himself he murmured, "I hope so."

Godfrey had gone to bed soon afterwards. Despite his tiredness Giles found it hard to sleep. He kept seeing Margot's smile and smelling her perfume. Her cheek had felt soft when she leaned it against his.

His late and broken night's sleep and the copious pints of beer he had consumed were having an impact this morning. Giles parked the tractor outside the village store. As was his custom Giles stepped out of his muddy boots before walking into the shop. He looked down and registered that his socks were odd. He picked up a pint of milk and a local paper and waited to be served. Emma chatted to the other customer in the shop.

"Oh yes, really famous and so so rich you know. Writes romantic novels, she's written hundreds of them."

Giles suddenly paid attention to the conversation in front of him. Romantic novels; now wasn't that what the gorgeous

Margot was talking about last night? Emma lowered her voice and leaned towards the old man in front of him. Giles strained to hear what she was saying.

"Writes mucky ones too, if you know what I mean."

"Really?" now the old man was interested.

Emma looked up and sensed Giles's interest.

"Is that all you want, Giles?" She held out her hand for the money.

Giles paid for his purchases and left. He looked at his watch; time to head back home. He pulled the tractor into the yard and saw that his sister's car was parked alongside the garage. He saw a couple of suitcases and a rucksack on the back seat. Giles pushed open the back door and walked into the kitchen.

"Alright, our Jean?"

"Oh hi, Giles. I was just telling Dad, he's not getting any younger."

"No you're right, none of us are." Giles waited for his sister's punch line, she must want something, she usually did.

"So I thought an extra pair of hands around the place, always useful when you're busy."

Giles could see where this was leading. He looked around for her son Gavin.

"What's he done now? Don't tell me; let me guess. There's a father with a shotgun looking for him."

"Giles, don't be nasty. He's a very good looking boy, as you well know – these young girls, well, they throw themselves at him. What's he to do?"

Giles was tempted to say "resist" but he didn't.

"How long is it for this time?"

"Just for the summer initially, until he can make up his mind what he wants to do with his life."

Godfrey took no part in the discussion between his son and daughter. Giles would be the one taking responsibility for the lad. It was up to him whether Gavin came to stay or not. Gavin had finished college a couple of years ago and was on an extended 'gap year', trying to decide what he actually wanted to do with his life. Despite his mother's pushing in various directions Gavin always came back to the farm.

"He's not expecting to get paid I hope."

Jean sensed victory. "No, of course not, it's family, but if you could see your way for a bit of pocket money, just to help him out a bit."

Giles nodded. Having sole responsibility for a son whose raging hormones and good looks got him into all sorts of scrapes meant that Jean's life was not always easy.

"OK, he can stay, but he'll have to pull his weight, mind."

"Oh thank you Giles, Gavin will be ever so pleased. I'll go and get him."

She walked through the kitchen and into the front room. Giles could hear raised voices, his nephew's sullen one and his sister's placatory tone.

"Might as well eat," Godfrey said.

Gavin and Jean joined them around the kitchen table for dinner. Gavin had the farmer physique and at six foot plus equalled his uncle in height. Like Giles he was hard muscle, the result of the gym rather than hard work. Giles had a soft spot for the boy. Jean had parted from Gavin's father soon after Gavin had been born. They never should have married in the first place. Jean was on the rebound – Bill had been the wrong person at the right time. Gavin had been a lovely kid but a nightmare teenager. Giles knew that he would come good in the end, but probably not until he had put his mother through the wringer first.

After dinner Gavin unloaded his gear and decanted into the spare bedroom. Godfrey wandered outside to check on the animals. Giles and his sister sat at the table drinking coffee.

"I'm ever so grateful, Giles, he's a good boy, just gets himself into scrapes."

"I know, Jean, I know," he patted his sister's hand. "To be honest I could do with a bit of help around here. Dad is getting tired."

"The farm's too much for the two of you. You ought to think about selling some of the land. There is this push to get affordable housing in the villages. I read about it in the local paper last week."

"Affordable housing, yeah that's what the council says just to get their hands on the land. Before you know it some greedy bastard has gone and built five-bedroom mansions with no garden and nowhere to park." Giles didn't name names but they both knew he was talking about Danny Bragg. "We should have bought Saddleback Cottage when we had the chance. If only Dad hadn't insisted on holding out to get it at a lower price. I tried to tell him but he didn't listen."

"I hear it's been sold to some woman from London." Jean lifted her cup and drained the coffee.

"Yes, some old dear, I nearly ran her over this morning."

"Well, at least Danny Bragg didn't get his hands on it."

Danny and Jean had been at school together and were briefly an item until Danny had gone off to the big city to make his fortune. Not long after Jean had met Bill and the rest was history.

The door opened and Godfrey came back in. Jean looked at her watch. "I'll have to be going, Dad. Thanks so much for having Gavin. He's promised that he won't be any trouble." All three men stood in the yard and waved Jean off.

As the tail lights disappeared down the lane the three of them turned and looked at each other. "Pub?"

"Why not?"

They walked to The Quarry Man. The Land Rover was still in the car park from Giles's visit the night before. Giles bought the first round – he usually did where his father and nephew were concerned. He would go easy tonight; his headache had only just lifted from this morning's hangover.

"With the boys tonight I see," Samantha smiled as she pulled on the pump. "Oh oh, you've got young Casanova again. Whose heart has he broken this time?"

"Hello, Mrs Savage, looking as beautiful as ever." Samantha smiled back.

'Now why don't I have that effect on women?' thought Giles. They walked over to a spare table. Giles sat with his back to the bar.

"Come on then, Uncle Giles, spill the beans. What's this Grandad tells me about you having a date?"

"None of your business," Giles sipped his pint slowly.

Gavin grinned at his grandfather.

"If you need any advice or tips, Uncle Giles, just come to me."

"Well for a start you can drop the uncle. Anyway I can't see what all these girls see in a skinny kid like you."

Suzie Savage walked over to them pad in hand. Gavin smiled at her but she ignored him.

"Did you want to order?"

"I'll have a burger."

The waitress scribbled on her pad, and looked at the others who shook their heads remembering the casserole they had consumed less than an hour earlier.

"What? I'm a growing lad." Gavin looked at the menu card. "You couldn't lend me a fiver could you, Giles?"

A little while later Gavin wandered to the end of the bar to get some cutlery and took the opportunity to speak to the waitress. Giles noticed the exchange, so did Samantha Savage. She stared at Gavin pointedly and gave her daughter a warning look. Gavin rejoined the others at the table.

"What was all that about?"

"Nothing, Giles, nothing at all." He looked back at the bar. "I can't believe that's little Suzie Savage; when did she grow up into such a gorgeous looking girl?"

"Gavin," Godfrey growled a warning at his grandson.

It didn't take long for Gavin's food to arrive. The waitress put it and the bill on the table. Giles was about to pick the receipt up when Gavin got to it first. He read the bill and smiled.

"Result I've got her phone number," he tore off the bottom of the bill, kept the small piece and passed the rest to Giles.

"Watch and learn, Uncle G, watch and learn." He bit into his burger. "If you see something you want, don't hesitate; go for it. Life's too short to sit around and wait for them to make the first move."

CHAPTER 6

Margot woke early. In the short time she had been living in Saddleback Cottage she had quickly settled into a routine. She would try to get three or four hours' writing done before lunch then walk down to the village shop to pick something up to eat. Her afternoons would be spent editing the morning's work. In London she would have worked straight through, but living in the village she felt a moral obligation to participate. Her ritual of walking to the shop and buying locally made her feel part of the community. Margot had given her talk at the WI and it had gone down quite well. She had sold several books on the strength of it. Margot had also arranged for Bragg, the local builder, to come and look at the piggery. She was keen to get the renovation going. Margot had not, as yet, met her immediate neighbours from the farm further up the lane.

The phone rang; it was her agent reminding her about the interview with the local journalist. The genuine article this time. 'Shame really,' she thought, she had quite liked the bogus one. Despite all her wanderings around the village Margot had not come across him. She had been tempted to visit the pub again but although she may have been happy walking into a London wine bar on her own, The Quarry Man was a different matter.

The doorbell went, Margot answered it. It was Danny Bragg.

"Hi, I've got an appointment with," he looked at his notebook, "a Miss Denning," he flashed her a big smile. Danny recognised the woman immediately. She was Giles Farmer's mystery girlfriend from the other night. No wonder Giles had looked so pleased with himself, she was an attractive woman.

"You must be Mr Bragg, come in."

Danny Bragg looked around whilst Margot made some coffee. She had made the cottage look really nice. It was a lot smaller than he remembered. Margot carried the tray into the sitting room. They quickly settled down to business.

"What I want is an estimate for an extension to incorporate the shed at the side of the cottage."

"Piggery."

"I beg your pardon?"

"Piggery. It's not a shed, it's a piggery."

"Really?"

"Yes, it's quite old, older than the cottage I think."

"Is that likely to be a problem?"

"It might be. Leave it with me. I'll need to submit plans to the Council. We'll see how it goes, shall we? And what did you want it converted into?"

"An office. I'm a writer and I would like to keep my work separate from my home if I could."

Danny Bragg leaned back in the chair; he was in no rush to get going. Margot drained her coffee cup and look pointedly at her watch.

"Well don't you want to go and measure it up or something?"

"Nah, I'll send one of my boys around to do that."

Danny Bragg would not normally have bothered to make a site visit for so small a job. He had been interested to meet the person who had beaten him to Saddleback Cottage. Having now met her and realised that she was Giles Farmer's mysterious date he was intrigued to find out more about her.

"Excuse me asking but didn't I see you with Giles Farmer in The Quarry Man the other night?"

Margot started to say something then thought better of it. Instead she picked up the tray and took it into the kitchen. Danny Bragg could smell prevarication a mile off and closed in on her, following her.

"Er, yes, I did have a meal with Mr Farmer. Why, do you know him?"

"Yeah, known him for years actually," he paused, "but I must admit, I did wonder how you and him, I mean you and he knew each other."

Margot was at a loss as to how to reply. She rapidly tried to think of something that wouldn't sound stupid. She smiled at Danny Bragg to take the sting out of her words.

"Ah well, that would be telling. Now if you could give me a rough idea as to how much this conversion is likely to cost then we could both get on with finishing our working day."

Danny took the hint. He wound up their discussion and left promising a quote within the week. Margot was quite glad to see the back of him. He had made her uncomfortable in a way that Giles Farmer never had. The meeting had put her all behind with her writing schedule so she would have to forgo her afternoon walk. If she and Giles Farmer were the subject of village gossip she needed to contact him, unfortunately she had no idea how.

On Sunday it was family service at the church. Margot went because she had been specifically invited by the vicar and thought it rude not to go. It was a lovely simple service and although it was cold people milled around outside afterwards chatting. She had spotted Giles almost immediately. He was sitting at the front of the church, whilst she was right at the back. He hadn't noticed her. She left before he did and waited a little way down the church path hoping to catch his attention. The final few came out of the main church door but no sign of Giles. He must have left by a different entrance. Then she saw him. He was standing by a gate the other side of the churchyard; he must have come out of a door by the altar. He was with two other men, one older and one much younger. Giles caught sight of her and lifted his hand in a wave. She looked around to check that the wave was intended for her and smiled back at him. Margot would have walked over but she was stopped by the vicar. He was asking her how she had enjoyed the service and how she was settling in. She replied as politely as she could. Over the vicar's shoulder she could see that the elder man was trying to get the others to leave, they appeared to be late for something. She saw Giles shrug and turn to follow the other two down the path.

"Oh, vicar, that man over there," the vicar turned, "is that Giles Farmer?"

"Yes that's Giles, three generations of the same farming family, the old man is Godfrey and the younger one is his grandson."

Grandson, so Giles had children. She had only caught a glimpse of the other two men but could see a family resemblance. All three were tall with dark hair but it was the set of their shoulders and the way that they walked that marked them out as being cut from the same cloth. Margot wondered if there was a wife around but felt that she couldn't ask. She glanced over the vicar's shoulder again. Giles and his family had reached the lychgate; Giles glanced quickly back at Margot then he was gone. The young man with him ran back towards Margot and the vicar.

"Excuse me," he looked pointedly at the vicar who shook Margot's hand for a second time and left.

Margot turned to face the young man. He smiled and handed her a slip of paper.

"It's his phone number," he grinned then hurried off after the rest of his family.

Margot looked around to see if anyone had noticed the exchange but everyone else seemed occupied with their own business. She thrust the slip of paper into her pocket and walked home smiling. Having the number was one thing, but having the courage to do something with it, well that was something altogether different.

Margot had always disliked Sundays; they seemed to emphasise somehow just how alone she was. Rural Sundays were even worse than London ones. At least up in town she could go and visit a gallery or a museum but here there was nothing, except her work. The novel wasn't going as well as she had hoped so she didn't mind using her 'dead' Sunday afternoon to write.

Margot placed the phone number on her desk. She actually picked up the telephone twice and even got as far as dialling the first three digits before dropping the receiver. What would she say? If Giles knew that she had been given the telephone number this morning would she look too forward by phoning this afternoon? Oh God she had never been any good at this sort of thing. How long should one wait before contacting someone after a first date or after you had been given their telephone number? Had she left it too long already? Would he think she wasn't interested? Margot had already transgressed the rule of only kissing on date three. She sighed; did the same rules apply when you were forty-three as opposed to twenty-three-years old? Margot felt more nervous now than she had ever done then.

Margot opened a bottle of Merlot to have with her Sunday evening meal. By the time she had eaten, washed up and poured herself another glass it was nine-thirty. Damn it, why not.

She picked up the phone and quickly dialled the number before her courage failed. It rang for ages and she was on the point of giving up when someone picked up at the other end. The voice was old, it wasn't him.

"Yes? Sorry who did you want? Giles?" The man moved his mouth away from the mouthpiece and Margot heard him shouting across the room.

"Someone on the phone for Giles, Gavin ask your mother to give him a yell, he's in the bath."

Before Margot could protest the old man had dropped the phone on to a table. She could hear a woman's voice shouting, presumably up the stairs. Margot didn't know how long it took Giles to get out of the bath and come down to answer the phone. By the time he did she was long gone. She had terminated the call almost immediately. It appeared that not only was there a son but also a wife. Disappointed she finished off the rest of the Merlot.

'Sod Giles Farmer,' she thought.

CHAPTER 7

"You did what?" Giles had to shout above the noise of the tractor even though Gavin was squashed in the cab beside him.

"I said, I gave her your number."

"Gave who what number?"

"That woman in the church, the one who was giving you the eye."

Giles turned, looked at the boy and then switched off the engine. The silence was more deafening than the engine noise had ever been.

"Say again, you did what and to whom?"

Gavin sighed as if talking to a difficult child. "When we were in church the other day, didn't you notice that woman, she stared at you virtually the whole way through. You must have noticed her, well dressed, not bad looking for her age. She was sitting right at the back. I kind of got the impression she was trying to attract your attention."

"So?" Giles didn't like the way this conversation seemed to be heading.

There was a wealth of controlled anger in that one little word 'So'. Gavin began to lose his confidence.

"Well, I noticed that when we came out she was looking over at us. I think she was going to speak but Grandad was rushing us home because Mum was coming for lunch."

"So?"

"So I ran back and gave her your phone number."

Giles started up the tractor engine and they continued in silence for a few minutes.

"Did she say anything?" Giles tried not to sound keen.

"No not really, just thank you and then she walked off."

They finished the work in the lower paddock as it was beginning to get dark. Neither of them mentioned the incident of the telephone number again. Godfrey had arrived home before

44

them and was busy reheating the casserole that Jean had left the night before. Giles casually asked:

"Any messages, Dad?" he noticed the envelopes on the table that his father had begun to go through. "Any letters or phone calls?"

"Just what's on the table. Oh and someone phoned for you last night but you were in the bath. I got Jean to call you but when I went to tell them you'd be a few minutes they'd gone."

"Did this er person say what he wanted?"

"No, and anyway t'weren't a man, t'were a woman."

Gavin didn't say anything but just grinned at his uncle. After dinner Godfrey started going through his mail.

"Well I'll be buggered," he looked up at the other two. "This 'ere's a letter from the Parish Council. Says the new owners of Saddleback Cottage want to convert the old piggery."

Godfrey automatically looked towards the big kitchen window. Were it not dark his view would have been across two open fields. The piggery was the first building that could be seen.

"What sort of a conversion? Does it say what she wants to turn it into?" Giles looked across at his father.

Godfrey reread the letter. "It doesn't say exactly, just that it's going to be converted. Danny Bragg is down as the agent."

"Don't worry, Dad, that's agricultural land, they won't get permission to build. If the Parish Council don't turn it down the District Council will."

"My father should never have let the cottage go. He was a fool; he had no right, leaving it to that," Godfrey spluttered, "that bloody woman."

The cottage had always been part of Home Farm. It was used to house the cow man who was employed in Godfrey's father's time. Unfortunately, George Farmer had a roving eye which had finally settled on Maggie Smith, a girl he had been at school with. Rumour had it that Maggie and George had had a 'thing' going for years. There was even some talk that Smithy was George's illegitimate son. It might have remained just conjecture, had it not been for George's will. George had left Saddleback Cottage to Will Smith, Maggie having passed on a couple of years before George himself. Folks reckoned that

George was keeping a promise he had made. Whatever the truth, the ownership of Saddleback Cottage passed from the Farmer family to the Smiths.

During the time that Will Smith had lived at Saddleback Cottage, he and Godfrey never spoke or even acknowledged each other. When Smithy himself died the cottage went up for tender. Godfrey reckoned that no one would pay the ridiculous asking price so he had held back, biding his time. Danny Bragg was a Smith on his mother's side and he too was after the cottage. In the event, they both lost out. Saddleback Cottage was sold by secret tender to the highest bidder. Neither Godfrey nor Danny Bragg knew by how much they had missed getting the cottage but the estate agent hinted that the cottage had gone for considerably more than the guide price.

"The owner's some woman."

Giles looked up, "Is there a name?"

"Yes, name of Dudd, Maureen Dudd."

"Miss or Mrs?" Giles asked.

"Dunno, I think she's a Ms, whatever that is. Stupid title if you ask me, neither one thing nor t'other."

"What are you going to do, Dad?"

"Object of course."

"On what grounds?"

"Oh, I know on what grounds, son; don't you worry."

Giles knew better than to ask too many questions. Over the years Giles had learned to keep his own counsel about the feud between his father and Will Smith. Personally Giles had never seen the point in holding grudges. However, in Middle Chippings grudge holding was an Olympic sport and one for which Godfrey held Gold, Silver and Bronze. George Farmer had not been a good sort. He had treated his wife very badly. Jean was terrified that Gavin might take after her wayward grandfather. Giles could understand his sister's concern but the lad was still young and there was nothing wrong with sowing a few wild oats.

Giles had been shy and tongue-tied with women when he had been Gavin's age. Gavin had a lovely easy way with girls. He had a charm that women seemed to instantly warm to, he didn't get that from the Farmer side of the family. Giles had had a few relationships in his time, but nothing he would consider 'special'.

"Fancy a drink, young Gavin?"

"I'd love to, Giles, but I'm skint, on account of the fact that I'm working for love at the moment."

Giles laughed, "OK, I'm buying."

"Then I'm drinking."

They grabbed their coats and climbed into the Land Rover. The pub was virtually empty although Gavin brightened up when he spied Suzie Savage, looking around Gavin saw Danny Bragg deep in conversation with one of his men. Giles sipped his pint; he knew that Samantha would come over and chat once she had finished serving. She was a good landlady. Samantha wandered down the bar towards him. He offered to buy her a drink which she declined. She looked across to Danny Bragg's table.

"Treats this place like his own personal office."

Danny was renowned for carrying out his dodgier deals after hours. Giles wondered what he was up to this time. As if sensing the attention Danny looked up. He picked up the empty glasses and walked to the bar.

"Two more pints, Sammy love," he nodded an acknowledgement towards Giles. "Met your girlfriend the other day."

"Sorry?"

"You know, Margot. Nice legs, nice arse, nice …"

Giles didn't rise to the bait and chose to ignore him.

Danny continued. "Lovely lady, I'm hoping to get to know her better myself, in a manner of speaking."

Giles tried to feign indifference and failed miserably. Bragg smiled, pleased that he had rattled Giles. He picked up the beer and returned to his table. Samantha put her hand on Giles's arm.

"Don't take any notice of him. Nice classy lady like her, she wouldn't give him the time of day."

Giles hoped that Sam was right. He knew very little about Margot Denning but what he did know was that he wanted to see her again. He also knew that Gavin was right. He couldn't just sit around and wait for her to contact him.

Giles turned his back on Bragg. Samantha wandered away to serve another customer. There was a full width mirror behind the bar. Giles could see the optics and glasses reflected in it. He could also see a middle-aged man who had let himself go. His hair was unkempt, his face unshaven and although Giles hadn't noticed it earlier his shirt could have been cleaner. What woman would be interested in someone like him? After his mother's death Giles had watched his father grow older and lonelier. Giles didn't want that to happen to him.

Gavin finally tore himself away from the young waitress and rejoined Giles at the bar. His glass was empty.

"Same again?" Gavin waved to get Samantha's attention.

"Well if you're offering."

Whilst they waited for to be served Giles turned to Gavin and asked:

"Do you think I look old?"

They were both facing the bar mirror so Gavin spoke to Giles's reflection choosing his words carefully. "No, you look OK for your age. You've still got a full head of hair and only the slight beginnings of a paunch. I'd say you looked spot on for your age." Gavin grinned, "How old are you, Uncle Giles?"

Samantha caught the tail end of their conversation.

"He's old enough to know better."

"Do you think he looks OK for his age, Mrs Savage?"

"Not bad, not bad at all, could do with a haircut and perhaps some more modern clothes. But apart from that, yes I'd say he's OK. He'll pass muster and while we're at it, don't keep monopolising my waitress, she's not paid to stand around and gossip."

Gavin grinned back at the landlady and said nothing.

CHAPTER 8

Considering what a small place Middle Chippings was Margot was surprised that she hadn't casually bumped into Giles Farmer. It hadn't been for want of looking. The brief glimpse after church had been the last time she had seen him. Perhaps it was for the best. She had always made it a strict rule never to become involved with married men.

Margot sat at her computer; she had just finished the first draft of her next novel. She always felt a sense of achievement at this point, closely followed by an ominous dread. She was thrilled that she had told the story but knew that the hard work of editing had to be undertaken. It was likely to be at least three months before she submitted it to her publisher. As she typed Margot kept the Internet open in the background. She tried not to be beguiled by it too much. It was an excellent time waster, but she also found it incredibly useful for checking facts. Margot was usually very self-disciplined with her time but the finishing of the novel meant that she could indulge herself with a bit of idle surfing and flights of fancy.

Margot clicked on to the 'Country Cousins' website. She had found it quite by accident when researching Internet dating for her current novel. What she particularly liked about this organisation was that as well as the website they also had proper offices in Exeter. You had the option of making an appointment with a real person or you could remain anonymous for as long as you liked. Margot logged on to the home page and hovered her mouse over the registration button. She hesitated.

"Oh what the hell," she said out aloud and clicked to open the online registration form. She stared at the screen for a few minutes before deciding that it might be fun to complete it.

Personal details, height, weight, hair colour were no problem. Margot resisted the temptation to lie, especially in the box marked 'weight'. Margot had to describe herself in one hundred words; 'surely for a writer it shouldn't be too difficult,' was her first thought. Her second was 'Help!' Margot couldn't decide between total honesty and fabrication. In the end she used both. Unfortunately her difficulties did not end there. Page four asked for her 'ideal' partner. She was tempted to put 'someone who is breathing and with a pulse', but decided that made her sound desperate.

Margot typed in her requirements in the 'What are you looking for' section. For height she put six foot plus. Despite being short herself she favoured tall men. Good manners were a definite must, as was a reasonable level of intelligence. She had no preference about what sort of a job her future partner might have. She hesitated about whether or not she minded someone who was divorced or who had children. That was a tough call. Margot pondered for a while. The chances were that a man within her required age bracket was likely to have some sort of personal baggage so she ticked all three boxes, single, divorced and widowed.

Margot placed her hand over the computer mouse and moved the cursor over the screen. Should she register or not? There was no other way she was going to find a man. She closed her eyes, and clicked. It was done. Within seconds she had received an acknowledgement to say that her application had been registered. Margot printed off her application form and placed it in a file. It was only later when she read through the paper copy that it dawned on her. The specification of her ideal partner was a description of Giles Farmer. She hoped that Giles Farmer wasn't the sort to register with an Internet dating agency. If he was she hoped against hope that he had chosen a site other than Country Cousins. Thinking about it logically Margot doubted that he could even switch on a computer, let alone surf the Internet. In any event, he was history. Margot did not do married men, end of story.

The following morning Margot decided to give herself the day off. She opened her wardrobe and looked through her clothes. She really didn't have anything suitable to wear in the country. The phone rang. It was her agent trying to arrange a meeting. She was reluctant to travel down to the country so Margot agreed to go up to London. The appointment was made for the following day. She looked at her watch; if she hurried she could catch the mid afternoon train and be in London by early evening. The novel had kept Margot so busy that she had not been clothes shopping for ages.

Margot telephoned Abi, one of her dearest friends, immediately.

"Oh Margot, what a lovely surprise, of course we would love to see you. No problem. We're off to a party tonight but you are more than welcome to come along."

Margot started to protest but Abi would have none of it. Abi and Margot had been good friends for more years than they both cared to remember. It didn't matter how long the gap was between meetings. They never had any problems catching up where they left off. Margot telephoned to book her taxi. She and Mr Leaker B. Quick, the taxi driver, had come to an understanding. He wouldn't overcharge and in return she would give him a generous tip.

Margot caught an early train and then a taxi to her friend's flat. Abi was so pleased to see her that Margot felt guilty at not being in touch. Abi was a public relations consultant. She dealt with all sorts of people and businesses. Although she earned a very high salary Abi envied Margot's glamorous life and she was eager for Margot's news. They chatted over a pot of tea and Margot asked about the party that she was being dragged along to. Abi was her usual vague self; she said that it was more like a reception. Her company were helping to promote a new government initiative aimed at invigorating the rural economy.

Margot had brought very little in the way of luggage but decided to treat herself to something new and glamorous to wear. Margot was disappointed that Abi was unable to go shopping with her. Oxford Street was as mad and busy as ever. Margot had forgotten how rude people in the city could be. She made her way to one of the big department stores. Margot hated the insecurity of not knowing what the dress code was for the evening's reception. She would have to opt for something 'safe'. She was pleased with the wide black trousers and the floaty top. They made her look slimmer than she felt. She also treated herself to some outrageous earrings to add an air of flippancy. It was such a long time since Margot had had a good night out. She felt really up for it.

The reception was held in one of the government buildings just off Whitehall. It was packed when Margot and Abi arrived. They squeezed their way through the mass of people to the bar. Margot picked up her glass of wine and tried to find somewhere less busy. This was not the sort of evening she had planned. The push from behind caused her to spill the wine. Margot turned angrily to remonstrate with the person who had pushed her. Instead she just gave a big grin – it was Giles Farmer.

"I'm terribly sorry …" he looked up, "Margot."

"Giles." There was no mistaking the pleasure in either of their voices.

"Fancy meeting you here," they said in unison and then laughed. They each waited for the other to speak.

"Well aren't you going to introduce me?" Abi looked from her friend to the tall man with a silly grin on his face.

"Oh sorry. Abi, this is Giles, Giles Farmer. He comes from Middle Chippings, the village where I now live."

"Look let me get you another drink, dry white, isn't it? You seem to have thrown most of that one down the front of your lovely outfit." Giles took Margot's glass, turned and pushed his way back to the bar.

"Well. Come on, come on tell all. Who is that lovely man?"

"I've told you, his name is Giles Farmer and he lives in the same village as me. I hardly know the man. There is nothing else to tell, honestly."

"So how come he knows what sort of wine you drink?"

Margot felt herself colour up. "We err, we had dinner together."

"And?"

"And, that's all; anyway he's married so that is the end of that."

Giles returned with the drink, plus a pint for himself. He and Margot manoeuvred themselves into a corner. Abi diplomatically wandered off. Margot smiled at Giles, what the hell, it was just an evening out. Married or not she would just enjoy his company.

"My father should be here really not me. Dad's been a Farmers' Union official for years but he couldn't come. I left him at home. Dad reckoned that we don't get a lot out of this government so I might as well use his invitation and get a free meal and a good night out."

"And has it been a good night out so far?" she smiled at him.

"Not really, but," he looked at his watch, "but with effect from five minutes ago it has got a whole lot better."

Giles steered Margot towards the food table. She had long since lost sight of Abi. They carried their laden plates to a corner table. Giles looked down at the food.

"I wonder how much of this is locally produced?"

It was something that Margot hadn't really thought about. When she went food shopping she bought what she needed and had never really thought about its provenance before. Margot sat and listened as Giles talked passionately about farming and organic food. Quite how they then got on to the subject of art she wasn't sure. But she was gratified to discover that Giles liked art, not the modern stuff but the good old-fashioned art. It was a complete reversal of their dinner at The Quarry Man when she had done all the talking. They chatted for over an hour, totally absorbed in each other.

Margot noticed that the crowd of people was thinning and the reception was breaking up. She just wanted the evening to go on and on. Abi came over to reclaim her.

"It was really nice meeting you, Mr err Giles," Abi held out her hand politely. Giles took it and smiled. Abi looked pointedly at Margot. "I'll just go and retrieve our coats, see you at the main entrance in about five minutes." Margot and Giles looked at each other, neither of them sure about the next move. They tentatively leaned towards each other, hesitated just a fraction too long and the moment was lost. Instead Giles cupped her hand in both of this.

"Thank you for a lovely evening. Er I don't suppose, what I mean is," he paused, took a deep breath and started again. "What I mean is can I see you again?"

Margot was about to reply when she caught sight of the young waiter clearing the tables, he was about the same age as Giles's son. She gently pulled her hand away.

"No, I don't think that would be a wise idea, do you?"

She turned quickly and went to find Abi. Margot could feel the tears threatening to spill over. She had so wanted to say 'yes'.

"Are you OK?" Abi glanced at her friend.

"Not really."

They drove back in the taxi in silence. Abi held back with her questions until they had reached her house.

"So, come on what's with the tears? He looked like a really nice man."

"He is a really nice man."

"So what's the problem?"

"He has a wife and a son."

"Oh."

"Now can we drop the subject of Mr Giles Farmer please?"

CHAPTER 9

Gavin lay on the bed and looked at the girl sitting at the computer. He lowered his voice; he was brave but not that brave. The last thing he wanted was to be discovered in her room. Suzie was a student, but for now she was also a waitress and general dogsbody working for a pittance for her mother. Samantha Savage would skin him alive if she knew Gavin was in her daughter's bedroom. Let alone what they had just been doing. Suzie's shift wasn't due to start for another hour or so. Gavin worked all day and Suzie worked all evening which didn't augur well for their relationship. The short time they did manage to spend together was usually spent having sex whenever and wherever they could, a situation that Gavin had no problem with at all.

"God, he's awful. All he does all day is moon after this woman. Did I tell you that he met her in London? I mean it's ironic really. Giles spends ages trying to locate this Margot woman and in a village the size of Middle Chippings you'd have thought that wouldn't be too difficult, yet he doesn't. Then they both go to London – for totally different reasons and finally they meet."

"What did he say about her?"

"Not a lot really. To be honest I got the impression that she gave him the brush off. Shame really, Giles seemed quite keen on her."

"Well, there's plenty more pebbles on the beach as the cliché goes." Suzie beckoned him over to the screen. "See what I've found."

Suzie had the screen opened at a list of Internet dating sites. Gavin was amazed at how many there were. She clicked back on to the screen to refine the search area and chose a specific geographical location. Four came up, she discarded the first three and logged into the fourth.

"Country Cousins? Who are they?" Gavin looked over Suzie's shoulder.

"It is an Internet dating site for people who live in the country and 'who may not get the chance to meet people in the conventional workplace situation'," she quoted. "It says in the blurb that it is 'very popular with farmers and other country folk'."

"I can't see Giles signing up for a dating agency. For a start there's no computer at Home Farm and if there was I doubt he would know how to use it."

"No, but we do," she grinned at him.

Gavin pulled up a chair and between them they inputted all of Giles's data, or as much as they knew. What they didn't know they guessed. Neither of them had a particularly clear recollection of what Margot looked like but from what little they both did remember they put her description in the section headed 'type of person you are seeking'. The pair were made for each other – well on paper anyway. Not wanting to use Giles's name they incorporated their initials and signed it GUS.

Gavin pulled Suzie to him. They rolled off their seats and on to the bed. Gavin had none of his uncle's inhibitions. He pulled her on top of him and pushed his hands up the back of her T-shirt. She was bra-less. In one deft move the top came off. Seconds later they had unzipped each other and pushed their jeans on to the floor. Their hands were all over each other, Gavin marvelling at her softness and Suzie excited by his hardness. They rolled over so that he was on top. He momentarily came up for air and hesitated for a fraction.

"What about err, what I mean is I don't have anything."

"Don't worry, I'm covered."

"You little beauty," he smiled down at her and proceeded to chew her lip whilst rubbing and rocking his hard body up against her warm pliant one.

Giles stood behind Samantha Savage in the post office queue; they chatted whilst they waited to be served.

"How's that young nephew of yours? He's been hanging around my Suzie. She's a good girl with a brain; she's off to university soon. She won't get stuck in Middle Chippings all her life," she paused wondering how to phrase the next bit. "What I mean is, tell your lad not to get too close, it'll only end in tears."

Giles smiled, "Don't worry he's a good boy, far too sensible to get himself involved. He's got plans for the future too."

The queue shuffled forward and it was Samantha's turn to be served. Giles was only half listening to the conversation. Samantha was complaining that her hair appointment had been cancelled but that it now meant she could return to the pub early and get things ready before the evening rush. Giles pulled out his mobile phone and rang home.

"Hi Dad, is young Gavin home? No? Oh I see, OK, no, it's not important."

Godfrey confirmed what Giles suspected. Gavin was at The Quarry Man. There would be hell to pay if Samantha caught them. He dialled Gavin's number and waited. It rang for ages before a sleepy voice answered.

"Yeah?"

"Gavin?"

"Yeah," he sounded marginally more awake.

"Gavin, it's Giles here. I've just bumped into Sam Savage about ten minutes ago; she's on her way back to the pub."

"When?" all traces of tiredness had gone.

"Now!"

"Oh God, I can hear her car pulling up. Got to go, she'll kill me." He was about to ring off when he said, "Thanks Uncle G, I owe you big time for this."

"Just get out before she catches you." The line went dead.

Giles finished mending the fence in the lower paddock and drove back to Home Farm as darkness fell. He noticed the light on in Saddleback Cottage. What was the woman's name who lived there? He couldn't remember but Godfrey knew. It was on the Parish Council notification about the planning permission for the piggery conversion. He would see the application although he would be unable to make a comment on it. The Farmer men always served on the Parish Council. It was one of those obligations that each successive generation took on. All village planning matters came before it but Giles would have to declare an interest and withdraw from the discussion.

He pulled into the yard and walked into the kitchen. Gavin sat at the table, a cup of tea in front of him. He grinned at Giles.

"That was a close call."

"Samantha Savage is not a woman to be crossed. Take it from me, I know."

"Really? Go on, spill the beans."

"Nothing to spill." Godfrey looked up from his newspaper and joined in the conversation. "He could have 'ad her and he let her go."

"It wasn't quite that simple, Dad, and you know it."

Gavin looked from one to the other and sensed a row brewing. "Hey Grandad, how about we have an Indian takeaway for dinner tonight? Uncle Giles and I can drive into town and pick one up. You could stay and get the table laid and the plates warmed."

Godfrey grunted his agreement. Gavin and Giles climbed into the Land Rover and drove off into town to collect the food.

"So what happened?"

"Well, I was in Suzie's room and we were just hanging out chatting. Not doing anything wrong you understand, but Mrs Savage, well let's just say I don't think she approves of Suzie and I being friends."

Giles shook his head, "Can I give you some advice, son?"

"Er yes," Gavin wondered what was coming.

"When you put your shirt back on, make sure it's not on inside out." Gavin laughed as Giles shook his head. "Don't worry I don't think your grandad noticed."

If Godfrey had noticed he wasn't saying anything. Whilst Giles and Gavin were on their way to get some food Godfrey had received an unexpected visitor. The woman from Saddleback Cottage had turned up on his doorstep. She introduced herself and he felt obliged to invite her in. She wanted to know what the holdup was with regard to the planning permission and was it anything they could discuss. Godfrey was not overly polite and asked her to leave. She would find out soon enough what he had up his sleeve. Who did she think she was, moving into the village, wanting to change everything?

By the time the boys returned Godfrey had calmed down and was beginning to feel just a little bit ashamed of the brusque way he had treated the woman. She had been unfailingly polite to him. He decided, on balance, not to mention the visit.

Gavin left it a couple of days before he felt that it was safe enough to return to Suzie. Samantha Savage was working in the pub and although not exactly welcoming she was civil to him.

"Alright if I pop up to use Suzie's computer, Mrs Savage? I just need to check something on the Internet."

"No problem; only leave the door open will you, in case I need to call Suzie to come down and give me a hand." The lines had been drawn and they both understood each other.

Suzie was sitting at the computer. Gavin stood behind her and casually slipped his hand down the front of her top, no bra again. He cupped the breast in his hand rubbing it gently; Suzie leaned back and felt him harden. She allowed the fondling to go on for a little longer, then with a sigh she leaned forward causing Gavin to remove his hand.

"Later," she whispered.

"You two OK up there, can I get you a drink or anything?"

"No thanks," their replies were in perfect unison.

"We've got a result," Suzie turned her head slightly to look up at Gavin.

"What do you mean?"

"For Giles, for your uncle, he has had a couple of replies."

"Really?"

"Don't be so surprised. By the time we had finished describing him anyone with a pulse would have found him attractive."

They logged into the Country Cousins website and then on to the page they had created for Giles. There were five messages in the inbox. Suzie and Gavin looked at each other and then clicked on the icon. They discarded two of the women because of their age, a third was married, divorce pending – too much baggage they decided. However, there were two that looked like good possibilities. Suzie clicked on one.

"Do you think it's her? The name is the same, Margot."

"I don't know, what do you think? What does she say about herself?"

"It says that she's single, lives alone and that she is a writer." Suzie turned to Gavin, "It has got to be her. Surely there can't be two."

"What shall we do?"

"Reply of course. Now what would your Uncle Giles say?"

They made their first reply quite short, saying how pleased they were that she had picked him out and that he was looking for …

Suzie turned to Gavin who had resumed his position behind her, his hand caressing over the shirt this time, just in case Samantha walked in. "What is he looking for?"

"Sex, friendship, sex, companionship, sex…"

"No, that's you," she slapped his hand away.

She sighed and decided to totally ignore Gavin's input. She typed that Giles was looking for a 'meaningful relationship with a mature attractive woman that he could converse with'. They both paused. It made him sound lonely, well actually he probably was. Suzie added 'and which he hoped would lead to a warm and intimate friendship'. They tried to use euphemisms that a man of Giles's age would be familiar with. They decided it was probably too soon to arrange a meeting. It wouldn't hurt for them to correspond for a while. Suzie hit the 'send' button.

Finally Gavin's prayers were answered. Samantha yelled up the stairs that she was popping out for about ten minutes. Ten minutes was all they needed. A 'quickie' suited them both fine. They were at it within minutes of hearing the door slam. After it was all over Gavin was very careful to check that his shirt was on correctly. In the event Sam was longer than she had said which gave them both plenty of time. Gavin left not long afterwards and returned to Home Farm. Giles was getting ready to go out. He didn't seem very enthusiastic.

"Parish Council meeting," Giles explained. "Hopefully I should be back early. There's a couple of planning matters which I won't be able to deal with because I have to declare any conflicts of interest. The chairman has put them at the end, that way I should be able to get away early."

The Parish Council meeting was tedious and overlong and Giles was quite pleased when they came to the last couple of items of planning. One concerned the knocking down of an old farm building which had been almost derelict for years. Godfrey had submitted it on their behalf. They wanted it demolished so that they could build an extra garage and the other concerned the conversion of the piggery at Saddleback Cottage. Giles might have stayed for this but he knew that Godfrey had sent in a letter of protest against the conversion. He therefore felt obliged to leave.

Giles crossed the car park and climbed into his Land Rover. He was about to switch on the lights when he saw them. Margot and Danny Bragg were walking across the car park and towards the hall. Bragg had his arm around Margot's back, their heads were very close and they were deep in conversation.

"Well I never…" he waited for them to go in before switching on his engine.

Chapter 10

Margot seethed as she stormed back to her cottage. The man had been so rude. It was her outhouse and she could do with it what she wanted. She had only called in as a matter of courtesy. She had barely got over the shock that the man who answered the door was the same one she had seen in church with Giles and his son. It was ironic that she had spent weeks trying to find out where Giles Farmer lived and all the time the one person who could have told her was her neighbour. Surely Giles couldn't be related to such an ill mannered old man. He hadn't even introduced himself, although he seemed to know who she was.

Margot's original idea had been to call into Home Farm to inform them that she had submitted plans for the conversion of the piggery. It quickly became apparent that she was too late; the old man had already received details about her proposal. Margot was then obliged to listen to the old man's diatribe about neighbourliness and about how, round these parts, you talked to people before you went ahead and did things.

Margot tried to explain that her intention was to keep the outside shell the same. She had even got the plans with her, which the old man refused to look at. No matter how reasonable she was he just wasn't listening. Mr Farmer senior was spoiling for a fight and would oppose the conversion no matter what. Margot would speak to her builder to see if she could get to the bottom of the problem. She had a feeling that this particular fight had little to do with her and much to do with matters she knew very little about. After her visit to Home Farm she had tried to get hold of Danny Bragg. In the end Margot left a message on his answerphone. He returned her call early the next morning.

"No, I'm not surprised at all. Old man Farmer always was a difficult old sod. I expected as much. Will Smith, the previous owner, wanted to extend out to the side a few years back but old man Farmer managed to put a stop to it. The plans got thrown out at Parish Council level on some technicality. If truth be told

Godfrey's never forgiven his father for leaving the cottage to Smithy's mother. Godfrey Farmer's been playing the waiting game, thought he'd be able to buy Saddleback Cottage with no problem, he knew that Smithy would eventually sell. I wish I had seen Godfrey's face when he found out that someone else had bought the cottage," he laughed. Margot wondered how Danny Bragg knew so much about her cottage and began to wonder whether he could be trusted.

'Bloody village politics," she thought, this whole business goes way back. In any event Bragg told her that the planning matter was to be discussed the following evening at the Parish Council meeting. He suggested that she attend and he offered to go along with her for moral support.

That conversation had been yesterday. Now here she was with Bragg going into the Parish Council meeting. The car park was full. Margot's mind, occupied with what was to come, failed to see the old Land Rover parked in the corner. Neither did she see the driver who appeared to be taking such an interest in her and Danny Bragg. They slipped in quietly at the back of the hall. They were just in time to hear a discussion about the demolition of an old farm building at Home Farm. This was passed without any dissent. There was one other planning application before hers which necessitated a discussion. Finally they got on to the conversion of the piggery at Saddleback Cottage. Several of the members seemed to think that it was a good idea, particularly as it was going to make use of a near derelict building. The chairman allowed the discussion to flow, taking care that everyone had their say and Margot felt herself relax. A few of the councillors looked across and smiled at her.

"However," the chairman opened a letter and began to read, "according to my information there is a preservation order on the piggery," he paused. "What this means is that it will have to go to district; even if we're happy with the plans it will be up to district to make the final decision."

Danny Bragg raised his hand like a schoolboy, "Excuse me Mr Chairman, does your letter give any indication when this preservation order was taken out?" There was a delay whilst the chairman scanned the rest of the letter.

"July 2005 by the looks of it."

Danny Bragg made no comment but just nodded. As he explained later to Margot, Old Smithy died at the end of July 2005 and had spent most of that month in hospital. He would have been in no fit state to organise a preservation order on the piggery. It just didn't make sense. Danny guessed that it had been done by someone else – his money would have been on Godfrey or Giles. Danny promised to investigate further and report back. He pulled his car up outside Saddleback Cottage.

"Don't worry, Margot, we will get this sorted."

He waited hoping to be invited in for coffee but he was disappointed.

Margot waited until Danny Bragg's car had pulled away. She then went inside and logged on to her computer. It was late and she didn't feel at all creative. Instead she logged on to the Country Cousins website. It had been just over a week since she had registered her details. There was one message in her inbox which she read three times. She wondered what was meant by 'warm and intimate friendship'. Was she ready for intimacy? Had she ever been ready for intimacy? Margot very rarely let people get too close. As a teenager she had been shy around boys. She also had an unrealistic view of romance. Her mother had blamed it on the idealistic nonsense that she read. Mother had told Margot that life wasn't like a romantic novel but was more akin to a kitchen sink drama.

Margot's problem was that she had never met anyone who came even close to what she was looking for. Then of course there had been the question of money. Margot was an extremely wealthy woman. Within five years of her first novel being accepted Margot had become the publishing house's most successful and prolific writer. She had been so busy chronicling other people's lives that she had very little spare time left to live her own. It was being on this treadmill that had prompted her move to Middle Chippings.

Margot looked around her lounge at the expensive furnishings and looked down at the expensive ring on her right hand. What it came down to was that all this wealth was meaningless without a special someone to share it with.

Margot turned back to the computer. He had signed himself 'Gus'. She typed quickly then sat and read what was on the screen. If this was a sentence in one of her novels she wouldn't have given it a second thought. However, this was not fiction, this was her life.

"Hi Gus, good to read that you are looking for someone you can converse with, I think good conversation is so important and what is the point of having a relationship if it isn't going to be meaningful. I would consider myself reasonably attractive but am not sure about your definition of mature though," she paused. "I'm in my early forties, is that too mature for you?" She signed her name.

Margot reread what she had written and wondered if she should have used her proper name but 'Maureen' didn't have the same ring about it as 'Margot' did. The name Margot Denning had been suggested by her agent who felt that it was more appropriate than her real name of Maureen Dudd. She hesitated momentarily, aware that she had told a little white lie about her age, but hey what woman didn't? Resolutely she clicked on the 'send' button. There, she had done it.

CHAPTER 11

The chairman of the Parish Council telephoned Giles to let him know that his application for the demolition of one of their outbuildings had been agreed. He also brought him up to date on the other planning matters he had missed. The chairman referred to the letter about the planning constraints on the piggery.

"I'm surprised you didn't mention it when you first saw the application, Giles."

"That's because I didn't know anything about it."

"Well that does surprise me, particularly since it was Godfrey who wrote the letter informing us."

"What? My father Godfrey?"

"Yes, I thought you knew. Well I'd better go; sounds like you and your old man need to communicate a bit more."

Giles could hear the chuckle in the chairman's voice. Giles finished the call; he needed to get to the bottom of this. However, it wasn't until after supper that Giles was able to quiz Godfrey.

"Since when has there been a preservation order on the piggery at Saddleback Cottage and how the hell did you find out about it?"

Godfrey avoided answering the question directly.

"Oh I think it's been there a few years." He deliberately ignored the second part of the question and avoided Giles's direct gaze.

"Dad?" Giles knew the old man was hiding something. Gavin looked from one to the other. He hadn't a clue what they were talking about but it sounded interesting. Gavin had been told what a womaniser his great grandfather had been and he knew that there had been enmity between Godfrey and old Smithy but not why. Gavin feigned indifference all the while paying close attention to the argument between his uncle and his grandfather.

"Dad, you had no right to interfere. That cottage was left to Will Smith all legal and above board. It was what Grandad George wanted."

"Bah, we all know what my father wanted. He broke my mother's heart then made matters worse by leaving the cottage to that," Godfrey spluttered and could barely get the word out, "that woman. At least she didn't have much pleasure out of the place; she died within a twelve month of my father. It should have come back to us, not be passed down to that bastard son of hers. He had no right to the place, he wasn't even family."

Local gossip would beg to differ on Godfrey's statement about Will Smith but none would dare mention it in their presence. Rumour had it that William Smith was old George Farmer's illegitimate son. However, within the Farmer family it was accepted that Smith was from his mother's first marriage and had no blood ties to them. The fact that he looked nothing like a Farmer helped, though not everyone was convinced.

"Anyways, I fully expected to be able to buy the place back when that man died."

"So why didn't you, Grandad?"

"Because those grasping solicitors sold it through a bloody London estate agent. Somebody made a lot of money on the deal and I have my suspicions as to where that money went," Godfrey paused, his anger dissipated. "In any event I had my little insurance policy." Giles and Gavin looked at each other and then back to Godfrey. They hadn't a clue what he was talking about. Godfrey shook his head and continued. "You probably won't remember, but a few years ago we celebrated the village jubilee or some such. Anyway this woman comes down from the County Museum and gives a talk about the old buildings in the village. It turns out that some of the old farm workers' cottages were built in Victorian times and therefore attracted listed building status."

"But Saddleback Cottage isn't that old; it was built in the late forties, wasn't it?" Giles knew that much.

"Yes, the cottage was, but the piggery, now that was a different matter. It is a genuine Victorian farm building and qualified to be listed."

"Hang on, hang on." Giles was having trouble following the conversation. "But how come old Smithy knew about this?"

"He didn't."

"But if he didn't know about how important the shed was how did it get listed?" Giles might have been slow on the uptake but the penny was beginning to drop.

Godfrey looked decidedly uncomfortable. "The man from the council may have come around when my father was in hospital. I can't remember."

Giles knew that his father had perfect recall. "And of course as he got worse my old Dad didn't know what he was signing," Giles finished for him. Godfrey made no comment. Gavin felt totally lost in the conversation but got the distinct impression that his grandfather had been involved in something underhanded.

"Anyway, what's said between these four walls stays between these four walls." Godfrey was defiant now. "Agreed?"

Giles made no comment. Gavin said, "OK, Grandad."

"Anyways, if that damn woman wants a bigger place to work in why doesn't she just sell up and buy something bigger, back in London where she belongs."

"That's not very kind or neighbourly, Dad."

"That's what she said."

"You mean you've spoken to her, you've met our new neighbour?"

"Yes, she came up here, bold as brass to tell me about her plans but of course it was too late. I already knew. She should've come to see me sooner. I could have saved her the trouble."

"What's she like, Grandad?"

"Bit full of herself, smart clothes, stupid shoes for walking in the country, I didn't like her much."

Giles was beginning to feel uncomfortable. "Did she have blonde curly hair and a lovely smile? Nice figure, nice legs?"

"How the hell would I know? She had one of those stupid hats on, she was wearing trousers and she certainly didn't smile the whole time she was here. Anyway, why does it matter what she looked like?"

"No reason, what did you say her name was?" Giles tried to ask the question in as casual a manner as he could muster.

"Dunce or something like that, no Dudd, that was it Dudd, Maureen Dudd."

"Did you think it was someone else?" Gavin tried to hide his smirk.

"No, no of course not."

Godfrey looked from one to the other, now he was missing something.

Gavin's mobile rang, it was Suzie; he listened for a while. "Really? She has? Yes, of course, I'll pop round later, what time do you finish?" Gavin ended the call and then looked at Giles. "Could you give me a lift to The Quarry Man later this evening Giles? I need to see a girl about her country cousin."

Giles didn't even try to pretend to understand what young Gavin was getting at but he was quite happy to pop down to The Quarry Man later. Truth be told, he had been going quite regularly since his first date with Margot in the hope of seeing her again. It had been such an unexpected pleasure to bump into Margot in London. Everything had just seemed so natural and easy. He knew he should have asked her about that first meeting and why she had picked on him. Things had been going so well and he hadn't wanted to break the spell of such a wonderful evening. But he must have said or done something because the minute he suggested meeting her again she became distant and withdrawn. Giles wished he knew more about women in general and that one in particular.

After the conversation with his father Giles felt obliged to sort out this Mrs Dudd who lived in Saddleback Cottage. Giles loved his father dearly but knew what a difficult cantankerous old sod he could be. Godfrey was allowing his bitterness over losing the cottage to affect his judgement, not to mention his manners. Giles decided to call in to see this woman and smooth things over.

Suzie had finished her shift early and was up in her room when Gavin joined her. Luckily the bar was quite busy so Samantha's attention was elsewhere. Gavin hugged Suzie tightly and gave her a long kiss using his tongue to caress hers. It was some minutes before they both came up for air.

"God, I needed that," she murmured huskily. "I've had enough of being ogled and fondled by that skittles crowd from The Bell. They're pathetic."

"Who's been bothering you? Shall I go and sort them out?" Gavin couldn't suppress the anger in his voice.

"Don't be daft and anyway it was nothing I couldn't handle."

Gavin knew she was right. This girl could certainly handle herself. He had been attracted to her firstly because she was the only half decent girl of his age in the village, secondly she was very bright but thirdly, and most importantly, he had fallen for her feisty no strings attached attitude to life. They had agreed that as Suzie was destined to go off to university, probably followed by a gap year, their relationship would be one of strictly fun and sex. However, Gavin was beginning to realise that Suzie meant more to him than just a summer fling. He was too frightened to ask if she felt the same way about him. He had his Jack the Lad reputation to think of. Suzie stood back and looked at Gavin.

"Are you OK?"

"Yeah, fine. Just pleased to see you. Giles and my grandad aren't exactly the liveliest of company."

"Oh thanks, is that all I am, a diversion from boredom?"

Gavin wasn't sure if she was teasing him or not, so he just grabbed her again and kissed her even harder.

"As diversions go you're the best!" he joked trying to hide the sudden revelation of just how much she meant to him.

Suzie laughed, "Anyhow, Giles is brilliant company, witty and chatty and well read."

"He is?"

"Yup he certainly is when we speak for him. Come and have a look, he's had a reply and I'm convinced it's her."

Gavin sat on the computer chair and Suzie sat on his lap. They read Margot's message.

"She's been a bit optimistic on the age front," Gavin commented.

"It is a lady's prerogative to lie about her age and anyway your Uncle Giles isn't exactly a spring chicken!"

They had a lively discussion on what their reply should be. In the end Suzie typed, "I just love the description you give of yourself. I am particularly fond of creative blondes."

Suzie paused "Does that sound a bit pervy?"

"Nah it sounds fine to me."

They closed down the computer. Gavin would have liked to close the door and make love to Suzie but with the ever watchful Samantha below he knew it would be impossible.

"As you're off duty how about I take you out for a drink?"

"Where do you suggest?"

"I know a lovely village pub, absolutely gorgeous waitress, landlady's a bit of a dragon and the beer's cheap."

"You've sold me on it!"

They walked down into the bar and immediately saw Giles sitting at a small table by himself. He looked a bit forlorn so they joined him. He insisted on buying them both a drink. Gavin went up to get the drinks and Suzie was left to chat to Giles. As confident as she was, she did not find it easy.

"So Mr Farmer, Gavin tells me…"

"Please, call me Giles, Mr Farmer is my father."

"OK, so Giles, Gavin tells me that you met your mystery lady in London. How did it go?"

Giles brightened up, this was just what he needed, a feminine perspective on things.

"Well I thought it was going really well. I mean I was a bit unprepared, I didn't really expect to see her at a National Farmers' Union do. She didn't really strike me as that sort of a person. She writes, I think," he paused, he really knew very little about her. "Anyway we chatted about this and that. She was really interested when I told her about my plans for the farm."

"Oh really?"

He looked at Suzie.

"Not the most interesting of subjects?"

"If you're a farmer yes, but otherwise…"

Gavin returned with the drinks, sat at the table and let Suzie and Giles continue with their conversation.

"Giles was just telling me about how he met up with Margot in London. Apparently he was chatting her up by talking to her about farming!"

Gavin gave his uncle a withering look.

"Well she seemed interested in what I was saying, although I don't think her friend was. In fact her friend disappeared quite quickly once we met up."

"Male or female friend?"

"Oh it was a girl friend of hers. Margot said that they went way back. She was staying with her in London. Apparently they hadn't seen each other in ages but…"

Suzie interrupted, "You mean that she abandons an old friend who she hasn't seen in ages just to spend the evening with you talking about farming? The woman is either slightly deranged or very keen on you!"

"Or both." Gavin felt he ought to contribute to the conversation.

"Do you think so?" Giles felt a spark of hope.

"Seems like it to me," Suzie continued. "Anyway, what you need is a plan of action. For a start off you don't even know where the woman lives or do you?"

"Well it must be a bit of a distance out of the village because she took a taxi home that first night. To be honest I've never seen her in the village." Giles looked at the empty glasses.

"I'll get us all another one, shall I?"

Whilst he was up at the bar Suzie and Gavin discussed the situation; they decided that one of their priorities was to find out just where this woman lived. Gavin thought that all they had to do was ask her online. Suzie pointed out that the exchange of a couple of emails did not yet constitute a relationship and one of the major warnings on the Country Cousins website was about the importance of not giving out addresses or information of a personal nature too quickly.

Giles waited patiently at the bar to be served. Samantha Savage was serving Danny Bragg. When Danny saw Giles he moved towards him.

"That was a real fast one your old man pulled. But he won't get away with it, you know. My client will fight him all the way; she's got the money to do it. You may think that you're Lords of the Manor but you're not. You're all just jumped up thieving farm labourers." Danny's voice raised, he was attracting attention. Samantha moved swiftly down the bar and around to

72

the other side where Danny and Giles were eyeing each other angrily. She stood between them.

"Now come on, boys, I don't want no rowing in my pub. If you've got issues then sort them out elsewhere."

Gavin walked to the bar. "Everything OK, Giles?"

"Yeah, just fine. I think I'll forgo that drink. I'm not too keen on the company here."

Giles stormed out of The Quarry Man closely followed by Gavin. "What was all that about?"

"Nothing to concern you. Grandad has prevented the woman who bought Saddleback Cottage from knocking the piggery down and replacing it with a summer house or an office or some such thing."

"So what's it got to do with Danny Bragg?"

"Bragg was contracted to do the job. I don't care what he says about me but I won't have him threatening my old man and anyway, he's got a damn cheek accusing your grandad of dodgy dealings. Bloody Danny Bragg wrote the book about dodgy dealings."

"Come on, Giles, let's get back home."

They had both had far too much alcohol to drive so they left the Land Rover in the car park and walked back along the main road to Home Farm. Gavin looked worried so Giles put his arm around Gavin's shoulder. "Don't worry about your grandad he'll be OK. I'm not going to let anything happen to him now, am I?"

A car came up behind them illuminating them in its headlights. Giles looked up, "Old Leaker's running his taxi late tonight." He had recognised the vehicle but failed to notice its occupant.

CHAPTER 12

Even though she had only glimpsed them for the briefest of seconds in the taxi headlights they had looked so comfortable together, father and son. Margot wondered where the mother – Giles's wife was. Perhaps she was still at home. Oh why, oh why couldn't she find someone single and available? For the first time since she had moved to Middle Chippings Margot seriously contemplated moving back to London. She had been lonely in London too but this was a different sort of lonely. Country living was not proving to be as conducive to working as she had hoped. Margot had spent the evening with a representative from her publishers. In all fairness she could not call their behaviour bullying but the woman had been very insistent. Margot had promised them a deadline and she knew she was way behind and in danger of not meeting it. She was letting thoughts of Giles Farmer obsess her to the point that it was affecting her work.

Added to her preoccupation was the stress of this building business. Margot was not even sure that it was worth it. The last thing she wanted to do was upset the old man up at the farm, particularly as he was related to Giles. Margot had tried to tell Danny Bragg that she was thinking of withdrawing the plans but he had been insistent that they see it through. Even if she did not do the conversion herself, to have outline planning permission would be a good selling point should she ever decide to move on. Margot could see the logic in this so she agreed in principle for Bragg to make some further enquiries on her behalf. She stressed, however, that she wished to be consulted at each stage, particularly if they started incurring legal costs.

The following morning Margot started early and was sitting at her computer by eight o'clock, raring to go. She blocked out everything except her novel. Margot was sorely tempted to log on to the Country Cousins website but resisted. If she could get a minimum of three thousand words out before midday she might, just might allow herself to log on. She missed lunch but by three o'clock she was famished. She had exceeded her word quota so gave herself the rest of the day off. After a quick sandwich and a cup of tea she picked up her bag and decided that she needed a walk. She would nip along to the village stores and get a few things.

Margot had just got to the gate when she realised that she had left her list on the hall table. She turned to retrace her steps when her name was called.

"Margot? Is that you?"

She had just been thinking about him and there he was. She turned and smiled at him.

"Are you going to see this Maureen Dudd?"

Margot picked up on the anger in his voice and was at a loss as to how to reply.

"Why? Is there a problem?"

"Yes, there most certainly is. The local grapevine says she is planning to go the local Council to make trouble about this bloody planning permission business."

"She is?" this was news to Margot. "And where did you hear all this from?"

"Emma in the village stores told me. She heard it from one of her customers."

"Really?" If there was one thing that Margot hated it was being talked about. Only Danny Bragg knew that Maureen Dudd was her real name and for some reason he had chosen to keep this fact to himself.

"Anyway," Giles seemed to have calmed down a bit, "are you going to see her or not?"

Margot had no idea why she said it but before she could think things through she found herself saying:

"I think she's out."

"Probably a good thing, the mood I'm in," he smiled at Margot, "but every cloud as they say. If I hadn't come to see her I wouldn't have bumped into you. That's got to be a bonus. You rushed off so suddenly in London. I had no idea how to get hold of you."

Margot could feel her resolve, not to get involved with a married man, slipping away. She found it so hard to resist that smile and she had a feeling he knew it.

"Are you free tonight? Could I take you out to dinner?"

"Yes and no. I mean yes, I am free, no you can't take me," she emphasised the word 'me', "out to dinner. But I would like to take you."

"OK," that smile was back again. "Where shall I pick you up?"

"I've got some work to finish; I've got a deadline I mustn't miss. My trip to London took out quite a chunk of my time. Perhaps I could meet you there, say eight thirty at The Quarry Man?"

"The Quarry Man?" he sounded disappointed with the choice of venue."

"Why is that a problem?"

"No, not at all, that will be great; I'll see you there then, later this evening."

They walked back down the path and she watched him climb into the tractor whilst she turned in the opposite direction towards the village. At the village shop no mention was made of the planning permission for Saddleback Cottage. Margot sensed a slight air of embarrassment on the part of Emma who hid behind the grille of her post office booth. Emma was unaware that Margot and Maureen were one and the same. Like many people in the village, with the exception of Danny Bragg, she was under the impression that Margot worked for Maureen. Quite where the woman had got this idea from Margot did not know but she was prepared to peddle it as truth and Margot was disinclined to put her straight.

As soon as she returned to Saddleback Cottage Margot phoned the pub to book a table. Margot had picked up that Giles was disappointed in the choice of venue. He probably wanted to go somewhere more private. The man had a nerve, to be seen twice having dinner with a woman who wasn't his wife and in such a public place; well that took some effrontery. Anyway, lovely as he was she knew that she would have to give him the brush off. There was no way she would allow herself to get involved with a married man!

Margot made herself a cup of tea then switched on the computer and immediately logged on to the Country Cousins website. There was a message awaiting her. It hadn't been there when she left to go to the shops because she had had a quick peak before she went. She looked at the time it was sent – about the time that she was chatting to Giles Farmer. Well that put paid to her theory. She had wondered whether Gus and Giles might have been one and the same person. With any luck her Country Cousins suitor was free and single.

The message was short, but so had hers been. She realised that he was reflecting back what she had said to him – cautious, she liked that in a man. To test her theory she wrote a three paragraph message explaining that she hadn't written too much before because she had been very busy trying to meet a publishing deadline. She added that she was going out for a meal with someone that she had been 'sort of involved with'. Did two platonic chaste kisses at the end of two evenings really constitute being 'involved' she wondered. Margot also mentioned in the email that after tonight she would be a free agent.

She paused before pressing the send button. Was that last comment a bit too forward? Did it sound as if she was angling for a date? She knew that she was, but she didn't want to make it too obvious. 'Damn it,' she thought. 'Why not go for it? What have I got to lose?' She clicked the send button before she had a change of heart.

Margot looked at all the clothes piled on her bed; she had been trying on outfits for the past quarter of an hour and still couldn't decide what to wear. She didn't want to go for flirty vamp but neither did she want to look like she was on her way to the office. She wanted to be 'smart casual' but in all honesty had never truly understood the meaning of smart casual, an oxymoron if ever she heard one. In the end she settled for a pair of dark trousers and a tight, but not too revealing, top, over which she wore a smart jacket. She could feel herself getting nervous. Margot knew that this was really silly; it was only a dinner after all. She would make it perfectly clear to Giles, in the nicest possible way of course, that she was only interested in men who were available. No that didn't sound right. In the end she decided to play it by ear and see how it went. She couldn't work out in advance what to say but she knew the outcome she wanted to achieve and that was what was important.

Margot was ready five minutes before the allotted time for the taxi (a quarter of an hour before the time she had requested). True to form Leaker turned up early. They had settled into a mutually agreeable routine which involved an initial nod to each other and absolutely no idle chit chat from Leaker. He would then receive a generous tip no matter the length of the journey.

Margot saw Giles as soon as she walked into the bar. He was chatting to the landlady, a pint of beer in his hand and a full glass of wine waiting on the bar top. Following the landlady's gaze Giles turned round and gave her his devastating smile which she found herself returning, how could she not? She walked towards the bar and stood next to him. He leaned down and unexpectedly kissed her on the cheek, an action which seemed to surprise them both.

"A dry white yes?" he gave her the glass. "Samantha's given us the table in the corner, bit more private," he smiled "otherwise it's like being in a fish bowl. Everyone comes in and jumps to conclusions."

"About what?" she was very guarded.

"About everything!"

They went over to their table and waited a while for the waitress to come over but she was nowhere to be seen. Samantha came over instead and took their order.

"Where's your young lady tonight, Sam?"

"Why don't you ask that lad of yours? She seems to give him more time than she gives me and I'm the one paying her wages! I'll give her a yell in a minute. I expect she's upstairs on that computer again."

The mention of Giles's lad was like a douche of cold water and Margot felt herself stiffen. Smile or no smile she would not go back on her plans – rule number one she never ever got involved with married men.

They picked up their drinks, sipped them and started to speak at the same time.

"No, you first," she smiled at him

"I was just going to ask, did you get your work finished and did you ever manage to get hold of the elusive Ms. Dudd, because I certainly didn't?"

"No, I'm afraid I didn't either. I spent a bit of time on the computer but having taken a break to walk down to the shops I lost my thread somehow."

"Emma at the shop, apart from gossiping about Parish Council business, told me that you're quite a famous writer."

"Well I've sold a few books," she said modestly. "I think the last one peaked at seven hundred thousand."

"Wow," he was suitably impressed. "Would I have read any of your books?"

She smiled, "I doubt it, unless you're into romantic fiction."

Giles grinned at her and closed his hand over hers as it lay on the table. "Not fiction, but I am into romance," he paused. "Was that as cheesy as it sounded?"

"Yes," she laughed and left her hand there for a few seconds before gently removing it.

"Giles, there's something I think..." She didn't finish, Giles had a puzzled look on his face and was looking at something behind her. She turned around. The young waitress was gesticulating towards their table and was obviously trying to get Giles's attention. "I think the young lady wants to speak to one of us. You I think."

"She probably wants to know where Gavin is – that lad is so unreliable at times and she's such a nice girl she doesn't deserve it and he certainly doesn't deserve her."

Giles decided to ignore Suzie so that she was forced to come over with her notebook under the pretence of taking a drinks order. She smiled at Giles and pointedly ignored Margot. Giles ordered some more drinks.

"Giles, could I have a word," she paused, "in private please." She waited. "Now."

Giles smiled an apology to Margot, "Excuse me a moment." Suzie pulled him over to the corner and whispered. "She's going to dump you, Giles."

"What?" it came out louder than he intended. "But how do you know?"

"I just do, er call it intuition, yeah that's it, a woman's intuition."

Giles felt relieved, was that all it was, for a moment there he thought it was something really serious. This was the closest he had been to Margot and there was no way he was going to let her slip away this time.

"Look Suzie, I'm really grateful for your advice, I know that you are only trying to help but well, er things are going OK at the moment. I'm going to ask her to come with me to the County Ball and I think she's going to say yes."

Giles returned to the table and Suzie caught her mother's angry look and returned to the bar to help serve. She was really angry. Giles was such a nice guy; he didn't deserve to be treated like that. Suzie served up their starters; she placed Giles's in front of him with a smile. She practically threw Margot's on the table. The pub quietened down halfway through the evening and Suzie took the opportunity to slip back upstairs to her room.

"Where was bloody Gavin when you needed him," she thought. She made the Country Cousins website reappear on her screen. She had to do something. She typed quickly, paused then amended her first sentence. It wasn't quite what she wanted to say but it was better than nothing. She heard Samantha yelling for her, she quickly pressed the 'send 'button then switched the machine off. Suzie walked back into the bar and glanced across at the table. The woman appeared to be doing all the talking and Giles did not appear to be enjoying what he was hearing.

"But why?" he was genuinely puzzled.

"Because I don't think we ought to see each other again. Please don't ask, I have my reasons. Now shall we just enjoy the rest of the meal and talk about something else?"

The door to the bar opened and in came Jean closely followed by Gavin. They walked over to the bar and Gavin bought his mother a drink. She stayed at the bar chatting to Samantha, they were old friends who went way back. Suzie had a whispered conversation with Gavin who looked across at Giles.

"Didn't you warn him?"

"I tried but he wouldn't listen."

"Judging by the look on his face I think she's told him, poor sod."

Suzie took their pudding course to the table and gave Giles a sympathetic smile which he did not return. They finished their meal in silence. Giles was at a loss as to what to say. Everything seemed to be going so well and then all of a sudden the shutters came down and whatever the issue was, it was non-negotiable according to her.

Margot just wanted the evening to end, it had started off so well but nothing had gone according to her plans. He had pre-empted her by pulling out two ludicrously expensive tickets for some big County Ball. She had been so taken aback that she hadn't known what to say. It didn't help that the waitress kept interrupting. It was like having dinner in a madhouse. She would get the bill and get out of here. Margot turned to catch the waitress' attention and saw that Gavin was at the bar chatting to a woman about her own age, perhaps slightly older. Difficult to tell from this distance. Margot couldn't see the face but had a shrewd idea of who the woman might be – the boy's mother and Giles's wife. The nerve of the man, flaunting a dinner date in front of his wife.

Suzie walked over with the bill and placed the saucer on the table. Margot glanced at it very quickly, opened her purse and threw the money into the dish. It was far too much she knew and the girl certainly hadn't earned a decent tip but she was desperate to get out. What if the woman at the bar realised she had just been having dinner with her husband and became abusive to her.

Margot half ran across the bar and would have made it to the door but the young lad stopped her in his tracks.

"Hi, it's Margot, isn't it?"

"Yes," she glanced nervously across to Jean who was showing quite an interest in her.

"We've not been properly introduced, I'm Gavin Farmer, Giles's nephew and this is my mum." He turned to the woman at the bar who was now smiling at her.

"My brother hasn't stopped talking about you for weeks."

Margot stood and looked at each of them in turn. She looked back across the restaurant to where Giles sat staring at her, the tickets in his hand. He wasn't married after all and she had just ruined any chance she ever might have had with him.

"I must go." The pitch of her voice sounded slightly hysterical to her ears. She pulled open the door at the exact time as Leaker pulled his taxi up to collect her. He was twenty minutes early and she could have kissed him. She sat in the back of the cab, totally mortified at what she had done. How could she have got it so wrong? She managed to keep her composure and gave Leaker a hefty tip for good measure. He had got her out in the nick of time. What a mess she had made of everything. But why hadn't he told her he wasn't married? He kept calling that boy 'his lad' as did everyone else. Even the landlady, when she was talking to Giles, referred to the boy as 'your lad'. It was no wonder she had assumed they were father and son. They looked so alike too. But that wasn't the worst of it. She had been so rude to that poor woman at the bar, Giles's sister. She had gawped, spluttered and then just turned and ran. In fact thinking about it, if you included the old man at Home Farm she had managed to offend virtually every member of the family.

She walked into the tiny bathroom and looked at her tear streaked face. Her mascara had run and her eyes were beginning to look puffy; she knew that by morning they would be so swollen that they would be mere slits in a pudgy mass of blotchy skin. She pulled a brush through her hair dragging out the curls she had so painstakingly created earlier in the evening. The heating had gone off and she was cold so she pulled on a faded long-sleeved T-shirt and a pair of old jogging bottoms to wear to bed. Pulling the duvet over her head she began to cry herself to sleep.

It would not be until mid morning of the next day that she would log on to the Country Cousins website. "Well!" she said reading the message, "Well!"

CHAPTER 13

Giles was confused, he had somehow messed things up without knowing how he did it. He and Margot seemed to be getting on so well, despite Suzie's constant interruptions. What was wrong with the girl? She had been incredibly rude to Margot. Suzie was behaving really oddly, when he asked her why she said that Margot was about to dump him. But that implied that they were 'going out'. Surely you could only dump someone if there had been some sort of a relationship and in all honesty he hadn't even got off the starting blocks. Did two meals and a drink constitute a relationship these days? It certainly didn't when he was younger. Then when he had asked Suzie for an explanation all she had done was mutter something about women's intuition. He would never fathom the female mind as long as he lived.

Giles had just got out the Ball tickets and had asked Margot if she would like to accompany him when Jean and Gavin had turned up. For some reason their arrival totally freaked Margot out. She shouted for the bill and threw the money at the table – far too much he noticed. Suzie's behaviour had most certainly not warranted a tip. Margot then tried to run out of the room but Gavin barred her way. From where he was sitting Giles couldn't hear what was said. What he did see though was Margot's reaction. She virtually pushed Gavin aside in her desperation to get away. Giles had so many questions running around his head but what he really needed were answers.

Jean was staying the night at Home Farm and had driven with Gavin to The Quarry Man to offer Giles a lift back.

"No, you go on with Gavin, I'll walk. Are you sure she didn't say anything to you?"

"Apart from 'excuse me' and 'I must go' that was it," Jean paused. "She doesn't have some sort of mental problem does she?"

"Not that I know of."

Giles looked around for Gavin who had disappeared with Suzie. Giles felt he was living in a madhouse. He left Samantha and Jean gossiping – no doubt about him. If he had hoped that a quiet walk home in the peace of the late evening would soothe him he was sorely disappointed. He actually felt angry but with whom he was not sure. Giles turned into Blossom Lane. As he drew level with Saddleback Cottage he saw that lights were on both upstairs and in the front room below. He wondered if the elusive Ms. Dudd was home. She might know where Margot lived or how he could get hold of her. He paused at the gate for a few seconds, took a deep breath and walked down the pathway to the front door.

He pressed the bell tentatively, and then waited; nothing happened. He listened and felt sure that someone was in. He pressed again harder and for longer this time. He heard something move within the house, someone was definitely there. He took his finger off the bell push for a few seconds then pressed for a third time. He would not stop until this damn door was opened. He heard footsteps down the stairs and a muffled voice said:

"Yes, who is it, what do you want?"

"Is that Ms Dudd, Maureen Dudd?"

"Why, who wants to know?"

"I do."

"And who are you and what are you doing knocking at my door so late?"

The voice though muffled sounded slightly alarmed. Giles suddenly realised the absurdity of the situation. Here he was shouting through a door at a poor woman who didn't know him from Adam and who was probably terrified or about to telephone the police.

"Look I'm really sorry. I'm after Margot, Margot Denning. Could you please give her a message? Please tell her Giles Farmer would like to talk to her, please, it is very important."

The catch in his voice when he said 'please' for the third time is what did it for Margot. She opened the door a fraction and looked at him.

"Margot?"

"Giles?" she opened the door wider. "Giles, I'm really..." she faltered and burst into tears. "I'm so sorry, I was so rude." She sniffed and rummaged around for a handkerchief. "S'all my fault." She finally found a crumpled tissue in the pocket of her trousers and dabbed at her eyes and nose.

Giles had never been good around tearful women. On the occasions when he was faced with one he usually made himself scarce. Some men were good in an emotional crisis but Giles was not one of them. He had only ever seen his mother cry once and she had not known that he was watching. She had stood in the kitchen sobbing and his father had walked in and just gathered her in his arms.

Giles stepped over the threshold and put his arms around Margot and they stood like that for what seemed ages, her sobbing, him holding. After a while her shoulders stopped heaving and the sobs became less frequent although the sniffing continued. Giles held her slightly away from him and looked down.

"Bed? Cup of tea? Both?"

She nodded, turned and walked towards the stairs. Giles closed the door behind him, switched off the hall light and watched as she walked up the stairs. He heard her go into the bathroom. He went into the kitchen and found what he was looking for in the first cupboard he opened. He made a pot of tea and waited a few minutes for it to brew. Giles didn't know if she took sugar in her tea, he knew so very little about her he realised. He put the milk jug and a sugar bowl with two cups on a tray and carried them up the stairs.

The time it had taken him to make the tea had provided sufficient breathing space for Margot to regain her composure. She had left her bedroom door open and the first thing he noticed was that she had changed from the old shirt and jogging bottoms into a silk pyjama type of outfit. It was a creamy colour. She had also scrubbed the tears from her face. He smiled, placed the tray on the little bedside table and poured out the tea.

"Sugar?"

She shook her head. He handed her the cup then looked around for somewhere to sit. There were no chairs in the room and very little space around the large double bed that dominated the small room. In the end he perched on the edge of the bed holding his cup. His anger had subsided though his confusion had not. He waited for Margot to offer some sort of explanation.

She began falteringly. "I thought you were married."

"Married? Me? Whatever gave you that idea?"

"That first time I phoned you at home I heard someone say 'Gavin, get your mother to tell Giles there's someone on the phone for him'."

Giles waited and made no comment.

"So I just assumed that Gavin was your son and that you were married."

Giles was beginning to understand.

"And then at the pub, the landlady kept calling him your lad. Even the vicar said so. It was no wonder that I thought that…"

"The vicar told you I was Gavin's father?"

"Yes, er no, I mean no. But he did say something about three generations of Farmers, so I assumed…" she trailed off.

"So you assumed I was married," things were becoming clearer to him now.

They sipped their tea.

"But what about before, can we go back right to the beginning, to that first meeting in the pub? I was just sitting there minding my own business when in comes this gorgeous woman who makes a beeline for me. I've never met her before but within minutes I'm buying the drinks, paying for dinner and hearing her life history," he paused. "No beeline's the wrong word. You hit on me; yes that's what you did. You hit on me."

"I did no such thing," Margot began to rally – the tea was working its magic.

"You certainly did, you were all over me and we hadn't even been introduced. You had no idea who I was. What was that all about?"

"Now that is not true at all. I did know who you were. Well I thought I did at the time." Nothing she seemed to be saying made any sense. "I was expecting to go to The Quarry Man to meet a local journalist who wanted to interview me about my move to Middle Chippings and my next book. It was all arranged by my agent, but that imbecile of a taxi driver turned up."

"A quarter of an hour early," Giles interrupted.

"Yes, but how did you know?"

"Everyone knows that Leaker always turns up fifteen minutes before he is supposed to. That way he's never late."

"Anyway," she continued her story, "I got to the pub, walked in and saw you sitting at the table, mobile phone in hand and a copy of the local paper in front of you so I put two and two together."

"Like you did about me and Gavin?"

"Yes."

"Not very good at maths are you?"

She smiled, "No, I'm much better with words."

"So what happened to the real journalist?"

"When I got back there was a grovelling apology on the answerphone from some chap who kept saying how sorry he was for cancelling at short notice, but I didn't get the message until I returned. So then I became really confused and couldn't work out why a total stranger would buy me dinner and sit and listen to me talking about myself all evening."

"Someone who was desperately hoping a beautiful woman would turn up."

Margot didn't understand what he was talking about but she registered that he had called her both gorgeous and beautiful within the space of a few minutes.

"Sorry, I don't understand. Were you waiting for someone? Were you stood up too?"

"Sort of," Giles was not prepared to elaborate. He nodded towards the tray, "Fancy another?"

She nodded and he carried the tray downstairs. She could hear him opening cupboards. She pulled open a drawer in her bedside table and pulled out a mirror. Checking her lipstick and smoothing her hair, she decided that it was the best she could do in the circumstances. Margot glanced at the clock beside the bed and realised that they had been talking for ages. She heard his footfall on the stairs and replaced the mirror quickly. She smiled up at him as he returned and perched himself on the edge of the bed. She noticed that he had moved a little closer to her this

87

time. He poured out the tea and passed the cup to her. They both seemed to have run out of things to say.

"Are you feeling better now?"

"Yes, much, thank you," she smiled and they both looked into their tea cups. Giles looked around the room.

"Nice room this. I didn't realise you lived here with that Dudd woman. Although I wouldn't have thought that someone like her would need to take in lodgers. She's not short of a bob or two by all accounts."

"I er…"

"Not a nice lady from what I've heard."

"Really? In what way is she not very nice?"

"According to my dad, and I know that he does have a tendency to exaggerate, she marched up to the house and demanded that he let the planning permission go through."

"She did?"

"Yeah, but dad said that he sent her packing. Not that it did him any good. Apparently she now intends to go the District Council and make a complaint about the Parish Council; all because she didn't get her own way. She sounds a bit spoilt if you ask me."

"How did you hear all this?"

"The Internet has got nothing on the Middle Chippings grapevine, it's amazing."

"Really?"

Margot was not sure that she liked being the subject of village gossip and anyway how did they know about her trying to reverse the Parish Council decision? As for going to the District Council, well that was news to her. She had left it to Danny Bragg to sort out. But the last thing she had said to Danny was to ask him to keep her informed before any decisions were made. She was annoyed that he seemed to be discussing it with people in the village before he discussed the matter with her. Damn the man, it was her outbuilding and her planning permission. He was just the builder.

"Anyway, it was probably a good thing that this Dudd woman was out when I called the other day. I don't mind telling you that I was pretty angry. Where is she by the way?"

"Oh, she comes and goes," Margot waved her hand around vaguely in the air.

They lapsed into silence again and Giles suddenly seemed to realise that he was sitting in a woman's bedroom. He jumped up.

"Is that the time? I'd better be going. Now are you sure you're OK?"

"Yes, I'm fine."

Giles wasn't sure but he thought that there was a slight frostiness that hadn't been there earlier. He stood awkwardly not knowing what his next move should be. She pulled the duvet across.

"I'll see you out."

"That won't be necessary. I can find my own way."

"Oh, I insist." She had suddenly become very formal.

Giles preceded her down the stairs. She opened the door for him and he turned.

"I am so pleased that everything has been sorted out. I really did enjoy our evening. What do you say to us starting again tomorrow with a totally clean and honest slate?"

Margot nodded aware that there was still one little lie that needed sorting out. The moment to tell him that she and Maureen Dudd were one and the same passed. She had missed the opportunity to come clean. Margot was too tired to think, let alone sort out any misunderstandings!

Giles swayed towards her and was pleased to see that she didn't make a move away from him. However, neither did she make a move towards him. She stood her ground waiting for him to make the move.

"Well, goodnight then."

He smiled down at her and there was no mistaking the admiration in his eyes. Before she realised what was happening he had given her a quick kiss on the forehead.

"Sleep well and lock up behind me."

The door closed firmly behind Giles, he paused then walked back down the path. It was much colder now. He looked at his watch, it was almost 2.00 a.m. He had no torch but had walked the lane so often he didn't really need one. He let himself into the back kitchen at Home Farm and noticed a light in the front room. Gavin was still up watching something on the television. He poked his head around the door.

"You're up late, Gavin."

Gavin grinned, "I could say the same about you. Anyway, where have you been, what time do you call this?" He tapped his wrist in mock seriousness.

Giles returned the smile.

"You've been with her haven't you? You sly old dog."

"Ask me no questions and I'll tell you no lies. I'm absolutely shattered. I'm off to my bed. See you in the morning."

Although he was tired Giles couldn't sleep. He couldn't get Margot Denning out of his head. Nothing ever seemed straightforward where she was concerned. He thought things had been going really well until the business about the planning permission had come up. He leaned across and switched off his bedside light. He would think about it in the morning.

CHAPTER 14

Margot overslept; she woke up feeling really tired. She saw the two cups on the bedside table. The emotion of yesterday evening was still with her. Well at least she now knew that Giles was single and available. He had come clean but why hadn't she? She had been on the point of telling him that she was Maureen Dudd then he made that ridiculous remark about Maureen being spoilt and selfish; it had put her back up immediately. How dare he make an assumption about someone he didn't know, purely on the basis of village gossip.

Margot got out of bed and put on her dressing gown. She took the dirty cups downstairs and placed them in the sink. She opened the front door to collect the milk and there laying on the step was a lovely bunch of daffodils. She smiled, picked them up and inhaled the scent. It was only when she looked down the garden that she realised that he had picked them from her own flower bed.

"Cheeky devil," she thought but it made her feel good – a kind, thoughtful gesture, even if they were stolen. The phone rang and she rushed to answer it trying to disguise the excitement in her voice.

"Margot? It's Danny Bragg here."

Margot tried to hide her disappointment.

"We need to talk about this planning permission business. I've got a feeling it could turn nasty. One of the Farmers, either Giles or Godfrey but I'm not sure who, has pulled a fast one with this listed building nonsense. But don't you worry. I'm sure that we can win. I feel really confident. I've got old man Farmer and his son in my sights and I'm not giving up until we get what we want."

"We, Mr Bragg, We? I don't remember anything in our discussions about pursuing this planning permission to the extent that I would be persecuting any of my neighbours."

91

Danny was surprised to hear the frostiness in her voice and decided to change tack. "No, no Margot, I didn't mean –" then he took a deep breath and rephrased his statement. "Godfrey and Giles Farmer own a fair bit of land in Middle Chippings, but they don't own the village. I just don't think that it is right that they can dictate what people do with their own property. I mean, it is not as if it makes any difference to them whether or not the bloody piggery is renovated."

'But it obviously means a great deal to you,' Margot thought.

"Look Mr Bragg. I am still keen to get the outbuildings renovated. I do love Saddleback Cottage but it is tiny so go ahead and do anything you can legally." She laid particular emphasis on the word 'legally'.

"Great, don't worry, Margot, you can rely on me."

"Oh and Mr Bragg, before I forget. Could you please discuss any developments as and when they happen with me first. I don't like hearing my business second hand via the Middle Chippings grapevine." Margot paused. "Is that clear?"

"Crystal, Margot, absolutely crystal."

Margot finished the call, had a quick shower and settled down to work. She found it incredibly difficult to concentrate, her mind kept wandering back to Giles's late night visit. She wondered what would have happened if she had asked him to stay. She had wanted him to, right up until the point he started complaining about her visit to Home Farm. But of course, he didn't know it had been her.

Maureen Dudd had never been a spoilt selfish person. She had been a sad lonely girl who lived her life through books and dreams. Margot caught sight of her reflection in the mirror and wondered what had happened to young Maureen. She wasn't sure who she preferred being. Margot had style and money but had she lost something along the way? Maureen had been a wistful romantic with dreams to fulfil. Maureen had made plans – meet someone very special, get married, have two beautiful children and live happily ever after. Unfortunately life hadn't quite worked out as Maureen had hoped. Once the romantic writing career took off so did Maureen, only to reappear as the accomplished stylish Margot. Margot's dreams were a lucrative career, foreign travel and a couple of homes, one in town and one in the country. Yes, no doubt about it, of the two of them Margot was by far the more successful.

Margot knew that she should have changed her name by deed poll but up until now, using her real name and her pen name had not really been a problem. Danny Bragg had insisted that she use her real name in the planning application so now Giles thought that there were two of them. "Oh God, was nothing about this relationship going to be straightforward?" she thought.

Margot switched on her computer but before she started work she logged on to the Country Cousins website. She was surprised to see that there was a message awaiting her attention. She read it. 'Well!' she thought. She read the message twice. Margot knew that she had to send a reply to Gus. She had given him the impression that she was about to become available. However, she didn't want to raise his hopes. If Margot's relationship with Giles was to develop it would not be fair for her to correspond with someone else. Gus wanted to know if she was now a 'free agent' and if so, would she like to meet up with him? Margot thought long and hard about what she was going to say. After several false starts she finally wrote that she was sorry but that, due to a misunderstanding on her part, circumstances had now changed. In view of this she didn't feel that it would be a good idea for them to meet up. She pressed the 'send' button.

Having sorted out Danny Bragg and her Country Cousins' admirer Margot settled down to work. Despite checking several times that it hadn't, by some fluke, been disconnected, the telephone did not ring. Margot's optimism of the morning began to dissipate. By mid afternoon the walls of the cottage were beginning to press in on her. Margot decided to go for a walk to the village shop. If nothing else the fresh air would do her good.

She could see the tractor parked outside the village stores, its engine running but no one at the wheel. The shop door opened and out came Giles, followed by Gavin, each of them munching on a hot pasty. Margot and Giles stood and grinned at each other, neither of them quite sure what to say.

"Hi, are you feeling better?"

"Yes, I am," she lowered her voice. "Sorry you caught me at such an emotional moment but it was the final straw for me. I'd had a terrible day and then in the evening I managed to inadvertently be rude to everyone and ..." she trailed off. Gavin was still waiting in the doorway trying to squeeze past Giles. Gavin gave him a gentle push and he fell forward into Margot.

"Oh I'm so sorry." Giles looked at the crumbs he had managed to shed across the front of her very smart coat. He put his hand out to brush them away, then realising that he would be stroking her breast he thought better of it. His hand dropped to his side. Margot brushed them away herself. Giles appeared at a loss of what to say, he looked up at the cab of the tractor where Gavin had now wedged himself into the corner.

"Er, I think I'd better be going, got lots to do."

"Oh, OK," she could not disguise the disappointment in her voice. "Thanks for the flowers."

He turned. "Flowers?"

"Yes, the daffodils."

He made no reply and she watched as he climbed up into the cab. He drove the tractor down the main high street; he didn't even wave, although with a pasty in one hand and a steering wheel in the other it would probably have proved impossible.

Margot felt a sense of anticlimax. It was as if he was a completely different person from the man she talked to last night. Midnight Giles had been chatty, kind and understanding but the one she had just met acted as if they were strangers. She didn't know what to think.

Margot entered the shop; Emma was behind the Post Office counter.

"How's the new book going, Miss Denning?"

Ever since she had given her talk to the WI, Emma had taken a great interest in Margot's writing career.

"I'm struggling a bit with this one. It is always difficult getting into a new book because I also have to promote the previous one at the same time. But this will be my twentieth so I am used to it."

Margot bought some bits and pieces and walked slowly back home. She hadn't been quite truthful about the reason why she was struggling. She was finding it hard to get started because of Giles. She knew it was stupid but she found herself thinking about Giles when she should be concentrating on her hero. She had had to rewrite three chapters because she found herself describing her current hero as a tall slim man used to the outdoors, a template of Giles. Normally it wouldn't have mattered but her main character had started the novel off as a sensitive concert musician. She was so used to living in the world of her novels and her creative writing that it threw her totally when the real world tried to intrude.

Back home Margot made herself some tea and carried the hot cup over to the computer. She switched it on and logged on to Country Cousins' website. She was taken aback to find a message waiting for her. It was from Gus again.

'So glad you sorted out your misunderstanding with whoever this guy was, he must be someone special. Shame that we won't be able to get together now but hey if you need any help or advice just ask away. I'm a man and to be honest we're not very complicated creatures.'

Gus must have read her mind. Boy oh boy did she need some advice. She was about to reply immediately when she paused. What sort of advice did she want? It wasn't as if she were even in a relationship yet. However, it would be good to have someone she could talk to; someone who was neutral. Yes, Gus could prove to be a great help should she ever need it.

She typed in a message to Gus, thanking him and offering to reciprocate should he find himself in a similar position and needed a woman's perspective. Margot finished her tea and settled down to work on her novel. After a couple of hours she knew she had reached a natural stopping point and switched her computer off. 'I really must get back to office hours,' she thought as she looked at the clock and realised that it was way past seven o'clock. In London she had kept to a strict timetable, even on those days when the words didn't come so easily. In Middle Chippings she was very aware that country living had its own natural rhythm. Work started early and finished once the light had disappeared. But she was not an agricultural worker; she was a writer and needed a much greater discipline than she had displayed of late.

After dinner Margot settled down to sort out her correspondence. She often left the post until the end of the day. Bills and requests for personal appearances took up far too much of her time. Experience had taught her that dealing with them first thing often took up more time than if she left them to the evening.

The invitation was on thick embossed card; it was from one of her publishers, a dinner at one of the rather grand hotels in London. She never bothered going usually but on the one occasion Margot had accepted she had been placed on a table with all the other 'singles'. She hadn't enjoyed it one bit. Margot knew that writing her novels was the easy part, the bit she enjoyed the most. What she did not enjoy was the promotional side. She was well aware that those who did go along to these publishing events were the ones who got noticed. They met the right sort of people and although Margot had confidence in her agent to get her a good deal she knew that she too ought to play her part.

There was a reply slip and prepaid envelope in with the invitation. She quickly scribbled her acceptance and in the section that said 'name of partner' she wrote 'Mr Giles Farmer'. There she had done it. She quickly slipped the acceptance into the envelope and sealed it up. All she had to do now was ask him.

CHAPTER 15

Giles finished eating his pasty one handed, he didn't speak. It was so noisy in the cab that even with the two of them sitting cheek by jowl it was impossible to hold a conversation. They drove down to the lower field; Gavin jumped out to open the farm gate then stood holding it whilst Giles drove through. Giles drove over to the corner of the field where the metal frame that held the hay was partially sheltered by a big wide tree. Giles switched off the engine and the pair of them transferred the hay from the back of the tractor into the feeding area.

"So?"

"So what?"

"So where did you get to after you stormed out the pub last night and before you came back home about three hours later?"

"Are you your uncle's keeper?"

"Well someone has to be."

Giles tried to ignore the question but Gavin was having none of it. He pushed that bit further. "You were with her, weren't you?"

"Oh for God's sake, I got the third degree from your mother this morning, I don't need it from you as well!"

"You were with her." Gavin's tone was triumphant. "I knew it, you sly old dog, you spent the night with her."

"I did not 'spend the night' with her as you so crudely put it. I called around to see her and we sat and chatted, that's all, though what business it is of yours I do not know. And, as you recollect you were still up when I came back so it could hardly be said that I was out all night."

"And that's all you did, chat?"

"What I did, young Gavin, was my own business to mind, nobody else's and I would ask you to do the same. Now can we finish this feeding and get back, please?"

They finished the job in silence; Gavin realised that he had overstepped the mark. The woman was most certainly getting under Giles's skin. When Gavin and his mother had returned to Home Farm without Giles, Jean had demanded to know what had been going on. She knew from Godfrey that Giles had been seeing someone. She hoped that it wasn't that rude woman who had rushed out of the pub. She was most definitely not right for her brother. Giles needed someone practical not ornamental. Gavin wouldn't give his mother much information, which either meant he knew nothing or that he knew a lot but wasn't telling. Jean had noticed that Giles and Gavin had become closer since Gavin had moved back to Home Farm. She was pleased but a small part of her felt excluded. With Gavin working back at the farm Jean was lonely in the house by herself. Still it was a good excuse for her to make frequent visits back to the farm; she always enjoyed coming home. Her father always kept her room free. With Gavin in the spare room there was nowhere to put visitors, not that it mattered. Godfrey very rarely had people to stay. Their mother had been the welcoming one.

Jean had spent much of her life trying to get away from Middle Chippings but as she got older she felt an undeniable pull back to her roots. However, some things never changed. Emma from the village shop spreading malicious gossip, the vicar polite to her face but who did not approve of a woman twice divorced. Samantha in the pub was friendly enough, but then they went way back. They usually avoided the one contentious topic of conversation that was likely to spoil their friendship – past indiscretions. They had both had flings with a certain builder by the name of Danny Bragg. In Jean's case neither her father nor her brother had approved of Danny so he was never made welcome and certainly never invited to the house. Both Jean and Samantha knew that Danny was not the settling down kind of a guy so they had both moved on and made bad marriages. Sam had one divorce to her two, but who was counting.

Jean looked up as she heard the tractor pull into the yard. She called for her father to come down for dinner.

Giles and Gavin were still arguing when they came into the kitchen.

"Look, just drop the subject, it's personal, OK."

"What's personal?" Jean looked up from laying the table.

"Everything is personal, unless of course you are a member of this family when everyone seems to think they have a right to know your business."

Jean looked at her brother, he wasn't usually this touchy.

"It's that woman isn't it? That woman from the pub last night, the one who behaved so oddly. She totally cut me dead and was really rude to Gavin when he tried to introduce us. Who is she anyway?"

"Her name is Margot Denning and she is a writer and I've met her a couple of times that's all." Giles felt that he had to give his sister something, just to keep her quiet.

"He met her in London too," Gavin added.

"That was by accident and..."

"She gave him the brush off," Gavin finished.

"Probably for the good, I mean, come on, Giles, she's hardly your type is she?"

"Look, can we discuss something else other than my love life please?"

"Oh so you admit you have a love life?" Gavin teased his uncle, enjoying his discomfort.

"Well where does this woman live then?" even Godfrey was joining in now.

Giles sighed, "She lives in Saddleback Cottage. I think she rents it from that other woman, the one you met, Dad, the one who wants to do something with the piggery. According to Margot..."

"Ooh, it's Margot now," Gavin teased but was silenced by a glare from his mother.

"According to Margot she is at Saddleback Cottage more than the other woman. It sounded a bit complicated when she explained it to me but I think the Dudd woman owns the place but Margot, I mean Miss Denning lives in it." Giles paused, it had seemed so clear when Margot had explained it to him last night but in the cold light of day it sounded just a little bit odd.

"From what I can recall Saddleback Cottage has only got two very small bedrooms unless of course they're what you call 'close' friends, lesbians like." It was now Godfrey's turn to be provocative.

"Take it from me she's not a lesbian."

Giles saw his sister exchange glances with Gavin and realised that he had walked into their trap. He decided to assert some authority over his family.

"Right, enough is enough. Let's just get on with dinner, shall we?"

Their family meals had always been like this, even when Giles was a little boy and his mother was alive. Jean often used to tease him and he had never been able to ignore it or learn how to get his own back. He hadn't needed to as his mother had always protected him from his quick witted sister. He loved them all but wished they would let him get on with his own life instead of always interfering. Not wishing to be unkind, his sister hadn't exactly made a success of her life thus far.

After the meal, when they had all washed up and cleared away, they sat in the sitting room watching television. Gavin was restless; he was only staying in because his mum was visiting. Giles could see that he was itching to get down to visit Suzie at the pub. Surprisingly it was Jean who gave them both the 'out'.

"Giles, why don't you and Gavin pop down to The Quarry Man, you both look bored stiff and there's a film I want to watch. I'll stay and keep Dad company."

"Well if you're sure Mum?" Gavin made a token protest.

They drove out of the yard and down to the pub car park. Giles switched off the engine but made no move. He pulled out his wallet and passed a five pound note to Gavin.

"Here have a drink on me."

"You're not coming in?"

"No, to be honest I just wanted to get out of the house. I love your mum but she does wind me up. Put the pair of us in a room together and after an hour or so we're at each other's throats."

"Did you see? As we passed, her light was on."

"Was it, I didn't really notice," Giles lied.

They both laughed.

"I'll pick you up just after eleven thirty, if that's OK?"

"Fine, good luck. Enjoy yourself."

Giles watched as Gavin walked into the pub. He wanted to go and see Margot but it was late and he wasn't sure what sort of a welcome he might get. If he drove the Land Rover back to the end of Blossom Lane he would have to find somewhere to park. The cottage didn't have a driveway and to leave the Landy in the lane would proclaim his business to all and sundry. Giles opened the glove compartment and withdrew the brown bag with the name of the ironmongers written along the side. He placed the bag and its contents on the passenger seat.

Gavin looked out of the window. Suzie's bedroom was at the back of the building and it overlooked the car park. He noticed that the Land Rover had not moved and that Giles was still sitting in the front. Suzie was not in a good mood. Gavin had caught her on the hop and she was aware that she hadn't done her hair and that she probably still smelled of food from the kitchens where up until five minutes ago she had been working. They weren't that busy this evening which was why Samantha had begrudgingly given Suzie time off. Samantha had long given up the effort of preventing Gavin and Suzie spending time in their room together.

"Come here," Gavin pulled Suzie towards him.

She made a token protest but let him pull her into his embrace. He kissed her long and hard and all the anger left as she gave in to his lustful eagerness. He wanted her even if she did feel that she wasn't looking her best. Gavin pulled away and walked towards the bedroom door, quietly turning the key in the lock. He smiled, "Just in case."

They turned to face each other; Gavin pulled the T-shirt over her head. She was wearing a pink lacy thing; he slipped his hand into the right cup and gently massaged her breast. Her eyes were closed and she suppressed a soft moan as her hands worked quickly and expertly at his belt and zip. She looked down.

"You really are pleased to see me."

With his right hand still caressing, Gavin awkwardly undid Suzie's jeans; in the end she did the job for him. They stepped out of their clothes and Suzie made to take off her bra.

"No leave it," Gavin's voice was husky with excitement.

Suzie made a move towards the bed but instead he gently pushed her against the wall. They had tried several positions but this was a new one. She parted her legs and he entered her; placing his hands behind her buttocks he lifted her up and she curled her legs around his waist. It was quick and fierce and a whole new experience for both of them.

When it was over he carried her back to the bed, she lay next to him. Suzie kissed his right collarbone, her teeth marks had broken the skin and there was a tiny trickle of blood. Gavin moaned as she slowly licked and caressed.

"Sorry, no can do, you can't expect miracles."

Suzie looked down at the flaccid penis. Without comment she kissed, licked and nibbled her way down from his ears to the top of his pubic bone. She bypassed his groin and started on the inside of his thigh, continuing right down to his ankle and then back up again. This time she did stop at his groin.

"Hallelujah," she mumbled as she bestrode him.

The muffled sound of the 'last orders' bell insinuated itself into his subconscious and he struggled to wake up. He was somewhere warm and comfortable but had a feeling that he ought to be somewhere else. Suzie stirred beside him; he looked at the alarm clock. With a start he realised that it was eleven fifteen. He carefully slid out of bed and quietly pulled on his clothes which had been abandoned on the floor. He looked down at the sleeping girl and felt really chuffed; that was only the second time ever he had managed twice in one night!

Gavin heard the sound of a diesel engine pulling into the car park. He looked out of the window just in time to see Giles pulling into a parking space. He smiled and hoped that Giles had had as much luck as he had tonight.

CHAPTER 16

Margot saw that there was no message from Gus when she logged on to the Country Cousins website. Perhaps he had been keener on her than she had thought. She hoped that she hadn't offended him by being honest about being interested in someone else. Margot was not in the business of leading people on but she had hoped to keep up some sort of dialogue. Saddleback Cottage might have been conducive to the peace and quiet required for her to write successfully but it was also a lonely place. She had really enjoyed the exchange of emails. It made her feel as if she were not so isolated. She switched off the computer and was pleased she did because otherwise she might have missed the tentative knock on the door. Margot checked the time, just after 9.30 p.m. A bit late for callers. She stood behind the door.

"Who is it?"

"It's me, Giles Farmer."

He heard the key in the lock and there she was, standing smiling in the doorway. He grinned back at her and for a moment neither of them spoke. Giles held up the bag.

"I got this for you."

He gave her the bag; she opened it and found it contained a chain and lock.

"I noticed the other night, when I called, that you didn't have one. I know that Middle Chippings is probably one of the safest places to live but even so..." he trailed off.

He pulled out some tools from his pocket and placed them on the bottom of the stairs.

"It'll only take me a few minutes."

"I'll get us a drink, shall I? I'm sorry I don't have any beer, will wine do?"

"Yes, that'll be fine."

Whilst Giles was putting the lock on the door Margot rushed upstairs to the bathroom and quickly washed her face, brushed her hair and put on a smear of lipstick. She didn't want it to be too obvious. She toyed with the idea of changing her top and decided against it. Oh well, perhaps one day he would see her looking nice, she had been in old baggy pyjamas the last time he had called and now she was in her comfortable, but far from flattering sweatshirt; she looked down, at least her trousers were clean. She stood at the top of the stairs and watched him working. She loved the breadth of his back; he had taken his jacket off and thrown it on the floor. His body shape was that of a typical inverted triangle. His jeans were slightly loose and a bit baggy; the bagginess enhanced rather than hid his tight little backside.

Giles opened the door to test the width of the chain and the blast of cold air made Margot shiver. She quickly came down the stairs and went into the kitchen. She opened a bottle of red from her wine rack and found two long stemmed glasses. She carried all three into the sitting room.

"Come and try it," he called from hallway.

He stood back whilst she hooked the lock into the slot. She couldn't quite manage it so he covered his hand with hers and guided her. His hand was rough and warm and safe. He was directly behind her and very close; she could feel the heat and length of his body against hers.

"There, done it," she slipped the lock into place then opened the door which stopped abruptly as it reached the end of the chain. She turned, but he had not moved or stepped back. Their faces were so close that she could feel the warmth of his breath. She looked up, he leaned down and they came together. The first kiss was gentle and tentative, their lips barely touched. Giles stepped back fearful that he had overstepped the mark. Margot's lack of response panicked him into thinking he had misread the signs.

It had been a beautiful kiss and Margot had wanted to savour every moment, to be kissed was such a wonderful feeling. She was about to make a move to kiss him back when he stepped away and the moment had gone.

The doorbell rang making them both jump. Margot went to open the door then remembered the lock and chain so she slipped them on. Giles stepped back further into the hall so he could not be seen.

"Margot, glad I caught you up."

"Mr Bragg, what do you want, it is rather late," the surprise in her voice was genuine.

"It is about that planning business."

"I don't think that now is the time to discuss it. Can you phone me in the morning please?"

"Oh," there was no mistaking his disappointment. "I thought you might be a bit lonely stuck here all by yourself like. Thought you might like a break from all your writing. I picked up a couple of bottles, wasn't sure what you liked so I got one of each." He lifted up both hands to display the bottles and gave her what must have been his winning grin.

"No, er I'm really sorry but it is not convenient this evening. I'm er busy," she smiled politely. "Perhaps another time."

"Now, are you sure, I don't like taking 'no' for an answer," he cajoled.

Giles stepped forward, slipped the chain and pulled the door open wide.

"I think the lady said 'No' quite clearly Bragg so if I were you I would just bugger off back to where you came from!"

The two men squared up to each other. Margot had a feeling that whatever was between them it had very little to do with her. Bragg smiled and looked from Margot to Giles, noting Giles jacket thrown carelessly on to the hall floor and Margot's flushed look.

"No problem, as you say, perhaps another time." He turned quickly and disappeared down the garden path. Giles slammed the door after him. He followed Margot into the sitting room.

"That's why you need a lock and a chain. You don't know what sort of undesirable people might call uninvited late at night."

She smiled. "You mean like the local farmer perhaps?"

He returned her smile. "Yeah, you want to watch the local farmer types; they're probably the most undesirable."

"Oh, I don't know," she muttered under her breath as she turned away from him.

Giles flopped down on to the settee and watched as Margot opened the bottle of wine. Margot could feel her hand shaking and hoped that Giles hadn't noticed it. She cursed under her breath, "Damn Danny Bragg, who did he think he was anyway?" She had given him no encouragement. He was a business acquaintance, no more, no less, but the way Danny had just behaved at her front door might have given Giles the impression that he was something more. She handed a large glass of red wine across to Giles and sat in the chair opposite him.

"Does he come round often?"

"Who?"

"Bragg."

"Well yes, he has been a couple of times to price up the conversion job and he and I went along to the Parish Council meeting when they discussed the planning application. But he has never come uninvited before." She sipped her wine.

"He's not to be trusted, you know."

"Oh I think I can look after myself."

"Man like Danny Bragg, preys on women and takes advantage of them."

Margot was not sure that she liked the direction that the conversation was taking. Anyone would think that she was an impressionable teenager instead of a successful businesswoman and writer who was more than capable of looking after herself. The closeness from earlier was disappearing. Bragg's appearance had angered Giles.

"Why do you dislike each other so?" The writer in her was curious to find out the history behind the antagonism.

"We are just totally different people. We were at school together you know. Then Bragg's family moved away to live in town. They only stayed there for a few years and returned back to the village but Danny had changed. He thought he was so much better than the rest of us, harder and tougher just because he had been to a different school. He was never able to fit back in. Of course the girls all loved him. Rough diamond and all that. And there's other stuff which I don't want to go into." Giles paused and seemed to make a decision. "Anyway, let's not talk about him."

Margot went to top up his glass but he put his hand over the rim.

"No more, I'm driving."

"Oh, I didn't hear a car."

"No I parked around the corner, just inside the field."

"Very discreet or just didn't want to be seen visiting the mad writer?"

He looked a bit sheepish. "My old Land Rover is quite well known around these parts. Don't get me wrong, I love living in Middle Chippings but sometimes it just gets too much. It's like living in a goldfish bowl; everyone wants to know your business."

Margot could understand his feelings; she had always hated being the centre of attention and had a morbid fear of being gossiped about.

"I know what you mean, that woman from the village shop seems to have adopted me as her own personal pet novelist. Every time I go in there she interrogates me."

They both laughed.

"It will be interesting to see how long we can keep this a secret."

"Keep what a secret?" She flashed him a quick glance then looked down carefully studying her wine glass as if it was the most important thing in the world.

"Us." He said it so quietly she was not sure that he had even said it.

She looked up.

"Us? Is there an 'Us'?"

Giles leaned forward and said, "Well if there isn't, I would very much like there to be." He gently removed the wine glass from her hand and placed it on the table by her side, next to his own. He placed his hands firmly on the arms of her armchair and leaned forward and kissed her. The pressure of his mouth on hers pushed her back into the seat momentarily until she returned the kiss, cupping his face in her hands. She pushed gently forwards, caught off balance he fell backwards and she followed tumbling on top of him. Laughing, Giles wrapped his arms around her and rolled her over so that he was now on top of her. He lifted himself away from her, all the better to look at her. "I have waited for this since that moment you walked into The Quarry Man."

She smiled back. "Was it worth the wait?" she teased.

"Every bit of it."

He kissed her again and for longer this time. Giles was now lying along side of her and they were face to face, eyes locked in mutual admiration. Gently they ran their hands up and down each other's bodies; gently at first and then more insistently. Giles stroked the side of her face and her throat and it just seemed natural for him to slip his hand into the neck of her top and for his fingers to move downward to the soft roundness. Margot stiffened and he stopped. She tried to laugh the moment off but failed miserably.

"I'm so sorry …" she trailed off.

He withdrew his hand.

"No, it's me who should be sorry. It's just," he searched for the right words, "you are just so beautiful, you're everything I have ever wanted in a woman." He paused then propped himself up on his elbow and looked down on her. "I have never been this close to a woman before and I don't know the rules." He smiled down at her gently. "My mother always said that my problem was that I wanted to run before I could walk."

Margot sat up and stretched across for the wine bottle. She topped her glass up and passed Giles his still full one.

"No, it's not you, it's me." She could feel tears pricking her eyes so she shut them tightly, praying that the tears would not fall. "It is just that I'm, what I mean is I've not…" she didn't get to finish what she was saying.

"You're crying, oh I am sorry I've upset you. I didn't mean it." The concern in his voice made her feel worse.

Margot sniffed, "This is stupid, I never never ever cry and yet this is the second time you've visited me and I've blubbed on both occasions." She pulled out her handkerchief and tried inelegantly to blow her nose.

Giles pulled her towards him, hugging her tightly and rocking her gently.

"There, there, it doesn't matter; it is all my fault. I presumed too much and I am so very very sorry if I have offended you." She made no reply but was content to be hugged to his chest and rocked like a child. "It is my charm and my aftershave Eau de Cowshed; it always has an effect on women. Please don't cry, Margot."

She pulled away and gave him a weak smile.

"Sorry, I am not usual this emotional, only in print."

Giles's mobile phone bleeped with a message. He ignored it but it bleeped again a few minutes later.

"Hadn't you better check that, it could be important?"

"I'm sorry, do you mind?"

She shook her head.

The message was a very succinct "Where RU?" It was from Gavin. Giles looked at his watch.

"Oh God, look I'm really sorry, I have to go. I have to pick someone up."

"Don't worry, that's OK."

He sensed that she was withdrawing from him, putting up barriers. They both stood up and walked to the hallway. Giles retrieved his jacket from the floor and picked up his tools. He turned.

"I'm really sorry but I need to pick Gavin up and…"

"You don't have to justify anything to me. Thank you for coming round," she nodded towards the door, "and for fixing the lock for me."

They stood facing each other, each unsure of the next move. Giles opened the door and turned to say goodbye. There was a stricken look on Margot's face which she was desperately trying to hide, but he had glimpsed it in a few unguarded seconds.

"Margot, I am really sorry if I messed anything up. Is there a chance er I mean, can I see you again?"

Margot's face lit up. "Yes, if you really want to."

"I would like nothing better." He stepped back into the house, threw his arms around her and swung her around. He replaced her back on to the floor. Margot knew that she was no lightweight yet he had lifted her up as if she were. She watched him hurry back down the path; he turned to smile and wave as he walked through the front gate and down Blossom Lane.

She shut the door. She knew that she would have to tell him, it seemed such a stupid thing but for her it was a big deal and the longer it had gone on, the bigger the deal had become. She had not told a soul. How could she explain, and more to the point would he believe her? Despite countless torrid love affairs, all in print, at forty-two years of age Margot Denning remained a virgin.

CHAPTER 17

On balance Giles could not decide if he had been pleased by Gavin's untimely message or not. He sensed that the evening was not going the way he had hoped, but then he wasn't sure what he was expecting when he called around. It had all seemed to go wrong when bloody Danny Bragg turned up. The bloody cheek of the man, turning up unannounced and uninvited. However, on the plus side Margot had said that she wanted to see him again. He could have kicked himself for moving too fast, for some reason it had spooked her. She was nervous around him and he wasn't quite sure why.

Giles wanted to talk to this Maureen Dudd woman as well about this damn piggery conversion. Giles had finally managed to wheedle the secret out of his father. Godfrey had tried to get Saddleback Cottage itself listed so that it would put off any potential buyers and leave the way clear for him to buy it back at a knockdown price. The house was very small and for anyone buying it their first thought would be to extend. Unfortunately, there had been nothing to distinguish the cottage; it had been built from scratch at the beginning of the 1940s. There was nothing particularly special about it and it met none of the criteria. However, the outbuildings were something else; they predated the cottage by a good sixty years or more. There had been a great deal of interest in industrial and agricultural heritage in the early eighties, particularly with regard to agricultural buildings. Local councils were keen to protect their local identity and heritage so were more than happy to slap preservation orders on old farm buildings and outhouses. It had been easy for Godfrey to get the old piggery listed. Unfortunately, the subterfuge he used to do this was now unravelling. Godfrey had not been the owner of the property at the time of the listing. It had belonged to his father George. Between George dying and the reading of the will Godfrey had enough wit about him to organise the visit from the listed buildings people. As he told Giles, "Twern't my fault if the man from the council thought it was my place, he didn't ask and I didn't say."

Giles suspected that his father had an inkling that Saddleback Cottage would be going out of the immediate family which is why he had planned it as he did. Godfrey had considered it 'insurance' just in case his suspicions proved founded. He had been proved right. Old George left the cottage to his mistress and she in turn passed it on to her son William Smith.

None of this would have come out had this Maureen Dudd woman not put in for planning permission to convert the piggery. That she had chosen Danny Bragg for the job made the situation even more difficult. If there was a chance to discredit a member of the Farmer family, Giles knew that Danny Bragg would not hesitate to take it.

Although his father had pretended not to care about getting found out he hadn't fooled Giles. Godfrey had no wish to be dragged to court for something he had done, albeit for good reason, many years before. Godfrey had taken the action in the expectation that Saddleback Cottage would eventually be his. William Smith had no emotional ties to the place like Godfrey had. Godfrey was a patient man and had been prepared to bide his time and wait for the property to be put on the market. The Farmers weren't the only people interested in the cottage. Danny Bragg wanted it too. Danny was distantly related to William Smith's mother through her first marriage.

However, what neither Danny nor Godfrey had counted on was that the solicitor would sell the cottage on the open market using a national chain of estate agents. As a result of this neither man had been quick enough to put in a bid for the place. Within hours of it going on the market a London agent had sold it. All of this Godfrey had told Giles over breakfast. Giles had been amazed at all the secrets that came tumbling out. He didn't know whether to admire his father for his actions in getting the order placed on the piggery or to be angry with him for the double-dealing.

Giles had a niggling feeling that there were more secrets to come out. When he and Gavin had got back to Home Farm last night Godfrey and Jean had been deep in conversation. Whatever the subject was, it was rapidly changed as the men walked through the door.

That had been last night and this was this morning. Despite yelling for Gavin three times the lad had stayed in bed. In the end he gave up. Giles was cross the boy was definitely dropping off. He would need to have a word with him. He seemed to be spending a great deal of time with young Suzie. They were too young to get too heavily involved with each other. Besides which Giles knew from Samantha at the pub that Suzie was destined for bigger and better things. Her university place was already booked. Sam Savage would kill rather than let her daughter pass up such a great opportunity to better herself.

Giles was mending a damaged fence in the lower paddock when he heard a car. He looked up and was surprised to see Jean getting out of her old runabout. She walked towards him. He waited until she was closer.

"Where's that lad of yours then?"

"He's back up at the farm; Dad's got him cleaning out the garage."

"Oh." It was a job that Giles had been putting off for weeks.

"Anyway, I didn't want him around. You and I need to talk."

"We do?"

"Yes," Jean paused as if unsure how to go on. "It's no good beating about the bush but Dad and I have discussed it and I'm moving back home to live."

Giles was taken aback, he hadn't known what to expect but it certainly wasn't this. "You're what? For how long?"

"For good."

Giles stopped what he was doing and faced his sister square on.

"So what has brought this on? Was I going to be consulted or asked what I wanted?" Giles could feel the antagonism of their childhood rising and he fought to control it.

"I've as much right to Home Farm as you have, Giles, and you know it. When Gavin goes off to college or travelling I shall be rattling around in that house all by myself," Jean stared defiantly at her brother, "and anyway Dad needs someone to look after him, to cook and clean."

"We've managed OK since Mum went."

"You mean you've managed."

"And what about Gavin, what does he want, what does he think about you moving back permanently?"

"He'll be fine with it."

"You mean you haven't told him yet?"

"No, I wanted to speak to you first, to get your blessing so to speak."

"You don't need my blessing. You and Dad have got it all sorted out. You only want my opinion as long as it agrees with what you want, so why bother asking?"

"Giles, I don't want us to fall out over this." She now had her placatory voice and changed tack. "Are you coming home for lunch? I've done a big casserole."

"No thank you. I'll have lunch out."

He turned to continue with the fence mending. It would take more than a bloody casserole for Jean to mend fences with him. Jean shrugged and walked away calling out over her shoulder, "Suit yourself, see you later."

Giles drove his tractor to The Quarry Man for lunch; he sat at the back of the bar with a pint and a sandwich. He didn't usually drink at lunchtime but felt that he needed one today. He wanted to think through the ramifications of having his sister move back to the farm. She might think that she had a right to return but it was Giles who had stayed working for a pittance in the expectation that Home Farm would one day be his. Giles knew that had either of Jean's two marriages stayed the course she would not be interested in moving back to Middle Chippings. For choice she would have lived up in town, making the occasional duty visits back home on high days and holidays only. Gavin was the key. Jean was securing her share of the farm for Gavin. Giles could not be sure that Gavin even wanted it. Farming wasn't in his blood in the same way as it was for Giles. He supposed that in the absence of anyone else Gavin was heir apparent whether Giles liked it or not!

"Hi, penny for them."

Giles looked up and saw Margot standing next to his table. He jumped up with a smile and made as if to kiss her on the cheek; she leaned towards him to receive the kiss then realising where they were they leaned away simultaneously aware that curious eyes were watching them. Instead he gently rubbed the side of her arm.

"Sorry I was miles away," Giles looked around, "are you here by yourself, do you want to join me?"

"Sorry, I've got a lunch date with your local reporter," she smiled at him, "the real one this time." She looked at him, "Are you OK?"

"Yeah, a few family problems that's all." He straightened up. "Nothing I can't sort."

"Would a sympathetic friend who is prepared to listen be of any use?"

"Only if she is a beautiful blonde with a gorgeous smile and brown eyes to melt into." Giles pushed his hands deep into his pockets. He just had an overwhelming desire to touch her.

"Dinner at eight followed by a sympathetic ear and most definitely no advice whatsoever."

"Sounds great."

They were interrupted by a polite cough. They both turned to look at the young man waiting patiently just out of earshot.

"Er, so sorry to interrupt, Miss Denning, but I think our table is ready now."

Giles watched her walk away; she had a lovely arse and the sexiest wiggle he had ever seen. All of a sudden his despondent mood had lifted. Giles finished his beer and climbed back into the tractor to return to the fence mending in the lower paddock. Gavin was there waiting for him.

"Giles, I didn't know, she didn't ask me. Honestly, if I had known then I would have said something."

"It's OK, Gavin, don't worry. You don't have to explain anything. I know that she's your mum but she's been my sister for a lot longer so I know exactly what she is like."

They started work on the fence where Giles had left off earlier.

Gavin started to explain. "Mum always talks about Home Farm and about how she misses it," he paused not wanting to be disloyal, "and to be honest the last couple of boyfriends she has had were rubbish. She doesn't find it easy making friends."

"I know."

"Well, most of the people in Middle Chippings she's known for years and I just think she'll be happier here."

Giles didn't say anything but the thought uppermost in his mind was, 'for how long? For how long will she be happy before she wants to move on?'

They got back to the farm just before six o'clock. Jean was in the kitchen laying the table for dinner and there was a lovely smell of a roast cooking.

"Dinner in twenty minutes, you've just got time to wash up."

"Nothing for me, I'm eating out tonight."

"But you didn't say," Jean tried unsuccessfully to curb her anger.

"You didn't ask."

They stared at each other for a few moments before Jean turned away and back to the stove. 'She might be moving back home but there was no way that I'm going to allow myself to be organised and bossed about by her. My life was my own and the sooner she realised that, the better,' he thought.

Giles lay in the hot soaking bath, the smell of the roast was tempting as it wafted up the stairs but the thought of a dinner with Margot was far more enticing. He took his time getting ready and spent ages trying to decide what to wear. He looked through his wardrobe. Perhaps he ought to buy himself some new and smarter clothes if he was going to do this more often. He popped his head around the kitchen door just before he left.

"Bye, not sure what time I'll be back. Don't wait up."

He left before they started asking him questions which he had no wish to answer. He could have walked to Saddleback Cottage but he was too early. He drove to the out of town supermarket. Half an hour, a bouquet of flowers and a bottle of wine later he parked the Land Rover discreetly around the corner from Saddleback Cottage. Giles switched off the engine and looked at his watch. He felt like an adolescent love struck teenager – nervous and excited. He locked the Land Rover then walked to the cottage. He rang the bell, he was three minutes early.

CHAPTER 18

The lunchtime interview had finished late so it was almost three o'clock by the time that Margot returned to Saddleback Cottage. She looked around her. The place needed tidying but more important than that, what on earth was she going to prepare for dinner this evening? Margot was not a brilliant cook; she wasn't even a good one. She had never needed to before. She opened her cupboards.

"Mother Hubbard eat your heart out," she said out aloud.

It was at times like this that she really regretted moving out of London. If she were in her London flat now she could have just popped around to the deli two streets away and bought the ingredients for a meal. All she would have then had to do was throw them all together, use her best china and crystal and that would be it. No one really cooked in London, why bother when you could eat out. She had eaten at The Quarry Man so many times now that she could quote the menu off by heart. It was typical pub food, not particularly imaginative and a bit on the stodgy side. She could take Giles to an expensive restaurant but the nearest one was at least half an hour away by car and she had a feeling that, at this stage, Giles would not feel too comfortable being paid for by a woman. No she would have to make do with what she had.

She rushed around the cottage as quickly as she could tidying and cleaning, paying particular attention to the matchbox of a bathroom. She firmly closed the door of the second bedroom; the one that Giles had assumed belonged to Maureen. Margot would have to confess that she and Maureen were one and the same but she wanted to choose her moment.

Before she realised it, five o'clock had come and gone and with it any chance she may have had to get to the village shop. She would have to make do with what she had in stock – there wasn't a lot she could do with a tin of tuna and baked beans. She telephoned her friend Abi in a blind panic.

"What can I do?" she wailed. "I've got three hours and I need to have a bath, wash my hair and do all the usual things that you do…" she didn't finish.

"In case you get lucky," Abi finished for her laughing. "Right what have you got?"

"Nothing!"

"Have you got onions, a tin of tomatoes, and some pasta?"

Margot cradled the phone between cheek and shoulder as she opened all of her cupboards.

"Yes, I've got all of that."

Abi then proceeded to tell her how to make a tomato and tuna-based sauce to go over pasta – main course sorted. Margot found a couple of tins of soup; Abi assured her that if she added some brandy and a few herbs on top that would suffice. All she was left with was a pudding. Try as she might, she couldn't find anything. She had some bits of cheese and some ancient crackers; they would have to make do. Wine was no problem, Margot always kept a supply of expensive Italian whites and French reds.

Abi wanted to know more about Margot's date and apart from telling her that, "Yes it was the good looking farmer that she met in London," Margot was not prepared to elucidate.

"Abi, I'll give you a ring tomorrow and tell you all about it, I promise, but I must go."

After putting the telephone down Margot reviewed her options. She needed to prepare dinner first. How she hated having a deadline for cooking. She quickly made up the sauce and drained off the oil from the tuna before adding it. Margot looked into the pan, it looked a bit oily but it would have to do. She opened the two tins of soup and put them in the saucepan, washing out the tins and hiding them in the bin. She sloshed in a generous glug of brandy and shook some dried herbs over the top. Margot laid the table with her best cutlery and crystal wine glasses, placing candles in the centre of the table. She couldn't decide if that was a bit too obvious but left them anyway. Margot checked her watch, seven o'clock. Not nearly enough time to get herself ready.

Whilst Margot ran the bath she flicked through her wardrobe. Since she had moved to Middle Chippings she had put

117

on half a stone and not a lot fitted. For Giles's last two visits she had looked an absolute fright and was determined that this time would be different.

Margot was so engrossed in choosing what to wear that she forgot the bath. By the time she remembered it had been overflowing for a good few minutes. Margot grabbed the towels to mop the floor. She pulled the plug to let some of the water away. She wanted to cry, time, like her bath water, was fast disappearing. Twenty minutes, twenty bloody minutes, that was all she had left. Margot poured her expensive bubble bath into the now tepid bathwater. She jumped in and out very quickly, so much for her planned leisurely soak. She looked down at her legs, she might have just enough time to deal with the stubble but her underarms would have to wait. She pulled out the lady shaver razor and quickly ran it up both legs. The telephone ringing startled her and she nicked herself, just under her right knee. Margot tried to staunch the blood but every time she moved the cut seemed to open up again. It needed a plaster. She hobbled down the stairs and into the kitchen. She was just in time; the tomato sauce had been left on too high a heat and had reduced to a third of what it had been when she started. There was a half opened bottle of wine on the side. Margot poured a generous portion into the sauce. There was a trickle of blood running down her leg so she opened the drawer where she kept the plasters. She only had the blue kitchen ones. Oh well, they would have to do. She quickly stuck one over the cut and rushed back upstairs. Five minutes, she had five minutes before he came. She put on her best underwear, just in case and because it made her feel good. She heard the front gate go. Oh God, he was early. She grabbed her long black skirt and pulled it on, the bell sounded once. In a blind panic Margot pulled a multi-coloured top with a low V neck over her head. It was the one that Abi called her 'tarty top' on account of the amount of cleavage it showed but Margot was past caring; the bell sounded a second time.

"Just coming," she shouted in the vague hope that he would hear her. She grabbed her hair brush and pulled it through her hair, looking longingly at the hair straighteners that she now did not have time to use.

She ran down the stairs and reached the bottom as the bell rang for the third time. She pulled open the door with a big smile on her face.

The smile froze, it wasn't Giles.

"Sorry, I know you weren't expecting me," Jean made a feeble attempt at a polite smile, "but don't worry he is still coming, but not until later."

"Is there something wrong?" Margot just managed to pull herself together.

"What with Giles? Good God, no, I just thought that you and I had better have a little chat so I left him a message to come a bit later. I hope that you don't mind?"

Margot did mind but it looked as if she had no choice in the matter. They stood either side of the doorway looking at each other.

"Well can I come in?"

Margot remembered her manners, "Yes, of course."

Margot waved Jean towards the kitchen, trying to shut the door on the lounge with its dimmed lighting and the softly scented burning candles. She had a feeling that this woman missed nothing. As she followed Jean into the kitchen she saw Jean glance at the empty tins poking out of the top of the bin. "I bet she uses fresh every time," thought Margot uncharitably. There was a tiny bistro table and two chairs in the corner of the kitchen and Margot waved Jean towards them.

"Can I get you a drink, wine? Tea? Coffee?"

"A glass of red will do fine thank you, if you've got a bottle already opened."

Margot pulled out two glasses from the cupboard and poured a glass for each of them.

"I suppose you're wondering what this is all about?" Jean sipped her wine.

"Has it something to do with this conversion?" Margot hazarded a guess.

"In a way, yes," Jean took another sip. "This is really nice," she lifted up her glass appreciatively. "Look I won't beat around the bush. There might have been some sort of complication when the piggery was listed. I'm not saying that it shouldn't have been done mind, but perhaps the way it was done could have been thought out a bit better. But you've got to remember that when my Grandad George died my dad was all over the place. If you dispute it and take us to court I've no doubt that we will win but it is going to cost us all a lot of unnecessary heartache and upset, not to mention a small fortune to the solicitors."

Margot looked blankly at Jean, she hadn't got a clue what the woman was going on about.

"The thing is, this place, Saddleback Cottage, means a lot to my dad and to my family so we would like to make you an offer. Just name your price, within reason of course. I mean, just look at you, you're not really cut out for the country life are you?"

Jean had hit on a raw spot. Margot, she had been asking herself the same question these past few weeks.

"How long have you and my brother been seeing each other?" The change of subject completely threw Margot. "Keen on him are you?"

"I think that is my business, don't you?" Margot decided to try to regain charge of the conversation.

"'Spose it is really. But from what Gavin and Dad say I get the impression my brother is quite keen on you."

"Oh," Margot didn't know what to say.

"Very honest and open is my brother and he expects everyone else to be the same with him."

"So? I'm sorry I don't follow you. Am I missing something?"

"Well he's putting all the blame for this building conversion business and the upset it is causing our family on to Miss Maureen Dudd. It is not the sort of thing that the lovely Margot Denning would do now is it?"

"How did you find out?"

"Well it was easy really. Dad described you, a quick visit to the library and all I had to do was read the biography at the back of one of your books."

"Well it is not a problem; in fact I was going to tell your brother this evening."

"Really?" Jean clearly did not believe her. "Do you know why Giles hated my grandfather?"

"I didn't know he did."

"Oh yes. Grandad George, not to put too fine a point on it, was a lying deceitful philanderer. He broke my grandmother's heart and then by leaving Saddleback Cottage to his fancy woman he denied my father what was rightfully his. The only way that Dad could regain any control was to have part of the place listed. He knew that it would be difficult to sell with that on it."

"But that's illegal, isn't it?"

"That depends on your point of view. Morally it isn't wrong but legally, well it is a moot point." She paused. "But I am going off at a tangent. The point I want to make is that Giles has very strong views on people who lie or who set out to deceive others."

"But I didn't set out to deliberately deceive him. It was a misunderstanding," Margot protested.

Jean finished her drink and placed the glass back on the table, "Well let's hope that he sees it like that shall we? Are you also going to mention the frequent visits made by Danny Bragg as well?"

Margot was outraged now. "Mr Bragg has been here in a professional capacity. Not that it is any of your business anyway." Margot was not prepared to justify her actions to this woman. "I think you had better leave before one of us says something we may regret."

"OK, but just think about what I said. We would be prepared to make you a very generous offer."

Engrossed in their argument they did not hear the footsteps down the front path, when the bell went it made the both jump.

"No need to mention to Giles I was here. He might ask for an explanation," Jean said to Margot gathering up her handbag. "Don't worry; I'll see myself out the back way."

Before Margot could make further comment Jean had gone. The bell rang again. Margot ran her fingers through her hair and smoothed the front of her top before she opened the front door. The smile this time was not as wide or unguarded as it had been earlier.

CHAPTER 19

Giles hadn't heard the telephone go whilst he was soaking in his bath. It was a good job that someone had though because Margot had left a message to say she was running late. He hadn't minded because it had given him a bit more time to go and choose the flowers and wine. Having parked his Land Rover discreetly he started to walk up Blossom Lane. He heard a car come along the main road and turned. It stopped at the end of the lane, hesitated then drove on. It had only paused momentarily but that had been long enough for Giles to recognise it. Danny Bragg, now what was he doing around here?

All the lights were on in the cottage when he arrived and he could hear someone inside. Even so he had to ring twice before Margot opened the door. Giles looked her up and down appraisingly.

"Hi, you look gorgeous." He handed her the flowers. "A bit cheesy I know."

Her smile widened. "No, they are beautiful, come in."

He had wanted to kiss her but she had turned away too quickly. He took off his jacket and followed her into the kitchen.

"Smells nice, can I do anything to help?"

"No, just get yourself a drink, glasses are up there," she indicated the cupboard. He pulled out a wine glass then turned to the table to pour some wine from the already open bottle of wine. He noted the two dirty glasses on the table.

"Did I interrupt anything?"

"Pardon?"

"When I arrived it sounded like you had someone here."

"Who me?" She became flustered, "No, no one just me. I was probably talking to myself; I do that when I'm nervous. Cooking for someone else always makes me nervous. Go on into the sitting room, I'll join you in a moment once I've got everything going."

Giles decided to let it go and walked into the sitting room. Margot remained in the kitchen clearing up. She automatically picked up the two dirty wine glasses; their significance suddenly hit her. Giles must have seen them and that was why he was asking if she had been alone. Oh God, how should she handle this now?

Margot returned to the sitting room. Giles was looking at the titles on Margot's bookshelves; surprised and impressed that she had written so many. He pulled one out at random and started to read it. He turned as she came in.

"Not bad, not bad at all."

"What have you got?"

Giles closed the book and looked at the title. "Deceit and Desire," he quoted. "A pretty powerful combination if you ask me."

Margot looked at Giles, "And which of the two would you say is the stronger?"

"The stronger or the most powerful?" he asked. She didn't reply so he continued. "Without a doubt deceit is a powerful and destructive emotion. I mean all relationships need trust and honesty. It should be a given." Margot held her breath and said nothing. "But as for desire well…" he walked towards her, a grin on his face. "Desire is a pretty powerful emotion too."

"Giles, there was someone here earlier."

"It's OK; you don't have to explain anything to me. Your life is your own; you can do what you want and see who you want."

"But…" She didn't get chance to finish as his tight embrace and kiss stopped any conversation dead. Margot just stood and enjoyed the feeling of his tongue urgently exploring her own and the feeling of his big hands as they ran themselves up and down her back. He placed his hands on her buttocks and pulled her in close to him, hips and groin welded together. Reluctantly he stood back from her.

"Oh boy did I need that," he smiled down at her. "If you knew how long I have waited for this."

He bent down again and gave her another deep kiss, a slower, gentler one this time. The depth of feeling surprised them both. When they stepped back from each other Margot realised that the moment for confession had gone, she had missed her opportunity to come clean about her visitor. She poured out the wine and they sat next to each other on the sofa, arms and thighs touching, wanting to be as close as they could. Giles twirled the glass in his hands. He had tried to rush things before and had been rebuffed; he knew that this time he needed to take matters more slowly.

"Well how has your day been?"

"Manic," she replied. "I always forget that everything around here closes down at five o'clock and as the buses are nonexistent there was no chance to get to the shops, so I'm afraid dinner is very much potluck."

"How was your lunch date with your journalist?"

"Fine, he was a nice young man, very respectful, asked the right questions did everything right except, I suspect, read one of my books. Why is everyone so stuffy about romance and romantic fiction? It is a damn difficult genre to work in, not everyone can do it."

"Come on it's got to be better than standing in a force nine gale freezing your whatsits off trying to mend a fence that you know will be down again within days."

Margot refilled his glass.

"To make matters worse I've got a nephew who spends his time avoiding the outdoor jobs. If he is not on the computer he's around his girlfriend's or both and as for my sister – well don't even get me started."

"Your sister, was she the woman I met in the pub the other evening? I think I was a bit rude to her actually."

"I shouldn't worry about it, our Jean is very thick skinned and stubborn, she's very much like my dad. I mean take this business about the planning permission to alter the piggery. To be honest I can't see why it shouldn't be done." Margot smiled. "But don't quote me on that. If it comes to supporting my sister and my old man against your elusive Miss Dudd then they'll get my vote every time."

"What, even if they're in the wrong?"

"It depends on what you define as 'wrong'. Morally I think that they have a point and you can't blame them for wanting to keep Saddleback Cottage in the family." Giles glanced around the room. "It broke my father's heart when it went to Grandad George's fancy woman. It didn't help that he lost out when old Smithy put it on the open market. The first we knew it had been sold was when Emma from the shop told us that someone from London had bought it." Giles sipped his wine. "Anyhow, I have to say my sister is not one of my most favourite people at the moment."

"Why, what's she done?"

"It is what she is about to do, she is moving back home to live. Back to Home Farm. I ask you, a woman of her age. It's ridiculous."

"Why? You still live at home; it's no more ridiculous than you living there is it?"

"It's not the same at all; I live at Home Farm because it is where I work."

A timer sounded in the kitchen and Margot ushered Giles into the dining room whilst she dished up the food. The dining room, which also doubled as the office, was softly lit by candles as well. Giles noticed that she had opened the bottle of wine he had bought and the flowers were in a glass vase in the centre of the table. Margot carried in two bowls of soup then went back for the bread basket. They sat down to eat.

They talked about everything over dinner, about books and music and the theatre. If Giles hadn't been a farmer's son he had wanted to be a teacher but his Grandad George died when Giles was just sixteen. An extra pair of hands was needed on the farm. There was no money to employ anyone. Beside they couldn't afford to subsidise Giles over the three or four years it would have taken for him to get qualified. Giles was regretful about it but not bitter. Margot listened, fascinated by his family stories and totally captivated by the soft burr of his accent.

The phone rang, Margot glanced up at the clock, it was very late. She made no move to pick it up and after several rings the answer phone kicked in. It was Danny Bragg. Judging by the background noise he was ringing from a pub and judging by the slur in his voice he had been there a fair time.

"Hi, Margot forgot to say earlier but we need to get together again. Give me a ring, you've got my number." There was a loud click as the call ended. Margot felt that she ought to explain but wasn't quite sure how to. Giles saved her the bother. He picked up the empty glasses and walked into the kitchen. He started to fill the sink with hot soapy water.

"Hey you'll get wet, put this on," Margot pulled him around to face her and put an apron over his head, she put her hands behind his back and tied the strings. It felt good having her arms around him. Giles allowed himself to be turned around to face the sink and the pile of dirty crockery. He washed whilst she wiped and put away. Through the kitchen window Giles could see the outline of the piggery. Damn thing caused more trouble than it was worth.

Margot had made the coffee, placed it on a tray with two glasses of brandy which she carried it into the sitting room. It was late and she was getting nervous. She really couldn't decide if she wanted Giles to stay the night or not. He walked in and flopped down on the sofa beside her.

"Thank you, Margot, that was a wonderful meal and the company, well it was even better."

"Giles, I…"

"Sh, no need to say anything." He took the brandy glass out of her hand and slowly placed it on the table. Gently he pushed her down on to the sofa and leaned over her, pinning her down. She cupped her hands around the back of his head holding his face so tight against hers that it hurt, he pulled away, then kissed the hollow in her neck and very slowly he pulled her top up and over her head to reveal the lace underneath. He slid his hands into the bra easing her breasts out and kissing them in turn.

Margot moaned with pleasure, she never knew it could be this good. He undid her trousers and slipped them over her hips, marvelling at the wisp of matching lace. Giles impatiently pulled his top over his head and undid his own jeans pulling them down hurriedly. Giles threw the cushion on to the floor and rolled off the sofa pulling Margot with him. She was momentarily on top until he rolled her underneath him. She could feel the hardness of his desire matched only by her own.

"Giles," she barely recognised the voice that came out. "Giles, I have to tell you something, something important," she paused. "This is my first time."

Giles stopped kissing the side of her ear and raised himself up on his elbows, looking down at her.

"Pardon?" he wasn't sure he had heard correctly.

Margot kept her eyes closed, she wasn't sure she wanted to see the expression on his face.

"I said it is my first time. I'm a virgin," she opened her eyes to face his look of astonishment. "I know, I know, it's pathetic but I always wanted er. I always wanted." But what had she always wanted, she had thought she had always wanted to save herself for marriage, for that commitment but now she wasn't so sure. "I always wanted to wait for the right one, the right person."

"Oh." Giles was at a complete loss as to what to say. The significance of what she said, not to mention the alcohol, suddenly had a catastrophic effect on his erection. "Oh," he repeated. He rolled off Margot and they lay there side by side, not touching, staring at the patterns made on the ceiling by the flickering candles. This was not going how he planned. He was astounded that at her age, what was she – forty, forty-two – she was still a virgin. OK, so he hadn't had that many partners or sexual experiences himself but he had more than zero.

Margot lay there, she was cold but didn't want to move to find something warm to cover herself with. She had blown it, completely and utterly. Why did she have to go and spoil the moment with the truth? She wanted to cry. She was ashamed and embarrassed by her inexperience. In spite of herself Margot shivered. Giles turned towards her.

"Are you cold?"

"Yes, a bit," her voice was suddenly very tiny.

Giles stood up and turned away from her. She looked at his naked back view, the tight buttocks, the long muscular legs and felt a great regret. She had lost her chance.

Giles gathered up his clothes. "I need the bathroom, won't be a moment."

The minute he had walked through the door Margot scrabbled for her clothes so that by the time Giles returned she too was fully clothed. He had got on his outside jacket.

"Look it's er getting late; I need to be up for work in the morning." He leaned towards her as she sat on the settee and gave her a quick kiss on the forehead. 'God how lame did that sound,' he thought but he couldn't think of anything else to say.

He saw himself out.

CHAPTER 20

Margot sat motionless as he let himself out and she heard his receding footsteps as they walked, nay practically ran down the front path. When she was sure that he had gone she allowed the tears to fall. Her sobs were loud and ugly. She had wanted him so much and she thought that he had wanted her. When she had told him that she was a virgin, she had meant it as an explanation, not an impediment. Margot felt humiliated. What if he told other people – no he wouldn't. If others found out she couldn't bear it. The sobbing which had subsided started again.

She would move, leave the village. She hated it anyway. The cottage was far too small unless she could extend out into the piggery and the chances of that happening were pretty slim. The people were nosy and wanted to know all your business, the shops were non-existent and there was no culture whatsoever. In fact, when she thought about it any other place on earth would be a better option than where she was. She lay down full stretch on the sofa staring at the black night through the window.

She must have fallen asleep at some point. The dawn chorus woke her up. For a moment Margot couldn't work out where she was. She was still in her clothes from the previous evening, albeit wrapped in a duvet which she couldn't remember dragging down from upstairs. Her eyes felt swollen and puffy and her head pounded giving her a pain over her right eye. 'Bloody birds,' she thought then wrapped the duvet tighter around her body and promptly fell back to sleep. The next time Margot looked at her watch it was past nine o'clock. Margot dragged herself up to the bathroom to run a hot bath. The long soak made her feel marginally better. She lay in the bath with two large circles of cucumber on her eyes in a bid to reduce the puffiness.

Margot didn't actually get around to switching on her computer until late morning and instead of opening up yesterday's work for editing she logged on to the Country

Cousins website. She hadn't checked it for ages and was surprised to find two messages from Gus. She opened the bottom one first.

It wished her luck and reiterated the point that he would like to remain friends and correspond with her. The second one was more detailed and had been sent earlier this morning. It asked how her date had gone, particularly as she had been so nervous and apprehensive. For a moment Margot wondered how Gus had known about her date. But then she remembered that she had emailed him about it when she got back from her interview with the journalist. She had been so happy at the prospect of seeing Giles that she had wanted to share it with someone. Margot couldn't remember what she had told Gus about her date but judging by his reply she must have communicated some of her eagerness and anticipation.

Margot tried to ignore the two emails but as the morning wore on the need to confide in someone became stronger. She could do with a friend she could talk to. Abi would have been ideal but she was busy in London. Anyway how could she explain to Abi, who was very experienced where men were concerned, that it had all gone totally wrong because of her admission? Margot had a feeling that Abi would not believe her anyway. However, Giles had. He had accepted, without question, that she was telling the truth. She clicked on the icon to write and send a message. She told Gus that, for reasons she did not wish to divulge, the evening which had started so well had ended in total disaster. At this stage Margot felt unable to go into exact details but she did make the point that she was the one to blame. She pressed the 'send' button, and then logged out.

There was still the message on her telephone answer machine from Danny Bragg. Margot rang him and they arranged to meet later to discuss the progress of the planning permission. Danny had assured her that whether she stayed or whether she went, if she had planning permission for the piggery she could increase the asking price for the cottage.

Margot was in a quandary. It had cost her a great deal to move out of London, money she would not recoup if she sold Saddleback Cottage so soon after moving in. Added to this, she would need to find accommodation for herself back in London.

Margot had already spoken to her solicitor and there was no way she could buy her way back into her own flat for at least the next six months. She had to face it; she was stuck in Middle Chippings at least for the immediate future.

All this emotional turmoil was having an effect on her work. She was already behind. Margot had a very strict working routine. She would start the day rereading the previous day's work making only minor edits and then she would start on the next part. But just lately even sensible editing had been beyond her. Margot tried to clear her mind so that she could get back to her new novel. She had left it at a critical moment when the hero was about to make love to the heroine. Margot was famous for her light deft touch when writing sex scenes. This was ironic, given her own personal track record. Margot started to describe the hero's body but realised halfway through that it was Giles she was describing. Those long powerful legs covered in dark hair, the tight little arse that he kept so well hidden in baggy jeans, these were images that came into her subconscious so that after an hour she had a mere five or six hundred words, most of which she knew she would discard in tomorrow's edit.

Margot had dialled Giles's mobile telephone number three times, replacing the receiver down before she had even punched in the last digit. She so wanted to talk to him but what would she say? Margot decided to abandon work for the day and she pottered around the house before walking into the piggery. She needed to be sure that its conversion was a project she felt passionate enough to see through. She stood in the middle and tried to imagine it as an extension to her tiny sitting room. As a lounge it would be enormous and although there were only two very small windows along one side of the building she knew that putting a picture window in would provide her with the most magnificent views. She ought to get Abi down for a weekend; Abi had vision and a wonderful eye for colour when it came to interior design. Although the piggery was very much a utilitarian building even Margot could see that it had potential to add space and value to Saddleback Cottage.

Margot had arranged to meet Danny Bragg at his office and Leaker picked her up in his taxi. The amount of money that Margot was putting his way she did wonder at one point if it would be cheaper to employ him as her personal chauffeur. Danny stood up to greet her as she entered his office. He had plans and drawings all laid out on his desk. By knocking through the side wall into the piggery the whole of the ground floor would be opened up. The kitchen and dining areas could be extended into what was now the sitting room, leaving the rest as one long enormous lounge area. It certainly looked impressive on paper.

"Ah, Mr Bragg, but you haven't told me how much all of this is likely to cost." Danny came up with a figure much more than she had expected. "Oh that is a lot of money."

"Yes I know but it is money that you will recoup if and when you decide to sell," he paused, "and there is a way that I could make it slightly cheaper, say by a couple of thousand."

"Yes?"

"Well if you were to enter into an agreement with me, all legal and above board like, giving me the first option to buy Saddleback Cottage should you ever decide to move," he paused, "well I could see my way to reassign the total cost of the conversion. If you follow my drift."

Oh she followed his drift right enough. Two offers in the space of two days, it didn't make sense. Margot had a feeling that there was a much bigger history to Saddleback Cottage, Danny Bragg and the Farmer family than she knew about. She would not allow herself to become embroiled in village politics.

"What about the hold-up with regard to listed building status, where do we stand on this?"

"Ah. I'm looking into that. It seems that when it was applied for a few years ago it may not have been," he paused, "how can I put it? It may not have been above board so to speak. I have someone looking into the matter. If it was done er illegally then we could contest it. Without listed building status we can go ahead almost immediately."

"Mr Bragg, what is so special about Saddleback Cottage?"

"Sorry?"

"Well you are the second person who has asked if I will give them first refusal should I ever decide to sell. Why? It is a nice little cottage but nothing special."

"Oh, who was the other person?"

"Jean, I don't know her married name but she is Giles Farmer's sister."

"Jeanie?" he couldn't hide his amazement. "I'd heard that she was back in Middle Chippings but I thought that was only a temporary thing."

"Not according to my information."

"Well, well, well. Fancy Jeanie Farmer come back to Middle Chippings to live."

"Do you know her?"

"Let's just say Jeanie Farmer and I go a long way back."

Margot noted the bitterness in his voice and waited for further explanation.

"Jeanie and I went out together for a very short time, only long enough for her father to find out and put a stop to it. I wasn't good enough you see. Wasn't rich or clever enough for the bloody Farmer family." He laughed, "Anyhow, that is all water under the bridge now. I've moved on with my life."

Margot asked to take the plans home so that she could think about things. She also took the estimate for the conversion with her. On the reverse of the estimate Bragg had written two prices, the lower one was four thousand pounds lower. Next to the sum Danny had written, 'First refusal price'. Margot had the money to pay both figures mentioned. She just needed to decide if she wanted to spend it on a project like this. She left Bragg's office and walked into the sunlight. Her meeting had overrun and Leaker was sitting outside in the taxi waiting. She climbed into the back.

"You 'avin some work done then?" Leaker nodded to the plans she had dropped on to the seat beside her.

"Perhaps," was Margot's non-committal reply.

"Little gold mine that place of yours."

"Gold mine? I'm sorry I don't follow you."

"You ask 'im, next time you see 'im."

"Who?"

"Young Danny Bragg, you ask 'im about the plans for the new houses in the village."

"Plans? New houses? I'm sorry but I don't have a clue what you are talking about!"

"You'd best find out then, before you go and spend good money on that cottage of yours."

Margot pressed him further but he would say no more. When they arrived back at Saddleback Cottage Margot leaned through the driver's window to pay him. Leaker looked up at her, "You go and ask Giles Farmer, he's on the council, he'll know all about what's going on. I'm surprised he hasn't told you already. What with you and him being so close like."

Before Margot could ask Leaker what he meant by the remark he had wound up his window and driven away. Margot brightened visibly, at least now she had an excuse, a valid reason to phone Giles but did she have the courage to do so?

Giles knew he had behaved badly; he had not handled it well, but talk about putting you off your stride. He had been dumbstruck by her admission. During the evening he had the feeling that Margot was trying to tell him something. Giles thought it might have something to do with the cottage or Danny Bragg or both. Either of those he could have dealt with – but being a virgin. That was something else. What was he supposed to have said? He had been so frightened of saying the wrong thing that a swift exit seemed the best option.

Their disastrous date had been over a week ago and he had still not been in touch. The longer he left it the harder it became. He had driven past the cottage several times in the hope of just bumping into her but had had no luck. She seemed to have gone to ground. He had casually asked Emma in the village shop if she had seen Margot recently.

"Oh yes, she did call in at the beginning of the week, said she had a deadline to meet and that we probably wouldn't see much of her. Such a nice woman, don't you think?"

Giles had mumbled a non-committal reply and left. He knew that he would have to get in touch with Margot somehow and soon if he were to stand any chance of making things up to her. In the meantime having his sister living at home was driving him mad. She hadn't got herself a job yet so she spent all her time cleaning and sorting things out. She had even gone into his room and moved everything around. Giles was not happy. Gavin was equally put out. His frequent visits to Suzie at the pub had been seriously curtailed and his mother was on his case about his future career plans. In fact the pain of having Jean at Home Farm seemed to be the main topic of conversation between Giles and Gavin these days. They were back mending the fence in the lower paddock.

"Look I'm fed up with your mother too, but I'm even more fed up listening to you moaning about her. She loves you and wants the best for you so it stands to reason that she is going to push this college business. I mean do you want to end up like me, lonely and broke trying to scrape a living from farming?"

"What about you and her, you know, you and the writer woman? From what you said I thought things were going well. Didn't you go round there for a meal last week? How was it?"

"Don't ask; let's just say things didn't quite go as I'd hoped. I haven't seen or spoken to her for about a week and a half."

"Whatever it was, just phone her and say 'sorry'."

"But I didn't do anything that I need to say sorry for."

Gavin sighed; his uncle could be very slow at times.

"Giles, it doesn't matter. Whether you were right or wrong, it isn't important. Let me explain it to you, Giles, I may only be young but trust me, I know women. One of you has to say sorry and the role of most men, and take it from me, I know these things, is to be in the wrong. So if you really like this woman just phone, or leave her some more flowers with a note that says 'sorry'."

Giles looked up. "More flowers? How did you know about the flowers?"

"You mean the ones she found on the step, the ones I expect you took the credit for? Come on, Giles, how do you think I know about them? I left them there."

"You didn't have to you know."

"Giles, let me ask you, was she pleased? Did you get a result?"

Giles remembered that first night which had been interrupted by Gavin's text. Yes the flowers had made an impact. Despite Gavin's advice Giles wasn't sure what action to take. He needed to think this through. He still hadn't made a decision by the time he went to bed that night so he decided to sleep on it and see what the next day would bring.

The next morning Giles had to go into town to get some parts for one of the tractors. He walked through the high street and stopped outside a florist's. Before he could change his mind he marched inside and ordered flowers to be sent to Margot at Saddleback Cottage.

"Do you want to write a card?"

"Pardon?"

"You can write a card to go with them. Here." She pulled a small card from a rack and handed it to him with a pen. He hadn't thought about a card or a message. He pondered, and then decided to take Gavin's advice. He wrote 'Sorry' and signed it Giles. Before the Sales Assistant had a chance to read what he had written he sealed it in the small envelope.

With Giles in town Gavin had taken the opportunity to sneak off to meet up with Suzie. She was on the computer surfing the Internet.

"God, my uncle's got no idea where women are concerned. I'd love to find out what went wrong with his date. Whatever it was Giles seems to think it can't be sorted."

"Well, why don't we find out? Let's ask her?"

"Ask who?"

"Ask this Margot woman. Don't you remember, I told you last week that she had written to Gus again and I have been replying to her, or rather he has."

Suzie clicked on to the Country Cousins website and scrolled back through the messages until she had located the one that Margot had sent the day after her evening with Giles. Gavin read it.

"Well. I wonder what happened."

"I've tried asking her, but she won't be drawn," Suzie stated. "Whatever he did or said it has obviously upset her quite a bit, that's for sure."

They discussed ways in which they could find out what had gone wrong but more importantly how they could put it right. Suzie had bumped into Margot earlier in the week; the woman had definitely lost her sparkle. Giles had been so morose all week that it was beginning to get Gavin down. They toyed with various options.

"Tell her you're sure that he still cares and that, whatever it was, he probably doesn't know how to handle the situation, which is why he hasn't been in touch. Tell her that men aren't very good at showing emotions, especially if they really care for someone."

Suzie typed as Gavin dictated. Although they were talking about Giles and Margot, Suzie detected a slight undercurrent.

She wondered if Gavin was trying to tell her something. Suzie pulled Gavin towards her. "Do you need some practice at showing your emotions, Gav?"

He slid his arms around her and pulled her down on to the bed. They rolled around giggling then Gavin's phone went.

"Don't answer it," Suzie whispered.

Gavin glanced at the number, swung his legs off the bed and answered it.

"Hi Mum. Yes Mum, no Mum," He looked at his watch, "About half an hour, is that OK?"

He flicked the mobile telephone shut and turned to face her.

"Half an hour, eh, you'd better get a move on then."

Gavin arrived back at Home Farm just before Giles. Dinner was imminent so no chance for a word with Giles beforehand. Jean seemed to be excelling herself with the cooking, perhaps to prove a point that Home Farm needed her. They had just finished dinner when the telephone went. Godfrey answered it.

"It's for you, Giles, some woman."

Giles picked up the receiver and turned his back on them.

"You did? Good, I'm glad. Look it's a bit difficult to talk now. Can I ring you later? Great."

Giles replaced the phone and turned in time to catch the rest of his family looking at him.

"What?"

"Nothing," Jean said speaking for them all. Giles avoided catching Gavin's eye. He went upstairs and phoned Margot back on his mobile.

"Hi, I'm sorry, the house phone is in the kitchen and we'd just finished dinner. I had a bit of an audience." He paused, unsure what to say next. "How have you been? I heard that you've got a deadline to meet." She was making him do all the running, ask all the questions. Margot was not going to make it easy for him.

"That's what the Middle Chippings gossips are saying, is it? The trouble with this place is that you have to tell people something, if you don't they'll just make it up." She finally replied after a long pause.

Giles was unsure what to say next so there was an even longer silence, neither of them wishing to break the deadlock.

"I've missed you," he said finally.

"Well I haven't been anywhere." Giles knew that he had disappointed her by his initial response and that he had managed to make things much worse by not getting in touch sooner. The silence lengthened.

"Well I had better let you get on," was all Giles could think of to say.

"Okay, fine," and she had gone.

Giles returned to the kitchen, his father and sister were sitting at the table with a pot of tea between them.

"Want one?"

"Yes, please."

"Looks like he could do with something stronger, if you ask me." Godfrey never missed a trick.

"Just leave it, Dad, eh?"

"I didn't say a thing, not a thing," he protested.

"We're just discussing this planning application business."

"Oh." Giles had had enough of the whole matter but listened anyway.

"The thing is if Danny Bragg takes it further then Dad could get into trouble."

"What on earth possessed you to apply for listed building status? Honestly, Dad, how did you think you would get away with it?"

"Look, I knew my father wasn't going to last much longer and, at the time, I thought, well won't matter because the cottage will be mine anyway so no one would be any the wiser. Of course when he left it to that," Godfrey spluttered trying to find an appropriate description, "that fancy woman of his I was glad I had done it. It prevented her from messing the place about. It was like a kind of insurance if you like. It would have worked if the cottage hadn't been sold on the open market. I blame that Danny Bragg; there is something definitely dodgy about him."

"Pots and kettles, Dad, pots and kettles," Giles laughed.

"Anyhow, what is done, is done, we can't change the past." Jean joined in the conversation. "What we need to do is persuade this Dudd woman not to pursue her planning application." She looked directly at her brother. "That's where you come in, Giles.

138

Do you think that you could exert any influence to get the planning application dropped?"

Giles remained silent; he wasn't sure what sort of influence Jean thought he had. Margot wasn't speaking to him at the moment and she was his way to get to Maureen Dudd.

"What about Danny Bragg, any chance of persuading him to drop the application? Couldn't one of you speak to him?" Godfrey asked.

"No!" Giles and Jean both answered together.

Jean leaned across the table and covered Godfrey's hand with hers. "Don't worry, Dad, we'll get it sorted. Giles seems to have made a big hit at Saddleback Cottage so if he uses his charm and winning personality I am sure she'll be putty in his hands."

Giles opened his mouth to say something but was silenced by a frown from his sister. He swallowed his reply.

CHAPTER 22

Margot put the telephone down and stared at the flowers. They were beautiful and, she guessed, very expensive. If only he had sent them a week earlier, then she would have been OK. But he had left it a week, a week during which he had been the last thing she thought of as she fell asleep at night and her first thought when she woke in the morning. Margot had done very little work, her concentration had gone completely. She was constantly checking her telephone and answer machine in case she had missed a call. Then just as she had given up he had to go and pull the master stroke of sending the flowers. It was no wonder she was confused.

Margot had felt so alone and desolate since Giles had walked out on her. No, 'walked out' was the wrong description. He had run as fast he could. She had even contacted an agency in London asking about rented accommodation. Margot had spoken to no one all week. It had taken a lot of courage for her to dial Home Farm, then to be dealt with so abruptly, well it had been upsetting. OK so he had telephoned her back almost immediately but that was not the point. By being curt and dismissive she had gained the moral high ground. Giles had had to work hard for every response she gave him. However, it didn't give her the sense of satisfaction that she had hoped; in fact it had made her even more unhappy.

"Damn you, Giles Farmer," she said out loud. She looked around her tiny sitting room. A long and boring evening stretched ahead of her. In her haste to put Giles in his place she had metaphorically shot herself in the foot. He'd never phone back and she didn't know how to retrieve the situation without losing face. She went to the computer and logged on to Country Cousins website. At least she could chat to Gus. There was an email waiting for her. Margot had written to Gus the day of her disastrous dinner with Giles. She opened it up. Gus was advocating that she give this man (she had never once mentioned

Giles's proper name) a second chance. 'Fat lot of good your advice is now,' she thought. It was too late now. She would be very surprised if Giles wanted to speak to her again, let alone have any sort of a relationship.

Margot needed someone to talk to so she typed a message back. She told Gus that she had blown it good and proper but she hoped that she would get the opportunity to make amends. Margot left it at that and sent the email. If she knew what to say she would have telephoned Giles but a mixture of pride, embarrassment and hurt prevented her. She could not believe that Giles was unaware of how much his hasty departure had hurt her.

By the end of the evening, and having put away three quarters of a bottle of red wine Margot was feeling rather maudlin. She decided that she would not telephone Giles but would write him a note instead. Margot rummaged around for a little card that would be appropriate. She found one of her promotional post cards. On the front was a photograph of herself at a book launch. She turned the card over and scribbled on the reverse.

'Thank you again for the flowers, they are really beautiful,' she paused in a quandary whether to put 'love from' or 'best wishes' or just sign it 'Margot'. There was a small blank space after her name so, before she could change her mind, she scribbled, 'I've missed you too.' She found an envelope and slipped the card into it. She wrote Giles's name on the outside, then left the envelope on the hall table. She would see how she felt in the morning before she posted it.

The next morning Margot awoke with a hangover which she knew would take ages to shift. Her cleaning lady arrived bright and early and proceeded to bang around. The noise of the vacuum cleaner was the last straw. Margot locked herself in her study. She could still hear the cleaning lady but the sounds were muffled and just about bearable. Margot was in the middle of a scene that she was finding very difficult to handle. It was the fourth draft but it just wasn't working so when her cleaner shouted something through the door Margot really could not be bothered to pay attention. The cleaner repeated herself.

"Yes, that's fine, whatever."

Margot heard the front door bang. Peace at last. She worked through the rest of the morning and had a late lunch. She had been thinking about the note she had written to Giles the night before. It didn't look like such a good idea in the cold light of day. She would rip it up and throw it away. Margot walked into the hallway. It had gone. She looked on the hall table and rifled through the post left there. She still couldn't find it. Oh God, where was it? A whiff of polish caught her as she walked through into the dining room. Her cleaning lady must have moved it. Margot flicked through the phone book looking for her number.

"Hi Linda. I seem to have mislaid an envelope. You haven't seen it have you?"

"The one with Giles Farmer's name on it?"

"Yes, that's the one," Margot paused as she listened to the reply. Linda had dropped it off personally at Home Farm.

Margot didn't know what to think, was she pleased or disappointed? Well if he telephoned tonight she wouldn't be in. She looked at the two tickets tucked behind her clock on the mantelpiece. She was going to a cheese and wine evening in aid of the church. Margot had bought the tickets weeks ago and had intended asking Giles to go with her. She would have asked him when he came round but she hadn't had the chance. She didn't mind wasting a ticket, she could afford it. Margot had bought the tickets from the village shop and knew that Emma would ask her where her 'friend' was. She would just have to say she had been let down at the last moment.

Margot got dressed early; all traces of her hangover had now thankfully disappeared. She had booked a taxi with Leaker for seven fifteen. He arrived on the dot at seven. The event was being held up at the big house and, if nothing else, Margot was curious to see inside. She asked to be dropped at the end of the drive so that she could walk slowly to the main entrance. She didn't want to be too early but judging by the noise and buzz of conversation others had been there for a fair time already. Emma was on the door, selling raffle tickets. Margot bought several. She walked into the main room; everyone seemed to be in couples or in groups. She looked around and realised that although she had now lived in Middle Chippings for several months she actually knew very few people. Margot wandered purposefully towards the bar and took a complimentary glass of wine. She stood there feeling like a spare part. She noticed that Suzie, the waitress from the pub, was serving the drinks; she seemed rushed off her feet but she managed a brief smile in Margot's direction.

"Well hello there, Margot."

She turned to face Danny Bragg.

"Hello, Mr Bragg, I wouldn't have thought this was your sort of thing."

"Ah, well, you'd be surprised. Support the local church and the community like, oh yeah I'm up for it."

"And he's hoping for the contract to re-point the church tower," Suzie interrupted. There had been a brief lull in her duties and she had obviously been listening to their conversation. Bragg smiled at the young girl.

"Business is business. Talking of which," he put his arm around Margot's shoulder and gently ushered her into a corner of the room. "Talking of which have you had any further thoughts about your extension? I think I can get that listed building order overturned; on account of the way it was illegally done. It might cost a bit though but I would be prepared to pay that part of it."

Margot was surprised; she would not have put Danny Bragg down as someone who would bear a legal cost unnecessarily. "Can I ask why you are prepared to be so generous?" She sensed a slight coolness in his mood.

"Well that's my business," he glanced around. "I'd rather not say, well not here anyway."

Margot's glass was empty so she excused herself and went and bought herself another, noting the extortionate prices. She looked around for someone to talk to and was cornered by Leaker. He had changed into his 'going out' clothes – a slightly less battered jacket than the one he wore when driving.

"Hello, Mr Quick, how are you?"

"I'm fine thank you, Miss Denning, well except that is for my arm, saw the Doctor only last week and he said, 'Leaker you are a martyr to pain,' he reckoned that a man of half my stamina would have given up years ago...."

When Leaker was driving Margot, in his professional capacity as a taxi driver he said very little but now, off duty, and having had a glass or two of wine, he was positively garrulous. She would have excused herself but Leaker never paused in telling the tale of his ailments so she didn't get a chance to get a word in edgeways. In the end Margot just stood there nodding and smiling in the right places, desperately hoping that someone would come and rescue her. Her situation was made more difficult by the fact that she had her back to the main throng of people so was unable to catch anyone's eye.

"Leaker, you might want to go and check your car. I think I heard a scraping sound as I arrived. It came from the direction of where you were parked."

Margot looked up grateful for the interruption and smiled. It was Giles.

Leaker rushed off to check his precious motor car. Giles looked at Margot's empty glass.

"Can I get you another one?"

"Yes, please. I think I've earned it. I lost the will to live two minutes after he started talking to me."

"See, that marks you out as a non-native, everyone else would have escaped after one minute or a minute and a half tops."

Margot laughed and walked with Giles back to the bar. Emma was there trying to catch people for raffle tickets.

"Oh Giles, I see you've met our Miss Denning. She bought two tickets like you did. Her friend couldn't come either."

Giles bought the wine and he and Margot manoeuvred themselves into a quiet corner.

"So," Margot paused, "you were let down too?"

"Not quite. I bought this ticket for a beautiful blonde but I didn't get the chance to ask her," Giles smiled down at Margot.

"Really? And why was that?"

"Oh because I treated her badly by running away and then I didn't know how to say sorry properly and to cut a long story short she was thoroughly pissed off with me. But I am hoping that she will forgive me because I truly am sorry, in fact I have a feeling that she already has."

Margot smiled. "And what, may I ask gives you that impression?"

"Oh the fact that her face lit up when she saw me, not to mention a little card that was delivered to my house yesterday."

"I wrote that under the influence of alcohol I'll have you know."

He looked down at her. "They do say that you always tell the truth when you are sloshed." Giles took a sip of his drink. "Anyway what about your spare ticket?"

"Oh I bought it for a farmer friend, but decided he didn't deserve it."

Their conversation during the evening was punctuated by several interruptions as various people came over to chat to Giles. He introduced Margot to all sorts of people, some of whom she knew by sight. It was good to put names to faces. Giles was obviously popular within the village. He was wearing a suit with an open-necked shirt, no tie. Margot looked around. She knew she was biased but he was the best looking man present. It felt good to be by his side. Margot noticed that she was receiving speculative glances and judging by the whispers people were wondering how she and Giles knew each other and more to the point whether or not they were an item. 'Let them guess,' she thought and just smiled back at them, giving vague answers to veiled questions. The wine was beginning to relax her.

Giles leaned down to whisper in her ear; his lips brushed her ear lobe.

"Do you fancy getting out of here? We've showed our faces so I think that we could escape with a clear conscience."

"Oh yes, please, before Leaker comes back to finish the conversation I was having with him earlier. We had only gone through his health problems above the belt; I couldn't bear to hear about the others."

"OK," he looked at his watch. "Synchronise watches, five minutes until departure."

"Oh good, that will give me time to find the toilet in this place. Someone said it's upstairs and I am dying to have a better look around." Giving Giles a smile Margot wandered off. There was a queue outside the bathroom and Margot exchanged chit chat with the two ladies in front of her. Looking at her watch she realised she had been gone a good ten minutes. Freshening up her makeup, Margot hurried back to the main room; Giles was nowhere to be seen. Margot wandered outside and saw the space that had been occupied by the Land Rover. He had left and without saying goodbye. She would not cry. She walked around the garden to calm herself and then went back into the main house to find Leaker for a lift home. Suzie the waitress approached her.

"Margot er, Miss Denning."

"Just Margot."

"OK, Margot. Margot, I've got a message for you from Giles. Whilst you were upstairs, Gavin called round, there's been an upset at Home Farm."

"Oh, nothing serious, I hope?"

"Jean sent Gavin to find Giles, the old man; I mean Mr Farmer senior has been taken ill, suspected heart attack. They've called an ambulance but he was asking for Giles, so he had to go."

"How serious is it, do you know?"

"No, that was all Gavin said. It must be pretty bad because Gavin looked really upset."

Suzie herself looked pretty shaken up. Whether that was caused by worrying about the old man or her concern for Gavin Margot wasn't really sure. Margot looked around, there was no sign of Leaker. However, she saw that the vicar was preparing to leave. She hurried over towards him.

"Oh course you can have a lift, my dear, I go right past the end of Blossom Lane."

During the short journey Margot explained about Giles having to rush off because of Godfrey's suspected heart attack.

"Oh poor man. He's been under some stress lately. This business about him and the listed building nonsense, well I know that it has upset him far more than he is letting on about." The vicar suddenly remembered who he was talking to. "Oh not that I am apportioning any blame, not if something was done and it was not above board then it should be dealt with, but one can't help but have sympathy for the situation."

Margot hadn't got a clue what the vicar was talking about. She would have asked more questions but the vicar had arrived outside Saddleback Cottage. "Thank you, vicar, for the lift, it was very kind of you."

He drove a little way up the lane and then reversed into a field entrance in order to turn around, she waited to wave to him as he drove past her. Margot went inside worried that her actions, or rather those of Danny Bragg on her behalf, could have caused Godfrey's heart attack. She looked around her sitting room. It was very small and her working space was miniscule but did she really need more space and was it worth falling out with her neighbours for? In truth she still was not one hundred percent sure that she had made the right decision in moving in the first place. Margot knew that it would not be difficult to sell Saddleback Cottage should she decide to return to London. She wished she had not agreed to Danny Bragg's suggestion that she leave the planning issue to him to sort out.

Margot felt tired, the combination of wine and disappointment hit her once she walked through her front door. She was in the bathroom with the fan going so failed to hear the telephone. She saw from the flashing answer machine that she had a missed call. She played the message. It was from Giles, from the background noise it sounded like he was phoning from the hospital.

"Hi, it's me, Giles. Look I think my dad's going to be OK but I'm going to be here for a while longer. As you're not answering your phone I assume you are still out. I'll be in touch tomorrow." There was a pause. "I really did enjoy this evening."

"So did I," she spoke out aloud to no one, "so did I!" She toyed with the idea of phoning him back but decided against it. He had said that he would be in touch tomorrow; she would have to be content with that. Margot looked at her computer; she was too tired even to switch it on to check the Country Cousins website. Now that she and Giles were becoming close again it seemed not quite right somehow, as if she was cheating on him. Margot knew she was being ridiculous but she didn't care. She crawled into bed excited about the prospect of hearing from Giles in the morning.

CHAPTER 23

Giles was desperate to get to the hospital but knew that he must be very close to the drink drive limit. He drove as fast as he dared without drawing attention to himself. He wished he'd had the chance to speak to Margot before he left. He had waited a couple of minutes after he got the call about Godfrey. As she still had not returned to the hall he had to make do with leaving a message with Suzie. He felt confident that she would pass it on to Margot.

It was so late he had no difficulty if finding a parking space; locating his father and Jean proved a little more difficult. Giles waited a good five minutes before someone appeared at the reception desk to deal with him. The woman then struggled to find her way through the database on the computer. Finally she confirmed that Godfrey had indeed been brought in as an emergency. They had processed him pretty quickly and he was now up on one of the wards. The receptionist gave Giles directions and he hurried through the maze of corridors as quickly as he could.

The ward was closed from the outside and Giles waited impatiently ringing the night bell several times. A young nurse came out to him and asked him to wait whilst she went and checked. Giles stared out of the plate glass window into the darkness but all he saw was a reflection of a worried man. The door opened and he turned expecting the nurse. Jean came through instead. She seemed to have aged since he saw her this morning.

"Jean, is he, what I mean," Giles couldn't get the words out quick enough.

"He's fine. Well he is now. Let's go get a coffee. There's a machine at the end of the corridor." Jean produced coins for the machine and got two cups of coffee in polystyrene cups. They sat down on red plastic chairs. She lowered her voice. "He's had a heart attack. Only a minor one but the doctor said we should consider it a warning." She sipped the coffee. "To be honest I was expecting something like this. Dad was diagnosed with angina over a year ago and has been on medication for months now."

"What? Why didn't I know, why didn't someone tell me?" Giles was angry and confused.

"He fell ill last summer, when you were away. Gavin and I came to stay with him, it happened then, the first time."

"Yes, but why didn't someone tell me?"

"Because he didn't want you to know."

"But you knew and you kept it from me all this time?" Giles could not contain his anger. He was a child again being excluded by his father and big sister in some sort of secret which they did not want him to be a part of. But he was no longer a child and had a right to know.

"Anyway that is not the important thing."

"It is to me," he interrupted.

"The important thing is that the attack was only a minor one. They're going to keep him in overnight to run some tests and we should be able to pick him up in the morning."

"Did they say what might have brought this heart attack on?" Giles was beginning to calm down a bit. He gave up being angry, it was pointless.

"It could have been anything. I think that it was a combination of hard work and stress about this business and Saddleback Cottage. He may have hidden it from you, Giles, but he is worried sick about being taken to court."

"But why didn't he talk to me?" Giles tried to disguise the hurt in his voice.

"Because he didn't want you to worry. What would you have done? Insisted that he stop pulling his weight on the farm? You know that is not his way. Why do you think I insisted that Gavin come and work for you over the summer? OK, so it was partly so that he could earn a bit of money, but I did think that having him here would lift the burden a bit off Dad."

"So did Gavin also know about Dad's heart problems?"

Jean hesitated. "Not as such, but I did say that I thought that his grandad was getting old and finding the work harder and more difficult."

"So every member of my bloody family knew except me."

"Giles, don't be so melodramatic." Jean was in bossy elder sister mode and her tone was beginning to grate on Giles.

"I'm going in to see him," he placed the barely touched coffee on the side table; he couldn't finish it. It tasted disgusting.

They returned to the ward and waited until the night bell was answered. Giles had calmed down and even managed a smile for the nurse.

"I've spoken to my sister and she's explained everything to me. Could I just see him for a few minutes, please?"

The nurse nodded and led him to a curtained-off area close to the nurses' station. He pulled the curtains aside and stood looking down at the figure on the bed. His father looked smaller and older. He was asleep and making snoring sounds. Giles smiled, at least something was familiar. Machines softly buzzed or hummed as they monitored Godfrey through the lines attached to his body. Giles didn't consider himself a particularly emotional man but he could feel his eyes pricking with unshed tears. Godfrey looked so vulnerable, with the sheets tightly bound across his chest, high under his armpits. His right arm lay on top of the coverlet, his left tucked in.

Giles leaned forward and covered his father's exposed hand with his own. The touch caused Godfrey to open his eyes.

"Hello, Dad, are you OK?"

"Hello, son, yeah I'm fine. Don't worry about me," he paused, talking was an effort. Giles guessed that he was fairly heavily sedated. "I'm in the best place." He closed his eyes and went back to sleep. Giles squeezed Godfrey's hand then leaned forward and planted a gentle kiss on the old man's forehead. He sensed the nurse hovering behind him.

"It's OK, nurse, I'm just leaving."

He returned to the corridor where Jean was slumped in the seat. She pre-empted his questions.

"Not now, Giles, not here, let's get home then we can talk properly."

They went out into the cold air and drove home in total silence. Each locked deeply to their own thoughts. As they drove past Saddleback Cottage Giles noted that it was in complete darkness.

"I went to see her, you know."

"See who?"

"That Dudd woman. I asked her to reconsider her conversion plans."

"And what did she say?"

"Not a lot, said it was in Danny Bragg's hands and that I should talk to him," her voice was flat and tired. "That would be a complete waste of time as we all know. Danny Bragg is highly unlikely to do any favours for the Farmer family. Especially the way that Dad treated him."

"But that was years ago."

"People like Danny have long memories. If anyone had a PhD in grudge holding it's our Mr Bragg."

Giles vaguely remembered the details, but Jean was going back over twenty years ago. It had something to do with the fact that Jean and Danny had been an item, for a very short time. Godfrey had soon put a stop to it. Giles's parents had been very strict with Jean, particularly where unsuitable boyfriends were concerned. There had been frequent rows during Jean's adolescence. Anyway, her heart couldn't have been that badly broken because from what Giles remembered Jean met and married her first husband quite soon afterwards. Then he went and left her before the year was out, abandoning Jean and her six-month-old baby. The marriage had been a mistake for both of them. Jean had returned to Home Farm but within two years of the split she had found someone else. This marriage lasted barely two years but this time Jean stayed put. However, she visited Giles and his parents regularly, particularly when she needed someone to look after Gavin whilst she worked. Giles's mother was only too pleased to help. Giles missed his mother so much. She had been the glue holding them all together.

They pulled into the yard. Although it was well past midnight the kitchen light was on. They walked in and made Gavin jump. He had been dozing in the old arm chair usually occupied by Godfrey.

"Is Grandad OK, Mum? Will he be all right?" Gavin had reverted to being a child.

"It's OK, Gavin, he's fine, he is in the best place. They just need to run some tests on him to check him over. He will be

OK," she repeated to reassure both her son and herself. "Now you get to bed, without Dad around you and Giles will need to get up early. Go on."

Giles had made a pot of tea but only put two mugs on the tray.

"Go on Gavin, your mum and I are just going to have a cup of tea. You get off to bed, then at least one of us will be fit for work in the morning."

Gavin nodded and left the kitchen.

"What are we going to do?" It was Jean's turn to ask the questions now.

"About what?"

"About Dad, about this damn planning business, about making sure he takes things easy. About making sure…" her face crumpled, "about making sure that he is going to be around for a lot longer." She let the tears flow and started sobbing quietly.

Giles was amazed; he had never seen his sister cry before. He got up from his seat and squatted next to her chair, putting his arm across her shoulder.

"Don't fret, Jeanie, we'll get it sorted. Don't you worry, the old man'll be around a lot longer yet, driving us both mad, you just wait and see." He stroked her back until she stopped sobbing. She scrabbled around in her pockets for a tissue then blew her nose loudly.

"Drink your tea, it's getting cold."

Jean sipped at the tea. "Can you speak to this woman and persuade her not to pursue this listed building business?"

"If you think it will do any good I'll go and talk to her."

"I'm sure it would help. Come on Giles, you could charm the pants off anyone," she smiled at her younger brother.

'Yes, but I haven't done too well in that department recently,' thought Giles, wondering what might have happened had he not been called away so abruptly earlier in the evening.

Giles washed up whilst Jean went upstairs. As she walked away Giles saw how tired she was. He looked at the clock, far too late now to call Margot. He was glad that he had taken the opportunity to call her briefly earlier on.

It was almost two o'clock in the morning when Giles finally crawled into his bed too exhausted and worried to sleep. He lay open eyed for another couple of hours before finally dropping off just before sunrise.

Despite his exhaustion Giles dragged himself out of bed at his usual time. He was surprised to find Jean already in the kitchen. She was preparing a cooked breakfast for him and Gavin. She looked up at her brother.

"Couldn't you sleep either?"

"Not really, I think I must have fallen off at about four or five." Giles moved towards the telephone.

"I've already telephoned the hospital. I got straight through to the ward. They said he had a comfortable night. The doctor is going to see him at midday so I said I'd be there when he examined Dad." She paused. "Would you like to come along as well?"

"No, it's fine; you talk to them and let me know. With Dad out of action there's a lot more to cover on the farm between the two of us."

"Giles, I'm sorry, I should have told you. I wanted to, but Dad insisted that I keep it quiet. Believe me, there were times when I came so close to telling you."

"It's OK, Jean, don't worry about it. I'm over it now. All we need is for Dad to get better."

Jean smiled and dished up the breakfast. She yelled for Gavin to come and join them. The three of them sat and ate together, conscious of the empty chair at the top of the table. For the first time in a very long while Giles felt close to his sister. The knowledge of Godfrey's heart problems had been a hard burden for Jean to bear alone and her relief at being able to share that burden was obvious.

Gavin and Giles were busy all day on the farm. Godfrey had been due to plough the large field at the north end of the farm and although Gavin could drive a tractor he was not so adept at ploughing. The monotonous furrows took Giles most of the morning. The rest of the day was then spent catching up on other jobs. He had no spare time to make a phone call. He hoped that she would understand.

Jean stayed at the hospital for most of the day. When she returned she came alone. "He's better but they want to keep him in for another day or so, just as a precaution. I thought that you and Gavin could go and see him this evening. He would like to see you both."

"Knowing Grandad, he just wants to check that me and Giles have done all his jobs," joked Gavin. Nonetheless Gavin went to change into some smarter clothes for the visit, leaving Giles and Jean alone in the kitchen.

"Is he really OK?"

"Giles, he's going to be fine. He will have to take tablets to control his condition. The consultant said that if he looked after himself and made some minor changes to his lifestyle there was no reason why he shouldn't go on for a good few more years yet."

"What sort of changes?"

"Well, this place for a start. It is far too big for him to manage. He really needs to move out to somewhere smaller."

"Like Saddleback Cottage."

"Yes, if you like, somewhere like Saddleback Cottage. But we both know that that won't happen. Although I did ask that Dudd woman if she would give us first refusal." Jean sighed. "The consultant also said to make sure that Dad wasn't unduly stressed."

Giles thought about Margot, he felt sure that she could use her influence with Maureen Dudd to get the enquiries into the planning business stopped. After all, from what he understood the piggery was being converted to accommodate Margot's writing, to provide more office space. If all she needed was a bigger office he would be more than happy to convert one of his outbuildings for her. It had been an idea that he and Godfrey had discussed in the past. Giles felt sure that he still had the plans lying around somewhere.

Giles let Gavin drive the Land Rover so that he could send a brief text message to Margot. "Sorry didn't get the chance to call, on my way to see my father in hospital. Will try again tomorrow. Miss you,' he added a few kisses then pressed the send key.

"She'll understand, Giles, I'm sure." It was as if Gavin had read his mind.

"Oh I know she will. At the moment Dad is my priority."

They drove around the car park three times before they found an empty space. It made them late. Godfrey looked considerably better than he had done the night before although he was obviously tired. He questioned them both about what jobs they had done and more importantly what jobs they had left. Giles and Gavin did their best to reassure Godfrey that the place was running quite smoothly without him. They stayed until the end of visiting, Giles didn't have a lot to say but Gavin was his mother's son and managed to chat about what was going on in the village. They both hugged Godfrey awkwardly as they said goodbye and left him sitting sipping a cup of cocoa provided by the cheerful night nurse.

"Shall I drive?"

Giles suddenly felt incredibly weary.

"Yes, if you don't mind." Giles climbed into the passenger seat and let Gavin take the wheel of the Land Rover.

As they drove past Saddleback Cottage they noticed the downstairs light was on. Gavin stopped the Land Rover in the middle of the road.

"Shall I drop you off here, Giles?"

"Yes, OK. I'll make my own way back, you go on."

CHAPTER 24

Margot awoke early and got straight to work on her computer. She hadn't worked on her novel for a few days so spent the first hour rereading and editing the previous couple of chapters. Margot's despair over Giles walking out and not being in contact had resulted in some powerful emotional dialogue between her heroine and the hero. Although her writing wasn't strictly biographical Margot knew that it was the lows in her own life that provided for much more interesting creativity than the highs ever did.

It had been wonderful spending the evening with Giles; he had been attentive and funny. He had introduced her to so many people that she had difficulty in remembering everybody's name. If only he hadn't been called away so suddenly yesterday who knows how the evening might have ended. Margot worked through until lunchtime. She checked her phone several times to see that it was still working. He had said he would be in contact and she did not want to miss his call. 'Oh God,' she thought, 'I'm behaving like some love struck teenager.'

The phone rang and she rushed to answer it. It was her agent reminding her about the awards dinner in London.

"Am I still OK to bring a guest with me?"

"Margot, darling, of course you are. Anyone I know?"

"I doubt it. OK, what was the date again?" Margot scribbled a date on a piece of scrap paper.

"I'll need a name for the other ticket and whilst we are on the subject of names what would you like us to call you for the evening?"

"Giles Farmer, that's the name of my guest and as for my name, what's selling the best at the moment?" Margot knew the answer already because she checked her royalties and sales figures on a regular basis. She wanted to check that her agent did too.

"Oh your Margot Dennings are doing really well, so I'll put you down under that name, shall I?"

"Yes please, and send both tickets to me please."

Her agent rang off and for a moment Margot wondered if she had been a bit presumptuous. The dinner was in three weeks' time and anything could happen in three weeks. Still, if by some reason, she and Giles weren't together she could always cancel. By mid afternoon Margot realised that he wasn't going to ring. She worried about Godfrey and wondered just how bad his heart attack had been. She was reluctant to phone Home Farm direct; Giles had promised he would be in touch so she just had to be patient.

Margot looked around the tiny room that she used as her office. Her initial misgivings about the room being impractical because of its size no longer bothered her. She strolled out into the garden and stood staring at the piggery. She opened the door, inside it was dark and it smelled musty. Danny Bragg had talked her through the plans a couple of times and there was no doubt that an office of this size would be very useful, but did she really and truly need it? Margot stepped back out into the sunshine and slammed the door shut. She returned to her kitchen to make a cup of tea and to give herself a break before she resumed her writing. The sun shone brightly through the kitchen window as Margot stood waiting for the kettle to boil. Margot's shoulder muscles ached through sitting hunched at the computer all morning. She switched off the kettle and decided to walk. With any luck she might bump into someone who might know how Godfrey was.

There were several people in the village shop; she guessed that it was pension day judging by the age of those waiting patiently in the queue. Margot heard Godfrey's name mentioned and unashamedly listened to the conversation.

"I hear it was pretty bad. They kept him in that intensive care overnight." Emma addressed her audience of a queue of four. "I spoke to young Gavin this morning. He said they might keep Godfrey in an extra day. Just for observation." The two women in the queue nodded, encouraging Emma to continue. She was interrupted by an old man standing behind the two women and in front of Margot.

"Giles will be busy running the place. I'll give him a ring later, see if there's anything needs doing."

Margot had not really thought about the farm work and realised that this was probably why Giles had not been in touch. She remembered that Giles had said that the farm was a three-man operation and with his father away he was down to a man and an inexperienced boy. Giles would have his work cut out getting everything done. As Margot listened to the continuing conversation it dawned on her how, nosy as they were, people in Middle Chippings genuinely cared for their neighbours. If she moved away from Middle Chippings she would miss this sense of community. She wished she could be of practical help but felt it wiser to keep her distance. Jean had accused Margot of adding to her father's stress by her planning application. She had a feeling that any sympathetic overtures on her part would not be warmly welcomed.

Margot looked at her watch, the queue showed little sign of moving. She swallowed a sigh and waited. She would be late for her meeting.

Although it was well past three o'clock The Quarry Man was still open. Danny Bragg sat in the corner of the bar, a folder of papers before him and his mobile phone clamped to his ear. He looked up as Margot walked in, smiled and signalled with four fingers. She presumed that he wanted her to wait. She ordered a filter coffee from the bar and looked around. Suzie was nowhere to be seen. She asked Samantha if she had heard how Godfrey was.

"No idea. Suzie has been trying to get hold of Gavin all morning to find out how the old man is but Gavin's phone has been turned off. Don't worry, Godfrey Farmer's fit for a man of his age, he will bounce back I'm sure."

She passed the coffee across the bar to Margot and nodded over Margot's shoulder.

"Danny's finished his call. I should catch him quickly before it rings again. That man spends half his life on that damn mobile."

Margot carried the coffee over to the table. Danny Bragg looked up but didn't stand when she walked over. She knew that

Giles would have done. After a very pointed pause she took the seat opposite him.

"Mr Bragg, don't you ever hold your meetings in a proper office?"

"Nah, I used to but as I do most of my business on the blower there didn't seem any point somehow and I like my clients to feel relaxed."

"Mr Bragg."

"How many times must I tell you, it's Danny."

"Mr Bragg, er Danny. I have come to a decision about the building work at Saddleback Cottage. I no longer wish to go ahead with it."

Danny's affable manner suddenly changed. "Can I ask why?"

"It's personal, Mr Bragg, nothing to do with you."

"Have the Farmer family put undue pressure on you to withdraw your planning application?" Margot hesitated a fraction too long. Danny Bragg jumped back in. "Look, they don't own Saddleback Cottage, you do. Even if you don't want the work done I would strongly recommend that you go ahead with the planning permission. It would be a good selling point er and talking of selling don't forget I'd give you a good price for the chance of first refusal."

Join the queue she wanted to say, but didn't.

"Mr Bragg, perhaps you could let me have a bill of the costs you have incurred so far on my behalf," she paused. "I may be interested in having some work done to the actual cottage itself. I don't like the idea of the door opening straight on to the path. I was thinking perhaps of having a porch done. Would you be interested in a job like that?"

Danny Bragg recognised a compromise when he saw one. Although he was angry about the bigger job being withdrawn he was not one to turn down any job – business was business.

"Yeah, we could do that. Let me know when you'd like it done. I'll send one of my boys around to measure up and give you an estimate. For a porch we might not need planning permission. The cottage was never a problem, only the piggery. Saddleback Cottage is a lot younger. The piggery originally belonged to Home Farm, but it was right at the edge of the

Farmers' land. At some stage someone got fed up traipsing down to sort the pigs every day so Saddleback cottage was built for the pig man. It was a tied farm worker's cottage."

Margot proffered her hand across the table. "Goodbye Mr Bragg, sorry, Danny. We'll keep in touch." Margot placed her empty cup on the bar and Danny was back on his mobile phone before she had reached the door. Margot gave a sigh as she left the pub. That had been easier than she had thought. It would probably cost her. She had no doubt but that Danny Bragg would charge for the time he had already spent and probably add a bit on to the cost of the porch, just to get his own back. But the money wasn't important.

It hadn't just been an emotional decision. Margot had calculated the cost of the conversion. She might be a wealthy woman but she was also a practical one. Things seemed to be going well with her and Giles but it was still early days. Margot was not quite secure enough or ready to seriously consider Saddleback Cottage as a long-term permanent home. In a few months the lease would be up on her London flat and she would have to make a decision whether to rent it out for a further year, sell it or even move back to London permanently.

It was almost dark when Margot returned to the cottage. She checked her answerphone, disappointed that there were no messages. Although she wasn't hungry she busied herself making supper. Halfway through eating Margot heard her mobile phone bleep. It was a message from Giles, just to say that he would be in touch. Margot decided she would write a note to Jean to say that she had decided not to proceed with the extension. She hoped that the news would be one less worry for them.

Although it was dark Margot no longer felt anxious or apprehensive walking along the unlit lanes. She took a torch but did not switch it on. A full moon gave her enough light to see by. There was a light in the kitchen and she noticed that the Land Rover was missing from the yard. As she approached the back door she activated a security light and a dog started barking furiously from within. Someone peered through the kitchen window but she couldn't make out who it was. Before Margot had time to push the letter through the letter box the door opened. Jean stood there.

"Oh hello," it wasn't exactly a friendly welcome. Jean was holding on to the collie dog's collar, she was pulling excitedly and barking. "Meg quiet," she yanked the dog back. "Look you'd better come on in. I'm afraid my brother's not here."

Margot walked into the back kitchen, the letter in her hand. "Well actually it was you or your father I wanted to see. Sorry," she corrected herself quickly, "sorry, I know that your father is in hospital er," she hesitated. There was something about Jean that put her at a disadvantage. "Look, I've written you this letter. I didn't think that anyone would be in. I've decided not to go ahead with the conversion of the piggery and I've asked for the planning issue to be withdrawn. Please tell you father. I wouldn't want him to worry unduly."

Jean stared at Margot then remembered her manners. "Would you like a drink, tea? Coffee?"

"Yes that would be nice, tea, thank you."

She sat down at the large kitchen table, the collie had placed its head in her lap and she sat stroking its silky ears.

"If she's being a nuisance just push her away. She's Giles's lapdog. He got her to work the stock but she was really useless." They both looked down at the dog that thumped its tail on the floor revelling in the attention. "Giles should have got rid of her there and then but he's a bit soft, my brother, but then you probably know that already," she paused, waiting for a response from Margot. "Well anyway he couldn't bear for her to be given away so we kept her."

The two women sat down either side of the table.

"How is your father?"

"He's OK. They've kept him in for further tests. Between you and me he has had heart problems for quite a while."

"Oh Giles didn't mention it."

"Ah, that's because Giles didn't know. And he is none too pleased that I knew and didn't mention it earlier."

"Oh."

"Dad made me promise not to say anything. Giles would have made him slow down and take things easy and that is not my father's way. That is why he wouldn't say anything. I was worried, of course I was, but when Gavin came to work on the farm I knew that would help to ease the workload."

"Giles said that Gavin is hoping to go to university."

"I hope so, he's got a place but he is enjoying having money in his pocket at the moment. Fingers crossed he won't change his mind."

It was very relaxing sitting at the kitchen table chatting about family matters. Margot actually felt part of their lives, although Jean was not one to give too much away. They stayed talking for ages. Jean asked Margot about her books. Margot could take a hint; the subject of the Farmer family was well and truly closed. They heard the sound of the Land Rover engine. The two women looked up, Gavin entered the kitchen alone. He was surprised to see Margot sitting with his mother.

"Where's Giles?" Jean asked the question.

Gavin was in a quandary about whether to admit he had just dropped Giles off at Saddleback Cottage. He didn't know how much his mother knew of the relationship between Giles and Margot. He had no desire to put his foot in it.

"Any tea in the pot?"

CHAPTER 25

It hadn't occurred to Giles that she might not be in, particularly as she had left a light on. To say he was disappointed was an understatement. He walked around to the back of the house. The kitchen was in darkness. Although there was a full moon the back yard was in the shadow of the piggery.

"Bloody piggery," he thought, "bloody father interfering. How did he think he could get away with it? Bloody Danny Bragg for stirring up trouble." Giles returned to the front of the cottage cursing everyone in his frustration. There was nothing for it, he would have to go back to Home Farm. He had no way of knowing where Margot had gone or how long she might be away. He covered the distance in considerably less time than it had taken Margot. He pushed open the kitchen door to be greeted by the sight of all three of them sitting around the kitchen table. Gavin looked up and said quickly.

"Hi Giles, I told Jean that you fancied a walk so I dropped you off at the bottom of the lane. Are you feeling better now?"

"What?" Giles was about to say something further when he caught Gavin's eye. He remembered just in time that Jean was not completely in the picture about his visits to Saddleback Cottage and Gavin was frantically trying to cover for him. "Oh yes, fine. Hello Margot."

"Margot here came to say that the building work on the piggery won't now take place. The planning application has been withdrawn."

"Well it will be. I cancelled my contract with Mr Bragg today."

Giles and Jean exchanged glances at the mention of Danny Bragg's name.

"Are you sure that's what you want to do?" Giles asked.

"Oh yes, financially it wasn't a good move and anyway, I'm getting used to having my office in the dining room. It is quite useful having everything to hand. I thought I'd let you know my decision. It might make your father a little less anxious. How is he?"

"He's fine now," Giles emphasised the last word shooting his sister a warning glance.

"Margot, I'm just going to make some supper for Giles and Gavin, won't you stay?"

"Well if it's not too much trouble I would like that, thank you."

Giles sat next to Margot, he was feeling very weary. When Jean's back was turned he dropped his hand below the table and gently caressed Margot's thigh. Margot dropped her hand and covered his with a squeeze. Gavin noticed but didn't make any comment.

Margot offered to help Jean, but she refused. Giles and Gavin were too tired to talk so Margot chatted about the progress of her novel. Finally supper was ready and Jean ladled out some sort of a casserole onto large white china plates. The food seemed to rejuvenate the two men who joined in the conversation. Margot relaxed and enjoyed the family banter. With Godfrey away in hospital Giles slipped easily into the role of head of the house. However, Godfrey's chair at the top of the table remained empty.

Giles was feeling incredibly tired, the hot food and the warmth of the kitchen, and Margot sitting next to him made him want to just lie down and sleep.

"Gavin, why don't you run Margot back to Saddleback Cottage in the Landy. Giles looks all in."

"No, it's OK, I'll walk back," Margot insisted.

Giles stood up, more than anything he wanted to be alone with her. "No it's OK I could do with the fresh air. I'll walk you home."

Giles took his coat from the hook and picked up Margot's, which he held out for her to put on. As soon as they left Jean turned on her son.

"Right, there's something going on. Spill the beans, because for some reason you obviously know. God the two of them could barely keep their eyes off each other, let alone their hands. How long has this been going on, Gavin, and how far has it gone?"

Gavin was caught and he knew it. He had never been able to lie to his mother.

"I don't know how long it's been going on, I think it started before I moved back to the farm and as to how close they are, well your guess is as good as mine. All I will say is don't wait up for him tonight."

Before his mother could interrogate him further Gavin yawned and stood up.

"Mum, I'm absolutely shattered. I'll turn in now."

Jean finished the washing up and tidied away. Perhaps she would leave the back door unlocked, she wasn't sure if Giles had a key.

Margot shivered as they left Home Farm. Giles put his arm around her, but the ground was uneven in places and it was awkward walking side by side. In the end he dropped his arm and walked in front of her. They were almost outside Saddleback Cottage when Giles turned to face Margot.

"Margot, I…"

There was no need for words. She closed her body to his and putting both her arms around his neck she kissed him long and hard. They stood enjoying the moment. They sprang apart as a car turned into Blossom Lane illuminating them in the headlights. It accelerated past them. They both turned to watch the disappearing tail lights.

"Who on earth was that this time of night?"

Giles who recognised Danny Bragg's car replied, "Oh nobody important. Come on let's go inside, it is getting really cold."

Margot led the way to the front door and Giles followed; as she put the key into the lock the car that had passed them minutes earlier drove past them. Bragg had probably turned in one of the field entrances after driving past the farmhouse.

The cottage was cold; the heating had switched off a couple of hours earlier.

"Do you want a nightcap?" she asked him.

Giles grabbed her and kissed her again. "No, I just want to go to bed." He went up and into the bathroom first. He didn't take long in the bathroom. He stripped naked and jumped into the cold sheets. He was so very tired. He closed his eyes for a few seconds whilst he waited for Margot. He didn't hear Margot go into the bathroom and he certainly didn't hear as she crept around the bedroom getting undressed. Giles didn't even feel her when she slipped into the bed beside him.

Margot looked down at Giles, already in a deep sleep. She wanted to run her hands over his face and down on to his muscled chest but she could see that he was exhausted. She doubted anyone could arouse him tonight. She placed a gentle kiss on his lips and snuggled her body into his. Unconsciously he threw a protective arm over her – she loved the weight of it across her body.

The last job that Giles had done before he crawled into Margot's bed had been to set the alarm on his watch for 6.00 a.m. He hadn't wanted to but he knew that he had no option but to get up early. The alarm woke him almost immediately and for a moment he wondered where he was, then he remembered. His naked back was hot from Margot's body, and for a moment he enjoyed the feeling of waking up beside her. Margot had just naturally curved her body around his and they had rolled into the centre of the double bed. The sign of an old saggy mattress, not that it bothered him.

Giles rolled over to face Margot. She was fast asleep and completely oblivious to his stare. He studied her face. Without her makeup he could detect faint lines but they seemed to Giles to add rather than detract from her beauty. He lay there eyes now wide open studying her as she lay next to him. Giles could feel an erection beginning but he was conscious of time, or rather in his case, the lack of it. He wanted her first time to be special and a rushed quickie first thing in the morning wasn't what he planned.

He gently slid out of her bed, collected his clothes and crept into the bathroom to get dressed. He looked around the bedroom door when he was ready. Margot was still fast asleep and didn't even stir. Giles left the house as quietly as he could and covered the distance to Home Farm very quickly. He was surprised to find the back door open. He let himself in then started to get things ready for breakfast. He was sitting at the table eating his when a very tired Gavin walked into the kitchen.

"God, Giles you're early," he peered at his uncle, "or didn't you go to bed last night?" He smiled, "Sorry, I'll rephrase that. Or didn't you go to your own bed last night?"

Giles chose to ignore him. "I'm not so much as early as you being late," he looked at his watch with a theatrical gesture, "and yes I did go to bed last night and I slept very well, thank you. Right you've got fifteen minutes to get some food inside you then I want you out, on the tractor and down in the lower paddock."

Gavin grunted his agreement but there was no way he would be fully operational in under an hour and they both knew it. Giles quickly finished his breakfast and dumped the dirty plate in the sink. He left the farmhouse and headed outside towards the tractor; he would drive it down to the lower paddock and make a start. He slowed down as he drove past Saddleback Cottage. There was a light on in the bedroom but the downstairs curtains were not yet pulled back. He smiled to himself. Giles could not believe that something he had been wanting for so long had actually happened. Well it had and it hadn't. He finally got to spend the night with Margot but all they had done was sleep. To be honest he knew he hadn't been capable of doing anything else. In his exhausted state an erection was the last thing he was capable of. But somehow, it didn't matter. It just felt so right and so good to wake up with her beside him. He hoped that she felt the same.

He had almost finished the muck spreading when he saw the figure of Gavin ambling down the lane, his mobile phone clamped to the side of his head. Gavin waited until the tractor drew level; it was now mid morning.

"That was a long fifteen minutes."

"Sorry, Giles, I'll finish now. Can you get back home? Mum's had a call from the hospital; I think that Grandad is ready to be collected." They unhitched the spreader and Giles drove the tractor back to Home Farm with Gavin riding shotgun. They kept the engine running after they parked in the yard. Giles jumped off and Gavin took his place behind the wheel. Giles gave Gavin a wave as he drove back to the lower paddock. Jean was in the kitchen preparing some food.

"Oh Giles, they said we can collect Dad anytime we're ready. If we go now we can come back and all have lunch together."

Giles quickly changed then he and Jean drove up to the hospital.

Godfrey was fully dressed and waiting impatiently for them to collect him.

"You took your time," he accused.

"Sorry, Dad, I needed to get on with the spreading in the lower paddock, it made me a bit late. Still we're here now. Right, where's your stuff?"

Giles picked up his father's bag whilst Jean wandered off to speak to the nursing staff to say that they were leaving. They drove back in comparative silence. This health scare had made Giles aware that his father was no longer a young man. In any other profession he knew his father would have been long retired. There was a saying that old farmers never retired they just passed away.

Godfrey looked across at Saddleback Cottage as they drove past. He broke the silence. "Well is she going ahead with it them?"

"Who?"

"You know, that woman from London, the one that bought the place."

"No, Dad, they've decided not to go through with it. They're withdrawing the application for planning permission."

Godfrey made no reply but just grunted. Within a couple of minutes they were back at Home Farm. The tractor was back in the yard. Giles carried his father's bags up to his room whilst Jean bustled around laying the table for lunch. Lunch was only soup and bread but it was a meal that they rarely ate together.

Giles stood in the doorway of his father's bedroom whilst Godfrey unpacked the small overnight bag.

"Dad, there's someone I'd like you to meet."

"Oh yeah?"

"Yes, her name is Margot Denning. She came round last night to let us know about the decision not to go ahead with the extension at Saddleback Cottage. You'll like her Dad, she's really nice."

"As long as she's not like that stroppy London woman who came round here causing trouble the other day. What was her name? Oh yes Dudd, Maureen Dudd."

"Well, Margot lives in Saddleback Cottage but she doesn't have a stroppy bone in her body. She is really lovely. As to your Maureen Dudd, well I've never met her although I think Jean has."

CHAPTER 26

Margot had sensed him moving even before he had woken up. She pretended to be fast asleep as he crept around in the half light collecting all of his clothes. She had been disappointed that he had fallen asleep before she had even come up the stairs to join him. He had looked so exhausted and vulnerable in her bed and she enjoyed having his naked body so close to hers.

This morning she let him slip away. There would be other opportunities, of that she felt sure. She was pleased that she had made the decision not to go ahead with the building work. It certainly relieved the pressure on Godfrey Farmer. Rumour had it that anxiety had been one of the causes of his heart attack. Margot knew that in the not too distant future she would have to come clean with Giles and admit that Margot Denning and Maureen Dudd were one and the same person. She was surprised that Jean hadn't told him already and wondered why. She had lived with her multiple professional identities for years. For her it was no big deal. If it weren't for the fact that she had been persuaded to apply for the building permission in her real name no one would have been any the wiser. "Oh why did life have to be so complicated?" she sighed to herself.

Margot heard the tractor driving down the lane but by the time she got to draw back the curtains it had gone. She smiled to herself, what was the world coming to when the sound of a tractor could excite her so much? She couldn't be one hundred percent sure but she thought that she heard the engine change key as it slowed by her house. She like the idea of him checking up on her.

After breakfast Margot switched on her computer. Before editing her last couple of chapters she logged on to the Country Cousins website. She felt a bit guilty that she had abandoned Gus, particularly as he had been such a support when things hadn't been going too well between her and Giles. There was one message in her inbox; it was from him. She clicked on 'open'. He had left a brief note saying that he was glad things were going well and to let him know how they progressed. She was in love and wanted to share it with the whole world. Gus had been a good friend to her over these past few weeks and months, she felt that she could confide in him. In the past he had been spot on with his advice. She thought for a moment then began typing.

She told Gus that she was head over heels in love and that she had never been happier. She omitted to mention that they weren't quite a couple in the biblical sense. Apart from being embarrassed about this she felt that it was only a matter of time. For her it couldn't come soon enough. She opened up her novel and began typing.

The post arrived late morning and with it the two invitations for the publishing party. She phoned Sasha and asked to be booked into a hotel for the night. She specifically asked for a double room. The girl made no comment and promised to organise a room in the hotel where the party was being held. Margot went online and booked two first-class train tickets. She didn't even wince at the cost. Money didn't really matter that much to her. She had more than enough but she instinctively knew that it would matter to Giles. Margot would need to think carefully how and when she broached the subject of the publishing dinner to him.

The doorbell went. Margot jumped up and gave a quick glance in the hall mirror before opening the door with a beaming smile of welcome.

"Well I don't know who you were expecting but it obviously wasn't me!"

"Mr Bragg, er come in."

Disappointed she led Danny Bragg into the kitchen and automatically put the kettle on.

"Mr Bragg, I am sorry I thought that we had dealt with the building business at our last meeting. You gave me to understand that one of your foremen would be coming to measure up for my porch. Is there a problem?"

"No problem, Margot," he took the mug of coffee from her and made himself comfortable at the kitchen table. "I just wanted to reassure myself that you had come to a decision about the building by yourself and that no one had put any undue pressure on you."

"No, Mr Bragg, there was no 'undue pressure' as you put it. I just looked at the finances and at my need for extra work space and decided not to go ahead with it. It was as simple as that."

"Oh," he sipped his coffee, "only I know how persuasive the Farmer men can be. Particularly Giles. Bit of a ladies' man so I understand."

"Really?"

"Oh yes…"

Margot did not let him continue. "Mr Bragg, I am not remotely interested in village gossip."

It was Bragg's turn to say, "Really?"

Danny Bragg had a way of wrong footing her and Margot tried to regain the upper hand. "If that is all, Mr Bragg, I really do have quite a bit of work to get through. If you will excuse me please." She stood up; Danny remained seated sipping his coffee. He had made his point and got her interested.

"Have you always hated the Farmers?"

"Yeah, they think they own the village. Old man Farmer thought he could play God with people's lives, and not just the people who worked on the farm but his own children. Telling them who they could and couldn't see, not letting his kids make their own decisions." Danny Bragg made no attempt to hide his bitterness. He paused for a moment before realising that he was probably giving more away than he had intended. "If things had worked out differently I could have been the owner of Home Farm you know."

"Really?" Now Margot was interested. "How come?"

"Jean Farmer. She and I had an understanding. I wanted to marry her but her father thought that I wasn't good enough so he stopped her seeing me. I moved away from Middle Chippings. When I came back she was married with a kid. The marriage didn't last five minutes."

"But surely that was a long time ago. I can't believe that in this day and age people can still hold a grudge for such a long time."

"Oh they can around these parts."

Margot wasn't quite clear whether Danny Bragg was referring to a grudge he held against the Farmers or whether it was the other way around. Danny finished his coffee and stood up to go. She had enough village gossip for one day.

"Mr Bragg, I am sorry to be so rude but I really must get back to my work. I've got a deadline to meet and I am in grave danger of getting seriously behind with it."

Margot showed Danny Bragg to the door. He paused in the doorway, stepped through then turned around assessing the front of the house. They both knew that the new porch was a compromise to save face. Margot suspected it would be expensive. She had a feeling that Danny Bragg would see to that.

Margot went back to her computer and had just begun to work on a particularly difficult scene when the telephone rang. She rushed to answer it. It was Giles.

"Hi gorgeous, how are you? Sorry I had to rush off this morning. How's your day been?"

"I've been busy working and I've just got rid of a visitor."

"Oh?"

"Yes, Danny Bragg called around. After I cancelled the piggery conversion I asked him to quote me for a small front porch."

"Don't let him bully you into having work done."

"I'm not," she protested. "I actually do need a small porch on the front of the cottage. I've never been entirely comfortable with the door opening straight to the garden. And any way I can make up my own mind you know," she laughed. "You're as bad as Danny Bragg. He accused me of allowing myself to be unduly influenced by you and now you're doing the same about him!"

"Sorry," he backed down. "Look I'm rushed off my feet today. My father isn't really up to helping with the major jobs yet so young Gavin and I are going to be fully stretched for most of the day but can I pop around at about tea time for an hour or so?"

"Of course, that would be great," she tried to hide her disappointment; she supposed that an hour was better than nothing. "I'll put the kettle on."

Margot busied herself tidying up; if he was coming straight from work he would probably prefer to sit in the kitchen. She wished she had some cake or something to offer him. She would have baked one if she had known how. Being practical was not one of her talents. As a farmer's wife she would probably be a real dead loss. Margot stood by the window as the time neared for Giles to call. When he did eventually ring the bell she was in the bathroom, so he had to wait for a few minutes before she opened the door.

"Hi," she suddenly felt shy, "come in, the kettle's on. You look all in."

Giles took his heavy filthy boots off at the door. She smiled at him.

"See, I do need a porch." Giles followed her into the kitchen. As Margot stretched up to reach the top shelf in the cupboard she felt his arms encircle her waist. He bent his head to nuzzle the back of her neck. "You smell good," he mumbled into her hair. He span her around and gave her a long hard kiss. She returned the pressure of his lips. Reluctantly they broke away from each other. The kettle clicked off and she gently pushed him towards a chair.

"Sorry, I'm filthy. I should have gone home first before I came here but I couldn't wait." She felt his eyes on her as she bustled around and made the tea; she opened a packet of chocolate biscuits she had found at the back of the cupboard and put them on a small plate. He wolfed them down two at a time. "I could eat a horse." He drank the tea then closed his eyes to relax. Margot wanted to ask him to stay this evening but felt strangely shy.

"Giles, I've got two tickets for a party in London. I don't expect you'll want to come er, it probably won't be your thing but they've asked me er well I've asked them," she realised that she was babbling.

"I'd love to come, when is it?"

"That's the thing, it is this weekend. Saturday night. It would mean staying over in a hotel, they've booked me er us into the hotel where the party is being held so it won't be a problem," she trailed off. This wasn't going quite how she had expected it.

"And how much is this going to cost me?"

"Nothing, nothing at all, the tickets are free and the publishers will pick up the bill for the hotel." This wasn't strictly true. They had organised the hotel booking but they would deduct the money from her sales figures. There was no such thing as a free lunch, especially in publishing.

"What time would we need to leave? Only there's a lot to be done with my father out of action."

"Well I need to be there for the afternoon. My publishers want to discuss the format for the evening so I know what to expect." Giles looked puzzled. "Well the thing is I'm up for an award and the party is actually an awards do, but the food is superb and the alcohol is free and…"

He laughed, "OK, OK, you've convinced me. How about I come up later on the train and then you can meet me and we can go together?"

Margot was disappointed but tried not to show it. She had hoped that they could be together for the whole of the weekend but she supposed that an evening and a night would have to do. Margot was beginning to realise just what a demanding job farming was. She got up to make a fresh pot of tea and in the warmth of the kitchen she saw Giles nod off. She made the tea then sat at the table watching him as he slept. There was a small high-pitched beep from his mobile telephone which made him jump. He woke up with a start and looked at his watch.

"Sorry, did I do it again? Did I fall asleep on you? I am so sorry, I am just so shattered."

"That's OK; just stay awake for me on Saturday night!"

"I promise. Look, I'm really sorry I must go. We've got to move some stock and Gavin can't do it on his own. I said I'd meet him at the top field," he looked at his watch again, "round about now." He stood up to go. She walked with him to the door and waited whilst he put his heavy work boots back on. He gave her a quick kiss, and started to walk away. She stood and watched him. He turned and retraced his steps. He took her hands in his and looked her straight in the face.

"I do want you, you know. But I want it to be right. When we make love," he paused not quite sure how to go on. "When we make love for the first time I want it to be special for you." He squeezed her hands then turned away. Margot wanted to tell him that the time and place didn't matter to her. As long as it was with him she really did not care.

Margot would have to work all through the evening, but she didn't mind. Her visitors had taken a chunk out of her working day. She found it hard to concentrate and her mind wandered to what she would wear at the weekend.

CHAPTER 27

Danny didn't often use the village shop but he had run out of cigarettes. Jean walked out of the shop door and straight into him. They each realised who the other person was. The words of apology never came. Jean would have walked off but Danny made her stay.

"How are you, Jeanie?"

"Fine, Danny and you?"

"Me, I'm OK, couldn't be better," he paused. "Er how's your old man? I heard that he was rushed into hospital with a heart attack."

"No thanks to you," she flashed at him angrily. "You knew he could get into big trouble over that listed building business yet you still went ahead and pushed that woman into applying for planning permission. How could you? He's an old man. What has he ever done to you?"

"Where do I start?"

"Come on, Danny, that was a long long time ago. You and me, it was never going to work out."

"It might have done, but thanks to Godfrey we will never know." There was no mistaking the bitterness in Danny's voice. Twenty-odd years and he still held a grudge.

The shop door opened and they were obliged to move to one side to allow someone to pass. Jean lowered her voice.

"You didn't care enough to stay and fight for me. You ran away, like you always do."

She physically pushed him out of her way and hurried towards her car without a backward glance. She had to get back for Gavin and her father.

Gavin, like Giles, did not go straight home that evening. Instead he called in at The Quarry Man. He knew that Samantha Savage would be organising the pub for the evening. As a result of this she would be far too busy to keep an eye on what her daughter was up to. Gavin slipped in the back way and straight up to Suzie's room. She was sitting at the computer.

"She's falling in love with him."

"Who is falling in love with who?"

"With whom, Gavin, with whom not with who," she corrected him.

"OK, OK, but who are you talking about?"

"Your uncle and the writer woman."

"How can you tell? Does she say so?" He stood behind Suzie and looked at the screen. He saw that she had logged on to the Country Cousins website. He read the message that Margot had sent to Gus and wondered how Suzie had managed to come to her conclusion from the few words that Margot had written. Suzie tried to explain to him.

"It is not what she says, stupid. It is what she doesn't say and what she leaves out. You mark my words; the woman is head over heels in love with that big lug of an uncle of yours."

"Words, words, bloody words" he swung the typing chair around so that she was facing him. "I'm an action man myself and I have to say, I don't have much time." He grinned then pulled Suzie on to the bed.

Giles had arranged to collect Gavin from the pub. He waited in the car park and looked at his watch for the third time. The bloody boy was late. If he could have done the job by himself he would have. Giles only had to move the sheep a short distance from one field to another but it was definitely a two-man job. Exasperated he pressed the heel of his hand on the horn. Within seconds Gavin ran out of the back of the pub and across the car park towards him, tucking his shirt in as he did so. Gavin saw the look of thunder on Giles's face and mumbled an apology.

'He obviously didn't get lucky like I did,' was Gavin's first thought.

They drove on in silence. It was getting dark and they would have to hurry. They parked the Land Rover in the middle of the lane next to the field gate. Giles jumped out and opened the gate. He sent the dog into the field to round up the sheep. Gavin walked a short way up the lane, pulling on a fluorescent waistcoat as he did so. He opened a gate on the opposite side of the road and waited in the middle of the road for the sheep to be driven towards him. They had to be quick because as narrow as the lane was, it was frequently used as a cut through by the locals. Gavin heard the roar of a car and stood his ground in the middle of road. He held his arms out as a signal to wait. He could sense the impatience of the driver behind him. 'He'll just have to wait,' he thought. Gavin threw a quick glance over his shoulder, there were now two cars waiting. Gavin recognised the second car, it belonged to Danny Bragg. The sheep came towards him and he walked from side to side, arms outstretched preventing them from getting past. He noticed that Giles had now climbed back into the Land Rover and was slowly herding the sheep towards him. The dog was nipping at their heels and making sure that none of them turned back. Gavin ushered the last couple through then waved on the waiting cars. He climbed back into the Land Rover. Giles seemed marginally more relaxed now that the job was done.

Gavin apologised again. "Look I am sorry, Giles, I just wasn't paying attention to the time. It won't happen again. I er, I had other things on my mind."

"I bet you did. But spare me the details. Your mother was expecting us home for dinner a quarter of an hour ago. You had better come up with a good excuse as to why we're late, my lad, or we'll both be in trouble."

When they arrived back at Home Farm they were in luck, Jean was behind with her cooking. They even had time to go upstairs to wash and change before dinner was served. Godfrey wanted to know what they had been doing. He was still under doctor's orders for light duties only. Giles listed the day's jobs that they had accomplished. He gave the impression that they had taken longer than they had, hiding the hour or so that he and Gavin had stolen to go and visit their respective lady friends. Giles and Gavin had come to an unspoken agreement to keep Jean and Godfrey out of their private affairs.

"Er Jean, you and Gavin are going to be around on Saturday night aren't you?" Giles asked casually.

"Why?" they spoke in unison.

"I've been invited to a party in London and the invitation includes staying over."

"Oh," was all Jean could think of to say. She wanted to ask more but knew that it was none of her business what her brother did or where he went.

"Someone you met when you went on that Farmers' Union do, was it?" Godfrey had no qualms about asking questions.

"Yes, someone I met there. Now come on, Dad young Gavin and I promised to take you down to The Quarry Man if you feel up to it."

"That I do, son, I've been going mad sitting in this damn chair all day looking at these four walls with nobody to talk to."

"Well thank you!" Jean commented sarcastically. "Nice to know that I'm nobody."

The men helped clear up after the meal then the three of them climbed into the Land Rover to drive to the pub. It was busy and they only just managed to get a table in the corner. Suzie was run off her feet in the dining room and only managed a swift smile in their direction.

Although she had made a fuss Jean was pleased to see the back of the men. They were hard work, especially Godfrey. Sitting around doing nothing did not come easily to him and he had been demanding and difficult all day. When she was sure that they had all left she opened a bottle of wine and took two glasses down. The knock on the door came dead on nine; punctuality had always been one of his virtues. She opened the door.

"Hello, Danny. Come in."

Chapter 28

Margot pulled the coat closer around her as she waited for Giles's train to arrive. It should be on time. She had debated whether or not to organise a taxi for him, but there was something romantic about meeting someone off a train. Giles had telephoned her for the last three nights before she had gone to bed but he hadn't been able to find any spare time to come and see her. Being away for the weekend meant that certain jobs had to be done before he left. Added to this her publisher had asked if she could come up to town a day early. Margot didn't mind. Not seeing each other had added an air of anticipation.

She watched as the train pulled into the station. Quite a few people got off. She couldn't see him at first, then she did. His tall figure strode along the platform towards her, he had a suit carrier slung over his right shoulder and in his left hand he carried a small holdall. She stood there grinning; he looked up, saw her and returned her smile. They were within a few feet of each other when he placed his bags down on the platform and opened his arms. She covered the short distance and he swung her up and around laughing. He plonked her back down and gave her a big kiss.

"I needed that," he said.

Giles picked up his bags and followed Margot. He turned to go down into the underground.

"No, that'll take ages, we will get a taxi."

They walked outside, there were a few people waiting. "Follow me," Margot instructed. They walked a little way along the road and then turned into another road which they crossed over. Within a couple of minutes a taxi came past. Margot had hailed it and they were in the back and away before Giles had time to catch his breath. Margot was obviously used to doing this type of thing. It only took about ten minutes to get to the hotel and whilst Giles was sorting out his bags Margot quickly paid off the driver. Giles looked up; she sensed that he was impressed with the hotel. Perhaps he had been expecting something smaller.

"I know, a bit grand isn't it? Of course I wouldn't normally stay here but they're having the awards ceremony in the banqueting hall and they've put all the nominees up in rooms here." Margot apologised. Giles, she noticed, had become very quiet.

They travelled up in the lift in silence. He followed her along the carpeted corridor. She stopped at room101 and opened the door.

"Would you like some tea? There's no proper milk, only the UHT rubbish."

"Yes, please, I don't care, as long as it is wet and warm."

Giles dumped his bag on the bottom of the enormous double bed that dominated the room. He turned to look around and saw the dinner suit hanging outside the wardrobe.

Margot had her back to Giles and held her breath as she heard him lift the suit down. She tried to keep her voice light.

"Oh I wasn't sure if you had a dinner suit, only it's a black tie do." She turned to face him. "I hope you don't mind." She held her breath.

Giles walked over to his suit carrier and opened it up to reveal an ancient, but perfectly good dinner suit with a white dress shirt and a bow tie. "You should have said, I could have told you that I already have one."

Margot tried to hide her embarrassment. "Oh well it doesn't matter." This was not going as well as she had hoped, yet again she had put her foot in it.

Giles took the jacket off the hangar and tried it on. It fitted well, she was obviously a good judge with regard to size; he doubted that he would have guessed her statistics as well.

"I'll wear this one as you've gone to all the bother to hire it. How much do I owe you?"

"Nothing, it's my treat." As soon as the words were out of her mouth she realised that she had said the wrong thing. She watched Giles as he looked around, she suspected that he was trying to work out how much all of this was costing.

"I may be a poor farmer but I can pay my own way."

Margot noted the edge to his voice. She finished making his tea and passed it to him.

"Sorry, I just wanted er I thought," she took a deep breath. "I just wanted everything to be right," her voice wavered.

Giles put his cup down and pulled her towards him. He held her close and very tightly in a hug. With her face pressed against his chest Margot screwed her eyes up in an effort not to cry. He kissed the top of her head.

"What time is kick-off?"

Margot looked at her watch. "We've got about an hour before we have to go downstairs and find our table"

"Great, just enough time to have a long soaking bath, get the smell of the farm and that train journey out of me."

Margot hesitated. "Er, I got us a bottle of champagne; I thought we could open it before we went." What had seemed like a good idea at the time now looked flash, as if she was flaunting her money.

"Champagne, what a treat. I'll just go and run the bath."

Giles went into the bathroom and Margot could hear the sound of running water. Whilst Giles was soaking Margot continued to get ready. She had already had her bath. All she needed to do was put on her makeup and put her clothes on. She sat at the dressing table and carefully applied her makeup and brushed her hair through. She had had it highlighted earlier in the day and was disappointed that Giles hadn't noticed. It was too early to put on her long black dress so she threw on her silk Chinese dressing gown and tied it tightly around her waist.

Margot took the bottle of champagne out of the cooler and carried it to the bathroom, two champagne flutes in her other hand. She knocked gently on the door.

"It's not locked."

She walked in. "Can you open this?"

He was half lying in the bath and he sat up and took the bottle from her. Quickly and expertly he popped the cork. Margot poured the champagne into the glasses and passed one to him. She turned as if to leave.

"No, stay and talk to me."

Margot perched on the edge of the bath facing him. She studied his upper body thinking how she would best describe it if he were a character in one of her novels. She sipped the champagne.

"How's your father?"

"Oh he's OK, driving us all mad. I tried to do as much as I could before I left but there are a couple of jobs that Gavin will have to do. What doesn't get done will still be there waiting for me on Monday. Now, tell me what's the format for tonight?"

Margot explained that the dinner would start at seven although they would be expected to be there a little earlier. She said that there were a couple of people she needed to speak to. These events were all about networking and keeping one's name firmly in the publishers' minds.

"At the moment I'm one of their top earners but believe me there are plenty of others coming up behind me ready to take my place." Margot leaned forward to top up his glass. As she did so Giles ran a wet finger from her throat and down into her cleavage. She shivered but leaned back. They really didn't have time. She smiled at him and swatted his hand away. "My friend Abi, do you remember her? She should be here tonight and I also need to speak to the commissioning editor, to remind her that I might now be living out in the sticks but I am still around." Reluctantly Margot stood up and picked up the now empty champagne bottle. "You've got precisely ten minutes to get out and dressed young man."

Margot returned to the bedroom, removed her bathrobe and put on her dress. It was a simple black silk sheath with a cowl neckline. The dress went in at her slim waist and skimmed her less slim hips. She loved this dress. She had bought it several months ago but until now had not had an opportunity to wear it. Quickly before Giles emerged from the bathroom she removed the hired suit hanging on the front of the wardrobe and put it in the back of the cupboard. She laid Giles's dinner suit out on the bed. She looked at it critically. It was obviously an old one but it had a classic style; he wouldn't look out of place.

Giles came out of the bathroom, naked except for a small towel tied around his waist. She stared at his long muscular legs and quickly looked away, such a shame they were up against a time deadline. She left Giles to get into his evening wear and went into the bathroom to put the final touches to her makeup.

In the lift going down to the banquet hall, Giles leaned down and whispered, "You look absolutely gorgeous."

She looked up at him and smiled. "You don't look so bad yourself."

The door opened and a woman of about sixty got in; her face lit up when she saw Margot.

"Mo dear, how lovely to see you!" the woman put her hands on Margot's shoulders and kissed her on both cheeks. The woman looked up and noticed Giles standing behind Margot. "And who pray is this gorgeous young man?"

Margot laughed. "Veronica this is my er this is..." what was he? How should she describe him?

Giles jumped in, "Hello, I'm Giles Farmer and I am Margot's date for the evening."

Margot was grateful for the interruption but was disappointed that he had only described himself as this evening's date. She wasn't sure what she had been hoping for, perhaps a bit more.

They reached the ground floor and the door opened into a small concourse area. There were lots of people milling around and greeting each other like old friends. Before she could prevent it Margot found herself swept up in a group of people leaving Giles standing in a corner. She looked over at him. He just smiled and waved her on.

"Hello again."

Giles turned, it was Margot's friend Abi.

"Hello, it's – er – Abi, isn't it?"

"Yes, we met very briefly at that Farmers' Union do a couple of months back."

"How come you were involved in that and now you are involved in this publishing junket? The two don't exactly go together."

Abi laughed. "I work in public relations and communications. The farming union employed us to organise their evening and we are doing a very similar thing here for the publishing house."

"Oh, I see," but he clearly didn't. They both looked across to where Margot stood chatting animatedly surrounded by several people.

"She's a very popular and successful author you know. She's already made several thousand pounds for the company, for the first half of this year."

Giles choked on his drink and spat some out. "What?"

"Oh yes, she's worth a very very tidy sum is our Margot. That was how she could afford to move out to the country and buy something right out. Of course, she has the rent coming in for her London pad. It all helps."

This was news to Giles who had assumed that it was the sale of Margot's flat that had financed the purchase of Saddleback Cottage.

"Hi, I'm sorry. Are you OK? I see that Abi is looking after you." Margot had managed to escape from the group and had come to retrieve Giles.

"Yes, Abi has just been telling me all about how successful you are. I had no idea."

Giles saw the glance that the two women exchanged and had the distinct feeling that Abi had overstepped the mark by telling him more than she should have done.

Margot smiled and took Giles's hand. "Come on, I'm afraid we have to have our photograph taken. It is for the company magazine. But don't worry I expect that they will use the photos of the glamorous young ones, they usually do."

They were made to pause in the entrance of the banquet hall for the photographer before making their way to the table. Margot had checked earlier where they were sitting and who they were sitting with. She had been pleased to note that Abi had been placed on the other side of Giles. She knew that she could rely on her friend to look after him if she was distracted elsewhere. Because of all the things going on around her Margot knew she would not be able to give Giles the attention that she felt she ought to. Perhaps it hadn't been such a good idea to invite him.

Although she hid it well, Margot was extremely nervous about this evening. Her books were not as popular as they had been say five years ago, despite her changing her style and content to keep up with the trends. When the publishers had contacted her to say she had been short-listed for an award she was thrilled to bits. She knew that professionally an award could raise her profile and have an impact on her sales. The food served was standard fare. Margot was too nervous to eat properly and just picked at the bits on her plate. She noticed with a smile that Giles ate everything put in front of him. Abi seemed a bit on edge but this event was a big deal for her too. These occasions were meticulously planned and Margot knew that the responsibility for this evening was very much on Abi's shoulders.

The dinner was over within a couple of hours then the main proceedings started. The chairman stood up and gave a speech about the Company's performance over the previous year. He highlighted some of the books that had been particularly successful. They then got on to the awards. Margot glanced across at Giles, he was struggling to stay awake, he'd been up since five this morning. She covered his hand with hers and squeezed it.

Various awards were given out, the best newcomer, best foreign rights, best historical novel, best romantic teenage fiction. The list just seemed to go on and on. The chairman began winding up. Margot was puzzled; they had definitely said that she would be getting an award.

"Finally, with the changing face of romantic fiction and with the content of such books becoming more explicit, we have decided to inaugurate a new award. This award is for the raunchiest, but none the less well written, sex scenes. The sort of writing that er gets people hot under the collar," he looked pointedly at his watch. "Yes, it is after the watershed." A few people tittered politely and he continued. "And we are all consenting adults. Well even I blush to read some of this X-rated prose." There were catcalls and whistles from some drunks across the room. The chairman waited for all of this to die down. "And the award for providing our readers with the best sex, well in print that is," he paused waiting for the laughter to die down, "the award for giving us the best sex without even taking our clothes off goes to our very own Margot Denning." There was a cheer and a round of applause and Margot found herself literally under the spotlight.

Margot was a rabbit caught in the headlights, not knowing which way to run. Everyone turned to look at her, some were smiling, some leering. She looked across at Abi who was picking an imaginary bit of fluff from the front of her dress, totally engrossed. "She knew," thought Margot, "she bloody well knew and didn't warn me." To calls of encouragement from the top table Margot found herself propelled towards the chairman to receive the award. It was a small bronze sculpture in the shape of a phallus wearing a condom. Mindful of its safe sex message the publishing company were careful to remain politically correct. She stood holding the award and the chairman's handshake for several minutes whilst photographs were taken. Unlike the other awards this one seemed to attract more than its fair share of photographers. She looked across the room. There seemed to be several extra people to their table. Giles appeared to be chatting to a couple of them. A least she didn't have to worry about him, she thought.

CHAPTER 29

As the conversation at the table became louder and livelier Giles found himself withdrawing and getting quieter and quieter. This was not his sort of a place and he damn well knew for sure that these were not his sort of people. One thing he did know for certain, the Margot he knew was not the same person as the glamorous successful businesswoman he was partnering for the evening. It started in the lift coming down when that awful woman had greeted Margot like some long lost friend. The false bonhomie sickened him. He was also uncomfortable about how much money Margot seemed to be flashing around. Giles hadn't got much of an idea about how much a dress suit cost to hire but knew that it probably didn't come cheap. Whilst he was waiting for Margot he had idly flicked through the hotel book left on the desk. It had fallen open on the room service page. He had been shocked to see the cost of the champagne that they had just drunk – it went into three figures. Margot was obviously very well thought of within the publishing fraternity and he was only just beginning to realise just how successful she was.

Margot tried to introduce Giles to lots of people but once they found that he was nothing to do with their world they lost interest in him. Giles found himself drinking rather more than he would normally. Matters didn't improve once they had sat at the table for the meal. Margot's friend Abi was assiduous in making sure that Giles's glass remained topped up.

Margot was trying to keep calm but even Giles could sense that she was excited and on edge. As the various awards were announced they joined in the enthusiastic applause as the recipients walked to the top table to collect their trophies. At last the chairman announced that he was about to present the final award of the evening. It had to be Margot's. Giles sat up in order to pay proper attention; he knew that in his befuddled state he would have to concentrate. He didn't know how Margot was feeling but he was damn certain that he was nervous.

Giles listened with total and utter amazement. To say he was shocked was an understatement. Margot who had admitted to him that she was a virgin. Margot who had flinched when he touched her. That very same Margot was now being celebrated for her erotic writing. He had thought that he knew her but he clearly didn't. People came up to him to offer their congratulations on Margot's success. Giles put his hand in his pocket and felt for the key fob. He had to get away. As he got up to leave he was approached by a man in a lounge suit.

"Hi, can I introduce myself, I'm Doug Jones and you are Miss Denning's?" he paused waiting for a reply. "You are Miss Denning's er partner yes?" He held out his hand and Giles automatically returned the handshake.

"Farmer, Giles Farmer. I'm a er close friend of Margot's, yes."

The man indicated the vacant chair next to where Giles had been sitting. "May I?" he had to shout because the noise level was quite high. They could barely hear each other speak.

Giles nodded and they both sat down. He noticed that Abi had disappeared.

"So, Miss Denning and you er you and Miss Denning, how long have you been together, as it were?" Doug Jones put his hand inside his jacket and withdrew a small flask; he unscrewed the top and poured some clear liquid into Giles's wine glass.

"Get that down you, make you feel better."

Giles took a sip from his drink.

"Wow, what on earth was that?"

"Oh just a little something to liven things up, don't worry it is legit. I drink it myself all the time see?" Doug Jones swigged from the flask himself before putting it back in his jacket pocket.

Giles looked around him; everyone seemed to be engrossed in what they were doing. No one but this Doug Jones was interested in him. He might as well have someone to talk to. He sipped his drink again. It definitely tasted better – smoother somehow.

"We were talking about Miss Denning – the romantic novelist – your friend." He spoke slowly like one would speak to a child or a rather slow adult.

Giles struggled to remember what Doug Jones's original question had been. He hadn't a clue as to why this man was bothering to talk to him; he knew nothing about romantic fiction. Giles looked across to the top table. Margot was sitting down surrounded by a phalanx of photographers and reporters. She was being interviewed; "No help from that quarter," he thought.

"You were telling me about you and Miss Denning."

"I was?"

"Yes you were saying how long you have been together."

"Margot and I have known each other for about four months."

"Four months, really is that all? Ah, whirlwind romance was it?"

"What?" a gale of laughter had drowned out the question.

"You and Miss Denning?"

"What?" Giles still hadn't heard him.

"Was it a whirlwind romance? Did you sweep her off her feet?"

Giles heard the last bit. "No she hit on me. Came straight over to my table; I'd never met her before in my life."

"But I bet you knew a lot more about her before the evening was out eh?"

"Oh yes, I certainly did." Giles was feeling very drunk.

"Would it be correct to say that you knew her intimately by the end of your first meeting?"

Giles thought about that first meeting at The Quarry Man when Margot had given him her life story. Yes by the end of that evening he knew pretty much all about her. What was the word the man had used? Intimately, well that was a joke. Giles noticed that this Doug Jones had a little notebook on the table and he appeared to be doodling on it.

"Yeah, I suppose I did. She pretty much laid herself bare." Giles liked the phrase 'laid herself bare' but wasn't quite sure where it had come from.

"And would you say you and she are close. I mean do you help her with her writing, research, that sort of thing?"

Margot's current novel involved a farmer who was one of her minor characters. She had asked Giles about a few technical points to see if what she had written was accurate.

Giles thought carefully before replying. "Oh yes, she tries a lot of it out on me first." He remembered Margot reading out bits of the novel to him.

"What do you think of Miss Denning's award?"

"What?" it was getting very noisy again.

"What's your take on getting an award for giving great sex?" Just as Doug Jones was finishing his sentence the noise level dropped and several heads turned in their direction.

"Oh it's well deserved." Giles was really tired now and feeling sick. All he wanted to do was get back to his room. He tried to stand up, swayed a bit then fell back down into his seat.

"Look, old man, you look like you could do with a coffee. How about I take you up to your room eh?"

Giles nodded gratefully and allowed himself to be taken out of the banquet hall. In the lift he half leaned, half slumped against the back wall. They reached his floor.

"What room number is it?"

Giles pulled out his key and passed it across to the other man. The two of them swayed along the corridor until they reached room 101. Doug Jones unlocked the door and walked in. The first thing he saw was the upturned bottle of champagne and two dirty glasses, one on its side. He quickly assessed the rest of the room. The bathroom door was open, towels were strewn on the floor and along the edge of the bath. Margot's dressing gown was thrown over a chair. Giles and Margot had been pushed for time earlier and had agreed to tidy up when they returned from the dinner. To all intents and purposes it looked as if there had been a party in the room. Doug Jones helped Giles over to the bed, where he fell face down. Checking that Giles was out cold Doug Jones walked over to the wardrobe, opened it and looked inside, nothing of note there. He opened a drawer now that was more interesting. The black basque was lying on top of some wispy pieces of lacy underwear; he gently moved things around and came across a suspender belt and black stockings. "What a bloody cliché," he thought. Jones had read some of the more saucy paragraphs which had resulted in tonight's award and felt a stab of envy. If Margot Denning did practise what she preached, or rather what she wrote, this country farmer was in for a really good night. Jones glanced across to the bed, judging by the state Giles Farmer was in he probably wouldn't be up to it.

Jones heard a key in the lock and slammed the drawer quickly, the door opened and Abi walked in.

"Who are you and what are you doing in this room?"

"Er, I'm a friend of Giles's here. I'm afraid he had a bit too much of the old red stuff downstairs; he needed to sleep it off so I helped him get back to his room."

Abi stared at the man. "Don't I know you?"

"I don't think so, my love," he smiled at Abi. "I'm sure that if we had met I would have remembered."

"Yes I do, you're that Douglas Jones from that downmarket rag the Gazette!"

"Was from the Gazette. I left them a few months back now. Slight disagreement about editorial direction, so we parted company. I'm freelance now. I specialise in what you would call 'human interest' stories."

"Sleaze you mean!" there was no mistaking the disgust in Abi's voice. "Anyway, what do you want with Giles Farmer? He's just a friend of Miss Denning's and a platonic one at that."

"Oh really?" Doug Jones looked around at the discarded bathrobe and the empty champagne bottles. He opened the drawer and pulled out the basque.

Hearing a groan they both turned towards the bed.

"'Scuse me, I don't feel too good."

He propelled himself off the bed and straight into the bathroom. They heard him being violently sick. Abi held the bedroom door wide open.

"I think that is probably time that you left, Mr Jones."

"OK, OK. God is that all the thanks I get for rescuing Margot Denning's lover on the night she gets the best sex award?"

"He is not Miss Denning's lover, Miss Denning does not have a lover." Abi raised her voice to reach Doug Jones as he walked away along the corridor. She returned to the suite and opened the bathroom door. Giles was sitting on the floor hugging the toilet bowl.

"Giles, did you say anything to that vile man about Margot?"

"No," he wavered, "no, I don't think so, I can't remember, I–" he threw up again, "I'm not feeling too good," echoed from the deep recess of the toilet bowl.

Disgusted, Abi closed the bathroom door on him. This was terrible. Margot had been worried stiff when she saw that Giles had disappeared. Abi was not only Margot's friend but she was also the PR person for the publishers. It was her job to keep the writers happy, especially the award winners. It was Margot who had given Abi the key to her suite and asked her to go and check on Giles. Although Abi worked in public relations she did not subscribe to the view that all publicity was good publicity. She felt guilty for not warning Margot about the nature of the award she was to receive, particularly as she knew what a private person she really was. Erotic writing, like the rest of Margot's novels, was pure fiction. Having read most of Margot's books all Abi could think was what a brilliant imagination she must have!

Abi heard the tap running in the bathroom. She knocked on the door.

"Giles, I'm going back to the hall to let Margot know that you are OK. If I were you I would just get yourself into bed. I'm sure you'll feel so much better in the morning."

All the way down in the lift Abi debated whether or not to tell Margot about the tabloid journalist. It could have been purely innocent. Giles had certainly needed help to get back to his room. He had been drinking during the meal but Abi felt sure that he wasn't that bad when she left him at the table. She would have stayed with him but she had been away from the hall too long already. "God, what a mess," she thought.

Abi returned to the hall. The crowd was beginning to disperse and she was able to have a quiet word with Margot.

"Here's your key, he is OK. I think. He has had too much to drink. He's sleeping it off." Margot made no reply so she continued, "Look I'm sorry I didn't warn you about the award, it was the chairman's idea. He wanted to keep it secret from you, said he'd get a more spontaneous reaction. It would look better and get the company maximum publicity."

"But you know that I'm not that sort of a person, the sort of person he said I was."

"Look, Margot, nobody is saying you are anything."

"Really? I've already been propositioned twice since the bloody man handed me the award. Good God, if it wasn't for their change of style in the first place I wouldn't have needed to spice up my books, but no, they have to pander to the masses. I had a perfectly good following for my books as they were."

"Had, Margot, you had a perfectly good following but things move on. These days relationships become more intimate quicker than they used to and the publishing house has to reflect this." Abi felt herself on firmer ground now. She wrote the publicity handouts and could quote facts and figures with confidence.

Margot lowered her voice, "Well I don't want the bloody award."

Abi could feel herself losing her temper. "Margot, just take it. Judging by the man upstairs in your room you have more things to worry about than a stupid piece of bronze – put it in your outside lavatory. I'm sure you have one in that cottage of yours!"

Two people walked past and stopped to congratulate Margot on her award, she nodded her thanks. Abi took the opportunity to slip away and join another group at the top end of the room. On balance Abi was glad that she hadn't mentioned the tabloid journalist, particularly with Margot in the mood she was in.

Margot made her way back to room 101. The first thing she saw was Giles stretched out on the bed. He had made a half-hearted attempt to get undressed but had given up. He was still wearing his dress shirt, which hung over his boxer shorts. Giles was trouserless, but for some bizarre reason was still wearing his shoes and socks. If she hadn't been so angry she would have laughed. She walked over to him and undid his laces and took off his shoes, she then folded the clothes he had discarded on the floor and placed them on the chair on his side of the bed. Margot wrapped the quilt around him. She pulled out her suitcase and started to pack; she pulled open her drawer with all her beautiful underwear and the silk nightdress she had planned to wear.

The tears ran down her cheeks. Tonight was going to be the night, the night when she would finally give herself to the man she had fallen in love with. The evening had started off so well, then there was that bloody stupid award and then Giles disappeared and here he was comatose in bed. What a bloody shambles. She just wanted to get away from here as fast as she could. Margot kicked the obscene bronze phallus across the room. How embarrassing the whole bloody evening had been.

She couldn't stay here tonight. Everything had been spoiled for her. She telephoned Abi, who joined her within ten minutes of the call. Margot had used the ten minutes to wash away the traces of her tears. Abi would notice but she was beyond caring about anything tonight. She waited outside the room; she didn't want Abi to see Giles in the state he was in.

"Abi, I can't stay here tonight, I…" she didn't get a chance to finish.

"You don't have to say anything, my spare room is made up and ready. Come on, it's been a very emotional night for all of us."

CHAPTER 30

Giles wanted to sleep. He wanted to sleep and never wake up, well not until the pain had gone. He opened his eyes then thought better of it. Movement seemed to make the pain worse and what the hell was that banging noise? He opened his eyes again; someone was knocking on his door. Gingerly he swung his legs off the bed and sat up – whoa, not a clever move.

"Who is it?" he yelled then winced as his voice reverberated back through his skull.

"Housekeeping, sir, I need to get in and clean your room."

Giles looked around him, of course, the hotel, Margot, last night. Oh God, he needed time to think. Risking further pain he yelled out.

"Can you come back later, please?"

"OK, half an hour, I'll come back in half an hour."

'Half an hour, not long,' he thought. Every part of his aching body told him to lie back down and to go back to sleep but his brain was slowly beginning to get into gear. His memory of last night was returning. Giles dragged himself into the bathroom and took a quick shower. He dressed in the clothes he had travelled up in. Where the hell was Margot? Why wasn't she here with him? He tried ringing her mobile but it went straight to voicemail.

"Hi Margot, it's me er Giles, it's about last night. Look, I'm really sorry. I er, we need to talk. Call me; let me know if you're OK, OK?"

It was Sunday so the publishers would be closed and he didn't have the telephone number of her friend Abi, hell, he didn't even know Abi's surname so there was no way he would be able to get hold of her. He swiftly, or as swiftly as the pain in his head would allow, packed his bag. He had two minutes to spare and met the cleaning lady as he walked along the corridor.

Giles went to the front desk and waited whilst the receptionist dealt with a couple of tourists. He looked across the foyer and saw the board announcing the publishing awards ceremony and bits of the previous evening came back to him. He remembered Margot getting an award and he had a vague recollection about talking about her to someone but beyond that there was nothing. He handed his key to the receptionist; she smiled and tapped something into the computer.

"Thank you, Mr Denning, nothing to pay, Mrs Denning paid for everything when she checked out."

He had neither the energy nor the coherence to explain that he was not Mr Denning but he did desperately want to know what had happened to Margot.

"Can I ask when my er when Mrs Denning booked out, please?"

The girl checked the screen again. "Certainly, sir, it looks as if she booked out very late last night. I can find out the exact time if you would like."

"No, no thank you, that won't be necessary."

"Can I call you a taxi sir?"

"No, I'll walk or catch the tube; the fresh air will do me good."

Giles walked out into the bright cold sunshine and instantly wished he was wearing sunglasses. The glare was not helping his headache. After two painkillers and a pint and a half of water to counteract his dehydration the headache was only just beginning to recede. His main concern was Margot, God what a mess he had made of everything. He had totally blown it. He only hoped that she would forgive him. She had gone to so much trouble, the champagne, the hotel suite, the sexy underwear he'd glimpsed in the drawer. What an idiot he had been. Giles tried her number again several times but each time it went straight on to voicemail. He left a second message for her.

"Hi Margot, it's me again. Look I just want to say how sorry I am that I messed up last night, phone me, please, I need to know that you are OK."

Giles fell asleep on the train journey and awoke with a crick in his neck. He had already sent a text message to Gavin asking him to pick him up from the station. Gavin was waiting, the engine still running. He had only just arrived.

"Hi Giles, did you have…" he looked across at his uncle. "Are you OK? You look like shit."

"Thank you, Gavin, and I can tell you I feel like it!"

"Good night was it?"

"Don't know, I can't remember!"

"And how was it with the lovely lady writer?"

"What is this? Twenty bloody questions? Just drive and get me home, I need a cup of tea and something to eat, I'm starving. Now would it be too much to ask for a nice quiet ride home please?"

Gavin opened his mouth to say something but then thought better of it. Back at Home Farm Giles went straight up to his room to unpack and phone Margot again, no luck. She was deliberately ignoring him. He had missed Sunday lunch and made himself a bacon sandwich. It was just what he needed. He hadn't eaten for nearly twenty hours, no wonder he couldn't think straight or function properly.

During supper later that evening Giles was quizzed about his night in London. He told them that Margot had received an award, although he didn't tell them what it was for. He said that Margot had booked him into a room in the hotel but that she had stayed with a friend. Giles intercepted a glance between Gavin and Jean. Let them think what they wanted, he was not about to elaborate.

Gavin delayed going down to The Quarry Man until after supper. Sunday evenings were not normally busy at the pub and he knew that Samantha expected Suzie to help out with the cleaning and restocking for the following week. He slipped in the back way; Suzie had left the door unlocked. He called out to her as he went up the stairs. She was sitting at the computer when he walked into her room.

"Suzie, you'll never guess what?"

"That your Uncle Giles really blew it last night in London?"

"Yes, but how did you know?"

"She's sent us, or rather Gus, a long email. God, did he make a fool of himself, poor woman."

"Why, what did he do?"

"Nothing, absolutely bloody nothing. Apart, that is, from getting blind drunk, passing out and ruining all her plans for the evening!"

"No! He didn't!" Gavin was beginning to see Giles in a new light.

"If you don't believe me read it yourself."

Suzie, or rather Gus, had sent Margot an email, early on Saturday morning, wishing her good luck. Margot's reply, which she had sent on Sunday afternoon, explained a lot; not so much by what it said but rather by its tone. The weekend had not been the success she had hoped. Reading it through Gavin began to understand why his uncle was in such a foul mood. Margot said that she had received an award but that it was an unimportant one and unfortunately her plans for a romantic evening had gone completely out of the window when her date got blind drunk and passed out. She said that she had been so upset that she had left and gone to stay with a friend. Margot concluded that all in all the whole weekend had proved to be a complete disaster from start to finish.

Gavin couldn't really believe it; he knew that Giles liked to have a glass or two but he had never seen him so drunk that he passed out.

"But why is she telling us all this?"

"She's not telling us you dummy. She is telling her online friend Gus, who she thinks is some anonymous man on the Internet."

Gavin still looked puzzled.

"Look, Gavin, it is like this. Sometimes you just want to talk to someone about your problems but you don't just want to talk to anyone. You want to talk to someone you can trust, someone who will listen and who won't judge you. And most importantly of all, someone who doesn't know you from Adam!"

"Well what about her mates? Surely she has a friend she could talk to?"

"Obviously not, or else she wouldn't be wasting time talking to Gus. Poor woman, I feel really sorry for her."

"I don't expect that Giles is feeling too great either." Gavin felt that he had to show some sort of male solidarity. He had never understood all this touchy feely woman's stuff and doubted he ever would. "Let's just hope that they can sort it out because I can't put up working with Giles in the mood that he is in. Should we reply, do you think?"

Suzie nodded and began typing. Gus cautioned Margot against jumping to conclusions and asked if her date was normally a heavy drinker. If he wasn't, Suzie, in the guise of Gus, asked whether there might have been a reason for him behaving as he did. The message ended by urging Margot to give Giles a second chance. When she had finished typing she called Gavin over to read what she had put.

"Is this blokey enough?"

Gavin read what she had put. "It makes Gus sound a bit girlie. Here let me," and he made a few minor adjustments. Margot had to believe that Gus was a real man or else she may not take the advice they gave. They sent the message. Gavin swung around and grabbed Suzie around the waist.

"Right, that's enough of my uncle's romance, now what about ours?" His head was level with her breasts and he pushed his face into them, she wasn't wearing a bra. He slipped his hands down and under her shirt lifting it up to reveal her bare breasts. Slowly he licked his way around each nipple until she could bear it no longer; she grabbed his hair and pulled him off. She bent down to his upturned face and stuck her tongue deep into his mouth. As one they stood then fell on to the bed. Samantha Savage was busy downstairs; they had all the time in the world.

Unlike Gavin and Suzie, time was the one thing that Giles was fast running out of. A weekend away in London had left quite a few jobs outstanding but at least he had finally made contact with Margot. She had sent him a text very late on Sunday evening to say she would be travelling back to Saddleback Cottage mid morning on the Monday. She had made no reference to Saturday night, nor had she suggested that they meet up, but at least they were communicating. It wasn't quite what Giles wanted, but in the circumstances it was all he was likely to get. He would get some flowers in the morning and leave them on her doorstep – a peace offering for when she returned.

Giles's final thought, as he fell into bed exhausted on Sunday night, was that he would see Margot tomorrow. Perhaps he could then explain properly what had happened, if he could remember. Bits were coming back to him, especially the man who kept asking all the questions, but he was damned if he could remember what they were or what he had said in reply.

CHAPTER 31

Margot sat on the train, emotionally spent and exhausted. Abi's spare bed had not been as comfortable as promised. Breakfast was a little awkward. Margot really hadn't properly forgiven her friend for not warning her about the award. She had tried to leave the bronze behind but Abi had insisted in packing it in the bottom of Margot's suitcase. In the end Margot had been too tired to argue. To say that Giles's behaviour had disappointed her would be a gross understatement. All the preparation she had undertaken, booking the suite, the champagne, her new underwear, and all for what? For nothing, that's what for, bloody nothing. Margot had asked Abi if Giles has said anything when she went up to check on him. Abi was adamant that nothing had been said but her vagueness about the whole matter rang alarm bells. Margot felt that she hadn't quite got to the bottom of it yet, but she would.

She had telephoned ahead from the train and Leaker was waiting for her in his taxi. He walked towards her to help with her suitcase.

"Nice weekend, Miss Denning?"

"Eventful!"

"So I hear."

Margot looked at the back of Leaker's head, what on earth did he mean? What had he heard? Before she could ask him he spoke again.

"Hear say you won an award."

"Yes, yes I did, but how did you know?"

"Newspaper."

"Newspaper?"

"Yup, it's in the newspaper."

They drove through the village. As they drew level with the village shop Margot asked Leaker to stop. She pushed open the door and walked in. Emma looked up from behind the counter, she was reading a newspaper, the smile died on her face when she realised that it was Margot.

"Miss Denning. What can I do for you?" there was no mistaking the frostiness in her tone.

"Er, a newspaper, I would like to buy a newspaper."

"I see. And which newspaper would you like?"

"I'm not sure really," she hesitated.

"I mean, do you want the one where you are on the front page? Or would you like the one where they put you on page three or even the one that has given you the centre page spread? Take your pick. I have them all." There was disdain in the older woman's voice. Margot was getting more and more confused by the second. She walked to the back of the shop where the newspapers were normally stacked on a long shelf. There appeared to have been a run on them today. Then she saw the headline – 'Local writer's nights of passion'. She picked up a different newspaper, it wasn't a lot better 'My sex homework', 'oh my God,' she thought, 'Could it get any worse?' She sensed Emma's scrutiny so she grabbed a selection of newspapers.

"I'll take these for now." She pulled out a five pound note. "Don't worry about the change," she turned to go but Emma called her back.

"You might as well take this one with you, I've read it."

Margot snatched the newspaper from the outstretched hand and climbed back into the taxi.

"Where to?"

"Home, of course."

"You sure?"

"Yes why?"

"Just asking."

They continued along the main road, then as they turned into Blossom Lane Margot could see why Leaker had asked. There were several cars parked along the lane and men with cameras lounging against them, reporters and photographers. Margot could feel the panic rising within her. She desperately needed quiet and privacy. Saddleback Cottage was unlikely to provide either. More than anything else she needed to read these damn newspapers.

"Straight on, Leaker, drive straight on," she shouted.

204

The taxi drew the attention of the reporters. As they drove past cameras flashed. Margot had slid down in the seat hoping that she hadn't been photographed. They drove swiftly past Home Farm and back on to the main road. Leaker checked that they weren't being followed. He appeared to be enjoying the drama of the situation. Margot made up her mind and gave Leaker some new directions. If he was surprised by the address he didn't show it, well not too much.

She paid off the taxi and walked into Danny Bragg's office. He looked up somehow unsurprised to see her. She noticed that he was reading one of the tabloid newspapers.

"Miss Denning. What a pleasant surprise. I've just been reading about your er triumph over the weekend." He smiled. "And what brings you to my neck of the woods?"

"Mr Bragg, Danny, I need somewhere to stay until," she waved her hands across the newspaper on his desk, "until all of this ridiculousness dies down. I can't go back to my cottage because it's got loads of reporters and photographers hanging around outside. I need somewhere er discreet."

Danny nodded, put his hand in his pocket and withdrew a door key which he swung tantalisingly in front of her. She stretched out her hand to take it but he withdrew it at the last moment.

"I seem to remember asking you a favour a few weeks back now, about whether or not you would give me first refusal on Saddleback Cottage."

She could see where this was going. She knew she had no choice.

"I wondered if you had a chance to come to a decision yet."

Margot took a deep breath; she needed this man's help. "Not quite, but having weighed up the options it is looking very favourable in your direction at the moment."

"Pity," he made as if to put the key back in his pocket.

"OK, you can have first refusal. Now just give me the damn key."

"With pleasure," he handed it over. "Now can I give you a ride, unless of course you would like me to phone Leaker to come and pick you up?"

"No, thank you, a lift will be nice," she paused, "thank you."

Danny Bragg drove Margot to his house, it was now mid afternoon and there were very few people about. He carried Margot's case through the front door.

"You can have the guest room at the back; it's got an en suite. My room is at the front. Now, if you excuse me I've got some business to catch up on." He turned to go.

"Danny?"

"Yes?"

"Nothing, just thank you. I'll only be here a couple of days, I couldn't stay at the cottage and there was no one else I could turn to." Her voice started to wobble which embarrassed them both.

"My pleasure," he smiled and left. "Help yourself to anything you need in the kitchen," he called as he walked out of the front door.

Tea, that's what she needed, a cup of tea and time to sit down and read the newspapers. She made the tea and settled herself at the kitchen table. She spread the newspapers out in front of her one by one and read them. With each successive article her horror grew. She didn't even bother to read the free newspaper that Emma had hurled at her as she left. A couple of the reporters had managed to get hold of the publicity shot that appeared on the back of her books. Although it had been taken about five years ago it was still very recognisable as her.

A reporter had described the publishing event, focussing on the tension and excitement as the awards were announced. Margot had been there yet barely recognised the description. The reporter had exclusively 'interviewed' Margot Denning's live-in toy boy lover who had refused to give his name, hiding behind the alias of Farmer Giles.

"That was no alias. That was his bloody name, you idiot," she said out aloud to the empty kitchen.

The reporter had made Giles sound like a young stud, instead of a farmer on the downhill run to middle age. The intimation was that he was much younger than her. 'Bloody cheek,' she thought. The lighting had been bad but not that bad surely. Giles would be flattered when he read that. What on earth was he thinking about, talking to a tabloid newspaper reporter? Come to that, what was Abi doing, her so-called best friend and public relations adviser, doing whilst all this was going on? Abi was supposed to be looking after Giles for God's sake. Part of her wanted to laugh it was so farcical, but a bigger part made her want to weep. What she and Giles had was personal, certainly not for public consumption. The newspaper had also reproduced quotes from her books, phrases completely out of context to make them sound more salacious than they really were. She wondered momentarily if she could sue them for copyright. The intimation in the article was that she pedalled porn rather than romance.

Margot stood up and made herself a fresh pot of tea. She tried to hold back the tears. Years and years of hard graft, writing countless novels, slowly building a reputation had now all gone. To be reduced to, how had that reporter described her? Oh yes, as the 'Queen of Porn' was just too much.

She needed to talk to the publishers, she needed answers from Abi. She ought to talk to Giles but was so angry that she knew that she would have to wait until she had calmed down. Margot made a list of jobs she had to do. She had already tried, unsuccessfully, to get hold of Abi, who was not answering her telephone. Margot tried the publishers direct. She got through to the chairman's office and spoke to his secretary.

"Oh, Miss Denning," she gushed, "what terrible things they wrote about you. It's scandalous, you should sue them. All those lies, how can they think they can get away with it? No, I'm sorry the chairman is not available at the moment."

Margot asked for either the chairman or Abi to phone her back as soon as possible. She told the secretary that she was in hiding because her cottage was under siege. Margot also knew that she would have to talk to Giles. She needed to know exactly what he had said to the tabloid reporter. Ten minutes later her mobile phone rang, it was Abi. She suspected that the chairman had ordered her to return Margot's call. Abi went straight on to the attack.

"Look, Margot, I've said I'm sorry already about not letting you know about the nature of the award ..."

Margot interrupted, "That's the least of my worries. Now what about these newspaper reports? In case you didn't know it I am splashed across every major newspaper, not to mention the vultures camped outside my cottage. I think I even saw a van from the local television company there."

"Yes, I guessed something like that might happen."

"You what? You mean you knew what was going on?"

"Well not exactly. It was just, well," she took a deep breath. She had hoped not to reveal the next bit. "Well, you remember when you gave me your room key to go and check up on Giles?"

"Yes," Abi sensed that Margot was barely concealing her anger.

"Well, he wasn't alone. There was a man with him. A reporter by the name of Doug Jones."

"Doug who? Should I know him?"

"Probably not, he is a tabloid newspaper hack who was sacked from one of the big red tops last year. He has been freelance ever since. Do you remember the scandal about the actress from that hospital programme last year?"

"Vaguely." She didn't really but didn't want to stop Abi from continuing.

"Well, he broke that story."

"So what was he doing at the publishing dinner and how did he know to focus on Giles?"

"Ah," there was a wealth of meaning in the sound. Margot waited. "That we're not sure about. The rumour about the publishing house setting up the award for the best sex writing has been circulating for quite a few months."

"Well how come I hadn't heard about it?" Margot interrupted.

"You might have done if you hadn't been living in the sticks so far away from civilised company and conversation. Anyway it doesn't matter. Doug Jones might be sleazy and underhand but he isn't stupid. He knows that you have won the Darcy award for romantic fiction. He was also aware of all the publicity about eighteen months ago when the publishers announced a new change of direction, so he probably put two and two together." Abi paused, "Or, we could have a mole in the publishing house who tipped him off. Then all he had to do was check at the hotel about which room you were in and whether or not you were alone. He had a bona fide press pass for the evening so getting into the ceremony was not a problem. It was also very obvious that you and Giles were together."

"What do you mean 'it was very obvious'?"

"Oh come on, Margot, you couldn't take your eyes off each other. When you did peel yourself away from him Doug Jones was able to step in and get his 'exclusive' interview. By the time I got to your room I don't think that he was getting much out of Giles. He was out cold on the bed, but I did get the impression that Jones had been having a bit of a nose around the room. It was lucky that I walked in when I did."

The rest of the story Margot knew and she didn't particularly want to talk about how hurt and devastated she had been that her plans for the most romantic night of her life had been totally and utterly ruined.

"Are you still there, Margot?"

"Yes, I'm still here."

"Right, do you want the good news now?"

"There's some good news in all of this?"

"Certainly, our sales people have been on the phone to me. Apparently, even after just one day, sales for your books particularly our 'contemporary' imprint, have rocketed. You know what they say 'all publicity is good publicity'."

Margot supposed that it was Abi's job to put a positive spin on things but she couldn't see it herself. She felt that this sort of publicity would alienate the core of her regular readers.

Abi decided to change tack. "What exactly did Giles say to this reporter?"

"I haven't got a clue."

"Don't tell me you haven't spoken to him yet?"

"I can't Abi; I am so angry that I am frightened of what I might say. He upset me so much by ruining Saturday night and then to have all this rubbish in the newspapers, well it has just gone from bad to worse."

"Oh Mo, I am so sorry," Margot wasn't sure whether it was the use of her childhood nickname, or just the sympathetic tone of Abi's voice. But whatever it was she could feel the tears pricking behind her eyes.

"Look, Abi I'll have to go, I've got so much to do. I'll call you later," she switched the phone off quickly before she broke down. Margot was unsure of her next move. She wondered how long those damn reporters would hang around outside her house. She walked upstairs to the bedroom. It was large with a tiny but perfectly functional en suite; Margot opened her case but didn't unpack. With luck she might only have to spend one night here. She knew that she would have to return to Saddleback Cottage sooner or later but she could not face it tonight. Margot lay down on the bed, closed her eyes and let the exhaustion of the last couple of days sweep over her. Within a few minutes she was asleep.

CHAPTER 32

At the same time that Margot was travelling down from London Giles was back in the lower paddock, the fence had been breached again. It was probably too soon to phone Margot. She had said that she would be back today so he would have to be patient. He debated whether or not to leave a note with the flowers that he was going to leave on the doorstep. He had already said sorry several times and was unsure if one more apology would improve the situation or make it worse. In the end he decided against it.

The flowers looked totally out of place in the cab of the tractor but Giles didn't care, no one would see them. He spotted the line of cars as he turned into Blossom Lane and wondered what on earth they were doing outside Margot's. He slowed as he drew level, stopped and called one of the waiting people over.

"What you after then?" he used his country voice. He found that people often said more if they thought they were talking to someone who was a bit 'simple'.

"We're waiting to interview the woman who lives here," he looked at his notebook, "a Miss Maureen Dudd. Do you know her?"

"No, can't say that I do."

"What about," and he checked his book again, "a Margot Denning?"

"Yeah, I know her, she lives here. Why, what's she done?"

"What hasn't she done," he leered, "if you know what I mean?"

Giles hadn't got a clue what the man was talking about.

"I don't suppose you know when she is due back, do you?"

"Not a clue, mate, not a clue. Anyhow, best get on." Giles drove away. What on earth was going on? He really did need to speak to Margot now. If she was in any sort of trouble she might need his help. But until he had an opportunity to sort things out there was still work to be done. Giles drove into the yard at

Home Farm to pick up the chain harrow. He connected it up to the tractor, raised it, then returned to the lower paddock. The tractor was very noisy and Giles, wearing ear defenders, missed the first couple of telephone calls. He stopped for a coffee from his flask and checked his mobile phone. He had four missed calls. He scrolled down the numbers. Three were from Jean and one was from Gavin – disappointingly nothing yet from Margot.

He dialled his sister's number.

"Giles, you'd better come home, there's something we need to talk about."

"What's wrong, is it Dad again?"

"No, he's fine, well he was until he picked up the newspaper."

"I'm sorry I don't understand?"

"Look just get straight back and Giles," she paused, "don't come in from the bottom of the lane, come in through the top, then you can avoid all those men waiting outside Saddleback Cottage."

Giles took a couple of sips of his coffee and then threw the rest out of the cab window. He unhitched the harrow and drove back to Home Farm as fast as the tractor would take him.

He walked into the back kitchen. "What's up then?"

Jean and his father were both sitting at the table reading newspapers.

"Giles have you seen this?" Jean looked really worried.

"Seen what?"

Before Jean could reply Godfrey jumped in. "Seen this piece about that woman in Saddleback Cottage? I told you she was no good. Didn't I say, after that time she came to have a row with me about the cottage? I said she was no good." Giles looked at his father and turned away ignoring him.

"Jean, what on earth is this all about?"

"Here, you read," she thrust the newspaper towards him. "I'll get you a cup of tea."

Giles read the newspaper article in silence, it went over two pages. He read it again a second time. He didn't have to speak; the look on his face said it all.

"I don't know what to say. I don't understand."

"Is it you that they're talking about?" Jean didn't beat about the bush.

Before Giles could reply Godfrey jumped to his defence. "Nah, it can't be. Says here that this Farmer Giles is her toy boy." Godfrey scanned the article again. "It doesn't give an age but this chap is obviously a lot younger than she is." There was hope in Godfrey's voice that it might, just might have nothing at all to do with them.

"That's not all they're saying," Jean muttered under her breath. She opened the back door. "Giles, now you're here you can give me a hand getting in the logs."

He followed her outside and closed the door behind him.

"Giles is it true what they're saying? About you and her?"

"Chance would be a fine thing, and anyway what exactly are they saying and who for God's sake are 'they'?"

"Giles don't pick a fight with me. They, the newspapers, are saying that Margot Denning writes dirty books and that her new boyfriend is responsible for the increase in the erotic content of the books."

Giles gave a grin. "Is that what they're really saying?"

"As near as damn it. And it is nothing to laugh about. We'll be the laughing stock of the village. That reporter called her boyfriend Farmer Giles. It won't take people long to realise that it should be Giles Farmer. Just tell me the truth, Giles; are you having a relationship with this woman? If so, why is she splashing details of your sex life all over the newspapers?"

Giles looked at his sister. "Whatever is going on is my business and nobody else's."

Jean made to reply but thought better of it. They both picked up an armful of wood and returned to the kitchen. They dumped the logs in the basket in the corner. Old Godfrey was not fooled. He knew they had been talking about what was going on and was aggrieved at being left out. Giles sat back at the table and read a different newspaper.

A photograph in the newspaper was allegedly of the back of Giles's head as he was being 'interviewed' by Doug Jones. Jones had a serious intent look on his face. The caption said 'our reporter agreed to anonymity for sex queen's lover'. It could have been the back of anyone's head. He looked up at his father and sister.

"Not one of you has asked about Margot, about how she must be feeling. All you're worried about is our bloody family name. People in this village will talk because that is what they do best, gossip, gossip and more bloody gossip. Now if you'll excuse me I've got half a field to finish."

Giles slammed out of the kitchen and climbed back up into the tractor. He drove down Blossom Lane, there were even more cars and people there now. 'Bloody vultures,' he thought. He drove fast past them and did not stop. Giles returned to the field and re-hitched the chain harrow on to the back of the tractor. He wished he knew where she was. She must be so upset with what they had written. Everything they were saying about her in the newspaper was untrue, unfair and unkind. It bore no resemblance to the woman he knew. It had taken a lot of courage on her part to admit that she was still a virgin. Even when he had handled it badly she had forgiven him and given him a second chance. He hoped she would be generous enough to forgive him this latest debacle.

Giles went over Saturday evening in his mind. He couldn't understand it. Normally he could hold his drink. He remembered how happy he felt, sipping champagne whilst he soaked away the sweat and grime of the day. She had looked lovely in that dressing gown thing wrapped loosely around her. He remembered wanting it to fall open, but it hadn't. He could taste the sweet floral scent of her. He sensed that she was ready to commit to him. He had felt excited and privileged at the thought that he would be the first one. It had all started to go wrong the minute that they left the sanctuary of their hotel room.

It had been even worse once Margot had gone up to collect her award; at least with her beside him he had had someone to talk to. Once she had gone there was no one. Then he recalled that man, Doug Jones, coming over. He remembered feeling grateful that someone was bothering with him even if the conversation was a bit odd. For instance, when he introduced himself the man seemed to think that it wasn't a proper name. He gave his surname first as he had been taught as in 'my name is Farmer, Giles Farmer'. Giles paused, in the noise and confusion Jones may have only heard the first bit.

Most people wouldn't have a clue as to his real identity, but the folk in Middle Chippings most certainly would. There was already gossip doing the rounds about him and the lady writer from Saddleback Cottage. A few had already commented about how close he seemed to the new lady writer who had moved into the village. Margot had hoped to keep their relationship not secret but at the very least discreet and low-key. For himself he didn't mind. He was happy to let people know that they were an item but he had respected Margot's desire for privacy. That would no longer be an issue. There was no way she was going to forgive him. It was bad enough that he had disgraced himself by drinking too much. He might just have got away with that, but talking to the press about personal matters, there was no way she would forget that.

He finished the field and unhitched the tractor. He stood with his mobile phone in his hand. He knew that he had to talk to Margot. He dialled her number; it rang four times then went on to voicemail.

"Hi Margot, it's me, look I've just seen the newspapers. Sorry seems so inadequate but I am so very very sorry. I'm sure I didn't say half the stuff that they said I did. In any event I think we need to talk," he paused then added, "I am so so sorry and I do miss you, please get in touch." He looked at the phone, how desperate had he sounded?

Giles drove back to Home Farm, passing Saddleback Cottage. There were only a couple of people hanging around, but then it was near the end of the day. Godfrey was sitting in his chair in the kitchen. Since the heart attack scare he had visibly aged. Farming was an unforgiving occupation. Meg the Border collie got up to greet him. He fondled her ears out of habit rather than affection.

"Hi Dad, how are you feeling?"

"Fine, son, fine, I'll be up and going again soon."

"Yes, Dad, of course you will." Godfrey was reading yet another newspaper.

"Er did you and her, did you really do what they said you did?"

Giles had never discussed his love life with his father before and had no intention of doing so now.

"Dad, you know what these newspaper people are like. What they don't know they make up. Anyway it doesn't matter now. After all this," he waved his hand at the newspaper, "I doubt she'll even speak to me again." He decided to change the subject. "Where's young Gavin? That spreader tank is still standing in the top field where I left it, full of muck waiting to be sprayed."

"I expect that he's down The Quarry Man with that young barmaid or waitress or whatever she calls herself."

"She's called Suzie, Dad; she is a very nice girl. She's trying to earn some money before she disappears off to University. I tell you what, I bet she doesn't leave jobs half done."

"No, not with that mother of hers as her boss. Samantha Savage won't allow any slacking. You're too soft with the boy."

'That was a joke,' thought Giles, Gavin was thoroughly spoiled by both his mother and his grandfather, but he was too tired to argue. "Where's Jean?"

"Out somewhere, said she'd be back later."

Giles climbed wearily up to the bathroom and ran himself a hot soaking bath. He carefully balanced his mobile phone on the window sill, just in case she telephoned.

CHAPTER 33

Margot's five minute lie-down turned into nearly two hours. She awoke with a start; if anything she felt worse rather than better for the rest. She located the sound that had woken her. It was her mobile phone; she had a missed call from Giles. Margot knew that she would have to speak to him at some stage but she just didn't feel up to it at the moment. She listened to his message and noted the desperation in his voice. 'Let him wait a bit longer,' she thought. 'He has caused this ghastly mess.'

The truth was that Margot didn't want to talk to anyone at this moment. She had been on the telephone almost constantly since the story broke, talking to the hotel, to her publisher and to Abi. She felt that she was beginning to get to the bottom of the whole business. Abi had done some digging with her contacts in the media. What Margot needed now was some impartial advice. She walked into Danny Bragg's hallway to retrieve the rest of her luggage and picked up her laptop, she would talk to Gus. As she turned she noticed a black and white picture in a silver frame. Margot peered closely; the boy could be Danny she thought. It was not so much the people in the picture that interested her but rather the background. The photograph had been taken in the front garden of Saddleback Cottage. She replaced the photograph on the hall table and carried her bags upstairs.

Margot logged into Country Cousins, paused and then began typing. She told Gus how she had felt betrayed by someone she trusted and had strong feelings for. Despite all that had happened she still wanted this person in her life. She finished the email by asking, 'Am I being stupid to trust him when he has let me down?' Margot wondered if she ought to spell out the nature of the betrayal but decided against it. She pressed the send button, left the laptop on and decided to have a bath.

As she lay soaking in the scented foam the tensions of the last few days began to ease. Margot tried to work out whether it would be better to have Giles in her life, or whether she just ought to give him up as a bad job. She could sell Saddleback Cottage and move back to London. She already had a buyer, in fact she had two. Margot heard the front door open. Danny Bragg yelled up the stairs.

"Are you hungry? I've got a take away and it is far too big for me to eat all by myself. You've got five minutes then I'm going to dish up."

Margot climbed out of the bath. It didn't seem quite right to put on her night clothes so she pulled on an old sweatshirt and loose trousers. By the time she got down to the kitchen all of the little foil trays were laid out in the centre of the table. The smell of the Chinese food made her realise that it was ages since she had last eaten anything. Danny had also opened a bottle of wine. For the first few minutes they ate in silence. Then Danny looked up.

"Margot, can I ask you something?"

"Depends what it is," she was on her guard again.

"Why me? Why did you come to me? Why not Giles Farmer?"

Margot thought carefully before answering. "Because he is part of the problem, a very big part in fact. To be perfectly frank there was nowhere else for me to go. I sense that you're an outsider like me."

"Actually you couldn't be further from the truth," he smiled at her. "My family has lived in Middle Chippings as long, if not longer, than the Farmers. Only difference is that they lived one side of the tracks so to speak and we lived on the other. My grandfather worked for George Farmer. Old George was a right bastard."

Margot accepted another glass of wine and settled down. She had a feeling she was going to enjoy this story.

"He led his wife a real dance. Had it off with several women, liked to spread himself around. Droit de seigneur and all that. He even tried it on with my grandmother, too, but she wouldn't have any of it. In the end his wife let him do what he wanted, as long as he came back to her. Keeping up appearances was really important to the Farmers. The old sod went and set up his mistress in Saddleback Cottage." He grinned at Margot. "So you see, the Farmer men have a tradition of keeping their mistresses just down the lane."

Margot did not rise to the bait. She knew that Danny was fishing for information about her and Giles.

"I thought we were talking about your family not the Farmers," Margot changed the subject.

"Well, after my grandma spurned George Farmer, my grandad really struggled to get work in the village. George's influence was really strong, chairman of the Parish Council, church warden and all that, despite his immoral ways. But he was a proud man was my grandad. He wouldn't be beaten so he stayed in the village."

"What did he do for a living?"

"He kept pigs."

Margot looked up. "Now, don't tell me, let me guess where he kept the pigs."

"Yup, Saddleback Cottage. Old Smithy's mother might have been George Farmer's mistress but she was also grandad's sister, my great-aunt. She knew that grandad had been treated badly so let him keep pigs at Saddleback Cottage."

"What about the next generation. Godfrey and your father, what happened between them?" Margot noticed a sudden change in Danny's manner.

"Oh them two, they're a pair bloody well matched. Useless buggers both of them. My dad actually worked for Godfrey. Believe it or not I used to spend a lot of time up at Home Farm as a kid, playing with Jean and Giles," he paused thinking for a moment. "Yeah, Jean and I were really close; but then my old man got too 'sick' to work so Godfrey gave him the sack, kicked him out of his job and me and my Mum out of our home. It was a tied cottage you see."

Margot nodded although she wasn't quite sure that she did 'see'.

"What was wrong with your father, was it serious?"

"A chronic case of idleness, though he said that it was a bad back. He had my mother running around him at his beck and call. She was worn out by the time she was forty."

"Are they still around, your parents?"

"No, I lost Mum about fifteen years ago, the dreaded cancer," he paused. "Sorry, even now I find it hard to talk about."

"Then don't," Margot said simply. "What about your father?"

"Oh the old sod is still around. He's got a little council retirement flat over in town. I pop in to see him every now and again, but it's not the same without my mum. What about you? What about your family?"

Margot paused, not knowing what to say but feeling she had to say something. Danny had opened up and it was her turn now. "I was a very late in life, unplanned child; my mother was in her mid-forties when she had me, my father older. To be honest they didn't really want a young child. Oh don't get me wrong they loved me, no doubt about that, but it was a love that came way after the love they had for each other. They always encouraged my writing, even if they did think that it wasn't a 'proper' job. They went within six months of each other. I knew my father couldn't survive without my mother."

"So, it was the ultimate love story was it?"

"Pretty much."

Danny walked over to the cupboard and pulled out another bottle of wine, Margot realised that they had finished the first. She cleared away the foil containers and dirty plates then sat back down at the table. She took a sip of her fresh glass of wine.

"Mm very nice."

"Shall we go into the other room?" She might be feeling a bit befuddled but she was still on her guard. Sitting at the kitchen table made the situation seem less intimate somehow. Danny seemed to have finished his family tale. Completely out of the blue Danny asked a question she was not expecting.

"What about Jean's boy, Gavin, what do you think of him?"

"Gavin? Well, I don't know him that well really. He has always struck me as a very polite young man and I know that Giles speaks highly of him."

Danny smiled, satisfied with the answer before moving on.

"What are your plans for tomorrow, will you try to go back to the cottage? Don't get me wrong, you're quite welcome to stay here as long as you like, well until the village busybodies find out."

"In this place that won't take long! No, I'm returning to London tomorrow, I need to talk to my publishers, not to mention my PR lady, who is also one of my best friends – allegedly. I don't suppose I could ask you one more favour?"

"What?"

"I've booked to go up on the early train. I could phone Leaker and book him but I don't think either of us want to advertise that I'm staying here, do we?"

"Speak for yourself, young lady. I'm sure that it would only enhance my reputation."

'And ruin mine,' Margot thought.

"Yeah no problem, I need to be over the other side of the county anyway tomorrow. I was planning on getting going at the crack of dawn. I can drop you off at the station on the way?"

Margot finished the wine in her glass and declined any more. "Excuse me, I really must get to bed, I'm shattered." She left the kitchen. Margot stood in the doorway and looked back at Danny Bragg. "You know Danny, I really am very grateful for you helping me out."

"Don't mention it, Margot, don't mention it."

Margot quickly took off her makeup, washed her face and fell into bed. She knew that she, was being silly, but as a precaution she placed a wooden chair against the back of the bedroom door. Better safe than sorry. Within minutes she was fast asleep.

If Danny Bragg had a hangover from their heavy drinking session the night before he certainly wasn't showing any signs of it. Margot, on the other hand, awoke with a pounding head and a very dry mouth. Danny's joie de vivre so early in the morning was almost too much to bear. Margot was not a morning person. She couldn't face breakfast. Two coffees and a bacon roll later, courtesy of First Great Western and she began to feel human again. Margot had had no more telephone messages from Giles. He had either given up or was waiting for her to return his calls. She suspected the latter.

Abi had organised transport to meet her at the station. 'Still trying to get back into my good books,' was Margot's first uncharitable thought. She sat back in the taxi and relaxed enjoying the buzz that only London can give you. Her editor and the sales director were both waiting in the office when she arrived. It had been the editor who had pushed her into making her love scenes more explicit. Although Margot had complied it wasn't something that she found easy to do. However, she had to admit that her erotic writing had come on in leaps and bounds since Giles Farmer had come into her life!

The sales director was effusive in his greetings.

"Margot darling, your figures, they've gone through the roof. Sadie and I were just discussing whether we ought to republish some of your earlier stuff on the back of all of this publicity." He picked up one of her earlier novels that she knew was now out of print. "Of course we would have to sex up the cover a bit."

"John, that book is about a love affair between two elderly people in the autumn of their lives. Putting a sexier cover on the front would be a gross misrepresentation of the novel." The book was one of her first and she had based the story very loosely on her parents. In sales terms it had been one of her least successful novels but it remained one of her favourites. The sales director's comment just confirmed what Margot had suspected all along, that the sales people very rarely read any of her books. They had a 'pile 'em high, sell 'em cheap' mentality. Undeterred, the sales director picked up another book.

"I was only using that as an example, but you know what I mean." He excused himself and left.

The rest of the meeting was spent discussing contracts. Even though Margot had an agent she also liked to go through her contracts personally. By the time her meeting finished it was almost lunchtime. Margot looked at her watch. She had arranged to meet Abi in a local wine bar.

Despite it being early in the week the place was packed. Margot got herself a soft drink and managed to find a small corner table. She wasn't ready to go back on the wine just yet. Margot read the menu through three times very slowly, sipping her fruit juice. Abi was notorious for her bad timekeeping. Margot placed her briefcase on the spare chair and had already been asked three times if it was taken before Abi finally turned up. Margot looked pointedly at her watch, thirteen minutes, not bad for Abi.

"Mo, I'm so sorry," she gave Margot a big hug. "Let me get you a drink, not one of those, but a proper one. Have you ordered yet?"

Margot laughed, Abi was always in such a rush. She gave Abi her food order and waited whilst she fought her way to the bar. For lunchtime it was incredibly packed, far more than what Margot remembered.

Abi returned with two very large glasses of white wine.

"Are we still on speaking terms? Have you forgiven me?"

Margot smiled. "Buy me lunch and we'll call it quits." Margot and Abi had been friends for years; she was easy to forgive.

"How are things? How's the book coming on?"

"Well if I could get back into my cottage and to my computer I could probably tell you. The place was crawling with reporters and photographers yesterday and I suspect that they're still there. I mean it is not every day that 'the Queen of Sex' moves into Middle Chippings."

"Oh Mo, don't worry, there's bound to be a scandal about to erupt somewhere and you'll be yesterday's news." She smiled at Margot. "I hear that the book sales are doing well, though."

"Well that's as may be."

"And how is Giles?"

"I wouldn't know and I don't really care." Margot tried hard to sound indifferent but Abi knew her too well to be fooled.

"You mean you haven't spoken to him since you walked out on Saturday night?"

"I didn't so much walk out on him as he passed out on me."

"Now you're just splitting hairs. Anyway, it wasn't all his fault."

"What do you mean it wasn't all his fault? Of course it was."

"Well, no it wasn't really. I've been doing some digging about Doug Jones. Apparently he is very well known for his underhand methods. It is highly likely that he slipped Giles something. Don't panic, nothing illegal or noxious, just something strong enough and fast enough to loosen his tongue.

That man can turn even the most innocent remark into a salacious lie."

"Who Giles?"

"No, you idiot, Doug Jones. To be honest I did think that it was odd. When you left the table to get the award I remember checking up on Giles because he hadn't really been chatting to anyone except us and it seemed a bit unfair to leave him by himself. He said that he was fine. Ten minutes and one conversation later with the gutter press and I find Giles out cold on your bed and the said Mr Jones snooping around your suite."

"So you think that he made up those lies, that Giles didn't say the things Jones said he did?"

"Yes and no. It's a bit tricky. We got our legal boys to contact Jones, to threaten him with libel but," Abi seemed uncomfortable and unsure of how to go on. "Jones taped the conversation he had with Giles and the words that were said were the words printed, but they were highly edited and taken totally out of context."

Their food arrived and Abi quickly changed the subject, keeping Margot entertained with stories and gossip about staff in the publishing house. Some of the names Abi was mentioning were ones she had never even heard of. In the eight months she had been living in Middle Chippings a lot had changed. With a start Margot realised that she was beginning to think of Middle Chippings and Saddleback Cottage as home.

"Do you remember that scandal about the finance director of that big multinational bank in London? You know the one where he was having an affair with his boss's wife and one of his cashiers at the same time?"

"Vaguely."

"That was one of Doug Jones's 'exclusive scoops'. I know someone from the bank's public relations department. They had to do quite a bit of damage limitation. It turned out Jones had got the cashier drunk and she had confessed all. Funny thing was she was normally teetotal, or so my friend said. Unfortunately, the bank didn't have any concrete evidence to go to the police about, so they let it drop. Let's be honest, Margot, it isn't as if someone has died or any great damage has been done, I mean, look what it has done to your sales. If you ask me you got off quite lightly."

"Yes, but it is not the sort of publicity I particularly wanted."

Although Abi appeared not to be in any hurry to return to work Margot knew that her time was limited. Once they had finished eating Margot declined another drink and said she needed to be getting back. Abi gave her friend a big hug.

"He's a very nice man, Margot; don't let other people spoil it for you. You deserve someone special."

CHAPTER 34

Conversation stopped as soon as he walked into the village shop. Giles picked up a packet of tea and placed the correct amount of money on the counter. As Giles was leaving Emma remarked to no one in particular.

"Well, you think you know folk and then they go and do something that totally throws you. I don't know what this world is coming to, I really don't."

Giles hesitated, about to turn and face her, but decided that he didn't feel that brave. He still needed to talk to Margot; he wanted to know where he stood with her. Giles knew that he would have to face people in the village at some stage. Jean had arranged a family meal out at The Quarry Man. He would rather not have bothered but Jean had been adamant.

"We've nothing to be ashamed of. Just because you had one drink too many and said too much, that's no reason why people around here should talk about us behind our backs. No, we go and face them."

Jean was a proud woman and Giles knew that she had been hurt more by village tittle-tattle than by anything printed in the newspapers. His father was upset, although he hadn't said too much. The only one who hadn't been offended was Gavin. His only comment was to yell out of the Land Rover window as he drove past Giles.

"Way to go Uncle G! Way to go."

The Quarry Man was quite busy considering it was midweek. They sat and ordered their meal. Giles went up to the bar to get the drinks.

"You OK?" Samantha asked.

"Yeah, I suppose so."

"We had one of those reporters in here asking about you and about Margot. I said I'd never heard of either of you. Then I introduced him to Leaker and he didn't stay long."

Giles smiled, Leaker could bore for England. One of the lad's from Danny Bragg's building firm sidled up to the bar and stood next to Giles.

"I'll have what he's having."

All three of them laughed and Giles realised that it would be OK. People who knew him would not believe what they read in the newspaper. His main regret was that his relationship with Margot was now public property, but it could be over before it had even begun, thanks to his stupidity.

Giles returned to the table. They had just started their meal when the door opened and Danny Bragg walked in. He looked over towards them and nodded at Jean. She pointedly did not return the acknowledgement. Gavin looked up.

"Who's that, Mum?"

"Danny Bragg. The man who is supposed to be doing the extension on Saddleback Cottage for that woman." She caught Giles's glance. "Sorry, the man who was hoping to do some work for Miss Margot Denning."

"Is he anybody important?"

"Well he thinks he is." It was the first thing that Godfrey had said since they arrived. "He's the one who went asking awkward questions and poking around with the Council about the damn piggery."

As if aware they were talking about him, Danny Bragg deliberately turned his back and chatted to Samantha at the bar.

They finished their meal; none of them had much of an appetite.

"Come on, you lot, get a move on." Jean was suddenly in a hurry to leave.

Godfrey put his hand on his daughter's arm. "Don't you let him bother you Jean, he's nothing to us."

"He's nothing to nobody," Giles muttered, now it was his turn to get a warning glance from Jean. 'What is this family coming to?' he thought.

Giles signalled to Samantha for the bill and they left soon afterwards, leaving a generous tip for Suzie. Gavin stayed behind, Giles promised to pick him up later. Giles slowed down as he passed Saddleback Cottage, the cars had all disappeared.

'Probably hounding some other poor devil,' Giles thought. The cottage was in complete darkness, so she hadn't returned then.

Gavin wandered over to the bar; Danny Bragg had moved to a table in the back of the restaurant area. Jean had warned her son about Bragg, saying what a devious man he was. The fact that his uncle and grandfather wouldn't give Bragg the time of day was a good enough reason for Gavin to shun him too. Gavin dragged out drinking his half of lager for as long as he could. The bar was full tonight and Suzie was kept busy. They were one waitress down. Samantha was flitting from behind the bar to waiting at tables. When she wasn't looking Gavin slipped behind the bar and through the door into the living quarters. He made his way up to Suzie's room. If he couldn't talk to her he might as well watch television or play a few computer games.

Gavin switched on the computer and had a couple of goes at zapping alien life forms but it was boring without Suzie. He decided to see how the Margot-Gus saga was going so logged into the Country Cousins website. There was nothing new, so he scrolled through the messages that Suzie had sent. He read them. Gus was very supportive to Margot and sympathetic to her situation, particularly in agreeing that Giles's behaviour in getting drunk was appalling and unforgivable.

"Bloody women sticking together," he said out aloud.

Gus was supposed to be a bloke wasn't he?' thought Gavin. Blokes stuck together, this wouldn't do at all. It took Gavin ages to write the message, but then he had all the time in the world. Gus told Margot that everyone made mistakes and that Giles should be given a chance to explain himself. Just in case she thought that there was something odd in this change of heart he added, 'I've been thinking about this a lot since you last wrote.' Gavin ran the spell checker and made some minor corrections. He sat staring at the screen for ages, wondering if he should send the message. Exchanging emails and pretending to be Gus had seemed like a harmless prank in the beginning. But having seen how cut up Giles was he was not so sure now. This was not a computer game; this was people's lives and relationships they were messing with.

"Oh what the hell." He pressed the send button seconds before Suzie burst into the room. She threw herself on to the bed.

"I am so exhausted, I stink of chips and cooking and I just want to sleep and wake up next week." She rolled over on to her back "What are you doing?"

Gavin had quickly switched to the desktop but the Country Cousins website was still along the tool bar at the bottom.

"Nothing," he tried to lie but he knew that she would find out. Suzie had a way of wheedling confidences out of him. He decided to come clean. "OK, I've just sent an email to Margot, or rather 'Gus' has."

"You're kidding me, right?"

"No, honest, I have just emailed it. I went back and read some of the other messages that we sent. They seemed a bit girly somehow and Gus is supposed to be a bloke after all." He was becoming defensive now, always a bad sign.

"You idiot." Suzie shook her head in disbelief. "Margot Denning is a writer, she will spot that your message is different from the previous ones."

"No, she won't, especially if it's something she wants to hear." Gavin was determined to stand his ground.

"See for yourself." He clicked on the site and displayed his sent message on the screen. She leaned over him and read. Suzie shook her head. Gavin hadn't got a clue about women. Still the damage was done now. There wasn't a lot she could do about it.

Gavin swung the chair around and hugged Suzie around her middle.

"Pooh, your clothes do stink." He slipped his hands down to the hem of her shirt. "Best get them off shall we?" He pulled the shirt over her head and hurled it into the corner of the room.

Suzie pushed him away. "I'm too tired and it's too late, Giles will be here soon to pick you up." She walked over to the crumpled shirt and pulled it back over her head. "How about I thrash you on my computer game?"

"In your dreams, girl, in your dreams."

Suzie pulled over a stool to sit next to Gavin as he set up the computer game. Gavin looked sideways at her. That was what he loved about her, as well as being a sexy girlfriend she was also a good mate. He would miss her when she went off to university in the autumn.

Godfrey had gone up to bed early leaving Giles asleep in the armchair in the corner of the kitchen. The sound of a kettle being filled woke him up.

"Sorry, Jean, almost fell asleep then."

Jean laughed, it was a family joke, it was what their father always said when he was caught out asleep in a chair when he shouldn't be.

"I'm making a drink, do you want one?"

"Yes, I've just got time before I pick up Gavin. It won't matter if I'm a bit late it always takes him ages to say goodbye to Suzie." Giles looked closely at his sister. "Are you OK, Jeanie? You look a bit tired." He wanted to say 'upset' or 'down' but their relationship precluded any sort of discussion about emotional issues.

"No, I'm fine, really. I'm not sure going to The Quarry Man was such a good idea tonight."

"Oh, I don't know, I enjoyed it and I'm certain that Dad did too." He paused. "You seemed a bit put out when Danny Bragg walked in."

"Did I?" she tried to feign indifference but Giles wasn't fooled.

"Don't let him get to you."

"Don't you worry about me. Sort yourself out first." She changed the subject. "Have you been able to speak to Margot yet?"

"No, but she has sent me a text saying she is likely to be back later this week. I just wish I knew when. Then I could find out if she is still speaking to me."

"Well if she sent you a text, she is still talking to you."

"She probably only sent the text to keep me quiet, so that I would stop bothering her." Giles stretched and yawned. "I'd better go and pick up young Gavin before Sam Savage catches him again."

Jean nodded her reply.

Giles drove the Land Rover towards the pub. As he pulled into the car park he swerved to avoid Danny Bragg accelerating away in the middle of the road. Giles hit his horn as a warning to

Gavin that he was waiting. He had just reversed into a parking space when Gavin came out of the back door of the pub. Gavin climbed into the Land Rover.

"Giles, can I ask you a question?"

"Yes, as long as it's got nothing to do with women. I haven't a clue in that department whatsoever."

"Well, it's about Mum."

Giles turned the engine off and turned to face Gavin.

"What about her?"

"What's with her and that builder bloke – Danny Bragg?"

"Nothing, as far as I know. Danny was at school with Jean, although I think he was a couple of years older. I'd just started senior school the year after he left. What little I do know I don't particularly like. There's been bad blood in the past between the two families. From what I remember I think that it was in my grandfather's time when it started, or it might even go back further than that. Why do you ask?"

"Oh no reason, it's just when he appears Mum goes all quiet and wants to get away. Suzie overheard Mum say to Sam Savage that if she had known Danny Bragg was still around she would have thought twice about moving back to Middle Chippings."

"Bragg only moved back to the village himself about six months ago. He's got one of those big mock-Georgian places on the new estate at the top end of the village." Giles paused. "Anyway, you know your mother when she's ready to tell us, she'll say something and not beforehand."

They pulled away and drove back to Home Farm. Giles had had a long, emotionally draining and fruitless day. He was no further forward with Margot than he had been at the weekend. He would just have to bide his time. All he wanted was to speak to Margot. Although he was dog-tired Giles couldn't sleep. The events of the weekend were on a permanent loop in his mind. If only he had done this or more importantly if only he hadn't done that. He got up a couple of times in the night and even went back down to the kitchen to make a drink. He wasn't sure of the exact time he finally got off to sleep. He slept through his alarm and didn't hear the sound of a piece of folded paper being pushed under his door.

Chapter 35

Margot hadn't wanted to stay an extra night at Danny Bragg's place but she felt she didn't have much choice. Whilst she was in London Danny had telephoned her saying that, although the majority of reporters had disappeared from outside Saddleback Cottage, there were still a few left hanging around. Consequently he suggested that she stay with him for a further night. He also offered to pick her up from the station personally so no one need ever know. Margot had left most of her stuff at his house, so although she had misgivings she knew that from a practical point of view it made good sense.

Danny picked her up from the station and then dropped her off at his house. He drove the long way around, avoiding Blossom Lane. He told her he was going to spend the evening at The Quarry Man so she would have the house to herself for the evening. By the time that Margot had had a long soaking bath there was not a great deal of the evening left. She had just gone to bed, placing the chair back against the bedroom door when she heard Danny returning. Margot heard him call out her name. She didn't answer. She did not want a repeat of the heart to heart they had had the night before. She was beginning to wish unsaid some of the things she had said. Danny Bragg was the sort of person who remembered every word in great detail; she had already learned this to her cost. Margot heard Danny walk up the stairs. He paused outside her bedroom door. She held her breath listening intently. Danny moved on and she heard his own door open and close. She exhaled a silent sigh.

Danny left early next morning; the bang of the front door woke her up. Margot lay for a few minutes in the strange bed in the strange room and tried to think out a sensible plan of action. She would have to return to Saddleback Cottage at some stage. She couldn't stay at Danny's another night. His overtures of friendship were making her feel very uncomfortable. She knew that she ought not to be like this. After all Danny hadn't hesitated when she had telephoned him. He hadn't asked too many questions, although he must have been dying to. She just had this feeling that he was expecting a payback and the payback was not just the agreement that she give him first option on her cottage. Margot had a feeling that Danny Bragg might expect reimbursement of a more personal nature.

Margot grabbed her silk wrap-around robe and wandered down the stairs. She stood in the kitchen waiting for the kettle to boil. When the doorbell went it made her jump. Her first thought was to ignore it; she reached across and quickly switched off the radio. The bell rang several times but she did not move, hoping whoever it was would go away. Finally it stopped; Margot tentatively tiptoed into the hallway. The door was a heavy wooden one with no glass so she couldn't be sure if whoever it was had gone. She hesitated, then turned the lock and opened the door a few inches. She was forced backwards as the door was pushed open.

"Hello Margot."

"Hello Giles." He looked at her. She folded her arms defensively across her chest. "You'd better come in." She hadn't heard a car and wondered whether he had walked. No, he couldn't have it was too far. More likely he had parked the Land Rover a discreet distance away. Danny's road might be in the more expensive part of the village but nosy neighbours were the same wherever you lived. Giles followed her into the kitchen.

"Tea? Coffee?"

Giles registered that she knew her way around the kitchen cupboards. "Tea, please," he paused, "and an explanation."

"Of what?"

"Of everything. You owe me that at least."

Margot decided that attack was the best means of defence. "Me? Owe you? I don't think so. I wasn't the one who spoke to the tabloid journalist, I wasn't the one who got blind drunk and passed out."

"No, but you were the one who lied to me about your writing, letting me believe it was romance when clearly it was porn.

"Erotica, actually," she corrected him but he ignored her.

"You also lied to me about owning the cottage and you let me believe you were inexperienced when clearly you aren't." Giles had raised his voice.

The kettle boiled and Margot took time in making a drink trying to calm herself down. She looked up at Giles.

"I did not 'lie' about my writing. It has been there for anyone to see, or for anyone who could be bothered to read it. As to the sex scenes, well they are no more explicit than some and a damn sight less than others I could mention. If you had bothered to find out about me as a writer you would have discovered Maureen Dudd is my real name. Not very glamorous is it? But it is the one I was born with and the one I use in my everyday life. It was you who jumped to the conclusion that there were two of us and to be frank you never really gave me the opportunity to explain otherwise."

They were both very angry, breathing heavily. Giles had his hands clenched by his sides. There was more he needed to know, he demanded to know.

"What about here, what are you doing here, in his house?" The disgust with which he said 'his house' spoke volumes.

"He," Margot emphasised the word, "has got a name, please use it." She was shouting at him now.

"I wouldn't give him the bloody satisfaction of speaking his name, after what he has done to my family!"

"And what about what your family has done to him, hey, tell me that?" Margot hadn't got a clue what she was talking about. It just seemed right to trade insults and to defend Danny Bragg, against what, she was not quite sure.

They stood either side of the kitchen table, shouting at each other. Giles walked around to Margot's side, put his hands on her shoulders and twisted her to face him. Their faces were inches apart.

"Talking of satisfaction I suppose that Bragg has been helping you out in that department." The ugliness in his voice was like a slap.

"You bastard!" She raised her hand to hit him across the side of his face but he grabbed her wrist, and then went for the other one as she tried to raise that. He pushed her against the wall.

234

"You want satisfaction; I'll give it to you." He bent his head and pressed his lips hard against hers, the weight of his body pinning her against the wall. She struggled trying to push him off. He raised his head and looked into her eyes. They were full of tears.

"Not this way, don't take me in anger please," she whispered feeling a bruise already forming on her upper lip.

He let go of her wrists and stepped back from her.

"I'm sorry, Margot, God I am so sorry." He looked down. "I didn't mean for that to happen believe me. I'm so sorry," he repeated. "Please forgive me, it won't happen again, I promise." He was beside himself with remorse.

"It's OK, it's OK." She put out her hand to touch him. "We need to talk. To talk properly but not here in Danny's house."

Giles took her hand gently and looked into her face. "I have never felt about anyone the way I feel about you," he hesitated. "There's no excuse for the way I behaved just now. You have the power to make me incredibly happy and unbelievably jealous."

Margot squeezed his hand. "You have nothing to be jealous about, trust me." She smiled. "Now drink your tea, give me five minutes to get showered and dressed, then you can take me back home. Back to Saddleback Cottage."

Margot went upstairs. Giles pulled out a chair and sat and drank his tea. He was ashamed at the way he had behaved. He had hurt her and not just physically. Giles picked up the two mugs, Margot hadn't touched her tea and it had gone cold. He poured it down the sink, rinsed out the mugs and left them on the side to dry. Margot yelled something to him down the stairs. He hadn't quite heard her so wandered to the bottom of the stairs.

Giles looked around the hallway, white walls, dark blue carpet, nothing of adornment except a silver-framed photograph on the telephone table. Giles walked over to it and picked it up. He stared at it intently for several minutes. Margot walked back down the stairs, her hair damp from the shower.

"It was taken in my front garden," she said.

"I can see that. Who is it? The child looks familiar." Giles had a feeling he should know who it was.

"The child is Danny as a little boy. I think that the other two are his parents, or grandparents or something like that."

Giles stared at the photograph for a few more seconds then replaced it on the hall table. He turned to Margot. "Here, let me." He put out his hands to take the case from her. "Is this all you have?"

"No, there's one more, from the weekend in London." She turned and went back up the stairs. When she returned to the hall Giles was still staring at the photograph although he had not picked it up again.

"You wait here; I'll get the Land Rover."

Whilst he was gone Margot wrote a quick note for Danny. "Thanks for giving me sanctuary. I'm OK now. I'll be in touch. Margot." She almost added a kiss, out of habit, but managed to stop herself. The Land Rover couldn't have been far away because Giles returned within minutes. He picked up her bags and threw them into the back, then helped Margot to climb into the front seat.

"Where to?"

"Home, Giles, take me home to Saddleback Cottage."

They didn't speak during the journey. They each felt that they had said too much already. Margot knew that she owed Giles an explanation as to what she was doing at Danny's. She wasn't even sure why she had gone to ground at his place. It had seemed like a good idea at the time. Equally, she had questions she wanted answered. The main question was how had he known where to find her? She lifted her fingers and gently ran them along her upper lip, it felt tender. Giles had frightened and excited her in equal measure. What had he said? That he had never felt about a woman the way he felt about her. She folded her arms, hugging his declaration to her as tightly as she could. Sensing her movement Giles glanced across at her and smiled. They swung into Blossom Lane; there were no waiting cars or reporters. Giles pulled up outside the cottage. He opened the back door and retrieved Margot's suitcase. Margot waited until he came around to her side. Giles opened the door and offered her his hand.

Giles carried the case up the front path whilst Margot hurried ahead to unlock the door. There was a pile of post and several business cards on the mat behind the door. She picked up a couple of the cards – reporters. Without even looking at them she threw them into a bin.

"Parasites."

"Where do you want these put?"

"Just take them upstairs and dump them in my bedroom, I'll sort them later."

Margot could hear the cases being dropped on the floor and Giles hurried back down. She persuaded him to stay for a cup of tea but he was impatient to get on. He told her that he would be working until late that evening so was unlikely to be back. With his father incapable of pulling his weight and Gavin unwilling to do so he was covering the work of three men.

"Look Margot, I'm really sorry but as well as a mountain of work on the farm there is another matter that I have to deal with. Family business."

"Nothing serious I hope?"

"Nothing I can't handle." He smiled at her. "There's someone I need to speak to. It's very important and really can't wait."

Giles sensed her disappointment, God knows, he wanted to stay but this other thing couldn't be left. He pulled her towards him and held her fast in a hug.

"I will be back, soon I promise. Tomorrow evening, just you and me and a bottle of wine, how about it?"

Margot smiled. "It's a date."

He kissed the top of her head, and then he was gone.

CHAPTER 36

Giles rolled over and looked at the time on the clock. It was mid morning and he had slept through a solid twelve hours. Physical exhaustion he could cope with but the emotional exhaustion of the past few weeks was something else. He threw back the covers and went into the bathroom, yelling downstairs on the way.

"Anyone there, a cup of tea would be great?"

There was no reply so he walked into the bathroom and revived himself with a scalding hot shower. He returned to his room and picked up and reread the note that had been pushed through his door the day before.

'You will find Margot Denning at this address.' Jean hadn't signed it but he knew her writing. She had added an unnecessary postscript. 'It's Danny Bragg's house.'

Bloody Danny Bragg, why couldn't he keep out of their lives and why had Margot turned to him, of all people? But much more to the point how did his sister know Margot could be found there? All Giles seemed to have at the moment were more and more questions, what he needed were answers and he was determined to get them, one way or another. He had been way out of order with his behaviour yesterday. He had been desperate to speak to Margot. What he hadn't wanted was the row. Giles could not believe that he had been so close to forcing himself upon her. He almost took her in anger – it would have been rape. Thank God he had come to his senses. Margot had told him to trust her, and he did. It was Danny Bragg he didn't trust. When he was with Margot he had no doubts but when he was alone, like now, they came crowding back.

Giles walked into the kitchen and made his own pot of tea. He looked around wondering where everyone was. He checked the calendar hanging on the wall. 'Dad, hospital visit' was pencilled in. Of course, he remembered now, it was the six weeks' check-up since the heart attack.

Giles went back up the stairs and into his father's room. He couldn't remember the last time he had been in there; it had been so long ago. He wandered over to the dressing table. In his mother's time the top had been covered with embroidered squares, which held bottles of lotions and scent. They were long gone. His mother's jewellery box was still there. Giles lifted the lid, a dancing ballerina popped up but she did not move, so he closed the lid, turned the box upside down and wound the key inset on the underside. He placed it back on the dressing table and lifted the lid. The ballerina began to turn in a jerky motion whilst tinny strains of Brahms Lullaby could just be recognised.

At the bottom of the jewellery box was a small ring box, Giles pulled it out and opened its stiff lid. His mother's engagement ring sat in a nest of cotton wool. Giles did not remove it but just looked and remembered the high days and holidays when she had worn it. He snapped the box shut and replaced it in the bigger one. He looked at the family photographs lined along a shelf above the dressing table. Professional photographs of him and Jean taken in the photographic studio in town were mixed with family snaps of the four of them on holiday. There were a few less faded baby photographs of Gavin. He had been such a sunny, happy little boy, doted on by his grandparents. There was a photo of the three generations standing outside the front door to Home Farm. Giles studied the picture closely. Gavin had been a small pudgy toddler with such a sunny disposition. It was only in adolescence he had grown tall and skinny and had begun to look like all the Farmer men before him.

The house telephone rang and Giles rushed downstairs to answer it.

"Did you find her?" direct and straight to the point.

"Yes, but, how…" he didn't get to finish.

"Giles, please don't ask me questions about how I knew, I just did. Let's just leave it at that shall we?" Giles recognised the tone in his sister's voice and changed the subject.

"How's Dad?"

"OK, I think. He is in with the doctor now. He wouldn't let me go in with him. Giles," Jean phrased her words carefully, "I'm worried that he'll keep things back from us. If I ask the doctors, they won't tell me anything either. You know how secretive Dad can be."

"Like a few other people I could mention."

"What's that supposed to mean?" She was on the attack now.

"Nothing, nothing. What time will you be back?"

"By the time Dad and I get away from here it is going to be late, I thought I might take him to The Quarry Man for dinner, he can pay. Gavin's going out with Suzie this evening. I only booked for two." She paused. "I had sort of assumed that you would probably be busy elsewhere."

"Yes, well I am actually," he sighed. "Let me know what the outcome is after he's seen the doctor. I may see you later but if not don't wait up. And Jean."

"Yes?"

"Thank you." He replaced the receiver. He would deal with his sister later. Giles sighed and realised that he would have to move pretty quickly to catch up on all the jobs that he had slept through this morning. He hadn't a clue where Gavin was, or what he was doing. He had a forlorn hope that Gavin might have made a start on the outstanding jobs, but he wouldn't hold his breath. There was a lot for him to get through before he could get back to Saddleback Cottage this evening. Giles drove around the farm and checked the stock, filling the troughs with fresh water and putting out extra feed. The afternoon sped by. He pulled into the farmyard for the last job of the day, checking that the hens had been shut up for the night.

A quick shower and a change of clothes, Giles felt like a teenager about to go on his first date. Leaving the Land Rover in the yard he walked down the lane to the cottage, nervousness and excitement mounting with every step. He walked up the garden path and rang the bell. Margot opened the door immediately. He had the feeling she had been watching and waiting for him.

"Hello beautiful."

She smiled back at him and stood aside for him to enter. He glanced into the dining room. The table was laid up with crystal wine glasses and candles.

"Sorry, I'm not quite ready yet, grab yourself a beer and come and sit in the kitchen whilst I just finish what I was doing."

Giles watched her preparing vegetables before placing them into a casserole. Emptying half a bottle of red wine into the dish with the meat and vegetables, she replaced the lid and put it all into the oven.

"Right, that'll be about an hour and a half." She busied herself washing up the cooking utensils. He just sat and watched. He stared at her back view and wondered what it would look like naked. She turned, as if reading his thoughts.

"Any suggestions as to how we can spend the time whilst we're waiting?" There was no mistaking the teasing in her voice. Giles smiled, parts of him were already rising to the challenge. But they had to talk first; he needed to get things clear. They sat side by side on the sofa. Giles wondered how it was that they could sit so closely together yet manage not to touch.

"You know, I am truly sorry about what happened at the hotel. I really can't understand what came over me. Normally I can take my drink and I honestly didn't realise that I had drunk so much."

"You didn't."

"What?"

"I think that you had your drink spiked by that journalist who spoke to you."

"But why? Why would he do that?"

"To get to me, to get at me, who knows? Someone tipped him off about the award and he saw it as a chance to make money."

"But how could he make money?"

"Romantic fiction is one of the most popular genres in the whole of the publishing world, but you wouldn't know it. It is treated as a joke by most people, especially the book reviewers. What they never address though is how much pleasure it gives to a lot of people. Doug Jones wanted something that would sell a few of his downmarket rags. Dishing the dirt on the woman who was awarded the best sex writing award was not a bad angle to go for. He was hoping to find some salacious skeletons in my cupboard."

"And did he find any?"

"No, not from me, which is why he thought he would pump you for information. He wasn't at all bothered about what was accurate and what was not. Why should the truth get in the way of a good story?"

"How did you find all of this out?"

"Abi, she did some digging around for me. She spoke to a PR friend of hers who works for a rival publishing house. Apparently Jones pulled the same trick on one of their authors."

Giles leaned forward and placed his glass on the low table in front of him, he turned and took Margot's glass out of her hand and placed it on the table next to his. He held her hands in his, rubbing his thumbs along the back of her hands in a gentle rhythmic way. They leaned towards each other and he gave her a gentle kiss. She winced slightly; her lip was still bruised from yesterday's encounter.

"I'm so sorry, my darling, about hurting you," his voice broke. "It is just that I wanted you so much and I was angry…" Margot didn't let him finish. She stood up and picked up the two half full wine glasses.

"Bring the bottle," she said softly and walked towards the stairs. Giles needed no prompting.

They didn't rush undressing each other but did it slowly and gently anticipating the pleasure yet to come: feasting with their eyes, tracing with their fingertips. Giles had thought of nothing else but making love to Margot since the first moment he had met her. He wanted to make her first time special. He had had women before but it had just been sex. This was different and he didn't want to spoil it for either of them. Finally they lay naked on the bed. She traced his face with her fingers; he traced her body with his. Giles pulled her on top of him and gently parted her legs. She straddled him and started to rock, gently at first. He let her control the pace but as it picked up he rolled her over so that he was now on top. His whole focus was on making her first time as perfect as possible. Her body caught this new urgent rhythm. Margot moved in time with him, arching her back so that he could go in deeper. It was as if nothing else in the whole world mattered except her and Giles. He brought her to a climax and followed it very closely with his own. His whole body shuddered with sheer pleasure. He lay, half on half off her but still within her. Her words were thick and barely distinct.

"Thank you. That was," she paused, "that was so beautiful." Her eyes were big and liquid full of tears which she allowed to run unchecked down her face.

"Don't cry." He kissed the tears. "Thank you so much for letting me be the first," he whispered. They lay still for a few more minutes holding. Giles closed his eyes satiated with warmth and pleasure, within seconds he was asleep. Margot lay there staring at him. She didn't mind him sleeping. It allowed her to study every part of his face. The frown line between his thick brows seemed to have softened. He looked younger and, dare she say it, happier than she had ever seen him. It might have been the warmth of his body or the fact that she felt so relaxed but she too fell asleep.

Giles felt himself being dragged from a happy place by a persistent bell. It was not the ring of a telephone, nor did it seem like the ring of a clock alarm, but it was there none the less. He opened his eyes and saw Margot's soft naked body beside him. He remembered why he was happy. He could hear the bell again. The cooker, bloody hell, how long had they been asleep, how long had the food been cooking? Giles gently eased his arm from under Margot and slipped out of the bed. He pulled on his clothes and crept down the stairs.

Giles walked into the kitchen and switched off the timer. The oven had turned off but was still warm. He opened the door and pulled out the casserole. It was a bit dry. He was feeling hungry now. He found a bottle of champagne in the fridge. He wondered if it was being kept for a special occasion. If so then this was it.

Carrying the champagne and two clean glasses back into the bedroom he walked in to find that she hadn't moved at all. He studied her for a moment; one of her breasts was exposed. It was large and rounded and the nipple was a delicious browny pink colour. Giles thought about how his tongue had felt around it and became aroused again. He wanted her so much, ever since she had walked into his life.

Sensing his scrutiny Margot opened her eyes and smiled at him.

"Hi."

"Hello beautiful. I thought we ought to celebrate and I found this in the fridge." Giles unwound the wire cage around the cork then he deftly popped it off. The champagne began to froth out of the bottle. Giles grabbed a champagne flute and poured it in.

Margot was sitting up now with a sheet tucked under her arms. Giles filled both glasses and walked over to the bed.

"A toast."

"To what?"

"I don't know, you choose."

Margot looked at him shyly and raised her glass. "To the virgin that I was."

Giles raised his glass and added, "And to the sexy woman that you are."

Margot gulped her champagne and it dribbled down her chin and on to her chest.

"Allow me." Giles gently pulled the sheet down, leaned forward and licked the rivulet of champagne. He was rewarded by a shudder.

Giles stood up, placed his glass on the side table and stripped off his clothes.

"Bugger the bloody casserole."

CHAPTER 37

The casserole did eventually get eaten, but not that night. The alarm went off early the following morning, Giles waved his hand up and down ineffectively before he realised that it was not his alarm, neither was it his bed. He glanced at the clock and then at Margot, there was just time. He gave her a gentle wake up kiss. He had set the alarm early so that they could make love again. This time it was quick but nonetheless pleasurable. Margot remained in bed long after Giles had left.

It was almost midday by the time she got herself up and going. She switched on the computer. Margot would not have believed that she could be this happy. She went straight through to her emails. She wanted to let Gus know how happy she was. Margot quickly read the message that Gus had left. There was something not quite right about it. She read it twice before she realised what was wrong. It had been written by someone different. As a writer herself Margot knew that most people had their own unique voice and this last message was definitely not written by the same person as the previous ones had been. How curious.

Margot went through her County Cousins inbox and reread all the emails she had received from Gus. She then printed them off and read them for a third time. On paper the difference was even more marked. But more than the voice Margot realised that a pattern was emerging. The emails mirrored almost perfectly the story of her relationship with Giles. The 'ups' were always commented on and when she had experienced the 'downs' it seemed that Gus was always on hand to stick up for Giles. Yet at no time had she mentioned Giles by name. She had deliberately withheld that information. Giles? Could it be him? Margot checked the times and dates of the emails. The last one was sent, yesterday evening. It was sent when she and Giles were making love. He was a very dexterous lover but even he couldn't manage an orgasm and an email simultaneously. At least three of the messages had been sent when Giles was actually with her, so it couldn't have been him.

Margot logged off the Country Cousins website and opened up her work in progress. She was behind again and needed to do at least three thousand words in order to catch up with her schedule. The phone rang.

"Hi beautiful."

"Giles!"

"Sorry, I was missing you, thought I would give you a quick ring. What are you doing?"

"Working. A certain person has put me all behind and I have deadlines to meet." She failed to hide the smile in her voice. "Giles, do you know anything about computers?"

"Me? Absolutely nothing, I'm a fully paid up Luddite. If you need any help ask our Gavin, or Suzie his girlfriend. They're brilliant at it. They seem to spend most of their time on the computer. Why, is there something wrong with yours?"

"No, I'll explain later when I see you. It's a bit complicated. When are you coming by the way?"

"I'll be round about six-thirty-ish. I'd like to come earlier but like you a certain person has put me all behind and I too have deadlines that I have to meet."

Margot laughed, "Oh really, like what?"

"Mother Nature is a real taskmaster and if I don't get the stock fed before it gets too dark then I'll be in trouble." Giles thought for a moment. "Actually can I make that seven please, I'd better call in and see Dad and Jean before I come down."

"Talking about feeding the wild beasts, do you want me to get you something to eat this evening?"

"That would be great." He rang off.

Margot continued working steadily and was just getting back into her stride when the phone rang again. She was tempted to leave it. The answerphone kicked in. It was Abi. Margot jumped up and lifted the receiver, pushing the 'cancel' button on the answer machine.

"Sorry Abi, I'm in the middle of working."

"I'm glad to hear it. How are things?"

"Things are looking good at the moment, thank you."

"Are we talking professional or personal?"

"Both. I received a letter this morning from the publishers; apparently my contemporary romances are selling very well, thanks to all this tabloid nonsense."

"Yes, so I hear. Have you listened to the news today?"

"No, should I?"

"Have you heard of Paul Marchant?"

"The name is vaguely familiar, isn't he a politician or something?"

"Was a politician, Mo. He's just resigned due to some scandal with him and rent boys."

"Sorry, Abi, I'm not quite following. What has this got to do with me?"

"Absolutely nothing, I hope. But he's on the front page of all the tabloids, it's the sort of story that will run and run. You, my dear, and the furore about the best sex writing award are next week's fish and chip wrapper."

"Well, whatever this politician has done I am more than grateful that he has knocked me off the front page."

By the time Margot had finished her chat with Abi she had gone off the boil with her writing. She decided to give up on it for the rest of the day. She had a meal to prepare and knew, for a fact, that she had very little food in the house. Margot walked down to the village shop. She stood outside the door, took a deep breath threw her shoulders back and marched in. Emma looked up and nodded a greeting; well that was an improvement on the previous visit.

Margot bought some bits and pieces for the evening meal and carried them over to the counter. Emma looked down pointedly at the pack with two chops in it and the double pudding pack. She pursed her lips, but said nothing.

'Let her think what she likes,' thought Margot, 'see if I care.'

Margot began preparing the meal as soon as she got back then quickly had a bath. She was halfway through drying her hair when the doorbell went. She rushed down to open it. Giles stood there with a big grin; he grabbed her around the waist and swung her around.

"You're early," she protested.

"Sorry, I missed you today and couldn't wait."

He followed her into the kitchen; on the table was a small box, wrapped in paper and with a stick-on bow. Margot picked it up and gave it to him.

"What's this?"

"A present, go on, open it."

Giles ripped open the paper and opened the box, inside was a key. He lifted it out and looked at Margot.

"It is my spare key. I want you to have it."

"Are you sure?" He looked up at her again. "You don't think that we're, er we're moving too fast?"

"Do you?"

"No. From the minute I first saw you, things just didn't move fast enough. Come here." He pulled her towards him and kissed her. They were both reluctant to pull away.

"Shall we?"

"No," Margot laughed, "dinner first. I don't want another meal ruined." She pushed him away. "Just sit down there and I'll dish up."

Margot had already opened a bottle of wine. Giles poured some into their glasses. During the meal Margot asked what his family had said about him staying over at Saddleback Cottage.

"Not a lot, none of their business really. I mean it's not as if I am a kid, is it? Bloody hell, I'm forty-three years old," he grinned. "I did warn Jean not to wait up. She seems to have something on her mind at the moment. She is very wrapped up in herself. But then she has always been like that. I was an open book compared to Jean. She seems to be worrying unnecessarily about Gavin, can't think why. The lad seems perfectly happy to me. Gavin has always been her Achilles heel. I suppose that is what comes from being a single parent. All in all I'm glad to get away."

They finished the first course. Margot moved the plates to one side and leaned forward towards him.

"Giles, I know it is actually none of my business and if you don't want to answer me just say so."

Giles leaned across the table and placed his hand over hers and gave it a squeeze. "Just ask away."

"You said that Jean was a single parent. What happened to her husband, Gavin's father, who was he?"

"Ah," Giles made the sound long and drawn out. He sipped his wine slowly, stalling for time; trying to work out what to say and how to say it.

"My sister has always been a stubborn secretive person, just like my father really. When she was twenty-four or five, she announced that she wanted to go to London to work, so she just upped sticks and left. My mum was very upset but Jean was always headstrong. Anyway a year or so later she turns up on our doorstep with a little scrap in her arms, and that was it."

"Oh my God, you mean that you didn't know – you didn't have any idea that she was pregnant even?"

"Nope, not a clue."

"What did she say about the father?"

"Nothing, absolutely nothing. She just said that it was a one night stand and that it was a big mistake. Between you and me I don't even think that she told the father that she was pregnant."

"But that is terrible. To go through that all alone, by herself in London."

"It was her choice. But it broke my mum's heart that she had done it. The only good thing to come out of it all was Gavin. My mother absolutely adored him, we all did, to be honest we still do, but don't tell him I said that."

"What about Gavin?"

"What do you mean, what about Gavin?"

"Didn't he ever ask about his father?"

"If he did, I never heard anything about it. But then he has a lot of his mother in him. He can be secretive when he wants to be. Anyway, why are you asking all these questions about Gavin?"

"Well, now don't get angry but I need to show you something. Have you heard of a website called Country Cousins? It is a sort of online dating agency for country people who don't get to meet a wide circle of friends."

"Can't say I have."

Margot sensed that Giles might not like what she was about to say. However, she ploughed on. Giles was such a computer virgin that she had to start from basics and explain all about websites and online chat rooms and social networks. He had heard of emails but had no idea how to go about sending or receiving them. Margot sighed; this was likely to be a long night. She first explained about logging on to the Country Cousin website, making it very clear to Giles that she had embarked upon this before they were an item. Margot explained how uncanny it was that in the exchange of emails Gus always seemed to say the right thing at the right time. It was almost as if he was orchestrating the way that their relationship developed.

Looking at his face, Margot realised that Giles hadn't got a clue what she was talking about.

"You go and make the coffee and I'll set up the computer. It will be easier to show you rather than explain everything."

Margot opened up the Country Cousins website and left it at the home page. Giles dragged up a chair and sat alongside her reading. She then showed him all the correspondence, particularly pointing out the date of her first one so he didn't think she had been 'two-timing' him. It took him quite a while to read through everything.

"But how do you know that this last message is different? They all look the same to me."

"When I realised that this last one wasn't quite right I reread all the others. The earlier emails had a very strong bias towards me, which makes me think they may not have been written by a man."

"But if it was written by a woman it doesn't make sense," Giles was getting more and more confused.

"I think it was written by two people. Two people who had an interest in our relationship."

Giles thought about the conversations and heart-to-heart chats he and Gavin had shared. He remembered too Suzie's encouragement when he felt everything was lost. Added to all of this some of the phrases used in the emails were familiar.

"I think I know who Gus is," he said.

CHAPTER 38

Giles couldn't decide whether he was angry or flattered by Gavin and Suzie's interference. Once the idea that it might be them had taken root Giles read the emails for a second time. Margot wanted to confront them both but Giles had a better idea. He got Margot to compose an email saying that she was desperate to meet Gus and asking him for a date. The reply, if there was one, should prove quite interesting to say the least.

Giles stayed that night with Margot. They made love twice. For a late starter Margot seemed hell-bent on catching up on what she had missed, but Giles wasn't complaining. He left early the next morning conscious that he had neglected some of his jobs. Margot also pointed out that he had been neglecting his family of late and suggested that he call in to see how they all were. She did not want to be the cause of any family rift.

Giles had finished by late afternoon and called into the farm. His father was outside moving some old bits and pieces from one of the open fronted outhouses.

"Hi Dad, thought you might need a hand."

"It's OK son, I might be old but I'm not dead yet."

Giles smiled at his father. "Where are Jean and Gavin, are they back yet?"

"Gavin's come and gone, off to see that young lady of his I don't doubt. And as for Jeanie, well she's gone to see some friend of hers. I'm not expecting her back for ages."

"It's a nice evening, Dad, how about we wash up and pop down The Quarry Man for dinner, save us getting anything."

"Jean's left a salad. I ask you, is that a proper meal for a working man?"

Giles laughed and went inside to get washed and changed. Within half an hour he and Godfrey were driving down to the pub. Suzie was not working this evening. Samantha informed them that Suzie and Gavin had gone to the cinema. The pub was not very busy and they wandered over to a corner table. It didn't take them long to order. They sat sipping at their pints whilst they waited. Giles started to reminisce about when he was an underage teenager trying to buy alcohol.

"When our Jeanie was about she used to buy me a cider, they knew it wasn't for her but provided it was only the one they usually turned a blind eye." He looked up and nodded at Samantha at the bar. "No blind eyes on our Samantha. Couldn't get away with it now. As annoying as my sister was I did miss her when she left. Did you and Mum mind her leaving the farm and moving to London?"

Godfrey sighed, "Your mother and I did miss her when she went, but you know your sister. She knows her own mind, always has done. Oh she kept in touch, although she didn't visit often. We were too busy to take time off to go to London. Then, of course, she came back with Gavin. It's not what we wanted for our daughter but, what can you say. You love 'em no matter what. To tell the truth your mother was thrilled to be a grandparent, and so was I. I was proud that Jean kept the Farmer name and followed tradition with his first name."

Giles paused; he knew he was treading on shaky ground, but he wouldn't get a better chance. "How did you and Mum feel about Jeanie being an unmarried mother?"

"What was there to feel? She was our daughter and we loved her. In my book you always stand by your family, no matter what."

"Did Jean ever say anything about Gavin's father?"

"Why are you asking all these questions? It happened years ago?"

"Oh no reason."

"She didn't want to tell us, so we didn't ask. We reckoned that when she was ready she would say."

"And was she ever ready to tell you?" Giles feigned indifference but was aware he hadn't quite carried it off.

"No, she never did but of course we had our suspicions," he looked across at Giles, "suspicions which we have never and will never share with anyone. At the end of the day it didn't matter one little bit. Gavin's a smashing lad and we love him. That's all that matters." He looked up. "Here comes our food now."

Giles knew that he would get no more information out of his father, so he settled down to enjoy his meal.

Suzie was reluctant to return to The Quarry Man. She got so few evenings off that when she did she always tried to make the most of them. She loved going to the cinema. They called into the Indian restaurant for a meal afterwards. Suzie was still a bit concerned about the email that Gavin had sent but as they hadn't heard back for a couple of days she was beginning to relax. It was all right trying to sort out Giles Farmer's love life but what about hers and Gavin's? Gavin was more than happy to take what Suzie offered him but that was as far as it went. He wasn't a bad boyfriend, just one that wasn't particularly committed. Suzie blamed his mother. Gavin's home life hadn't exactly been conventional. At least she had a dad, albeit one separated from her mother. She was always surprised at Gavin's lack of interest in knowing who his father was. She had given up asking questions; if Gavin wasn't bothered then why should she be?

They returned to Home Farm. Gavin could see that the lights were on in the kitchen and the Land Rover was in the yard. Damn he was hoping to invite Suzie back to his room. He might have sneaked her past Giles and his grandfather, but there was no way his mother would approve. Gavin grinned at Suzie.

"Sorry Suz, but they're all in. We'll have to go back to yours tonight."

"Gavin, have you ever thought about getting a place of your own?"

Gavin seemed genuinely surprised by her question. "No, what would I want with a place of my own? I am perfectly happy at Home Farm. In any case I don't exactly earn a fortune."

Before Gavin could turn the car around the kitchen door opened and the farm collie bounded out followed by Giles. Giles lifted his hand in a wave and walked slowly to the car. Gavin wound down the window.

"Hello, are you two going to sit here all night? Why don't you invite your young lady in?" Giles totally ignored the looks that Gavin was giving him.

"Why thank you, Giles, that'll be really nice," Suzie replied.

Before Gavin had time to think of an excuse Suzie was out of the car and in the farmhouse. Gavin switched off the ignition and followed them in. Giles had opened a bottle of wine and offered a glass to Suzie. They sat around the table chatting or rather Giles and Suzie were. Suzie was telling Giles all about the film that they had just seen.

"You ought to get him to take you out more often. He is a bit of a lazy sod is our Gavin. You ought to do things like proper couples."

"Proper couples? Sorry Giles, you've lost me totally." Gavin hadn't got a clue what Giles was on about.

"Well, these days people do this Internet dating thing. Don't really understand it myself. I mean surely part of any attraction is what you see. I fancied Margot the minute I clapped eyes on her. How can you fancy someone if you've never even met them?" Giles pretended not to notice the glance that went between them.

Suzie finished her drink, thanked Giles and said that she needed to be getting back home. In the car she turned to Gavin. "What was all that about? Do you think he knows anything?"

"Who Giles? Nah, it's impossible. He can't even turn a computer, on, let alone work one. No, it is just a coincidence, I'm sure of it." He paused. "Have you checked whether or not 'Gus' has had a reply?"

"I checked yesterday morning and there was nothing. Do you think that she is on to us? I said you should have left the emails to me!" They were still arguing when they arrived back at The Quarry Man. "Well there's only one way to find out, come on, let's go upstairs and check."

There were still a few stragglers in the bar and as Gavin sneaked up the backstairs, Suzie popped her head around the bar door and said to Samantha, "Gavin wants to check something on the Internet, I said he could." There was a slightly defiant edge to her voice.

"I'll be finished here in about ten minutes," Samantha said in a loud and pointed voice. "He'd better be gone by the time I've finished."

"Thanks, Mum."

When she got to her room Gavin had already switched on the computer and logged on to the Country Cousins website. He opened Gus's inbox. "Oh shit," he said as he read the message. "Oh God, Suzie, she wants to meet Gus."

Suzie leaned over his shoulder and read the message. "What are we going to do?"

"I don't know, but give me time to think." Suzie tried to quell Gavin's panic.

They sat in silence. "Email her back and say that Gus is very busy at the moment and it may not be possible." Gavin looked doubtful at this suggestion. "Look leave it to me, I'll do it later."

"Do you think it will work?"

"No, but it will stall her and give us time to think about what to do."

Samantha yelled up the stairs. "I'm nearly done here."

"You had better go. I'll try to think of something."

Gavin grabbed the car keys that he had dropped on to the desk, gave Suzie a kiss and left. His mind was racing on the short journey back to Home Farm. All he could think about was how the hell they were going to get out of this predicament. And another thing, if this Margot and Giles were as loved up as Giles's soppy grin indicated why was she arranging to see another man? He would never understand women as long as he lived. He noticed his mother's car back in the yard; she must have just got back. He pushed opened the kitchen door and saw Jean making a pot of tea. There was no sign of Giles.

"Hi son, do you want a drink? I'm just making one myself."

"No, Mum, it's OK." He sat down at the table and watched his mother pour out one for herself. "Mum, do you think that Giles is keen on this writer woman?"

"Judging by the number of nights he hasn't slept in his own bed I would say he was very keen. Why?"

"Oh no reason, I was just wondering. What about her, do you think that she is keen on him?"

"I wouldn't have a clue. Although it wouldn't surprise me if she was."

"Really? Why?"

"Well it stands to reason; she's a single woman just the wrong side of forty, and that is being kind. He's not a bad catch is my brother. Not bad looking, nice manners, generous, she could do a lot worse." Jean paused, sipping her tea thoughtfully "Yeah, it's lonely being single."

Gavin looked up sharply. He had a feeling that his mother wasn't only talking about Margot.

"Anyway how's Suzie?"

"Tired, but then she always is. She works long hours for rubbish pay. Trouble is that I work days and she works evenings, doesn't exactly make for a perfect relationship."

"Everything is all right between you though?"

"Yeah fine, Mum. You worry too much." Gavin stood up and gave Jean a hug and a kiss on the cheek. "I'm off to bed. I'm shattered and I've got an early start in the morning."

Jean watched her son walk away and sighed. He was a lovely lad and she was very proud of him. She wondered how things might have been had she stayed with his father. But it hadn't been an option then. She sighed. 'Why did life have to be so complicated?'

CHAPTER 39

Margot had now been waiting over three weeks for feedback from her editor about her new book. For the first time ever, she had not met the promised deadline, although she had only missed it by a couple of weeks. She wondered if it was their way of making a point about her tardiness; she would not have put it past them.

Margot gave herself a week off which she spent pottering around Saddleback Cottage, sorting out her garden and having very frequent sex with Giles Farmer. On the Monday following her break Margot started on her next book. She had put off starting it and now that she had she was struggling to get into the new one. She couldn't decide if it was the characters she didn't like or the setting. The letter box clattered. Margot stopped what she was doing and went into the hallway to retrieve the post. There was a letter from her editor. She recognised the heavy embossed envelope and its postmark. Margot read it twice before its meaning sunk in – they didn't like her last book, felt 'it wasn't up to her usual standard'. She didn't know whether to laugh or get angry. They wanted her to make some major changes.

When she had first started out on her writing career Margot had occasionally received letters like this. However, because she had an unerring knack of knowing what her readers wanted, for the last ten to fifteen years her books had been accepted with little or no change at all. She was really taken aback. There was nothing for it she would have to speak to her editor direct. She toyed with the idea of making them wait but decided it was childish. Margot phoned the publishers and arranged to go up and see them the following morning. She then telephoned Abi to see if she could stay with her. This needed sorting out and sorting out quickly. She was cross with herself that professionally she had been found lacking. If she was honest Margot knew that she had been neglecting work recently. Her relationship with Giles was taking up a great deal of her time. She smiled to herself, but hey it was damn well worth it.

Giles came around to see her later that evening. He told her about Gavin and Suzie's reaction to his throw away comments about online dating.

Margot smiled. "Let's keep it going for a little while longer. Let's make them sweat for a bit."

Giles was disappointed when Margot told him later that evening that she didn't want him to stay over. She had booked Leaker to pick her up at 8.15 a.m. and she didn't want to risk him finding Giles in residence so to speak. She didn't tell Giles the reason for her trip, just that she needed to speak to her publisher.

Giles wrapped his arms around Margot as she stood at the sink washing up, cupping her breasts in his big hands and nuzzling her neck. Margot leaned back into him, enjoying the pressure of his hands.

"How about we go upstairs now instead?"

Margot turned her body into his; she could feel his hardness and his hunger. The fact that he wanted her so much and made no pretence at hiding it always excited her. As she kissed him, her wet soapy hands entwined around his neck; he slid his hands down to her buttocks, pushing them hard into his groin.

"You've got such a great body," he whispered. "It's no wonder I can't keep my hands off it."

Margot laughed and pushed him away but not before she had given him a long and hard kiss. Cooking for Giles almost every night, she had put on weight, but if Giles noticed it he made no comment and she loved him even more for that. It was well past midnight when Giles, very reluctantly, returned to Home Farm. After he had gone Margot struggled to get back off to sleep. The words in her publisher's letter were going round and round in her head. Her professional pride had been severely dented by the letter and although she was a wealthy woman she still needed to earn a living from her writing.

The following morning Margot struggled to respond to the alarm clock. She looked in the mirror, she felt old and tired and what made it worse was that she looked it. She had a quick shower and put on her makeup trying to disguise the dark smudges under her eyes. By the time that Leaker arrived Margot was looking and feeling marginally better. She couldn't face breakfast so had given it a miss. Leaker carried her small suitcase down the path to the taxi.

"Going to London again?"

"Yes, I need to see my publisher."

"Oh."

Pleasantries exchanged Margot sat back in the taxi relieved that no more conversation would be required. Leaker dropped her off with a good ten minutes to spare. She waited whilst he pulled away and before she could walk into the station Giles pulled up in his Land Rover. He rushed over to her and gave her a big hug.

"Did you miss me? I missed you."

Margot laughed. "Don't be daft; you only left me," she looked at her watch, "six hours ago."

"Just wanted to say good luck."

"Good luck, but how did ..." she paused.

He smiled at her, "There's something bothering you, whatever it is it can't be that bad. It is only a job, not a matter of life and death. Just remember I'll be here waiting for you when you get back." He gave her another hug and carried her bag on to the station platform. There were several people waiting for the train so Giles just dropped the bag and with a wave he was gone.

Margot took a taxi to the publishing company and the receptionist asked her to wait in the foyer. As one of their top novelists Margot was not used to being kept waiting and it irked her, although she did her best to disguise the fact. The editor kept her waiting for almost a quarter of an hour. Margot had no interest in the magazines scattered on the table, so she sat and stared. A couple of months ago she was receiving awards, albeit ones she didn't particularly want, for her work. Now she was being kept waiting. Such was the fickleness of fame.

"Miss Denning, you can go on up now," the receptionist called across to her.

Margot walked straight into her editor's office, this time there was no sales director in attendance. Margot sat at the desk and saw that her manuscript was on the table.

"So, Jennifer, what is the problem?" Margot went for the attack.

Jennifer paused as if trying to get the right words in the right order. "To be honest, I am struggling to put my finger on it exactly. This last one" she turned the pages over to read the title, "'Moroccan Lover' lacks the er freshness and originality of your previous novel. I have to say that there is quite a marked difference in your," she paused again weighing up her words, "er your, more intimate scenes."

Margot waited; there was no way she was going to help this woman out. Let her struggle for her euphemisms. Margot just looked puzzled and waited for further explanation. She was rather enjoying Jennifer's discomfort and embarrassment.

"It is just that, well, having received an award for your sex scenes. A very well deserved award I must say. The sex in 'Moroccan Lover' seems a bit, well boring and pedestrian."

"I see," said Margot, who clearly didn't. Not that it mattered; the bottom line was that they were not going to publish the novel in its present form. "Let me have the manuscript back and see what I can do. How long do I have?"

Jennifer relieved that the interview was at an end, was prepared to be generous. "Oh whenever, I mean any time in the next month or so. I'm sure that working together we can sort something out."

Margot scooped up her manuscript and placed it inside her bag. "Thank you for your time, Jennifer, I know that it is precious. I will be in touch."

Keeping her anger in check she walked out of the office with as much dignity as she could muster but she was bloody angry. She caught the tube into Covent Garden and found a coffee shop. She ordered a hot chocolate and a doughnut, her lack of breakfast had made her ravenous. She started to flick through the script. Part way through she realised what the problem was. Pre-Giles love scenes were written from her imagination, post Giles they were written from her experiences. Even she had to admit her writing had changed. Margot disagreed with her editor; this novel was not any worse than her previous ones, but it was different and in her opinion actually better written.

Margot wasted the rest of the day pottering around town. Since she had moved to Middle Chippings, London no longer held her as it once did. Margot had a spare key to Abi's flat and although she was quite happy to let herself in she preferred to wait until Abi was back from work. Shopping in Oxford Street filled her afternoon quite happily. Coffee in one of the large department stores restored her equilibrium. She arrived at the flat minutes after Abi. There was a smell of food cooking, or in Abi's case, food being reheated. Abi walked into the hallway to give her friend a hug.

"Oh Mo, it is so good to see you. How did you get on today, no don't tell me yet, tell me over dinner. Go unpack then mix us both a drink." Her orders issued, Abi retreated to the kitchen. Margot dumped her bag in the spare room and prepared a couple of gin and tonics. She had never been keen on gin so made herself a very weak one and a stronger one for Abi. She carried the drinks into the kitchen.

"Oh great, I needed that," Abi took a gulp from the drink. "Two minutes and we can sit and eat, and then you can tell me all about your visit."

Over dinner Abi listened carefully as Margot recounted her interview with Jennifer. They ate and worked their way through the bottle of red wine that Margot had picked up from the off-licence down the road.

"Well it stands to reason that the books you wrote what five, ten years ago are likely to be different from what you are writing now. Life experiences are bound to have an effect on how and what you write."

"Sorry Abi, you've totally lost me."

"Oh come on, Margot, you can't tell me that making love to the lusty farmer every night doesn't make you look at things in a totally different way."

"Abi!" Margot blushed.

"Well it's true, isn't it?"

Margot sipped her wine before replying with a smile, "Well perhaps not every night."

The following morning both girls felt decidedly worse for wear. When they saw the empty bottles stacked on the draining board they realised why. Abi left for work with a promise to come and visit Margot at Saddleback Cottage. Margot was eager to get back and decided to catch the early train. Just as she was leaving a cramping pain in her stomach pulled her up short. She realised that her period had started. "Damn and blast," she thought. They had been sporadic over the past year or so. She knew from her doctor that she was pre-menopausal. She would have to change. Margot looked at her watch, not enough time to catch the early train. She would wait for the next one.

On the train journey down Margot resumed reading her manuscript. Yes, the novel was slightly different to her previous offerings but basically it was a good sound story. Margot thought about something that Abi had said the night before. In her job it paid for Abi to keep in touch with trends. She had suggested that perhaps it had been the choice of publisher that had been wrong rather than the novel itself. The more that Margot thought about this the more she thought that Abi might be on to something. This was the final book in a three book contract that she had signed four years ago. Perhaps now was the time to move on. In the meantime she would have to grit her teeth and just make the changes that her editor had requested.

When she arrived back at the station Margot was surprised to see Danny Bragg get off the train; he had been sitting in a seat a few carriages up.

"Hello Margot? Business trip or pleasure?"

"Business, Danny, although I did catch up with an old friend, and you?"

"Not quite sure what you would call it, probably family business would be the best description." They walked through the station and out into the car park. "Do you need a lift back Margot? I've got my car here."

Margot glanced around quickly, no sign of any taxis. "Yes, that would be really nice, thank you very much."

As they drove out of the car park Margot failed to notice the battered red car with the young man sitting in it. Giles was busy so Gavin had offered to come and pick Margot up from the station. He did not like what he was seeing. If you included Gus the bloody woman had three men on the go. He waited for a few minutes before driving back to the farm, trying to work out what he would say to Giles.

CHAPTER 40

The date for the vet's visit for the animal testing had been booked for ages. As much as he would have liked to meet Margot from the train Giles knew that he couldn't. Gavin was at a loose end so he decided to send him instead. Gavin was back sooner than he had expected.

"Did you pick her up OK?"

"Er no, she seemed to be travelling with someone and er he gave her a lift."

"He?" Giles feigned indifference. "Anyone we know?" Giles kept his eyes lowered studying the clipboard on which he was writing.

"That Bragg bloke, you know the builder."

"Oh so no one important then," Giles tried to make a joke of it. "Anyway can't stand around chatting; this vet is costing me money."

Giles kept busy and didn't allow himself to dwell on Gavin's news. Margot had not said anything about going to London with anyone. She had been alone when he saw her off. He decided not say anything; he would wait for her to tell him. Giles ate at home that evening and didn't wander down to Saddleback Cottage until quite late. He let himself in and walked into the lounge. Margot was asleep on the settee, the manuscript by her side. He bent down and kissed her.

"Wakey wakey, sleeping beauty."

Margot opened her eyes, clasped her hands around the back of Giles's neck and pulled him back down towards her. She gave him a long kiss, holding him tightly.

"Mm, I needed that."

"You were fast asleep when I came in."

Margot yawned, "Sorry, late night last night, I'm shattered."

Giles moved the manuscript and sat beside her. "Too much to drink?"

"I think I might have," she smiled. "To be honest I can't really remember. We had a girly night in. Abi and I had a lot of catching up to do."

"So it was just you and Abi and you didn't happen to bump into anyone else?"

"No. Should I have done?" Margot sat up. "Why all of these questions?"

"Gavin came to meet you today from the station."

"Oh," she waited.

"I sent him because I thought you might need a lift. He said that you had something already organised, so he came back home."

"Already organised? And what is that supposed to mean?" Margot sat up. She did not like Giles's tone one little bit.

"I don't know, you tell me."

"There is nothing to tell."

The conversation was going in a direction that neither of them had planned.

Margot knew what it was all about – Danny Bragg, though neither of them mentioned his name. "Giles, either you trust me, in which case we have a relationship, or you don't in which case we might as well call it a day now."

Giles had been stewing all afternoon since Gavin's return. He had to do something before the situation escalated. He stood up.

"Excuse me a moment."

Giles walked out of the front door and closed it behind him. He waited outside for about ten seconds before putting his key in the lock again. Margot had not moved.

"Hi beautiful. Did you have a good time in London?" He leaned forward and kissed her. "I really missed you."

Despite herself Margot laughed. "What on earth are you doing"?

"Starting again, I thought it would be a good idea to rewind the last few minutes."

Margot shook her head and smiled.

She went into the kitchen and got a beer out of the fridge and a soft drink for herself, the hangover hadn't quite disappeared. They sat on the sofa and Margot told Giles all about the editor's meeting and her very boozy evening with Abi. At no point did she mention Danny Bragg. Although desperate to ask about him Giles kept quiet. He'd overstepped the mark once and only just got away with it. He stayed over that night but they did not make love, Margot was asleep before he had finished in the bathroom. Giles lay wide awake beside her. He recognised the knot in his stomach as jealousy and was not proud that he had let it get to him.

Giles was up and out the door early the next morning. Before he left he made a cup of tea and took it up to Margot. She sat up still half asleep, taking the tea from him.

"Got to go."

Margot called him back. "Giles, I met Danny Bragg on the platform as he got off the train. He was as surprised to see me as I was to see him. We weren't even in the same carriage. It was pure coincidence. He said he had been to London on family business. He offered me a lift home, no more, no less. That's all there was to it."

Giles nodded and turned. The knot in his stomach loosened.

"See you later?"

Margot smiled and sipped her tea and heard the front door bang shut.

After a busy morning Giles went back to Home Farm for lunch. Godfrey was already sitting at the table eating a sandwich that Jean had prepared and left for him.

"Did she leave me anything?"

"Was she expecting you back for lunch?"

"Probably not." He opened the bread bin and proceeded to make his own. Godfrey watched him without comment.

"Fallen out with her have you?"

"No, everything is fine. And 'she' has a name. I wish you would use it, Dad."

"Fallen out with Margot have you?" he repeated. Giles didn't like the way Godfrey said her name.

"Do you have a problem with Margot, Dad? Because if you do, you had better get over it. She is the one I have chosen and you will have to like it or lump it!"

"Sorry I spoke," mumbled Godfrey. He took another bite from his sandwich.

265

Gavin had opted to nip over to The Quarry Man for his lunch, not in the bar but upstairs with Suzie. He quietly entered through the back door and then up the stairs into Suzie's room.

"Hi babe," he stopped in his tracks taking in Suzie's red swollen eyes and the opened envelopes on her bed. "What's up?"

"I have just had the biggest row ever with my Mum."

"Oh, it wasn't about me was it?"

"Gavin, my life does not revolve around you, even if you think it does."

"Sorry, sorry I spoke." He took a deep breath. "Right, what was it about?"

"University?"

"What about university?"

"Mum was cleaning my room and found these unopened letters about me going in September. I should have returned my forms ages ago."

"Suzie, why didn't you?"

The tears that she had just stemmed threatened to overwhelm her again.

"Because I am not sure it is what I want anymore."

"But why, you've worked so hard to get there?"

She shrugged her shoulders.

They heard footsteps coming up the stairs. Gavin instinctively stood close to Suzie. Samantha came in.

"Oh it's you." There was no mistaking the contempt in her voice. "I suppose she's told you she's not going to university. I bet this is your doing."

"It's nothing to do with Gavin. I told you. I'm just not sure that it is what I want anymore."

Sensing an ally Samantha turned to Gavin. "What is there for you here in bloody Middle Chippings? Don't you think she ought to go?"

Gavin slipped his arm around Suzie's back. "I think that Suzie has to make up her own mind. Whatever she decides I will support her." He always felt intimated in Samantha's presence.

Samantha turned to Suzie again. "I've just had a booking for a large party. I need you downstairs, in the kitchen. In case you've forgotten money doesn't grow on trees. Without a good education you'll need to earn every penny you can." She stormed out.

Gavin pulled Suzie towards him. "Don't worry, she'll calm down eventually."

Suzie's face was muffled against Gavin's chest. "You had better go; I don't think that you are one of her favourite people at the moment."

The row had unnerved Gavin. He returned to Home Farm upset and hungry. He pushed open the back door to find his uncle and his grandfather sitting at the table eating sandwiches.

"Any for me?"

"I thought you were having lunch at The Quarry Man," Giles mumbled between mouthfuls.

"Well so did I but, well let's just say things are a bit dodgy there at the moment."

"Not you as well?" Godfrey looked from his son to his grandson. "In thirty odd years of marriage your mother and I never had a cross word, God you two can't even manage it before you're married."

"Who said anything about being married?" Gavin asked, cutting himself a large slice of bread.

"Sorry I spoke," Godfrey mumbled to no one in particular.

They finished their lunch in silence, Gavin and Giles deep in thought. "We'll leave the washing up to you, Dad," Giles said. "Gavin and I need to go and finish sorting out the lower paddock."

They left the house and both climbed up into the tractor. For the first few minutes neither of them spoke.

"Did you sort it out with her?"

"Yes. She said she met Danny Bragg getting off the train, end of story."

"Oh." Gavin couldn't think what else to say. They had looked pretty friendly to him. But if that is what she said and what Giles wanted to believe, then who was he to say otherwise?

"What about you? Why didn't you have your lunch at The Quarry Man"?

"Suzie and Sam had just had a big row and then I got caught in Suzie's room," he trailed off. "Anyway I thought I'd better beat a hasty retreat."

"Good move, I wouldn't take Sam Savage on when she's in a good mood let alone when she is in a bad." Giles paused to negotiate a tight turn, "But you and Suzie, you're all right, are you?"

"Yeah, I think so. I thought that something had been worrying her these past couple of weeks. She has been a bit ratty and on edge. Apparently Sam found a couple of unopened letters from universities in Suzie's room. Mind you what she was doing snooping around her room in the first place I don't know. Anyway, Suzie said she's not sure that she wants to go away to university after all and Samantha just exploded."

"So the decision was nothing to do with you then?"

"Suzie never even mentioned about changing her mind about going to uni. The first I knew was when Sam went for me at lunchtime."

"Well you can't blame Sam. She's brought that girl up virtually single-handed since her husband walked out. Sam wants something better for her only daughter. Running a pub is damn hard work and I can understand why she wants Suzie to go to university to get on. Only a mad person would want their child following in the family business." He paused realising what he had just said. He looked at Gavin and they both burst out laughing.

They finished in the lower paddock just as it was getting dark and returned to Home Farm. Gavin was in no hurry to get back but Giles was. He was going to see Margot tonight. She had warned him that she would need to be up early the next morning. She had planned a day in town shopping. Margot had been to London only a few days ago and here she was arranging a trip to Exeter. She was still very put out about the novel being rejected. Margot's answer to feeling down was always a little bit of retail therapy.

Gavin didn't seem in a rush to go to The Quarry Man that evening. He probably didn't want to run into Suzie's mother until she had calmed down. On that point Giles was with Gavin all the way, Samantha Savage could be a pretty scary lady. If she thought that Gavin was influencing Suzie not to go on to university there would be hell to pay.

CHAPTER 41

Margot waited until she heard Giles leave the house. They had made love the night before to make up for the evening when they had argued. She had told Giles that she was spending a day shopping, which was partly true.

As soon as she heard the front door slam she was up and in the shower. Margot had booked Leaker for nine forty-five. He was on the dot at nine-thirty.

"Where to today?" She had told him when she had booked but repeated it.

"Exeter, like I said last night when I phoned you."

"Exeter, London, it's all the same, full of busy city types who haven't time to pass wind let alone pass the time of day with other folk."

'And who don't keep asking personal questions all the time,' Margot thought. She knew that it was a bit of an extravagance going by taxi, although Leaker had given her a 'special deal' of a day rate, or so he said. He implied that the special price was a favour to her – as one of his best regular customers. Margot happened to know she was his only regular customer. She may have only lived in Middle Chippings for a short while but she had already picked up on the fact that Leaker never did anyone any favours. She suspected that he had another booking in Exeter but she didn't really care.

As they drove out of Middle Chippings Margot saw a lone figure waiting at the bus stop. It was the young girl from the pub, the one who was going out with Giles's nephew.

"Waiting for the Exeter bus, I don't wonder," Leaker commented.

Margot tapped him on the shoulder.

"Turn around; we can give her a lift."

Leaker reversed back down the road, pulling up at the bus stop. Margot jumped out.

"Hello, it's Susan, isn't it?"

The girl looked up surprised. "Yeah but everyone calls me Suzie."

"I'm going to Exeter and Leaker seems to think that you might be waiting for the Exeter bus. I wondered if you would like to share my taxi."

The girl seemed unsure how to respond. "Er, well, it's kind of you but er I've only got the return bus fare."

Margot gave a slightly embarrassed laugh. "Oh, no, I don't mean for you to pay. No, it would be nice to have some company. I've already paid Mr Quick so it doesn't really make a difference how many of us there are."

"'Cept I'm only licensed to carry four," Leaker mumbled.

Suzie hesitated momentarily. "Oh OK, the bus will be ages anyway, thank you."

Suzie climbed into the back of the taxi. They chatted, or rather Margot talked whilst Suzie made the very occasional comment. The girl seemed a bit withdrawn and ill at ease. Leaker dropped them off in the town centre.

"Meet you back here at five, is that OK?" Leaker asked.

"Yes, that is fine," Margot turned to Suzie. "You're most welcome to come back with us if you would like to."

"Thanks, I'm not sure how long I'll be."

"Well we'll be leaving here at five o'clock if you want to join us."

Leaker drove away and Margot and Suzie walked towards the main high street. They stopped at the first crossroads. Suzie turned and smiled at Margot. "Sorry, you must have thought me really rude. I am grateful for the lift. Must rush, got a lot to do."

Margot wandered along to one of the large bookshops and found the romantic fiction section. She looked along the rows and could only find three of her books. She surreptitiously pulled them out from the serried ranks and left one on a large table that was advertising current promotions. She wondered if she ought to speak to the manager to see if they would like her to sign some copies. Some bookshops were quite keen to stock 'local' authors but then she decided against it. She spent a while browsing, checking the opposition. Margot liked to do a bit of market research. The shop was quite stuffy and Margot could feel a headache just beginning to build up. She opened her bag and rummaged for an aspirin. She didn't have any. She left the bookshop and found a large chemists a few doors down.

Margot grabbed a wire basket and wandered around the chemists spending ages at the makeup counter trying to decide whether or not to buy a cream that would 'stop the ageing process' and make her young again. 'Yeah right,' she thought and replaced it. She picked up a couple of other things, including her aspirin and looked around for the checkout. She could see the sign for it. It was behind a stand selling surgical appliances. As Margot walked around the display she literally bumped into someone, knocking their purchases from their hand. It was Suzie.

"Oh I'm really sorry, let me," Margot bent down at the same time as Suzie.

"No, it's all right really, no please don't."

Margot picked up the small box that she had knocked out of Suzie's hand. It was a pregnancy testing kit. She handed it back to Suzie.

"I'm so sorry. I didn't know." She looked up and could see Suzie trying very hard not to cry.

"Please, please don't say anything or tell anyone."

Margot made a decision and lifted the magazine that she had placed in her basket to reveal an identical pack.

"Snap."

"You too? But you're er what I mean is…"

"That I'm too old to get caught?"

"Sorry, I didn't mean to say that."

"You thought it, so why not say it." Margot's tone had been sharper than she intended. Suzie's tears were threatening again.

"Look I think that we need to sit down, perhaps have some lunch somewhere. Let's pay for these things and find a place where we can talk."

They waited in the checkout queue in silence. In a side street not far from the cathedral was a nice little restaurant that Margot had discovered on a previous visit. There were lots of spare tables but Margot asked for one at the back. Neither of them wanted to sit near the window. The waiter brought over the menus. Suzie looked at the prices.

271

"Lunch is on me. Don't worry, I can afford it. Have whatever you want." Neither of them spoke until after the waiter had taken their order.

"Have you told Giles?" Suzie asked the first question.

"Told him what? I don't even know if I am. I have missed a couple of periods but then at my age it could be the start of the menopause I really can't be sure," Margot yawned. "But I have been feeling so lousy this past week that, to be honest, if I'm not pregnant there must be something else wrong with me."

"How far gone do you think you are?" Suzie asked in a whisper.

"I don't really know, but I think probably about two and a half months," Margot was beginning to suspect that it had happened the night she lost her virginity. They had both been so carried away by the moment that contraception had been the last thing on their minds. After that first time, they had taken precautions.

"What about you? Does Gavin know?"

"No, he hasn't got a clue, but I am dead worried that my mum suspects something. She will kill me when she finds out. No, on second thoughts she will kill Gavin first, and then kill me afterwards."

"Surely not, she'll understand and support you, won't she? Anyway, I thought you young girls went straight on to the pill." Margot hesitated. "I'm sorry that was very rude of me. It is none of my business."

"I am, but a few weeks ago I had a really bad bout of sickness. I threw up so much, I reckon I lost nearly half a stone. When I read the leaflet, after I missed my next period, it warned that in cases of severe diarrhoea and vomiting other precautions should be taken." Suzie sniffed and started to sob quietly. "Mum got pregnant with me when she was my age. She had plans for a career and everything. Instead of which she ends up as a single parent working all hours she can just to make ends meet. She wanted something better for me and here I am, history repeating itself."

Margot covered Suzie's hand with hers and squeezed it. Her sobbing was beginning to attract attention.

"Sh, sh, don't worry we'll think of something." The waiter walked towards them, an anxious look on his face. With an imperceptible shake of her head Margot waved him away.

"Right, let's be practical, shall we? At the moment we both only suspect we are er," she was reluctant to say the word.

"Up the duff?"

Margot laughed, "Well I wasn't going to put it quite like that."

Suzie grinned back. "Sorry, saying the first thing that comes into my head has always been a problem with me."

"Mine is always that I think very carefully and analyse every word before I utter it. I'm not sure which of the two is worse. People think that I am stuffy and boring and…"

"No, you're not, you're really nice," Suzie sighed. "This has been eating away at me for the last couple of weeks. I haven't been able to talk to anyone about it."

"Me too."

"I mean it's not as if we could go down to the village shop and buy a pregnancy testing kit is it?"

Margot laughed, "Do they sell them?"

"No, but I bet they could order you one if you asked."

"And how long would it be before the whole village knew do you reckon? A day, a week?"

"Half a day tops."

Their food arrived, the waiter smiled pleased that whatever had upset the young lady seemed to have passed.

"I'm so hungry, I feel so sick in the morning that I can't eat a thing until later in the day."

Suzie nodded in agreement. "I don't feel sick as much as that I am just totally exhausted. I go to bed tired and I wake up even more shattered."

"Giles tells me that your mum wants you to go to university. How do you feel about it?"

"It's funny, I was really keen on going originally but I don't want to get into too much debt so thought I'd take some time out to earn a bit of money. Meeting Gavin has made me question whether I want to move away." She took a tissue out of her pocket and blew her nose. "Course none of it matters now. The decision's probably been made for me. But now because it looks like I may not be able to go I am desperate to take up my place. It is really weird. What about you?" Suzie looked around to make sure no one was listening and she lowered her voice. "Would it be so terrible if you were er?"

"Do you know, I honestly don't know how I feel at the moment, apart from being numb. I am forty-three years old, I have a very fulfilling career and, to be truthful I never thought something like this would happen to me. Giles and I have only been together for a few months and it's still early days."

They both fell silent, the waiter took it as a signal and came up to clear their plates away.

"Can I get you the dessert menu, ladies?"

"Yes please," Margot answered for both of them. She looked up at Suzie who was beginning to cry again.

"Sorry, don't you want a pudding, you don't have to have one if you don't want to?"

"No, it is not that it's…" she didn't get the chance to finish as the waiter returned with the menus.

"Two large ice cream sundaes, please," Margot ordered for both of them.

The waiter glanced at the young girl and swiftly moved away.

"What is it, what's wrong, Suzie?"

"It is something bad that I, I mean we, me and Gavin have done and have been doing."

"Oh you mean Gus. Don't give him a second thought."

"You knew?"

"Well yes, but not straight away. It took a while for the penny to drop."

"When did you realise?"

"The last couple of messages, particularly the last one, the tone was different somehow."

"Bloody Gavin," she looked up. "I told him that you would guess."

"But why did you do it?"

"Gavin absolutely adores his uncle. He hasn't got a clue who his real Dad is and Giles has always been there for him. When you and he met it was obvious to someone with even half a brain that Giles had fallen madly in love with you."

"Really?" Margot was genuinely surprised.

"Which is why," Suzie paused unsure whether to step over a line or not. "Which is why Gavin got so upset when he thought you were seeing that builder bloke Danny Bragg. He couldn't bear for Giles to get hurt."

"Appearances can be deceiving you know. I had literally bumped into Danny as I got off the train. I don't know what the Farmer family have against Danny Bragg. All I know is that he has been a good friend to me and I am very loyal to my friends."

The dessert arrived and they both tucked in. Halfway down Margot gave up but the younger girl managed to finish hers. Margot looked at her watch; it was well past three o'clock. She looked around; they were the only customers still there.

"I think they want us to leave," Margot looked up and made a signing motion at the waiter who brought the bill over. Margot handed over her credit card. "What do you want to do now? We've got a couple of hours before we get picked up. Unless you wanted to go shopping on your own?"

"No, to be honest I only came for the kit. Part of me wants to get back as quickly as I can find out. But another part of me wants to put it off for as long as possible."

"I know how you feel. My heart isn't in shopping really. How about we go together? We could find somewhere to stop for afternoon tea."

"OK, but if we do, it is my treat."

"It's a deal."

The two of them wandered through the town window shopping. They walked past a shop selling beautiful baby clothes but didn't linger. At four thirty they found a little tea shop near to the pick up point. Margot let Suzie order the tea; she declined a piece of cake.

"When are you going to do it?" Suzie came straight to the point.

"Tonight I suppose, what about you?"

"Well, it is difficult. Privacy at The Quarry Man is a rare commodity and I'm not sure I want to face everyone straight away. Once I know I'll need a bit of space to get my head around it."

"You could always come back to Saddleback Cottage to do it. To be honest I'm not exactly looking forward to doing the test. We could do them together as soon as we got back."

They finished their tea and Suzie excused herself to go outside and use her mobile phone. She returned minutes later, just in time to prevent Margot paying the bill.

"I said that it was my treat. If we're going to be friends you are going to have to accept that I like to pay my own way."

"Sorry." Margot backed off not wanting to offend the young girl. "Was your mum OK about you coming back with me?"

"Yeah, I said that you had given me a lift and that we had ended up shopping together and that you had invited me for tea."

They walked around the corner to find Leaker waiting for them, parked on a yellow line, his engine running. They climbed into the back of the taxi. He noticed their lack of shopping bags.

"I thought you were having a shopping spree? A bag each don't look like much of a spree to me."

"Oh don't worry, Mr Quick, we've got the essentials and that is what matters." Suzie answered for the both of them.

They didn't chat much on the journey back; they had said almost everything to each other that needed saying. Leaker dropped them both off at Saddleback Cottage.

"Do want a cup of tea first? It might help er…"

"Do you know, Margot, I've spent all day dying to go to the toilet, but now, when I need to produce something, I don't want to go."

They had a cup of tea, sitting opposite each other at the kitchen table. The light atmosphere of earlier had now gone.

"Right, me first," Margot went up to the bathroom, opened the packet carefully and read the instructions. It would take four minutes. She did the test and left it on the window sill. She hurried out. "Your turn now, but be quick."

Suzie ripped open her pack and rushed into the bathroom. When she had completed the task she placed the wand next to Margot's.

She shut the door and went downstairs. Margot was stood poised by the cooker. She set the timer to five minutes.

"This calls for champagne. Whatever the outcome, the situation calls for champagne. You get the glasses, they're in the top cupboard, I'll open the bottle."

"I can never get those bottles opened, even when I'm working behind the bar I have to get someone else to do it." Suzie faced Margot, a glass in each hand.

"Practise, dear. Years of being single and having no one to do it for you makes you very adept."

Margot turned the wire then expertly flicked the stopper; there was a bang as the cork flew out and it hit the wall. She quickly filled two champagne flutes and handed one to Suzie.

"To us."

"To us," echoed Suzie. They both took a long sip and before they had lowered their glasses, the cooker buzzer was sounding. They looked at each other and carrying their glasses they climbed up the stairs. They went into the bathroom together and looked at the window sill. One indicator was blank but on the other was a very distinct blue line.

Chapter 42

Gavin was not in a good mood – Suzie had cancelled their evening together.

"For goodness sake, can't you go out with one of your mates or something?" Jean said to her son.

"Nah, don't want to." Gavin's relationship with Suzie had become so exclusive that he had neglected his friends who had drifted away. Either that or they were into relationships themselves and not free. Come to think of it the only male friend he had been out drinking with of late had been Giles.

"What about you, are you going out with your er friend tonight?"

Giles turned to his sister and repeated what he had said to his father. "Her name is Margot and she is more than just a friend. The sooner members of this family accept this fact the better it will be."

Giles stormed out of the kitchen slamming the door behind him.

"Sorry I spoke," Jean yelled at the door.

Gavin felt obliged to stick up for Margot, even though he barely knew her.

"He's right, you know, Mum. I don't think you all realise how much this Margot means to him. I mean, he spends virtually every night at her place and take it from me, when he's not with her he's either thinking about her or talking about her. I think you and Grandad better get used to the idea that she could become a permanent fixture."

Jean kept her own counsel. It was her who had told Giles where to find Margot when she had gone to ground. Despite Giles's insistent questioning, however, she would not tell him how she knew that Margot was staying at Danny Bragg's place. Jean knew Danny of old. She would not trust him an inch and she was none too sure about Margot either. Rumour had it that it was Danny doing the pushing for an enquiry as to how, why and who had instigated the listing in the first place. But why would he continue it, particularly when the conversion had been cancelled? Giles assured everyone that Margot had stopped the application as soon as she realised that it could cause problems for Godfrey. Withdrawing the building application would not necessarily stop people prying into the whys and wherefores of the situation. If an enquiry did go ahead Godfrey could be in big trouble.

Having slammed out of Home Farm Giles arrived at Saddleback Cottage earlier than he had arranged. As was his habit he range the bell twice before letting himself in and shouting as he went.

"Hi it's me!"

"Won't be a moment, I'm upstairs in the bathroom."

Giles automatically wandered into the kitchen, the first thing he saw was the champagne bottle, about a third full and two unwashed champagne flutes on the kitchen table. He took a deep breath; he would not jump to conclusions. Giles put on the kettle and got a couple of mugs out of the cupboard. He was now comfortably familiar with her kitchen.

"Hi Giles."

Giles turned and the first thing that he registered was that she had been crying.

"Margot, whatever..." he didn't finish but just opened his arms. "Come here, what's wrong?" He held her tightly as she sobbed quietly into his chest. He let her cry for a few minutes before he held her away.

"Come on, whatever it is, it can't be that bad."

"No, it isn't, in fact," she took a deep breath. She and Suzie had made a pact not to reveal the results until they'd both had time to come to terms with them. Margot hugged Giles. "I'm just exhausted after a day's shopping and a bit emotional about the run-in with the publishers. You've caught me at a bad moment. But on the plus side, I've made a really good friend today."

Giles looked pointedly at the two glasses. "So I see."

"Now, it's not what you think. Go on, grab yourself a glass and help me finish the bottle."

Whatever it was that had upset her, Giles had the distinct feeling that he wouldn't get to the bottom of it this evening,

Giles had picked up very early on in their relationship that Margot would always share things with him but only when she was ready. Whatever it was that had caused the tears he wasn't about to find out at this precise moment. He got out a clean glass and Margot poured the frothing champagne into it. She emptied the bottle by topping up her own glass.

"I met Suzie from the pub; I gave her a lift into Exeter. We kept bumping into each other and ended up having lunch together. She came back in the taxi with me and I invited her in for a drink. She is such a nice girl. She was telling me all about her dilemma about whether or not to go to university."

"Yeah, she is a lovely girl. Our Gavin is more than just a little bit fond of her. Her mother won't be happy if she ducks out of going off to university and stays in Middle Chippings instead."

"Well, who knows? Now are we eating in or out tonight?" They compromised and Giles phoned a take away order through. He left ten minutes later to pick it up. Whilst he was gone Margot laid the table and made herself a cup of tea. She tried to calm herself down. She had been close to telling him everything.

By the time that Giles returned Margot was much more herself than she had been earlier. When the meal was over and they were clearing away, Giles said:

"I've got something to show you."

He went into the hallway and took a photograph frame out of his jacket pocket. He passed it to Margot and waited for her response. She had a really good look at it.

"What do you think?"

"But where did you get it? This is the picture from Danny Bragg's hallway."

It was the reaction he had half expected. "Look again."

Margot stared at the photograph a little while longer.

"The little boy is the same I think but the two adults are different."

"It is a different picture all together, although both of them were taken in front of Saddleback Cottage. Look," he leaned over her and pointed out the house behind the trio of people in the photograph."

"I'm sorry, I am totally confused now. Who are these people?"

"The people are my parents. See my Dad hasn't changed that much, in fact I think he still wears that old waistcoat."

"Well who is the little boy?"

Giles paused unsure whether or not to share his suspicions with Margot. Damn it he was sharing everything else with her.

"That is Gavin."

"Gavin, but he looks just like…" Margot didn't finish, the realisation of what she was about to say suddenly hit her. "He looks just like Danny as a little boy."

"Yeah, I know, I spotted the likeness the first time I saw the photograph in Danny's hallway." Giles took the photograph back and led Margot into the sitting room. "Jean is five years older than me and when you're a teenager that always seems such a big gap. Jeanie was just my big sister. Believe it or not she was a very popular and attractive young woman." Giles saw the look of surprise on Margot's face. "Yes, looking at her now I know that it is difficult to imagine but she was a real party girl in her time was our Jean. She was always falling in and out of love. As I said before one day she just upped and left, said she wanted to live in the city. She met someone, got married and had Gavin within the space of a year. Her husband Bill was a nice enough man but no match for my sister. To be honest no one was surprised when they split up. Bill showed no interest in his son whatsoever after the split and when Gavin was five Jean announced that, with her ex-husband's agreement, Gavin's surname would revert to ours. No one around here made any comment. They just assumed that it was something to do with Jean wanting Gavin to inherit the family farm eventually. I mean it is not as if I'm likely to have children now is it?" He looked up at Margot but her head was down and she was deeply engrossed in the photograph.

"Have you spoken to Jean about this?"

"I've not spoken to anyone. All I had was my suspicions, especially after I saw the photograph at Danny's. You add that to the fact that Jean won't even have his name mentioned in the house well…" he trailed off.

"What are you going to do?"

"There is nothing to do, really. It is up to Jean."

"Do you think Gavin knows?"

"No, I don't think so, but I can't be sure. I think that my mother suspected that Jean's first husband wasn't Gavin's father."

"What about Danny, do you think he knows?"

"Again, I haven't a clue but he's not stupid, even he can count up to nine months. Jean was really angry when she found out Danny had bought a big house just outside the village."

"I must admit that when I stayed with him he was asking me all sorts of questions about your family. Come to think of it, he was asking about Gavin quite a bit."

Giles ran his hands through his hair. "Let's go to bed, this thing has been going around and around in my head. To be honest it is a relief to be able to talk to someone about it, although you must promise not to breathe a word to anyone."

"Of course I won't." This was the second secret she had been asked to keep today.

"Not that it is anyone else's business but ours," Giles added.

As they climbed the stairs to go to bed the thought went through Margot's mind. She could think of a certain young lady who might be interested in Gavin Farmer's true parentage, but she said nothing.

CHAPTER 43

Giles had wanted to make love to her last night. All Margot had
wanted was to be held. She knew that Giles had been
disappointed. Instead they had set the alarm for half an hour
earlier so that they could make love before he went to work.
After Giles had gone, she lay in bed, naked and relaxed. She ran
her hands over her stomach, it was slightly rounded, but then it
always had been. Her huge disappointment at not being pregnant
had surprised her. Margot had never consciously wanted a child;
she was one of the least maternal people she knew. She
wondered how Suzie was faring and whether or not she had told
Gavin or her mother about being pregnant.

Margot finally got up to have a shower and settled down to
work. She wasn't even a third of the way through the new novel
but knew that she probably wouldn't finish it. Her heart wasn't
in this book. She could not pinpoint why, but she felt very little
empathy for her characters. If she felt nothing for them then how
could she expect her readers to? The doorbell went: a welcome
distraction. Margot opened the door. She wasn't expecting
anyone, especially not the person standing there.

"Jean. What a surprise. Come in please."

Margot opened the door wide. "Go on into the kitchen, it's
through there."

"I know where the kitchen is. My family have lived in this
cottage a fair few years."

"Yes of course, how silly of me." Margot was flustered.
Jean had a habit of wrong-footing her. "Can I get you a cup of
tea?"

"Yes that would be nice, thank you. I'm not stopping you
from work am I?"

"Well, I was about to have a break anyway and to be
honest, it's not going brilliantly."

"I've read some of your books, I enjoyed them. You're
really quite good."

Margot wished Jean had not sounded so surprised, but she was flattered by the praise. She busied herself making the tea. Jean pulled out a chair and sat down. Neither of them spoke again until the tea had been poured out.

"I er expect you're wondering why I'm here." She paused waiting for a reply which didn't come. "It's about Gavin, my son."

"Oh." Margot held her breath. She was holding so many secrets about this woman's son that she dared not say anything.

"It's Gavin's birthday on Saturday."

Margot's, "Oh," held a different tone this time and if Jean noticed she did not comment on it.

"I thought that we would have a family party, at The Quarry Man, I've booked a table. I wondered if you would like to come. If you are to be part of this family perhaps you had better get to know us, warts and all."

"Thank you. I would love to come." She could not resist asking, "Er who else will be there?"

"My dad, Giles of course and Suzie Savage, Gavin's girlfriend. Well she is at the moment. I think that they've had some sort of a fall out but I daresay that by the weekend it will all be sorted out one way or another."

"I've met her; she seems like a lovely girl."

"She is OK, but she will probably break my Gavin's heart. According to her mother Suzie's planning to go away to university."

Margot didn't know what to say. "Well people's plans change."

"I also have another reason for coming to see you." Jean bent down, opened her handbag and pulled out a letter. She placed it on the table. Margot could see that it was addressed to Mr Godfrey Farmer. "Do you know anything about this?"

Margot looked up. "What is it?"

"It is a letter from the District Council about the piggery and its listed building status. They want to ask my father some questions about who registered it and for what reason."

"Well it has nothing to do with me I can assure you. I withdrew my planning application several weeks ago. If anyone is pushing this issue I have to say that it is probably Danny Bragg."

"But why, what is it to do with him? It's your house."

"Well yes, it is now, but if I sell it in the future I have made an agreement with Mr Bragg that he will get first refusal."

Jean looked at Margot angrily. "When I asked you to give me first refusal you turned me down. Why him and not me?"

"I'm sorry, that's my business." Margot was not prepared to go any further. Jean lifted her mug and said in a tired voice:

"Any chance of another?"

Margot made a fresh pot of tea. Jean sat staring and rereading the letter in front of her. She didn't speak again until the mug reappeared on the table. She picked it up.

"I don't know what's going to happen. I know that Dad shouldn't have done what he did but I can understand why. Saddleback Cottage should be ours, the Smiths had no right to sell it behind our backs. Dad's not in good health, if they should start investigating him who knows what might happen. Danny Bragg has to be stopped." Margot could see that Jean was fighting back tears.

Margot tried to choose her words carefully. "Could you not speak to Danny yourself, appeal to his better nature?"

"He doesn't have a bloody better nature." Margot was taken aback by the anger in Jean's tone.

Margot sipped her hot tea slowly and thought even more carefully about what she was about to say.

"Do you have anything Mr Bragg wants?" she paused. "Anything that he wants so desperately that he would be prepared to drop his investigation?" She looked up; Jean looked at her long and hard. Margot could feel her insides churning but she held Jean's gaze.

"You know, don't you?"

"About Gavin's father? Yes I do."

Jean made no attempt now to check the tears. Margot got up and found a box of tissues which she placed in front of her visitor. Jean pulled several out, blew her nose and seemed to compose herself.

"Does anybody, I mean who else knows?"

"Just Giles and me, as far as I know."

285

She nodded. "How did you find out? Did Danny say anything to you?"

"No, I haven't spoken to Danny Bragg about it and I don't think that Giles has either." Margot stood up and opened a cupboard; she pulled out a photograph and passed it to Jean.

"Where did you get this? It's Mum and Dad with Gavin when he was little."

"Danny Bragg has an almost identical photograph of himself as a little boy, standing in front of his grandparents. When Giles came to collect me..." She looked up at Jean again. "It was you who sent him, wasn't it?"

Jean nodded.

"He waited for me in the hallway and the photograph of Danny as a child was there. Giles spent ages looking at it and he put two and two together and, as they say, the rest is history."

"I would like it to remain history too." Jean seemed to be regaining some of her fight.

"So Danny doesn't know that he has a son?"

"No." She hesitated then repeated, "No," in a firmer tone.

"And what about Gavin, does he know that Danny is his father?"

"Absolutely not. How can I tell him? He thinks Bill my first husband is his dad. Anyhow, Gavin doesn't need a dad. He's got my brother and my father. They're all the role models he needs."

Margot made no comment.

"You won't say anything to anyone will you? Especially not to Danny Bragg?"

Margot thought very carefully about what she was about to say. "Danny Bragg may be a lot of things but he is not stupid. Do you think that Danny might er, might suspect?"

"No, why, do you know something?"

"It was just when I stayed with him whilst my cottage was being besieged; he talked a lot about your family. At the time I didn't really think too much about it. He seemed to know a lot about you all. He asked questions about Gavin, not that I was much help because to be honest, at that point, I had barely met your son."

Jean slumped defeated into her seat. "He knows, the bastard knows. What sort of a sick game is he playing?"

"I'm sorry I don't follow."

"Everyone wondered what had brought Danny back to Middle Chippings. His business is in doing up properties and building new ones. There's not a lot of call for that in Middle Chippings. He came to see me you know. It was the night that Giles took Dad and Gavin down for a pint. He knew that I would be alone. He asked me outright if Gavin was his. What a bloody cheek. Twenty years ago the bastard dumped me without even looking back. Then he tries to walk back into my life."

"What did you tell him?"

"I denied it of course, I threw him out, said I'd phone for the police if he didn't leave." The bluster suddenly left her. "God was I frightened."

"And do you think he believed you?"

"What about calling the police or Gavin being his?"

"Both."

"I did at the time but now I'm just not so sure. Sam Savage said that Danny had been asking lots of questions about me. She thought he was just trying to catch up on all the village gossip." Jean made no attempt to hide the derision in her voice. "All he was really after was information about Gavin."

They both turned as they heard the front door open. Giles walked into the kitchen, looked at the two women and the photograph lying on the table between them. He didn't need Margot's warning glance. His sister's tear-stained face said it all.

"I've told Jean that it was pure guesswork on your part. That you put two and two together after seeing the photo at Danny's," Margot explained.

Jean could not meet her brother's gaze. Margot stood up to allow them some private time together but Giles lifted his hand for her to stay.

"Why didn't you say something, anything? We would have understood, no one would have judged you?"

"I couldn't. I did what I thought was best at the time. Let's be honest, Mum and Dad never made any secret of how much they hated Danny and then keeping the secret just became a habit…" she trailed off.

"Are you going to tell them?" Giles sat next to his sister and Margot made a fresh pot of tea.

"Who?"

"Gavin and Danny Bragg."

"I don't know. I might have to. I was going to tell Gavin, but in my own time, when I felt that the time was right. Now there is this damn business about the bloody piggery. Danny could cause Dad a lot of trouble." She began to sob quietly.

Giles looked towards Margot, women's tears; he was well out of his depth. Margot squatted down next to Jean's chair. She put her arm around the sobbing woman.

"Look you don't have to make any decisions at this precise moment. Let's just take one step at a time. The first priority is to get Danny off your father's back, then it is up to you what and when you tell Gavin. If he wants a relationship with his father then that will be up to him. All you can do is support whatever he decides. As for what you tell Danny that too has got to be your decision. But whatever you decide, Jean," Margot looked towards Giles for confirmation, "we will support you no matter what. You're not alone in this you know."

Giles plonked three mugs of tea on the table. Jean looked from one to the other and gave a small smile.

"I can see why my brother has fallen for you hook, line and sinker."

CHAPTER 44

The table at The Quarry Man was booked for eight o'clock. They had been given the largest one in the restaurant area. Samantha Savage was serving behind the bar and would be joining them for a drink at the end of the meal. They went in two cars. Giles picked up Margot. Jean drove Gavin and Godfrey. Suzie was waiting for them at the bar when they arrived. Margot looked at her questioningly, Suzie shook her head. The pregnancy was still a secret.

The meal was lovely and just as they were all on the pudding course Sam Savage appeared with a couple of bottles of champagne.

"A toast to the birthday boy," she said.

"Sam, that's very generous of you." Giles stood up to take them from her. "Only one of them is from me. The other is from a well-wisher who wishes to remain anonymous." Jean glanced across at Giles and Margot, no prizes for guessing who the well-wisher was.

Sam continued, "Tonight is a bit of a family celebration for us too. My Suzie has something to tell everyone."

Whilst Sam busied herself opening the two bottles of champagne Margot glanced at Jean and saw her seeking out someone. He was at the bar, a drink in his hand. Danny Bragg caught Jean's eye and imperceptibly raised his glass in a silent toast. Jean turned her gaze quickly back to the table.

"Dad make a toast, you're head of the family."

"Yeah, go on Grandad."

Godfrey held his champagne glass awkwardly; he would have much preferred a pint mug.

"I've got two toasts I'd like to make if nobody minds." He looked around the table. "Firstly and most importantly please all raise your glasses to the best grandson a man ever had." He lifted his glass. "To Gavin."

"To Gavin," they all echoed. Gavin looked around at everyone and grinned.

"Now, for the second toast. Apparently, the District Council has decided to drop their investigation into the damn piggery so you'll be pleased to know that you will not be visiting me in jail."

There were murmurs all around. Giles looked at his sister who just shook her head, as if to say, "Ask me later."

"To Grandad," Gavin stood up swaying slightly before he fell back into his seat. They all laughed but lifted their glasses in salute to Godfrey.

"My turn now," Sam Savage interrupted. "My toast is to my clever daughter to wish her good luck at university. To Suzie."

Everyone lifted their glasses except Margot. Before they could join in with the toast Margot blurted out, "To University, but you can't. You're pregnant."

"Pregnant!" Gavin, Sam and Jean spoke in unison.

Suzie smiled. "No I'm not," she paused, "but you are."

"Me, pregnant?"

"What?" Giles stared at Margot in disbelief, then back at Suzie who was smiling.

"I'm so, so sorry, Margot, but I switched them, I switched the wands over."

"Wands? What wands?" Giles was well out of his depth.

"But why?" Margot could not believe it.

"Will someone please tell me what is going on?" Godfrey's voice cut through the stunned silence.

"And me," said Jean.

"Me too," said Gavin trying not to slur his words.

Sam Savage just looked around the table at all of the Farmers. "I think someone needs to do some explaining," she looked pointedly at her daughter.

Suzie had everyone's attention. "Margot and I met last week in Exeter. We had both gone into town to do some shopping but primarily to buy pregnancy testing kits." Suzie looked pointedly at her mother. "Come on, Mum, don't be naive, you must have known that Gavin and I weren't just holding hands. Anyway to cut a long story short, we met up and had a

290

nice lunch." She smiled across at Margot. "You were so kind and lovely to me and I did a really mean thing. I swapped those wand things over. The one with the blue line was yours, not mine."

"But why?" Margot repeated.

"The champagne, the tears, all that emotion. Everything was going too fast for me. If it was me who was pregnant I needed some time to myself. I just needed some space to think. When it wasn't me I was so relieved. I was going to tell you there and then but you made such a fuss of me and tried to hide your disappointment and then the phone went and," Suzie looked around, it seemed so silly now, "and the time to come clean had passed. I didn't get time to explain…" she tailed off.

"Now let's get this clear, I," Giles looked across at Margot who appeared to have lost the power of speech, "we are going to have a baby?"

"Yes," her reply was barely audible.

Margot stared straight at Giles – the others might not have been there. She waited. Giles broke into the widest smile she had ever seen.

"I'm going to be a dad," he laughed and turned to the others. "I'm going to be a dad."

He pulled Margot out of her chair and crushed her to him. Everyone started to talk at once. Someone banged on the table to get order.

"A toast to Giles and Margot's baby." Samantha felt that someone ought to say something. She looked around the group encouragingly and caught her daughter's eye.

"To Giles and Margot's baby," Suzie echoed her mother. The others followed suit. Margot drank her champagne down quickly, and then looked horrified at the empty glass. "Oh my God, I shouldn't be drinking should I?"

They all laughed. There were a few minutes silence whilst everyone took in what had just happened. Godfrey looked up and said, "I think I'd better get back home, I've had more than enough excitement for one night." He looked around the table. "Unless anyone else has got a bombshell they'd like to drop."

The party broke up. Jean drove her father back. Gavin was bundled into the back of the Land Rover slightly the worse for wear. He slumped into the back seat.

"She's not going far," he mumbled.

Margot turned around. "Who's not going far?"

"Suzie, she's going to Exeter, only an hour away. I can see her whenever I like."

Giles stopped outside Saddleback Cottage. "You go on in. I'll just take this young man back. I won't be long." He leaned over and gave her a kiss. "A baby, we're having a baby," he whispered.

"I know," she smiled at him.

Margot heard the Land Rover pull away. She went straight up into her bathroom and looked at herself in the mirror. She didn't look any different. She placed her hands over her stomach – a baby, they were going to have a baby.

Margot was ready for bed by the time Giles returned. He called out to her from the bottom of the stairs.

"Margot, Margot, where are you?"

"I'm in bed, come on up."

"No, you come down here, I need you down here."

Margot climbed out of bed and pulled her dressing gown close. She walked to the top of the stairs. Giles was in the hallway, on one knee. She walked down towards him.

"Miss Margot Denning, would you do me the great honour of becoming my wife?" He held up a small ring box.

"Oh Giles, yes, yes I will." She almost fell down the final few stairs.

Laughing Giles jumped up and gave Margot a big hug, followed swiftly by a long hard kiss. She leaned away from him. "You're not just asking me because of the baby are you?"

"Margot, how do you think I could have obtained an engagement ring at," he looked at his watch, "two hours' notice, on a Saturday night? I bought this ring two days after I met you. I knew even there and then that I wanted to marry you."

"Really?" she smiled up at him. "Bit sure of yourself weren't you?"

"Oh yes, no doubt about it. I loved you from that first moment you walked into The Quarry Man and hit on me."

"I did not 'hit' on you."

"Yes you did."

"Did not."

"Did."

"Did not."

Giles laughed at her and squeezed her again. "Come on let's go to bed." As he climbed up the stairs he sung at the top of his voice, "Eee Aye Addyeo, the Farmer's got a wife." They then sang the next verse, "The wife's got a child, the wife's got a child, Eee Aye Addyeo, the wife's got a child."

Later in bed Giles explained why he had taken so long. It had taken a while for him and Jean to put Gavin to bed. Jean had then told him of the price that Danny Bragg had extracted for not pursuing the listed building issue. Jean had agreed to tell Gavin about his real father. Sending the bottle of champagne to their table had been Danny's way of reminding Jean of her obligations. It would then be up to Gavin to decide whether or not he wanted a relationship with his biological father.

Margot and Giles were both tired but too excited to sleep.

"Georgia for a girl and Gordon for a boy."

"Gordon? You must be joking."

"Well at least we don't have the problem of letting everyone know," Giles said pulling Margot towards him. "I think that the whole village knows by now."

Margot's final thought as she drifted off to sleep was that perhaps she ought to give up writing romantic fiction and go in for family sagas – no research needed, she just had to look around.